The Lone War Cry

A Western Novel

George E. Miller

The Lone War Cry: A Western Novel

Cover art by Pamela Askew, Tuscaloosa, Alabama

Published by Wheatmark®
610 East Delano Street, Suite 104
Tucson, Arizona 85705 U.S.A.
www.wheatmark.com

International Standard Book Number: 978-1-60494-138-8 (paperback)
International Standard Book Number: 978-1-60494-139-5 (hardcover)
Library of Congress Control Number: 2008929194

Acknowledgments

I GRATEFULLY ACKNOWLEDGE Dr. J. D. Askew, for his technical assistance, and my wife, Suzanna, for all her support.

Book 1

1848

1

THE COLD, RELENTLESS WIND pushed up the forested mountainside, whistling through the trees as it went. Soaring effortlessly above, a golden eagle climbed with it, covering the same ground the man below, leading his horse, had labored over all afternoon, in just a few minutes. The man's chest heaved from his exertions, and his lower back ached. Pausing, he watched as the eagle crested the rise above him and disappeared. The rhythmic thud of the horse's hooves behind him refocused the man's attention on the task at hand.

Finally stopping at the edge of a small, steep clearing on a level rock outcropping, he took the opportunity to rest while he pulled out his long glass to scan the lower elevations behind him. His large black horse swung its head down and began to immediately graze on the remaining grasses from the previous summer. Sweeping the glass slowly back and forth over the imposing wilderness, he did not see anyone, but Corby knew they were out there. Climbing as he had for the last two days, he was tired and sore of leg. Then, realizing, like the horse, that he had not eaten in some time, he reached into his saddlebag and took out another rock-hard biscuit to chew on before replacing the long glass and rededicating himself to the arduous chore of continuing his climb.

From high on the mountainside, two small, brown valleys, overwhelmed by the surrounding countryside, were visible below. Mountain after mountain swallowed up the view, and the sky felt low and close. Way down by the valleys, the Middle Fork of the Salmon River wound its way through the rough terrain. Boulders and cliffsides towered above the rapid flow, as if sentries, warning interlopers that this country was not meant to be disturbed. In fact, few people did manage to ever climb this far into the Salmon River Range in what was still just claimed territory of the United States. It was too remote and rugged, even for big game hunters, who could find plenty of elk, bear, and cougar down in the Sawtooth and Lost River ranges, one hundred miles as the crow flies to the South, closer to the Snake River and civilization.

Pushing North, it was unlikely Corby would see anyone for weeks, other than an occasional Indian, and he sure didn't want to see them either.

The wind seemed to always blow this high up, but now there was the threat of weather in the darkening skies above. It was late October, and the peaks already had a light mantle of snow. If it snowed now, Corby figured it would be a wet, driving snow, making travel more difficult. What with the wind and the ground cover of dry leaves that kicked up as he trod forward, he was making far more commotion than he wished to. At least the oncoming storm conditions would make it more difficult for anyone else to surprise him, unless, of course, he walked right into them. Wet weather would be uncomfortable but helpful to his purpose.

He had been leading his horse most of the day as he had climbed. This was exhausting work. The horse wasn't too taken with the exercise either. He stopped again on a large table of gray granite rock, where he could find a level perch, and examined his gear for the approaching snowstorm. Partially sheltered from the increasing wind by the rock wall rising behind the table, he reopened his saddlebag, took out his wool scarf, wrapped it over his head and ears, around his neck, and back down into his coat. His hat didn't fit well like this, but that's what the pull strings were for. With the back of his head now covered, he angled his hat brim low over his face for more protection from the advancing weather. Even though he was sweating under his coat, climbing and pulling as he was, he now put on his work gloves, knowing how quickly cold, wet weather would affect his hands. Then once again he examined his rifle and ammunition. It was time to find cover for the night and build a small fire. He headed around the mountain, toward some ledges still visible in the fading light, hoping to find a hideaway ravine, curled back into the mountain and out of sight.

APPROXIMATELY ONE THOUSAND feet below and two mountainsides behind, five men had already set up camp on a small, sloping meadow, deep within a mixed forest of quaking aspen and Douglas fir. A cold, steady rain made a large fire imperative. The storm was howling through the upper branches of the surrounding forest, with occasional snapping of limbs accenting the commotion. The men huddled around the roaring fire, sipping coffee and generally looking miserable. Two hours earlier they had sent down the balance of their party and equipment, save for their mounts and two pack mules, posted at the edge of the clearing.

Donovan surveyed his remaining charges and was not pleased. Besides Luther, who was a good man but getting too old for this kind of work, he had the Bridges, father and son, dead set for murder, and Quaid, who obviously was very capable, but basically an unknown volunteer. Quaid bothered him the most. Why would an outsider wish to hunt down Corby? God knew that they could use the help, but this was stretching the concept of a Good Samaritan. This was deadly work in what was fast becoming dangerous weather. He studied the man. Quaid was not big, but he was not small either. You got the impression that he could move with surprising speed and strength. And then there were those eyes. Donovan read people through their eyes. He could see indecision, or hatred, or cowardice at critical moments, instructing him to take the appropriate actions, but Quaid's eyes told him nothing. This was a man to be watched carefully.

"Marshal." Donovan turned his gaze to Ben Bridges. The elder Bridges was a stern man who generally kept to himself.

"How far behind you figure we are now?"

"Hard to say, Mr. Bridges, but I'd place it no more than half a day."

"How long we gonna lie up here?"

"No point in traveling now with this storm moving in. Corby's got to stop too. If we're lucky, it's snowing higher up … slow him down … track him easier. We've pushed pretty hard; a little rest ain't gonna hurt." Donovan pointed over to Bridges's son, Zeke, who had curled up alongside a fallen tree trunk, looking for more protection from the rain. Ben Bridges squinted over at his boy with clear disapproval, and then threw a stick into the fire.

"My boy Tom could have tracked Corby down alone," Bridges said, as much to himself as to the Marshal.

After twenty years as a U.S marshal in Missouri, Donovan had headed West, like so many Americans of the day. Drifting into the vast Oregon Territories, he had continued as a part-time lawman as he searched for a suitable new life. Working out of Old Fort Boise, run by the Hudson's Bay Company on the Oregon Trail, he had plenty of work sorting out disputes, between the newly established frontier towns along the trail, the wagon trains of immigrants bound for California and the West Coast, and the remaining fur traders and trappers in the region. This was work he did not intend to do for long.

Donovan nodded, and thought Tom Bridges probably got what he deserved, while the younger surviving son, Zeke, now whistling as he slept against the log, was even more unlikable. The Bridges boys had always been a pain, Tom a bully, and Zeke a cheat. Zeke was destined to fall farther in his father's estimation in comparison to his dead brother. Ben had always doted on Tom, especially since their mother had passed on some years ago. If Corby hadn't killed Tom, someone would probably have had to, maybe even himself.

Luther ambled over, tucking his chin down into his coat, looking like a half-drowned tomcat. Luther's coat looked more worn than Luther.

"It's too damn cold to be raining," he said as he examined a hole in his glove. "We're gonna have to shoot some game tomorrow too. Plenty of fixin's, but low on meat. How about an elk?"

Donovan nodded. He figured they were still far enough behind Corby that he wouldn't hear a shot. Not that he really thought they would overtake Corby in these mountains, but one never knew. The best hope was to cross his trail in the next day or so, once they got up a little higher, making a wide circle below the handful of mountain passes. This would at least tell Donovan which direction Corby might be going. Corby had to head for more supplies and a place to winter. Once the posse got back down to Fort Boise, he would send posts to the possible towns on Corby's path. Of course Corby knew this too and would try to mislead Donovan.

If Corby chose to turn North and try for Canada, Donovan figured the chase was over; either the Blackfoot or the elements would kill Corby this late in the year, or he would make it and never be heard from again—two more days of this weather would take the chase out of any hunting party.

If Corby turned back West, they would eventually hear about it. His guess was Corby had no reason to stay in this part of the country and would try looping around them, heading West once he felt he was free of any pursuit. It was a national pattern to keep moving West, particularly for those who had problems. Donovan wondered what were people going to do when there was no further West to go? For now, it solved a lot of headaches. Donovan would earn his money the next few days, but had no real interest in bringing Corby in. Better for all if they never saw him; a wound this far into the mountains could turn fatal for anyone. With luck the trail would prove too cold to follow.

Somewhere past the picket line, there came a sharp crack; the horses reared and whinnied. A second later they all recognized the sound as the splitting of a tree, caused by the tempest's rising winds. One of the large firs had probably snapped off high up, common enough in these mountain storms, but creating alarm throughout the camp. Time to pitch a secure tent and retreat for the night.

"Better hobble them horses, Luther."

"Uh huh."

THE GRIZZLY BEAR wasn't going anywhere. His coat had thickened all fall, and he was comfortable in this weather, even though he didn't like all the noise from the storm. The elk had already moved farther down the mountain, instinctively, before the heavy snow started to fly. Up above the treeline, the great bear turned into the storm, rose up on his hind legs, and smelled the gusting wind. It was a wet snow, but the bear could tell the temperature was dropping fast. By morning, the mountain would be well covered, and the bear seemed to sense that this storm was just starting. He turned one last log over to dig out some grubs and then, as if in resignation, lumbered toward the trees. The night was too dark to see the new snow well, and his eyesight was never much anyway. It was likely that the bear would stay out several more weeks before hibernating.

Morning found the great bear approximately a mile farther away in the forest but only a few hundred yards below the treeline. As always his hunger was central to his thinking. It was still snowing, but the wind had subsided. The temperature was now well below freezing, and the landscape was remarkably transformed. Fresh snow covered everything, hiding the trails that crisscrossed the mountain, as if no living creature had ever passed by before. The sky was still overcast with sullen gray snow clouds, but the whiteness of the night's work was in sharp contrast to the dark edges of the remaining landmarks in the morning's dim light. The bear, however, continued unaffected in his hunt for food, rolling over snow-covered rocks and logs, and constantly sniffing the air for hopeful signs of other sustenance.

THE SNOW HAD so covered the lean-to Corby had constructed the night before that he awoke in the dark with a start, knowing that he had overslept. He had found a nice overhanging ledge, wedged into a steep ravine. There was adequate room for both his horse and the lean-to on the sloping underledge. He had put up the lean-to at the tightest end, where the two ledges came closest together. It proved to be a cozy box under the circumstances, partially buried by snow, but unfortunately it kept out the morning light.

It was cold, and his legs were stiff and sore, but he was instantly alert and anxious to get going. The snow would potentially complicate travel, but if it kept coming down, it could help secure his escape. Corby was no stranger to winter hunts, but an extended stay at these altitudes was not something anyone tried to do. He moved swiftly to break camp, rubbing down his horse's legs and checking his shoes before resaddling him and leading him across the small creek dividing the ravine. His life depended on this big black horse, and once again he took great pride in his animal, stroking its neck, feeding it by hand. Like many westerners and Indians alike, his horse was his prized possession, sole confessor, and best friend. He had purchased this big black when it was a yearling, not knowing it would grow to such a stature. Now it stood a full sixteen hands high, and was broad and strong as any horse he had seen. He had taken to calling it several pet names, depending on whether he was happy or mad with it, but always introduced the horse as Midnight.

"So tell me again how you are going to fix this mess, huh, buddy?" he asked the horse as they climbed out of the ravine to start the morning's climb. Fortunately the new snow was not too deep, rising only to midboot. As he walked he thought over his morning strategy. The last danger would be when he broke out of the alpine treeline for the high passes. If a posse had guessed the right pass and pushed hard the last three days, there was the possibility he could step into their sights. This was unlikely, as he had pushed hard himself, and the storm would have stopped anyone last night. But how long had the sun been up? It was impossible to tell in the morning's overcast sky. Swirling snow continued to drift downward, though there were lulls in the onslaught.

"I'm thinking sunny California. Any objections to that, you big galoot?" Midnight snorted and shoved his nose into Corby's back.

The snow was wet underneath with a dry inch on top. This made climbing treacherous, as footing was slippery. Fortunately, he was high enough that the mountain seemed to be tabling off. He found a ridgetop and stuck to it in a slow, silent ascent. The snow crunched quietly below his feet, the horse breathed heavily in his ear, and the ever-present wind blew through the increasing gaps in the high forest. The firs were shrinking in size and thinning out as he climbed. He thought he recognized juniper and bristlecone pine now mixed in with the hemlocks and Douglas fir. He knew he would reach the timberline soon, and he became more cautious. The cold was nipping at his ears and nose, even as he was sweating, but most important, his feet were comfortable.

There it was, the broken and bare alpine zone and the passes he knew would be above it. He stopped a dozen feet below the end of the continuous forest. The timberline was not an abrupt boundary, but rather the stands of trees now rapidly decreased in number and size in a broad transition to open space, rockslides, and severe climate. Corby waited and watched. Time was precious, but he stood still as the minutes ticked by. The snow was blowing more than falling now. Ten minutes turned into twenty. Still he didn't move. Something caught his eye, movement at the edge of the forest half a mile away. He strained to see more. Nothing moved for another two minutes, then again he saw something. The grizzly bear stepped out in the open and tested the wind. Corby was downwind, and watched. The bear rocked back and forth for a minute and then headed up-mountain. It was the assurance Corby had been waiting for. He led his horse out and headed up-mountain too, bound for a pass downwind of the grizzly at a brisk pace, using what cover he could find. He stuck close to a rocky ridge, hoping to protect himself on one side anyway. The back of his head and neck felt exposed, and he kept turning around in anticipation of discovery. Once while looking behind, he tripped on the loose rock and landed hard on his elbow. He watched his feet more, and resigned himself to a slower pace and possible discovery from behind. He realized the Bridges weren't about to yell out and warn him, so wasting time looking for them while he covered this critical ground was futile. He plunged ahead, into the mountainside, gusting wind, and uncertain future.

After half a mile, he was able to top a bench and remove himself from lower gunsight line. He paused to catch his breath. His chest was heaving from the exertion and thin air. The pass was still not in sight, but he knew he was getting closer. The snow had drifted deeply against the back wall of the bench. The wind had blown the front of the level ground free of snow. It looked like either rock or snow the rest of the way up. He could tell the air was turning colder, and his legs were aching some. Maybe there was a mile more to go, straight up, and then temporary freedom, lower elevations, and he could breathe more freely.

He walked over to the edge of the plateau behind a large boulder and snuck a peek back down the mountain. There was the jagged line of weather-tortured trees, only a small distance behind, but a measurable safety zone nonetheless. He could now see far down the mountain to his right, but his view was effectively blocked to his left by the ridge he was tucked under. The bear was not in view. He looked up the mountain and planned his next path. Looking for secure footing and as much cover as possible, he would weave in and out of a large boulder field until the mountain topped out of his range of vision again. If he could get to the next level undetected, he would feel fairly secure.

Forty-five minutes later, he cleared the boulders and crested the rise. Time to sit down, rest the horse, eat something, and relax. He was laboring to breathe, wet with sweat, and his legs were quivering slightly, now that he had stopped climbing.

He fed and tethered his horse, pulled out some beef jerky, and lay back against a granite slab, rubbing his hands and thumping his legs. His view was much enhanced now, both above and below. He could now see two passes available to him. Still a hard climb, both over a mile away, but no place for an ambush. The towering peaks had worn the passes clean with their rubble of rocks, and hard weather. So far the wind had kept the passes free of most of the snow. Looking down the mountain, he could see the lower elevations were under assault from the storm. Snow clouds blocked out everything from view on the bottom two thirds of the mountain. To the West he could barely see two mountain tops away. On his own mountain, he could see the bear, still near the treeline, and a small gray lake downhill southwest of his position. The bear was well beyond rifle range, and as he watched, the great bear helped him again. It kept looking back to the East where he had emerged from the forest. Sure enough, five men and seven pack animals broke out of the treeline momentarily and then retreated to cover, milling about at the edge of the forest. He went to get his spyglass.

"DAMN IT, BRIDGES, you're going to get us all killed!"

"Look, Marshal, I didn't come this far, get this close, to turn tail now!"

Ben Bridges strained against the hold Donovan had on his arm, and was starting to boil over.

"I'm not saying we give up, just not get killed. If he is still up there above us, it would be easy pickin's, knocking us off climbing up to get him. If he is over the pass, he's gone."

Quaid now stepped up to the two men. "Now that's not 100 percent true, Marshal. He could turn and follow us back down in any direction."

"Now why in hell would he do that when he's safe where he is?"

"This is a killer, right? Who's to know what's in his head?"

Ben Bridges pulled his arm free. "Me and my boy are going after that son of a bitch, with or with out you!"

"OK, OK, but let's at least make it a little more difficult than shooting clay pigeons." Donovan looked back up the mountain, planning a path that might allow adequate cover. This was beginning to get out of hand.

"I'll go first. Stay behind me by a good two hundred yards, spread out among yourselves, and move from cover to cover. Stop if I yell to stop. If he starts shooting, work to cover first and then flank him if possible."

Donovan looked up the mountain yet again. How could you flank someone on this open terrain? It was just dumb luck when they crossed Corby's trail this morning, half filled in with new snow. But the boot heels had been unmistakable in the semi-shelter of the big trees. He should have known better than to let the posse split up, leaving him with this group. He began to have a very uneasy feeling about his companions, other than Luther.

"Luther, you're second, behind me. Keep a keen eye on me." The men moved to mount their horses. Donovan grabbed Luther's arm and said so only Luther could hear him, "This is bad business. These boys aren't thinking right, if they ever did. You and me may have to make a play if it gets bad. You with me?"

Luther looked caught by surprise but nodded grimly. He pulled out his mountain rifle and filled his pocket with extra revolver cartridges. He was suddenly and decidedly not feeling well. Maybe the weather would get real bad on their way up, forcing them back.

The five men and seven animals soon were spread out over a quarter mile, weaving through the diminishing cover. Donovan was peering as hard as he could up the slope and through the now intermittent snow. He felt naked and foolish, and that made him mad. Corby could be anywhere above him, waiting to take an easy shot. He zigged and zagged as best he could, slowing down the climb. Soon a small bench was just above him and he could see beyond it to where the mountain now presented a rugged boulder field to his left. If he could get to the big boulders, they would have more cover. But coming out onto the bare table bench exposed them badly. If Corby was waiting for them, this was the spot. He hung just below the lip of the rise and signaled the others to come up to his position.

CORBY COULD NOT believe these men could follow him in this weather to this spot, and then dare to mount an offensive over sparse cover into his gun sight. He was a fair shot, but even a poor shot held all the cards on this terrain. He could probably shoot the horses, pin them down, and, unobserved, slip through the pass with the only remaining horse. He certainly could pick off a couple of the riders, if they dared to top the bench at the bottom of the boulder field. Well, they weren't giving him much choice. He had to be ready to defend his position. He laid out his powder caps and balls, by his Hawken large-bore percussion rifle. Lying on his stomach facing downhill was the perfect setup for the heavy-barreled .54 caliber gun.

THE POSSE HAD dismounted to discuss their situation. Donovan knew he had to be persuasive to avoid a possible disaster.

"Look up the mountain. If Corby's up there, we don't have a move. If he kept going, he's to the passes by now, and as slowly as we would have to work our way up, we would lose him on the other side."

"You mean he might be right up there? He's almost in rifle range. Five guns to one. Let's go." Old man Bridges turned back to his horse abruptly.

"Damn it," Donovan yelled. "You're not hearing what I'm saying here! You can't reach him without getting shot!"

Bridges turned around holding his pistol level to Donovan's chest. "Get on your horse, lawman. You're leading this ride. Zeke, take his sidearm, rifle too."

Zeke advanced, pulling his handgun out, with an evil smile on his face. "Why, Marshal, I do believe we have new leadership."

"Now, boys, there ain't no need for this. I—"

"Shut up, Luther. Just do as my pa says. You're gonna stay right up front with the Marshal. I'll be taking your gun, too."

Ben Bridges then turned to Quaid. "Mister, you've done good sticking this thing out. I figure we've got a fair chance making a rush for them big rocks, and then it's a shootin' contest. Sorry, but I gotta know if you're with us or agin us?"

Quaid said, "Five guns are a lot better than two or three."

"That's for sure, but the Marshal here has gone real careful on us."

"You get the Marshal killed, the territory's gonna be after you."

"If the Marshal gets killed, he was a hero." Bridges spat on the ground. "Now I ain't got no more time. You in or out?"

THE POSSE HAD held up just under the ridge. Corby figured they would be having a pretty good discussion on their next move. It was a fair bet they would give up once they assessed their odds, but he hadn't figured them to get this far. Must be Donovan. No doubt the Bridges would be with him, in the party of five pursuers. There were no more sorry folks than the Bridges. Corby had seen his share of "Bridges" down in Missouri, cattle rustlers, gun hands, cardsharps, and the like, used to making their own law. Problem was, there was no reasoning with people like that. They only saw what they wanted. Well, the riders would have to do something soon. It wasn't getting any warmer.

QUAID EVALUATED THE situation. Two guns out and well spread between them. They would likely be asking for his gun next. If he rode with them under those circumstances, the Marshal, Luther, and himself would be no more than front cover to the boulders. A bullet in the back was likely.

"Too long, mister," Zeke said as he shot Quaid in his side. Quaid crumpled to the ground in a heap. "Now that was one slow thinking son of a bitch, hey, Pa?"

"Shut up, son, and get these boys mounted. I didn't figure it this way, Marshal, but you gave me no choice. No choice. Now the fat's in the fire for sure. We are going to rush those rocks. You stop, you get shot. Understand? You could get lucky, and that son of a bitch up there might get my boy and me. Now mount up!"

THE GUNSHOT REVERBERATED all over the mountaintop. Corby ducked instinctively, recognizing the echo of a Colt revolver a second later. He twisted around and raised his spyglass over the gravel mound he was laying on. What the hell was going on down there? Almost immediately, four horsemen charged over the ridge, headed for the cover of the big rocks. Where was the fifth rider? He took patient aim on the first rider. The crack from his rifle resounded over the scrambling horse hooves on the rocky ground. Down went the first horse like a dead weight on top of his rider. The second rider was veering off from the group and wildly waving one arm.

The stacatto crack of more small arms fire rang out. The second rider pitched forward in his saddle. Corby then realized they were killing each other. He lost precious time as he reloaded and readjusted his sights on the final two horsemen. They were halfway across the tabletop, now at a full run. He had time for one good shot and maybe a quick second shot. As he targeted the third horse, he recognized the squat body and gray hair of Ben Bridges. With some satisfaction, he squeezed off a round, and a second later he saw the horse's front legs buckle, throwing Bridges out over its head onto the hard rock-covered ground. The fourth rider was now barreling for the cover of the large boulders, and appeared like he would make it before Corby could fire again. Corby twisted back over onto his back and slowly reloaded his rifle. Well, there was no way he could head over the open ground for the pass now. He would have to deal with the gunman in the boulder field. Four men probably dead or dying, two horses down, and he had fired only two rounds. He surveyed the battlefield. The first rider was still alive, but clearly injured and pinned under his horse. Rider number two appeared to be dead in his saddle. His horse had stopped running near the end of the bench and was nervously stomping at the ground. The reins had fallen loose from the rider's hands. Ben Bridges wasn't moving where he had hit the ground, but his horse was still thrashing on the rocky shelf beside him. Corby took careful aim and ended its torment.

"Pa," someone yelled. "Pa, where are you?" Corby figured the fourth rider to be Zeke Bridges; from the boulders, he would be unable to see where his father lay on the cold ground. Corby took a fix on the location and moved down the western side of the boulder field, as it allowed him to cover any attempt to outclimb his own position. He figured he could slowly move down the mountain, squeezing off movement to his left, and keeping Zeke in front of him. He moved carefully from boulder to boulder, trying not to push any loose gravel and alert Zeke to his whereabouts. Ten minutes later, he was about halfway down, when he saw Zeke bolt from the far eastern end of cover, crossing the bench at its shortest point, and plunge his horse recklessly over the rise, racing down the mountain. Corby rose up to take aim, but really had no shot. He shot anyway, not coming close, but ricocheting on the ledge rocks behind Zeke. Hopefully that would spur him on to break his neck! True to form, Zeke had left his father and the others to save his own hide. By the time Zeke got back to Fort Boise, he would have quite a story to tell, none of it true.

The sun was now high in the sky and distinguishable through the overcast as Corby cautiously approached Ben Bridges. A spiteful old man, with two no-good sons, it was more than possible that Bridges could be playing possum, hoping for Corby to come close. As he drew near, however, he could see that the old man was in such an awkward position, it appeared he was dead. On close inspection, he looked to have broken his neck, possibly his back, and he was most certainly dead. Corby had a hard time just looking at the man, as if his hate followed him even in death. He momentarily considered leaving him for the bear but knew he wouldn't. Even this man deserved a burial.

Next he walked toward the dead man in the saddle. The roan was still wide-eyed, but settling down, as Corby reached for the dropped reins. It was old Luther, who sometimes helped the Marshal and mostly ran errands for the officials down in Fort Boise. He'd been shot low in the back and high in the shoulder. The back shot had killed him, most likely with a lot of pain. He was probably along to handle the trail chores, as he certainly was no gunman.

Corby pulled him slowly over onto himself and then to the ground. He'd be doing a lot of digging in what was very hard, rocky ground. Maybe he could find a site in the loose gravel area, for quick burial. Trail pay wasn't worth the price Luther had paid.

The next object of his attention was the lead rider, down under his dead horse and still struggling. He couldn't see the rider, as the horse was in between and the land slanted downhill where it had fallen. Holding the roan, he yelled out.

"Is that you, Donovan?"

"Get this goddamned horse off of me!" came the angry reply.

"Slow down, Marshal, are you holding iron? I can't see getting shot trying to free you."

There was a pause, and then Donovan called back. "OK, I see your point. I can't move. I've for sure got a busted leg. Help me and we'll have a truce, until I'm well again."

There was a longer pause, and Donovan started to wonder if Corby had simply left him there. Pinned as he was, he was in worse shape than a turtle on its back. Without help, he was a dead man. A wave of frustration swept over him again, adding to the great weight of his horse and the pain of his injuries. He pounded his fist into his saddle.

"Now, Marshal, I don't think that's gonna help." Corby was directly behind and below him, although Donovan couldn't see him, unable to twist around, pinned as he was. Corby leaned over, a gun in one hand, and patted around with his other hand, searching for a concealed weapon. "I don't figure you could take me in, in your condition, but you might figure different."

After satisfying himself that the Marshal couldn't pull a gun out, Corby sat down next to the Marshal, facing downhill where the lawman could see him, flipped his collar up, and placed his back to the weather. "Got any ideas how we can get warmer?" he asked as he handed the Marshal a stick of jerky out of his coat pocket. Looking the Marshal over, he remembered what he had heard of Donovan, a hard, mostly honest professional, good with a pistol, but quick to hit and ask questions later. Corby could see the toughness in his face: a couple of small scars on his left forehead, and unfathomable black eyes that studied him but also seemed to look past him. Now about fifty years old, Donovan was twice as irascible as he had been at twenty-five, just as dangerous but far more efficient. There was nothing in his bearing to suggest that one would enjoy his company. There was something else; the Marshal was embarrassed. Lying helpless as he was, he wasn't afraid, resigned, or feeling pity for himself. He was clearly put out over not being in control, and ashamed of his condition in front of a stranger.

"I heard one horseman ride downhill," Donovan ventured.

"Zeke" was the laconic reply.

Donovan grunted to show his lack of surprise. "The old man riding behind me?"

"Dead, shot twice in the back. You want to tell me what happened?"

"You want to get this goddamned horse off of me?"

THE STORM WAS re-intensifying as Corby rounded up the sudden wealth of animals and gear. A quick count revealed seven rifles, four pistols, a saddlebag full of caps and balls, a large tin of powder, a full trail kit of cooking and camping gear for five, and, of course, two horses and, better still, two mules that had been tied down and left just below the bench. The dead body below the ridge, the man named Quaid, had fifty dollars in coins in his bags, some very nice weather gear, a fancy knife in his belt, and a revolver and holster. Ben Bridges had been carrying Luther's guns, so Zeke must have Donovan's. Donovan wouldn't like that bit of news.

BURYING THE BODIES had been relatively easy in the loose gravel around the boulders. He had rolled larger rocks on top, but if the grizzly could smell through, they wouldn't help. Under the circumstances it was the best he could do. If they didn't get off the mountaintop soon, there would be two more dead. He walked back over to where the Marshal was propped up against his dead horse. Donovan had been carving on a crude crutch to be used later, but for now, it would serve as part of the travois they would use to drag the Marshal off the mountaintop. As best as Corby could speculate, the Marshal had a broken left leg, maybe a separated shoulder, and some degree of shock, maybe accelerating his drop in body temperature. Even wrapped up as he was, extra blankets were no substitute for shelter and a fire. It was high time to travel. The Marshal wouldn't like it, but Corby was going to take him over the mountain. It would add an hour to the ride to cover from the storm, but it would secure him for the winter against any pursuers. If he was to lay up for the winter with the Marshal, he had to be hidden from any further pursuit out of Fort Boise.

The gusting snow stung their faces as they crossed over the high pass and looked down the other side. There wasn't much to see in the storm, but both knew they would get some relief once they were back in the trees. Neither had been this deep into the wilderness, and both were thinking Indians. Not that they would be out in this weather, but this was Indian territory, and few Indians were friendly anymore. The ride was particularly uncomfortable for Donovan, but Corby had secured him to the travois well, and the bottle of liquor Donovan was consuming from Luther's camp pack was kicking in. Donovan felt slightly disconnected from the reality and events of the moment, but he knew he wasn't happy. It was just getting harder to remember why.

WHEN DONOVAN WOKE up, he found himself in one of the trail tents, on top of several blankets, and covered by several more. It was night, and a fire was burning a few yards in front of his tent. A new bottle was set out next to him, and he realized his leg was strapped to a splint. One boot was off, and his foot was covered in bandages and slightly raised. Then the pain hit him, and he quickly reached for the new bottle.

2

ORBY WAITED PATIENTLY FOR the elk to reemerge on the other side of the small rock outcropping. She was one of seven cow elks slowly grazing toward his position. As he fired he realized that these elk had probably never heard gunfire before. He walked over to the downed animal and began the long, hard task of gutting and bleeding her. The mules he had brought with him were a godsend for this kind of work. Fresh meat in camp would be a welcome change from the hardtack and beans he had been eating since taking flight from Fort Boise. This was rugged but beautiful territory. He had dropped several thousand feet down from the peaks into a parklike setting of meadows and streams to pitch camp with the Marshal until the man was capable of being moved some more. He had elected to not head out of the mountains until he had scouted around more. He figured the Indians, if there were any around, would be at lower elevations too. Snow had drifted in some areas to make travel difficult, but he was learning his neighborhood and navigating better each day. Staying in camp with an angry lawman added to his eagerness to hunt and explore.

Several hours later as he was leading his pack animals back toward camp, he crossed a fresh trail in the snow, a lone Indians moccasin imprints. He got down off of his horse to examine it further. The left foot turned in a bit and left a heavier imprint in the snow than the right. The track ran up the valley, paralleling the stream. He was pretty sure he would have seen this trail earlier had it been there, so he surmised that this Indian had passed through here after his morning trek. That would mean that the Indian had run across his trail and could be anywhere. It was strange to see just footprints without a horse track, unless they were close to some encampment.

"Just great!" he mumbled to himself "On the run, with a layed-up lawman, and now some Injun knows I'm here."

Was there some black cloud following him around this past year? Things were just getting worse and worse, and damn if he didn't feel that it just wasn't right. What was he going to do with winter coming on? They couldn't stay in the tents, and they couldn't keep traveling indefinitely, but now they would have to leave the area due to Indians. Maybe he could get lucky and pick off the Indian while he was still snooping around. With a horse and two mules loaded with elk meat in tow? Looking around rather nervously, a cold chill ran up his spine. Best to get back to camp and talk to Donovan.

WHITEMEN WERE STUPID but lucky. Lame Elk was once more trying to reason out how a race so stupid could prosper so well. He concluded once again that Whitemen must be very lucky. He himself had just had a run of bad luck. He was a great warrior, known throughout the Shoshone lands, both the lands the Shoshone claimed and other tribes did too. But he was a good distance from home, with no luck traveling with him.

In early Fall, he had led five braves on a horsestealing raid northwest of his territory, deep into Nez Perce lands. They had stolen twelve good ponies and had been circling East to escape home when the dirty Flathead people ambushed them. They should have been able to smell them, but bad luck had the wind blowing behind the Shoshones.

Lame Elk looked down on the Whitemen's camp some three hundred feet below him. These were rich Whitemen. He would be able to steal a couple of good horses and be long gone by tomorrow's sun. He was very tired of walking, as it was a constant reminder of his failed raid, and humiliating to his warrior pride. A great warrior never walked, having superior ponies, won in battle and stolen from his enemies. But Lame Elk wasn't lucky of late. Even when he escaped his captors one moon ago, he hadn't been able to steal a horse, and he had escaped alone. Well, he would be back with plenty of braves to avenge this mishap, even if he wasn't sure where the Flathead camp was, as he had escaped as they were being dragged and beaten en route to it. More bad luck!

The sun was going down, and the rocks Lame Elk had been lying against were losing their heat. He would steal some good blankets too, and plenty of the fresh elk meat just brought into camp. Whitemen were lucky hunters too. They seemed to stumble on their game and then kill more than they needed. But Whitemen were stupid, and you could steal their blankets off of them as they slept the night away. Lame Elk lay back to wait for the stars to come out in the late night sky.

His mind drifted again to the Yellowstone country he had been born in, his wife Dancing Cloud, and their small boy, Beaver on the Rock. He had only one wife, which was unusual for a recognized warrior, but Dancing Cloud was an excellent wife, good to look upon, a hard worker, and a good mother. She also got along with Whispering Trees, his mother, no small task. He could almost feel the buffalo robe Dancing Cloud would pull over him when they coupled on a cold night. He could imagine the smells and sounds of his people.

Lame Elk could still send fear into the young warriors when he stared his stare of death. But he was not the fierce, reckless warrior of some years back. His fighting skills were diminishing, from lack of interest and use. What he was most known for was his ability to track. Some warriors were good horse thieves; others were good at hunting, or killing enemies of the People. Lame Elk was a very skilled tracker, as his father and grandfather had been. He had studied the various markings of all the animals, great and small, for years, with his grandfather Swiftsnake. When the game was scarce, the People would turn to Lame Elk to lead the hunting parties.

His father had been killed by a rockslide as a young man, and Lame Elk spent even more time with his grandfather. Together they traveled many places in search of answers to his grandfather's curiosity about the fellow creatures of the mountains. In time he found he had the same curiosity. What made the elk so silent in their travels? When would the big winds accompany the snows? The old women, who told the stories, found Lame Elk was their best audience. Even when he didn't believe the stories, he was respectful. Often when he returned from his travels, he would ask the old ones many questions about what he had found, and if they knew more or had heard anything about his latest discovery.

Often the old ones talked about the Ancient People, the time the Earth trembled, or the possible evil spirits that explained the unexplainable. Lame Elk was not sure there were so many evil spirits around as the old ones alluded to, but he was careful to stay away from most strange or possibly haunted areas spoken of. It was the stories of the animal spirits and the Ancient People he was most interested in. To be a great tracker, you had to respect the abilities of the animals you sought. The Ancient People were said to be great trackers, with a deep understanding of the world they had lived in. It was said that some of them could foresee the events of their times, communicate with the beasts, and find the places where the Living Spirits would visit most.

Lame Elk was interested in finding those places too. He had hoped to some day speak to his father again, perhaps in a dream or a vision. He had climbed the most notable peaks, and indeed had felt the nearness of the Spirits. From time to time he would suddenly feel like he was in the presence of a greater force when no one else was around. He was fairly sure he had passed close to an ancient site of importance or was near a Spirit. He would carefully and reverently look around when he felt that way, often discovering a cave or mound, unearthing arrowheads, and other ancient relics. He had a small pouch in which he kept his most important finds that were small enough to carry. His lodge had other ancient treasures, and he often gave pieces to the old ones and the Shaman, mostly to keep a political peace.

THE WHITEMEN'S FIRE was out, as the night was nearing its loneliest hours. Lame Elk moved between the Whitemen's horses, slowly and carefully reassuring each animal that he was not a threat. Two horses would be good, but three would greatly speed his way home. But first he had to get the blankets and meat. A weapon would be good too. That would mean he would have to enter the tent of one of the Whitemen, and cross through the center of the camp. This would be a story he could tell with some pride, back at his lodge. Lame Elk moved without sound and surprisingly fast across the camp up to the front flap of the nearest tent. He quickly slipped inside so as to not allow the cold to follow him in.

WHEN LAME ELK stepped into the tent, Corby was sitting up facing him with his rifle folded across his chest. Both men were quite startled by the sudden meeting. Corby, like Donovan, had been sitting up waiting all night for this exact possible encounter, but he had not heard Lame Elk until he was inside the tent, three feet away. He wasn't even sure he trusted what he saw until Lame Elk ran back out of the tent.

"Donovan!" he screamed. "Injuns!" It took Corby only a few seconds to get to his feet and throw open the tent flap, but Lame Elk was already out of sight. He ran over to Donovan's tent still yelling and opened the flap to see Donovan pointing the rifle he had given him, braced up against some of the gear.

"Get to the horses, boy!" barked Donovan. "They'll want them animals most."

As Corby swung around toward where the horses and mules were picketed, he could hear the animals snorting and stamping, so he knew Donovan was right.

He looked to the right and left as he ran the short distance to the animals. One horse and two mules were loose, and one horse, his black, Midnight, was gone. He quickly tied the animals back up. Corby decided that there was only one Indian, and due to the surprise, the Indian had made off with only one horse in the wild dash back across the camp. Corby moved into the trees and started angling away from the camp, listening for the Indian and his stolen horse. There were deep shadows from a big moon, but no sounds to give the thief away. It was cold, probably below 20 degrees, and very quiet, with no wind. Corby could hear the snow crunch under his boot, along with twigs and needles. He crouched and listened again. Slowly he worked his way in a semicircle around the camp, away from the short side facing the mountain cliff. Nothing. He worked his way back again, concentrating on finding tracks this time. There they were, back at the picket line, running right to the mountain. The Indian, leading his horse, had run behind the camp under the mountain as Corby had run to the picket line. A bold move but, in retrospect, a smart one. He was long gone. He must have thought out the possible escape avenues, depending on the circumstances. Just like a damn Indian to take the best horse, his horse. The loss was acute, and he sat down in the soft falling snow boiling with rage.

LAME ELK WAS still cold and hungry. He still believed Whitemen to be stupid and lucky. But he was happy, as he now knew he would get back to his people, even if not in the grand style he had contemplated earlier. The horse was a strong, large animal, not to his liking, not the swift, surefooted paints his people raised and traded. Still, this horse would travel far and be much admired for its size and strength. His spirits rose as he headed home into the breaking day.

3

TRUE WINTER WAS ONLY a month away. The cold would pen everyone in. Little work would be done in the high country towns once the snows came to stay. The wagons of the immigrants would not be seen again before late spring. The trappers would hole up in either their mountain cabins or teepees with the friendly Indians. Confined areas around the old fort already stood out in dirty contrast to the surrounding wilderness. Smoke seemed to always hang over the little towns, and garbage was hauled less and less distance away as the cold crept in. Fort Boise was settling in for the protracted gloomy season.

Sheriff Tom Jackson had just completed his interview with Zeke Bridges, after hearing the story from everyone else he saw in town. Zeke had been barnstorming the two saloons, railing against this fellow Corby, lamenting the demise of Marshal Donovan, apparently a good friend if one believed it. Tom Jackson did not. Not that it mattered, as Zeke had come back alone. It was just that Zeke was such a blowhard, apparently a thoroughly despicable liar and cheat by all accounts. Sheriff Jackson knew Donovan too. Didn't like him much, but respected him. He instinctively knew a man like Donovan wasn't going to befriend a character like Zeke Bridges. Everyone in town pretty much felt the same way, but Zeke was having an effect on the winterbound inhabitants. It gave everyone something to talk about through the long, cold nights, and Bridges was buying more than his share of drinks.

The sheriff looked across the saloon at the back of Zeke Bridges, now mingling with the local drinking crowd in Murphy's. Bridges was a prime candidate for a hunting accident some day. There were hunting accidents that took less than desirable citizens from time to time. The West was very much a raw frontier, and local lawmen like Sheriff Jackson were often not seen in surrounding small communities for months at a time. Sometimes a town just couldn't wait for the slow arm of the law to take care of consensus problems.

Sheriff Jackson had ridden at a leisurely pace down from Payette when the news had arrived in his town. He was paid to investigate such crimes on a job-by-job basis when no one else was available. Fort Boise was about the farthest he would go, but with Donovan himself missing, he had to come this time. He needed to finish his work here and get back to Payette before the really bad weather started, and it would come fairly soon. Now he studied Zeke some more, knowing he would have to visit the scene of the crime with this man come Spring. Maybe he could turn it into a couple days of good hunting, bring along a friend or two to balance out the distasteful time spent with Bridges.

AT THE BAR Zeke felt the lawman's gaze. He pretended indifference, but started asking himself the same nagging questions. Would the bodies and bullets still be there in the Spring, and would the evidence raise questions about his story? He had killed Quaid with Donovan's Colt, and covered his tracks by explaining Donovan had uncovered Quaid to be Corby's friend. Why else would a stranger volunteer to ride posse? The town had bought that piece of fabrication, as no one knew Quaid. But how to explain Luther, shot in the back by his pa? Or had Donovan been killed when he went down under his horse? What if evidence showed Donovan was killed by a close-up shot by Corby, or had only had a broken leg, and had been left to die by Zeke? Zeke knew his tale of chasing Corby up over the mountain before losing him had some holes. He would have to get up the mountain first, dig the graves he had told everyone about, and, if necessary, keep going if his story came undone. He breathed a deep sigh of resignation. Leaving the territory wasn't such a hard thing to do. He really had no friends, and now he could sell-off the family possessions and travel elsewhere to make a fresh start. A familiar loneliness swept over him. He didn't really mourn the loss of his father and brother, who hadn't treated him very well since his mother had passed on. His mother had really been the only one to laugh with him and care about him. He would go visit her grave before he rode back to the empty house at the edge of town. But first he would have a few drinks, tell a few stories, and visit one of the girls at Maud's Place.

Two drinks later, he was embellishing his adventure to a traveling gun salesman. He showed him Donovan's worn black-handled Colt Walker, which he now wore in tribute to the "dead hero." He told his story with a real passion now, and it fit like a hand in a glove in his reconstructed memory. He was beginning to feel legitimately wronged and somewhat heroic in his ever-improving version of the chase.

DOWN THE WINDSWEPT street, Sheriff Jackson stamped the snow off of his boots before entering Maud's Place to see who was employed there since his last visit. The town could damned-well pick up this tab too, he thought as he selected a young companion for the long, black night ahead. A prudent man, Jackson was Maud's first customer of the early evening, earning himself the widest selection on a limited menu.

BY THE TIME Zeke would get to Maud's, he would be drunk enough to really not care about his options. His mind was swimming with conflicted emotions, a foreboding that ate at him, and a growing emptiness of soul he could feel but did not understand.

4

THE LATE MORNING SUN was melting the new snow on the bare patches of ground as Lame Elk pushed East to the Yellowstone. The surrounding mountains were now familiar, and he saw old signs of his people as he trekked toward the tribe's winter campgrounds. The Yellowstone Shoshone, like many tribes, broke into smaller bands to forage in the winter. But unlike many tribes, they didn't range very far, due to the unique qualities of the Yellowstone River valley. Game was plentiful in the valley, and he once again knew the strong pride his people had in living here. His Yellowstone Shoshone were not a large tribe, and he knew that many of his relatives in distant Shoshone bands lived on much harsher lands, in less conflict; but no Arapaho or Ute, or even the mighty Blackfoot, could claim such a wonderful homeland as the People had along the Yellowstone. Lame Elk thought the Shoshone were not as fierce as the Comanche, or as handsome as the Cheyenne, but they were resourceful. There were no better horse breeders, trainers, and traders than the Shoshone. The People prospered, and allied themselves to many other tribes. His people were just plain smart. Who else lived by the Earth's Water, in the misty valleys, comfortable through the harsh winter months? When other tribes starved and froze, the People had the buffalo and elk come to them to winter by the warm waters.

Since the time of his grandfather, however, the Blackfoot had been pushing closer to the Yellowstone with their summer hunting parties, and expanding their claims to the land. His people had slowly been pushed to the South by the more aggressive and larger tribe. Warfare had not broken out, due to the comfortable distance still between the two base territories, but there was no love lost between the two tribes. Lame Elk feared the day the Shoshone might have to give up the wonderful winter campgrounds of his ancestors, and live out by the summer hunting grounds of their cousins the Lemhi and Bannock, closer to their enemies, the Crow, or the Whiteman along the Snake River. The Yellowstone hunting grounds had been such a good provider that the People had not even bothered to travel to the traditional fall gatherings of the other Shoshone tribes for many years now, feeling secure in their mountain valleys along the headwaters of the Yellowstone River.

Whitemen, another problem, were showing up everywhere to the South too. Their distant relatives the Paiutes were in serious conflict with Whitemen. Word had come that more Whitemen had been seen in their wagons in Bannock lands and even as far North as Cree country in the Canadas. Many of the tribes were calling for an extended war to drive back these interlopers, and there were stories of great defeats and large decimations of other tribes to the distant East, primarily from the diseases the Whitemen brought with them.

No, the People were wise to stay in the land of rising steam and hot mud pools. The Creator had long ago led them to this magic and wonderful land. Lame Elk knew, as had his father before him, that his life's path was to keep him forever in these beautiful mountains.

The big black horse of the Whiteman had carried him well these last days, showing great stamina, if not the swiftness of his People's ponies. Still, the horse was well trained, and Lame Elk wondered how the horse might perform on a long run. He crested the high ridge and looked down on the People's winter hunting grounds. Soon the last of the summer camp would break up, and the smaller groups would spread out over the territory for the winter. They were probably just waiting for his band to come home. There, far below, were the teepees of his people, the smoke from dozens of fires, and the horses grazing by the river flat. He wanted to yell out his welcome, but knew he was too far away and high up to be heard yet. Turning his horse, he rode to the South following the ridgetop, looking down on the peaceful scene and visualizing his ride into camp.

Something caught his eye on the near side of the camp. He reined the big horse to a stop and stared hard at the once benign landscape. There, again, and now other movement. His heart stood still. He yelled out with all his might. If he only had a gun, he might warn them. There they were, a large war party of Blackfoot moving slowly through the trees from the northwest, thousands of feet below him. He recognized the attack strategy. Small bands of Blackfoot would be circling the area, eliminating what sentries there might be, set to capture and drive off the horses. Only this was more than a raid. There were too many Blackfoot warriors massed in the woods. The Blackfoot intended to drive the Shoshone from the Yellowstone for good, and that meant killing as many Shoshone as they could.

Lame Elk kicked his horse over and over, yelled his war cry, and watched in helpless horror as he raced across the mountaintop. The Blackfoot were now surging forward out of the woods, and he heard the distant gunfire. Most of the fighting would be done with bow and arrow, lance, and war club, but both sides would have a few guns. He lost sight of the battle as he was forced over the crest and down the mountain trail into the forest. Time seemed to stand still as he recklessly plunged down the mountain to the distant village. He could imagine Two Crows and Wind in His Hair rallying the Shoshone warriors to counterattack, or hit and run after the large Blackfoot war party, but he knew what the conclusion to the battle would be, long before he would reach the valley floor. Hopefully some would escape to preset hiding spots, or be left for dead in the carnage, but the Yellowstone Shoshone would be slaughtered this day. His wife and son came to the forefront of his terror, and his heart hammered as if it would explode.

CROOKED CLAWS LOOKED back over his shoulder and signaled Small Bear to ride forward.

"Take twenty warriors and relieve Blue Heron and his band. The Shoshone dogs will be barking at our heels all the way home. Send a rider if there are problems. Do not lose any more of my warriors."

The Blackfoot chief was feeling very powerful and smiled to himself. His plan had worked, just as he had explained it would to the Council of Elders. He was bringing back over a hundred ponies and a couple dozen women and boy captives. Already a great war chief, he was now a legend in the making. His people would retell the story of today's great victory, and his name would grow with the years. Sitting on his black and white pony, with his three owl feathers woven into his long raven hair, Crooked Claws was a picture of strength and confidence, which his warriors both admired and feared. His bear coat covered a tall, thick frame that intimidated most warriors by its size alone. But there was much more to be careful about with Crooked Claws. He was a skilled warrior, fearless in battle, and unforgiving of failure. Many a Blackfoot had felt the blow of an unhappy leader, and some had not fully recovered. As a consequence, Crooked Claws's warriors were a force to be reckoned with, and the Shoshone had been brutally butchered. Perhaps fifty to a hundred Shoshone had escaped and scattered. At least that many more had been killed. The survivors would probably join other Shoshone tribes further to the South and West. As a fighting force, the Yellowstone Shoshone had been effectively eliminated.

Crooked Claws admired the rich hunting grounds he was passing through and began to formulate a plan to break away with a large following to occupy this newly won and mysterious land of misting waters. The Blackfoot had long been envious of these lands, and as their power grew, they had begun to consider how they might expand into this Shoshone stronghold. Many were fearful of the many alliances the Shoshone had, including their feared southern cousins, the Comanche, but Crooked Claws had convinced them that these Yellowstone River Shoshone were women that he could subdue, and the great Blackfoot Nation need not fear anyone. In the end, the old men of the Council had feared Crooked Claws more than any reprisals. Besides, they were greedy, and looked forward to the spoils of conquest. Crooked Claws also knew that should he fall in battle or return home defeated, the old men would be happy with that too. He shifted his weight on his pony, once more looking at his new wealth, and then settled on a new seat for the long, slow march home to the North. Riders had been sent ahead to tell the tale of victory, and the camp would be ready to welcome home the warriors with great feasts and dancing. Crooked Claws began to think how he would consolidate his power to rise above the old men.

LAME ELK ANXIOUSLY asked the aged Small Hand and his band of refugees if they had seen what had happened to Dancing Cloud and his son, Beaver on the Rock, during the Blackfoot raid. Small Hand and approximately twenty women and children were rummaging through the burned and trampled remains of what had been the summer home of the Yellowstone Shoshone for untold generations. Bodies of warriors, women, and children were widely scattered in the wreckage and beyond. Smoke still rose from dozens of smoldering fires, and the small group was slowly identifying the dead, amid much wailing and sobbing.

Small Hand looked up at Lame Elk in somewhat of a stupor, and exclaimed, "Lame Elk! You have come home. The People will be happy."

Then he slumped back down, realizing the ridiculousness of his statement.

"Lame Elk, where will we go? Wind in His Hair is dead. Our warriors are gone. My son too." The older man sat down on the ground heavily, as if he would never get up again. Lame Elk knelt down beside him and asked about his family again.

Small Hand pulled himself together somewhat and looked in the younger man's eyes.

"Many children were down by the river when the attack came. Some women too. You might try looking there. Your mother was killed in the first sweep of Blackfoot warriors, over by your lodgepole. She stood by her cooking pot while others ran in all directions. She went down with the first blow.

"Wind in His Hair and fifty or so braves stood at midcamp when the

Blackfoot ponies stampeded through the People's camp. Not one of the warriors was standing after the first riders rode through the camp.

"The Blackfoot chieftain had great power, and none could stand against him. His warriors were the fiercest I have ever seen. Only young women and some boys were taken prisoners. Perhaps your wife and son were taken too."

Small Hand then lost focus and looked off into the distance. He did not have any more to say. Lame Elk stood up and hurried down to the river, his eyes sweeping the foreground as he moved forward. There were many bodies of all sizes strewn about. Clearly the Blackfoot had intended the worst on this campaign. Then he saw the crumpled body of Dancing Cloud. She was face down and twisted in such a way that Lame Elk knew immediately that she was dead. A few yards away, Beaver on the Rock lay sprawled out, his head crushed in by a warrior's blow. Lame Elk's heart constricted in such pain that he fell numb to the ground, oblivious to the noises around him.

After some time he felt a hand on his shoulder and saw that Small Hand was sitting next to him. The old man was crying for him.

5

I T WAS A TEDIOUS and slow process as Corby and Donovan traveled West, but getting out of the mountains was imperative. The plan was to find some outlying homestead or community where Corby could wait for Spring and then push further West into unknown territories. Donovan could rest up and recover, and they would go their separate ways. Donovan had heard the full story from Corby's perspective, and considering the treachery of the Bridges, along with this young man's efforts to help the Marshal, the deal had been sealed.

Corby's current circumstances had put him on a path to head West much as he had wanted to anyway. He wanted to see the untouched wilderness he had heard about his whole life. But first, navigating back to civilization and a road would take all their attention.

Donovan was pretty sure they would reach the Snake River today or tomorrow, and some little homesteads or settlements wouldn't be far off. He would send word of his situation downriver to Payette, and of the need to arrest Zeke Bridges for the murder of Quaid. He made a mental note to get his gun back when they took Bridges in. His Colt Walker had been a gift from the government for serving twenty years in the U.S. Marshal Service, and he damn well wanted it back.

This Corby kid was beginning to grow on him. Donovan had been a lone wolf for so many years that the forced companionship had kind of snuck up on him, and he found he enjoyed talking to Corby and passing on his own insights.

Corby, for his part, was happy to learn from such an experienced and famous lawman. Corby too had been alone too much, and life had been pretty tough so far. It was a good feeling to have a partner, even under these strange conditions.

They made an early camp that night high above the deep gorges the Snake River cut in this part of the country. Finding a way down to the river would be tomorrow's big challenge. Donovan was sitting a horse, but not so well, and any descent too steep would probably unseat him.

After dinner Corby walked to the edge of the camp and surveyed the terrain below. It was going to be an interesting day tomorrow. Those two mules would prove their worth again in the morning.

Among the contraband taken from the mountainside gunfight had been Quaid's revolver and holster. Corby had been wearing it since he picked it up. Ben Bridges had had the revolver stuck in his belt. Having a five-shot revolver was a huge step up from his single-shot pistol. The gun slid in and out of the used holster with ease and speed. Corby lined up some imaginary targets and drew on them, practicing his draw and trying different adjustments. He heard a grunt behind him, and Donovan hobbled over.

"That there is a Texas Paterson Colt." Donovan indicated the gun Corby was handling. "Had me a Colt Walker, one of the few outside of the army, until that little snake Zeke Bridges took it from me. Show me your draw again."

Corby flexed his hand and looked over at a tree. He drew quickly.

"Not a bad draw, kid, but you are most likely a dead man," Donovan panned.

"Well now, not the way I see it," Corby retorted.

"The draw is quick enough, but you ain't no gunfighter."

Donovan shuffled over closer, right into Corby's face. Corby, like most westerners, involuntarily took a step backward at Donovan's encroachment. As he did so, he felt a gun barrel stick him in the ribs.

"Bang, you're dead," smiled Donovan. "You see, kid, that was a damn slow draw, but you never saw it. Don't have to be much for aiming at this range neither. Swing radius is cut down big for a second target, and you've got the all important element of surprise to boot!"

"You mean if you draw first, Marshal. Ain't that murder?"

Donovan gave Corby a hard look and said, "When it's you or them that's got to die, you better be the first to draw, boy. And the closer in you get, the better your chances are."

Thus began the casual schooling of a gunfighter, as conversational topics were limited at best.

6

BY NIGHTFALL, THE WHITEMAN'S big black horse had caught him up to the raiding Blackfoot camp. Lame Elk had removed the noisy Whiteman's horseshoes to better evade notice. There were many guards posted and hidden, as befit a raid of this size. Some surviving Shoshone warriors would undoubtedly attempt small counterattacks or possible rescue missions directed at the retiring victors. Lame Elk crept forward yard-by-yard over a two-hour period, listening, assessing, and planning. He estimated a warrior force of nearly two hundred. It would be easy to kill a few unwary enemies, but Lame Elk knew that would fall into the Blackfoot chief's plan, and he would probably be caught trying to get away. His blood ran hot, but his mind was exceptionally clear and cool. These were enemies to respect, even as he hated them past any hate he had ever experienced before. He worked his way back to the horse and started a wide circle ahead of the Blackfoot in the remaining night, his mind so intent that he did not feel the biting cold.

Over the next day, he caught a glimpse of what appeared to be a Shoshone war party of maybe twenty warriors, but decided he would rather fight alone. He watched and waited until he was sure there were three advance-scouting parties the Blackfoot were using. Each had six warriors and frequently signaled each other. Consequently, their range of vision was quite extensive, and provided the security coverage the main party required. Lame Elk assumed that there would be other outriding bands on the flanks and to the rear. A dangerous but lethal plan began to take shape in his mind. Knowing it would be very difficult to penetrate the perimeter of the band, he thought there might be a way to position himself so the band would come to him unaware. He searched the terrain in front of the oncoming Blackfoot until he found a sizable rock outcropping directly in their path that would provide both his horse and himself a reasonable chance at staying hidden while the advance parties passed by him. Since they were looking for counterattacks, he hoped the rock hole he found, which was barely large enough to hide a single horse and rider, would be overlooked due to its size. He led his horse up a sharp twenty-foot slope to the selected spot and waited.

By midmorning, he heard the advance parties approaching. First, a group rode hard to the top of his rocky area for first looks forward, and then he heard them circle down on either side of him. Would the Whiteman's horse give him away? Would the other ponies smell them? The advance parties continued on. He waited while the main group passed by, and was sure a young Blackfoot wanted to come up his hill, but he didn't. After the main body passed, he calmly mounted and rode up behind the stragglers. He picked his first victim carefully for clothing and weapons, allowing himself some disguise. Settling on a method of killing, he casually approached when someone lost contact with the group, and moved up to point-blank range before firing an arrow through the back of his neck. He took his time, and moved back and forth behind the band, killing ten warriors before there was a general alarm.

The rear guard came up quickly to inform the main group that they were finding the dead warriors, and wondered why no one had signaled them of any attack. As they came forward, it was relatively simple to slip out the back door.

THE SLOW MARCH back to Blackfoot territory was now four times two days old. The Shoshone counterattacking war party had abandoned the fight and retreated home to salvage what was left and prepare the People for leaving the Yellowstone. Lame Elk understood their thinking, and hoped that the People would find refuge and peace. He, however, had no such need, and continued his one-man crusade with a religious fervor.

His namesake, the elk, was part of the spirit world he drew his particular strengths from, and in small ceremonies, he would call to his spirit brothers to deliver him the abilities to hunt the Blackfoot. He needed the stealth and elusiveness of the elk. Many times he had marveled at the large animal's ability to vanish into thin air or appear without a sound. Many times he had chased the animal, sure of the kill, until it had vaulted down a steep cliffside in a full run, ending the hunt in sudden fashion. So it was that Lame Elk concentrated on stealth and sudden death, while melting away before his pursuers could locate him.

Lame Elk decorated all his arrows, as did all braves, with his own signature markings. The circular elk horn he normally carved onto his shaft was now painted black to signify his new purpose. The Blackfoot who pulled the arrows out of their comrades' necks thought the elk horn was a black hand of death sign. They began to refer to the killer as the Black Hand of Death, and then shortened it to Blackhand.

Lame Elk worked to perfect his hit-and-run techniques, and by the time the Blackfoot finally reached their home camp, many in the war party were spooked into believing Blackhand was not a normal man but some kind of vengeful man/spirit who could not be seen or caught.

CROOKED CLAWS HAD arranged a huge reception for the returning conquerors. The warriors had stopped outside the Blackfoot home campsite to put on their fiercest war paints and battle regalia. A slow, majestic parade into the Blackfoot camp, leading the captured slaves and ponies, was greeted with cheering families and much kowtowing from the old Council members.

The Blackfoot camp was pitched along a lake next to a low-rising mesa. Behind the mesa was the beginning of a range of mountains to the West, and across the lake began the endless grasslands of the upper plains. Like the Shoshone, they were getting ready to break up the camp for the winter and depart in smaller groups for winter foraging, but they had awaited the return of their warriors. Large fires were burning in preparation for feasting and story telling. The women and children ran out to taunt and beat the prisoners. In particular, the young women captives received heavy abuse from the Blackfoot women. After a while Crooked Claws had to stop the beatings, to prevent his new wealth from being permanently damaged. Crooked Claws took on the air of a new king, receiving gifts and dispensing justice with a certainty that made the old men cringe with hidden animosity.

The feasting and storytelling went on all night, as did the display of war booty. Of course the subject of Blackhand was carefully discussed out of earshot of Crooked Claws, but eventually reached the Council members, who broached the subject with the great war chief. Crooked Claws dismissed the concerns as nothing but the fears of his youngest warriors, and assured the camp that there would be no more minor attacks now that the war party was home. He then stood with great dignity and headed for his wives and tepee. Orders had been given to leave all the prisoners and captive ponies alone for further division of spoils in the morning. It was, however, understood already what property was Crooked Claws's. Normal guards were posted, and the partying broke up just before light.

With all the fires and noise, it was easy for Lame Elk to kill some more Blackfoot. Anyone who wandered near his well-chosen hiding place for a romantic interlude or the call of nature received the trademark arrow. It was necessary on two occasions to use his knife quickly to silence the struggle, but the victims never heard or saw "Blackhand."

The next morning when the bodies were discovered, the Blackfoot camp was stirred like a hornet's nest. The luster was off Crooked Claws great triumph and the Council of Elders was demanding action to end the plague Crooked Claws had led right to their home camp. Crooked Claws was furious, as he realized that his next plans for power were placed in limbo, if not outright danger. He had to kill this Blackhand fast. He picked his ten best warriors, gave each a new pony in advance, and warned them to either track down and kill this Shoshone dog or face his eternal wrath. Needless to say, the warriors were not thrilled with the assignment, as it would further delay the breakup of the summer camp. Nonetheless, they were confident they could accomplish this task and gain more wealth and glory.

After provisioning themselves for a week of possible pursuit, the manhunting party left camp around midday to find Blackhand. The party chose to now dress in its winter campaign clothing, as the weather was turning colder, with intermittent light snow showers even at these lower elevations. Wolf and beaver hats, deerskin shirts and pants, and buffalo robes were worn along with a few trading post blankets taken from the Crow. Each man had his talisman or pouch with him to protect him in battle or give him advantage in the hunt. The ponies were painted for the task; some matching the paint symbols on the men, depicting accomplishments in battle each had won. This seasoned group of warriors each had their own band in peaceful times that traveled and hunted together. It was only when the bands came together for ceremonies, buffalo hunts, and war considerations that each of these braves submitted to higher authority. There the band leaders joined warrior societies of different notoriety, and the ten riders were of the most elite warrior society, the Bulls. The bull buffalo was a powerful symbol in the life of the Blackfoot, and the Bulls had a very distinguished history as fighters and leaders.

The Bulls to a man were great warriors, and most chaffed under the bullying of Crooked Claws. Although Crooked Claws was a great fighter and a natural war chief, he was not generous, or easy to live with. The Bulls were ready to disband and go their separate ways as soon as this business with Blackhand was settled and the war prizes were distributed. As such they headed out of camp with the mentality of haste and impatience.

Lame Elk watched the band ride out to the South, and there was no doubt in his mind that they were looking for him. These were the toughest-looking warriors he had ever seen, and he knew in open combat he was no match for any of them. Lame Elk had been one of the Shoshone's best warriors for many years, but the Shoshone didn't practice the warrior cult as a way of life like these Blackfoot did, nor did they have the strength of numbers the larger, more aggressive tribe did. His survival now depended more than ever on his skills as a tracker and hunter, only now it was time to use those skills to hide and evade. Undoubtedly the Blackfoot search party would fan out to pick up any sign of his passing and would work as a unit to flank and surround him when they did. Any isolated track would give him away, particularly one as large as his black horse's. The horse was also showing a tenderness in its hooves since Lame Elk had removed its horseshoes. As big and strong as the animal was, the big black would not be able to run hard on his tender hooves in an all out race.

So, the option of outrunning the Blackfoot was gone. He also realized that, outnumbered as he was, the Blackfoot could rotate riders and eventually wear him down and overtake him. No, he had to sneak away to survive. He mounted and looked for a traveled path leading away from the Blackfoot camp to the West. Despite the need to distance himself from the camp, he knew that a slow, careful retreat would serve him best.

THE BROWN HORSE seemed to drift in and out of the trees along the streambed. High brush covered much of the sloping ground that led down to the stream itself, so Lame Elk lost sight of the oncoming pursuer intermittently. The rider was hanging over his mount, studying the ground as he came. He was a big warrior with a wolf skin pulled over his head and shoulders. He had been following the same stream Lame Elk had chosen to ride up an hour earlier. It didn't appear that this warrior had picked up his trail, nor had he signaled to any other potential hunter in the last half hour. Lame Elk continued his stalk from the other side of the stream. He knew there was a steep rise ahead that would require the rider to dismount to continue. He ran ahead to get in position for his ambush.

Time dragged by as he waited for the Blackfoot warrior to reappear. He began to worry, as the warrior should have arrived by now. He wanted to move to see what had happened but knew he couldn't risk it. He listened for any indication of the advancing rider, over the sound of the small waterfall next to his ambush spot. There, finally, was the slow clip of a horse's hooves on rocks just downstream. The rider came into view, still studying the ground, but now looking up at the large rocks and rise in the stream. Then suddenly, the warrior decided to cross the stream to Lame Elk's side. The easy shot Lame Elk had planned was gone, and worse, so was his view of the warrior. In fact the warrior seemed to be within feet of him on the other side of the big boulders, and Lame Elk had no idea where he would reappear. Lame

Elk gently lay down his bow and picked up his war club. He rose to a squat, with his back against the big rock and held his breath.

The big Blackfoot warrior was leading his pony with one hand and using his other to climb up the rocks. His head popped up to the right of Lame Elk like a duck rising out of the water. Lame Elk swung down with all his might as the wolf head swiveled around to see him.

THE BULLS WERE using a crisscross weave to cover the surrounding area, trying to cut the trail of the Shoshone while staying in workable range of each other. Two Horns was more or less the leader, due to his natural abilities and the respect of the others, but each of the warriors was capable of taking command as needed. Two Horns suggested the tracking strategy, which the others quickly accepted, but he didn't direct the search, out of respect to the others. They all knew what was expected of them and how to do it.

Late in the afternoon, Two Horns rode up to Red Horses, who sat in a grove of ponderosa pines. Red Horses offered him some elk jerky, and they discussed the ongoing search.

"This Shoshone Blackhand is a fine hunter. He moves quickly, decisively, and disappears," grunted Two Horns. "No one has picked up his trail, and it will be dark soon."

"The riders to the North and East will be returning now to our meeting place by the Eagle Rock," opined Red Horses. "I should call in our riders to the West and join you there."

"Can't you signal both of your western riders?" asked Two Horns.

"I will have to go after Stone Bear, who we saw climbing the Gray Woman Mountain awhile back."

"Did you signal him to come back on the circle?" Two Horns asked.

"Yes, but he did not see me," said Red Horses. "He is probably returning by now."

Two Horns thought about the climb Stone Bear had made, and asked Red Horses where on the Gray Woman he had last seen Stone Bear. Red Horses picked up on Two Horns's concern, and the two swung their horses back in the direction of Stone Bear.

Awhile later, following Stone Bear's track up the stream, they heard a horse snort, and saw a very large black horse standing by the stream watching them. A little farther upstream, as they now expected, they found Stone Bear with his head caved in.

Two Horns slid off his horse to the ground and picked up the warrior, tied him to the strange big black horse, and, without saying a word, headed for the meeting place. This Shoshone had now made it personal with the death of one of the Bulls. Red Horses cursed a steady monologue all the way back to the meeting rock. Two Horns felt more of the anger he had been carrying with him since this campaign of Crooked Claws's had begun. Stone Bear had married Two Horn's wife's sister and had often accompanied Two Horns's small band on the winter hunts. He had been a quiet giant, slow to anger, perhaps not the most intelligent of the Bulls, but very dependable in battle and easygoing. His death seemed pointless.

7

THE TOWN AROUND FORT Boise was becoming less friendly every day. Zeke was no longer a celebrity with a new story to tell. Old animosities were rearing their ugly heads, and some citizens were openly questioning Zeke's tall tale. His sense of survival rapidly surfaced, and one cold morning, having sold everything he could, he quietly left the area. First East and then South, Zeke set a leisurely pace in the deepening Fall weather. Somewhere warm and sunny would be a nice change. Perhaps eventually New Orleans, or even Mexico City sounded appealing. He had enough money to live well for a year or so, from selling his pa's possessions. Right now he just needed to disappear from this part of the country. The buffoons in Fort Boise would wait all winter to take any action, and in retrospect, his decision to leave now was really quite intelligent. He would be too far gone for anyone to pursue him when and if they ever decided to do so. Why he had bothered to stay around even another day mystified him now, considering the possibilities and future he would have in far more entertaining environments. So he traveled, feeling rather well about his circumstances, and other than being cold from time to time, the slow travel was rather pleasant, as each step took him away from a past he had hated, toward a future that was already richer.

Zeke's father had married above his station in life. His wife had been a well-educated daughter of a Boston lawyer. Her family had frowned on the marriage, but tried then to make the best of it, including offering employment to the new son-in law. Ben Bridges had worked as the manager of her family's estates for ten years, and both of their boys had gotten a good start on their education. But Ben had resented living on the good graces of his father-in-law, and one day took his family West, partly out of pride and partly out of spite. One disappointment after another had finally led them all the way to the frontier, on their way to California, when Zeke's mother had taken ill. Stuck in Fort Boise, and still receiving some money from his wife's family, Ben started a small freighting business between the local frontier towns and settled into the community. When his wife died, he no longer had the ambition to travel on to California.

The boys, Tom and Zeke, due to their formative years, looked down on the local, mostly uneducated population. Both felt they were destined for a better life than their father's, and were waiting for a chance to leave the backwater town they had been living in. Tom's arrogance had prompted his demise. Zeke had almost followed his big brother into oblivion, but had now escaped. Had he been religious, he might have considered the events that led to his rebirth providential.

About three weeks into his travels, Zeke found himself somewhere southeast of the Great Salt Lake, when he saw a thin column of smoke rising in the dry canyon country ahead. Although Zeke wasn't greatly accomplished on living off the land, he had enough practice to be careful concerning Indians and other potential dangers of the West, so he quickly got off the road he was following and edged slowly closer to the smoke through whatever cover was available until he could see what was happening. The canyon terrain was sparse with vegetation, but rock outcroppings and arroyos were sufficient to hide anyone wishing to do so, and Zeke was able to get a good look from a fair distance before he ventured out into the open again.

The wagon train was partially burned, and widely scattered over about a mile. Seven wagons in all, some tipped over and others standing upright, were scarred from the battle that obviously had taken place. Clothes and personal possessions, along with the mutilated bodies of the white men and their families, were haphazardly lying around on the ground. The smoke came from two smoldering wagons apparently set on fire sometime before. There were indications of some night animals having visited the site, and a lone coyote skulked off when Zeke rode up. Magpies and other birds were less intimidated, and continued with their gruesome meals. Zeke could tell the danger had passed and that no one had survived. He decided he should salvage whatever he could before more Indians might return. So he swiftly and systematically began a search throughout the wreckage.

It became evident that these were Mormons, probably en route to Salt Lake City when they were ambushed. Zeke couldn't identify the Indian tribe and he didn't care, quickly moving through the wagons and bodies. He was able to find some money and jewelry, but nothing significant, until he reached the lead wagon. It had turned over, and he could see that there was a long box built under the driver's seat. It had no lid that he could see, but he was now very excited, as many stories floated around the West of wagon trains' attempts to hide their wealth in hidden compartments. He found a wheel jack and began to smash in the box. The noise made him nervous, and he kept looking up to see if it had alerted anyone to his presence. Eventually he was able to split a board enough to wedge the jack under and pry open the box. Inside were a large tin and several bundles tightly wrapped in rawhide. Zeke grabbed them all along with his earlier finds and quickly exited the massacre scene. The coyote slinked back as Zeke spurred his horse South.

That night, at camp, Zeke retallied his newfound possessions. The rawhide packages were a major disappointment, holding religious writings and icons, and Zeke threw them in his fire to destroy any evidence of theft, but the tin held coins and banknotes, jewelry, and stones. Zeke did not know how much they were worth, but he did know he was suddenly a rich man. Campsites were about to be traded for hotel rooms.

Two months later found Zeke, now Zachary DuPort, living in style in his new home overlooking the Mississippi River in New Orleans, garnering a reputation as an eastern businessman with a penchant for gambling and an eye for a quick dollar. Mr. DuPort's considerable appetite for investments overcame any concern about his mysterious background and unorthodox business practices. In fact, Zachary DuPort was spending a great deal of money, and consequently, made many new friends. His mother had been from Boston, and while never saying so, he allowed his acquaintances to assume he had come from there recently too.

As yet his business skills were rather paltry, but he was learning through buying his way into a variety of ventures, some good, some bad. Whereas Zachary may not have had an abundance of scruples, he was not stupid, and learned from his mistakes. He had a thirst for prominence and worked for the first time in his life without being threatened, for his own interests. He found he actually enjoyed the machinations of business, and wanted to be known as a good businessman. Unfortunately he was unwilling to get there over time and through hard work alone, and saw no problem with cutting corners and enriching his own pockets when the opportunity presented itself. To Zachary, the objective was to make money, period. Still looking down his nose at even experienced businessmen, Zachary was on a steady course to burn through his money or someone else's, unless one of his investment schemes paid off large in the coming months. As of yet, there seemed to be ample cash to continue his grand lifestyle, and he was sure that more money would come just as easily as before.

8

NEEDLESS TO SAY, WHEN word reached Fort Boise that Zeke Bridges was wanted for murder, no one was particularly surprised, and no one had a clue where the law might try to find him. The next spring Sheriff Jackson took his hunting trip up into the mountains, where he bagged a handsome elk and verified the approximate gravesites per Donovan's communiqué. On the way down, his hunting friend shot a large mule deer hiding in a grove of aspen. The case was for practical purposes closed, except in the minds of Donovan and Corby. The two had spent the winter together, and by springtime, Donovan was able to walk and ride again, but with a noticeable limp. He had heard for months of Corby's desire to see the farther West, and eventually decided that he was tired of the lonely life as a marshal and would travel with Corby for awhile, until maybe he found a homestead he could buy in good country for hunting, fishing, and maybe breeding horses.

So when the weather was right, the two former antagonists mounted up the best horses available, and with the two mules of unknown ownership, loaded with provisions, headed deeper into Oregon Territory, leaving the Oregon Trail and using a compass to make a beeline West. As they traveled, the lessons of life continued in a vague fashion, and the friendship deepened. Donovan actually started to enjoy himself, and rediscovered a little part of the boy he had buried in himself many years before. He took something of a vested interest in Corby, and felt a compulsion to teach Corby as much as the latter was willing to listen to. Corby, for his part, began to feel a sense of responsibility for the tough older ex-lawman, and could envision the small working ranch Donovan kept describing as his ambition for his old age. He knew he would help Donovan get squared away in a cabin before he took off to see more of the West. The ride West was a comfortable affair for the two now-compatible adventurers.

A month's travel found them climbing up the eastern slope of the Cascade Mountains, following the headwaters of the Deschutes River. This was ponderosa pines forest, and easy, open woods for the most part. Neither had ever seen trees this big before, some more than thirty feet around and higher than anything in the Rockies. Mule deer were abundant, as were cougar and bear. The bear were of many different colors and sizes, including a cinnamon color neither had seen before. And the fishing was incredible in the many lakes and streams they passed. But Donovan wanted to cross over and down into the Oregon Valley everyone had heard so much about. So they climbed up the gradual eastern slope at a sedate, steady pace, enjoying the natural beauty of the area. At the top of the summit, they encountered the most dramatic lake they had ever seen, in an old volcano's cone, and not far past, another natural lake, somewhat larger and surrounded by a Douglas fir forest, that shimmered like a diamond and had fish jumping in the early evening light. They decided to camp by the second lake for a few days to rest the animals after the climb to the top.

This was prime elk territory at the top of the range, particularly as it was summer, and the abundance of wildlife was amazing. Beaver, eagle, and both white tail and mule deer abounded. Had it not been the top of a mountain range, Donovan would have started his homestead right there. What a wonderful hunting and fishing ground. The trout were spectacular for dinner that night, and Corby had spotted a bunch of turkeys to try for tomorrow's hunt.

The two travelers lay down by the lake later that night, watching the night sky full of stars, at peace with the world. Corby reflected on his life and began to realize he had rarely found days such as this, where all was good and he didn't have to worry if trouble was following. All of his early life he had been burdened with an abusive, alcoholic father, the disdain of the community, and a mother he could not adequately protect from either his father or the communities' contempt. Too many fights won and lost at an early age had left their mark on him, and he had not begun to grow self-confident until these last few years out on his own. Yet still he was in bondage to his past, reliving over and over the emotional low points of his youth. His behavioral direction was a work in progress, and his anger was quick and often violent. He realized this was not good, but to date, he did not know what he could do to control it. As he experienced adult life in the West, he saw he was not the only one prone to physical solutions. But innately he knew that frontier behavior probably didn't represent man's best effort. He was ashamed of some of his actions, and he was afraid of becoming as bad as some of the characters he had hated as a child. Watching Donovan, he saw a man of some integrity, rough to say the least, maybe even a little pessimistic, but he had a philosophy he held to, and was obviously quite sure of his actions when he took them. His example was a considerable step up from Corby's hit-and-miss moral compass. Corby felt the time he was spending with Donovan, observing how he reacted to things, was more valuable than the variety of skills Donovan wanted to teach him.

Donovan, on his part, also was reflecting on their relationship. How many young bucks had he seen, both good and bad, cut down before their time? How many had he helped or hurt himself? The West was full of hard customers, for all kinds of valid and invalid reasons. His profession had forced him to sweep the streets clean of any potential dangers to the citizens, often based on very limited information. He had relied on his gut instinct, his experience to eye future trouble, and the need to stay preemptive or end up paying for it. As such, he had learned to use his authority aggressively, in the hope that by doing so he would avoid a larger problem later. Sometimes he would regret the particular outcome of such behavior, but he never wavered in his belief that this was how he had to perform his job to be effective. Many a young man like Corby had felt the butt-end of Donovan's gun as he had made his point. Some probably didn't deserve it, others had. Donovan wasn't losing any sleep over which had been wronged.

This young man had some sand in Donovan's mind; he wasn't afraid, he wasn't boastful, he wasn't selfish, and he wasn't a burden. Donovan saw a larger man in there, and due to so many years of knocking people down, he suddenly had an urge to help someone up, and it made him feel good. This new, wild country made him feel good too.

After a good rest of several days, they followed the western-running stream from the lake, down the windward and much wetter side of the Cascade Range. As gentle as the climb had been on the eastern slope, the western side was the opposite, with a very steep and rugged falloff. The stream grew into a rapidly falling river; they would later learn the river was named the Umpqua, after local Indians. The trees grew larger and larger as they descended down jagged ravines. This was virgin Douglas fir and hemlock forest, with trees over a century old, some probably two. Many were fallen from age and storms, and with the steep grade, travel was slow and often perilous. There were large granite walls in tall, lush canyons, with swift brooks at the bottom of each. The river grew in size as they made their way down to the yet unseen valley floor. Donovan and Corby kept a keen look out for Indians. As the terrain began to level out, they began to see more signs of Indian life, from old fishing camps and cooking fires to trails and pottery shards.

Two days later, the Umpqua suddenly seemed to hit flat land, where it deepened and widened somewhat. The river slowed down and straightened out some too. There were now glimpses of open fields after the descent of deeply shaded, forested canopy. The men let the animals feed on the open grass and take in some sunshine. Corby scouted ahead, staying on the highest ground near the river and in cover of the trees. Rounding a turn in the river, he could now see a mile ahead, where the river now cut through rolling hills and patchwork forest. A group of Indians was fishing off a large, sloping gravel bank. Men, women, and children were at work spearing the largest river fish Corby had ever seen, in what appeared to be very shallow water. There also was a white man with the group. Corby had heard of squawmen, trappers and such that took up with the Indians in order to live in their lands. This man however didn't look like a trapper. He wore a plaid shirt that looked clean and a sombrero style of hat. Corby could tell they were all having a good time, as the children often screamed, laughed, and ran around, as children tend to do. He rode back to Donovan to tell him about the first people he had seen all summer.

9

ZACHARY DuPORT, THE FORMER Zeke Bridges, was on an extended losing streak. He had been unlucky at cards, unlucky in his latest business venture, and unlucky in love. None of the established families in New Orleans with pretty daughters seemed to care that he had money and charm. In fact, some had straight out told him he would not be welcomed should he come calling. At the same time, they were quite willing to play cards with him, and in some instances, do business if the returns were substantial enough. Well, so be it. There were plenty of exciting women in New Orleans that didn't come with a pedigree, and Zachary was actively making their acquaintances. Zach, as he allowed his friends to call him, was not overly concerned about his recent run of bad luck. He had plenty of money still, and lots of contacts and ideas to make more. Still, the collapse of his foray into the shipping business, with assorted limited partners, was not raising his popularity at the moment. His partners had belatedly found out that Zach had not secured the Boston trade necessary to purchase their cotton shipments and make the venture viable as he had guaranteed when soliciting their funds. Nor had Mr. Zachary DuPort invested the 15 percent capital required on his end per the original verbal agreement. With their own shipping line failing to materialize, his partners were scrambling to find other arrangements to transport their overdue cargoes, and looking to legal recourses to recover their monies and punish Zachary. However, like all good conmen, Zach had used the New Orleans businessmen's greed, muddying the waters sufficiently enough, to make that very difficult to do. In his calculations, Zach had spread the pain out as to not severely hurt anyone in particular. These rich businessmen could take the loss, and with some good salesmanship, some might even gamble with him again.

What Zachary didn't know was that two of his associates in the failed shipping venture could not afford this particular loss at this particular time. Charles Augustus Loucheur and Jean Paul Mirabeau had parlayed the assumed savings from the proposed shipping venture into purchasing a highly desirable piece of Mississippi bottomland together that they had coveted for years, and were therefore strapped for cash on many of their other ventures. Monsieur Mirabeau was now in jeopardy of losing his cotton gin business, a key component to his empire, while Monsieur Loucheur had overextended himself with his young wife, whom had become accustomed to an extravagant lifestyle. Ironically, it was Madame Loucheur who had introduced Charles to Zachary DuPort. Gabrielle had many young friends that Charles disapproved of, but Mr. DuPort's plan of owning their own shipping line had made good sense, and he had not been alone in wanting to get out from under the burden of freight costs that seemed to keep rising all the time in the cotton trade. Now in hindsight he clearly saw the impulsive rush he had made. Worst of all, it was he who had introduced Zachary DuPort to Monsieur Mirabeau, and it was he Monsieur Mirabeau held responsible, even if it had never been said aloud.

Charles Loucheur sat in his study, going over his finances once again, but it was his beautiful young wife that really troubled him. How had he allowed things to go this far? He slumped down in the high-backed chair and looked out his window to the garden. Bougainvillea of orange and purple covered the wrought iron fence, and the hibiscuses around the fountain were a riot of bright colors against their green backdrop. Normally he would admire his splendid flowers, but today he didn't see them as he stared into space. Was he an old fool too? Was Gabrielle unfaithful or just immature? Thirty-five years her senior, he had no illusions as to why she had married him, but he had felt a connection between them, and couldn't bring himself to believe Gabrielle would be so silly as to bring dishonor on the two of them. She had been the only daughter of a good friend of good family who had recently died, rumored quite wealthy. The girl and her father had been inseparable. He knew she still mourned for him. He was aware of her flirtations and constant need to socialize, hoping and believing they would fade as her grief would. He had extended himself to accompany her when he could, despite finding her choice of company to be pretentious and self-indulgent young people. Perhaps it was just her age. Her friends however seemed to Charles to never tire of their pleasures, and when his business demanded his attention, he was relieved to escape the never-ending social demands. When Gabrielle attended anything in his absence, he made sure appropriate associates accompanied her. The money loss would hurt, but he would survive. A scandal would be both personally and professionally devastating. He had to know what else could befall him.

BILL FITCH STEPPED back into the doorway and lit up his pipe. Following Madame Loucheur was an easy task, and it paid well. Hopefully he could string this assignment out awhile before anything conclusive took place. On the other hand, Monsieur Loucheur was prepared to pay well for a quick and decisive report. The handful of minor indiscretions he had witnessed so far he had kept to himself, in case he wished to give a glowingly clean account of the behavior of Madame Loucheur. A happy and relieved husband often rewarded good news well.

Gabrielle was saying goodbye to her friends now and climbing back into her carriage. It was still early afternoon, and she was headed for the River Road. Her brief fling with Zachary DuPort had been exciting, but he really didn't fit into her long-term plans. Now he was pestering her to find out what Charles was going to do about the problems they had with their business venture together. He would have to understand that this was not something she wanted to be associated with anymore. Charles was not stupid, and she did not wish to implicate herself with any further unpleasantness that might result from this unfortunate incident. She had planned a sweet au revoir, to distance herself, at least until Charles was feeling ebullient again over his next business success. Besides, she had a very intriguing rendezvous next Tuesday for brunch with Rochelle, who would be accompanied by her very handsome brother, Dabert Justin Beauvais, just returned from the Continent, handling family business. In the back of her mind, she knew that she was treading on thin ice, but one thing about Gabrielle was her undaunting nature. Even as she experienced guilt over a decadent lifestyle that had quickly become something of a habit, she did not fear the consequences, as her own assets were significant, and her father had raised a fighter in his only child. Still, brains, beauty, and wealth were not serving her well at this juncture in her life.

When she arrived at the DuPort estate, Zachary came out to greet her. He had received a letter from the legal offices of J. Pierpoint Buchanon, Esq. requesting his appearance next week, at the insistence of Messieurs Loucheur and Mirabeau, to discuss the recent collapse of DuPort Shipping Associates. Inc.. Zachary had been quite distressed, until he saw the lovely Gabrielle step down from her carriage. He ushered her inside, and realized that some things took precedence over others. As the Madame seemed possibly interested in an afternoon tryst, his questions and planning could wait an hour or so. They sat down in the parlor for brandy and sweets.

Mr. Fitch took his time moving up to the house undetected, as was his trade. He positioned himself to listen if not always see. He had found through trial and error that listening usually was more important than seeing, and would indicate when one might move into an observing post.

10

ED HORSES WAS VERY angry, and passionately argued for pursuing the
Shoshone immediately. The Bulls were in council around a fire at
the meeting place by the Eagle Rock. They had taken the news of
Stone Bear's death hard and as a personal affront to their own abilities. These
powerful warriors had experienced much together, including past tragedies,
and their personal bond to each other was strong. Stories were told of Stone
Bear's bravery in battle, his loyalty to the Bulls, and even his childhood
pranks and humorous mistakes. Red Horses swore to take care of his wife
and daughter, a bond taken in front of his warrior society, and thus a sacred
trust. Two Horns understood his friend's sense of responsibility for the death
of Stone Bear, and the Shoshone warrior's escape, and also realized his enemy, this crafty Shoshone was counting on their impulsiveness. This was a
bold and canny opponent to calmly impersonate Stone Bear and affect his
escape. This Blackhand now knew they were tracking him and would likely
pursue him until they killed him or lost him. If they were to kill this lone
warrior, they would have to use his own tactics against him. Two Horns
calmly began to explain the situation as he saw it to the others, and soon all
saw the wisdom of his plan, even though it meant a protracted campaign.
Red Horses understood the wisdom of his friend's plan, but that did not
temper his foul mood.

Two of the Bulls were dispatched back to the Blackfoot camp for more
supplies and to tell the Council of their plan. In the early morning, the
remaining seven braves set out, five to the South in a ride calculated to
bring them back to the old Shoshone camp where they would wait for this
Blackhand in ambush. The other two, including Red Horses, were to try
and track the Shoshone, and send word if he was not headed to his former
home.

Two Horns had an admiration for this lone warrior, who had been so
cool and cunning. With his escape into the mountains to the West, however,
Two Horns saw an opportunity in staying on flat ground to the South to

circle ahead and lay in wait. It would be far better to be in position and waiting to surprise this wily warrior, than trying to catch a fox on the run.

When their supplies caught up with the main band by late afternoon, the
pace picked up a couple of notches. The seven warriors spurred their horses
on with a purpose; angry over their fellow Bull's demise, while oblivious to
the massive suffering they had inflicted on the Shoshone tribe only a short
time before. Only Two Horns reflected on the Shoshone's motives and realized they were most probably driven by terrible grief and now hatred. Two
Horns had not seen the wisdom in annihilating the peaceful tribe to their
South. Like most tribes, others surrounded the Blackfoot, which often led
to warfare. The Crow, the Flatheads, the Cree, the Cheyenne, and the Sioux
were all powerful tribes. He was not sure his people could inhabit the new
area safely after the news of the attack spread. This conquest stretched his
people far to the South of their home range, and could be interpreted as a
dangerous incursion by others. He thought that Crooked Claws was greedy
and petty, and was not thinking for the tribe. When this was over, Two Horns
thought something must be done about the war chief. For now, however, he
put those thoughts aside and began to envision how he should set the trap for
this wounded animal, this Black Hand of Death. He had tried to put himself
in this Shoshone's mind, and thought, the most natural thing for the warrior
to do, once the bloodlust was over, was to grieve, and that would bring the
warrior back to his lost ones. There was a responsibility to know that his family had been properly prepared for the next life. Two Horns would find the
Shoshone burial ground and set the trap.

LAME ELK LAY flat on the big rock watching the meadow well below him.
After exchanging horses to help cover his identity swap, he knew the Blackfoot would be following once they discovered their dead warrior. When the
Blackfoot came, they would have to cross this open area to stay on his trail.
He wanted to know how many would be coming. He wanted to see their pursuit strategy. He wanted to kill their best killers. It was cold, but the sun was
out today, and the rock began to absorb some heat. Resting for the first time
since climbing the mountain, Lame Elk felt the tension begin to leave his
body, even as he felt the soreness of his recent activities. He hoped he could
recapture the big black horse. Since the crushing blow of losing his family, he
had unconsciously attached himself to the only other living thing with him,
the horse. The horse had been his co-conspirator as he had wreaked his revenge on the Blackfoot. He felt that the horse should be with him. There was
almost a guilt that he had given up the horse and that the Blackfoot had this

fine animal. At the same time, he realized the big black's tender feet would have probably led to his demise. In time the hooves would toughen, and such a fine animal should not be captive to his hated enemies.

ABOUT MIDMORNING HE snapped alert as two Blackfoot warriors patiently and carefully followed the trail Lame Elk had purposely left behind. They would have a much tougher time following him over the rock above. He waited some more to see if they signaled back to others, but they apparently were alone. Suspicions immediately leaped into his mind. Had more warriors outflanked him as he lay in wait? Were they now advancing up the mountain from many sides to meet somewhere? He studied the two warriors some more and was convinced they were in no hurry.

RED HORSES HAD partnered up with Shining Crow. It was a good team, as Shining Crow was easy company, a good tracker, and a dependable fighter. The Shoshone had been pushing up the mountain hard by all signs, and was at least half a day ahead assuming he had stopped for the night. Two Horns had been right; this Shoshone dog was running for home. Red Horses hoped he would be there for the kill but realized that was unlikely. He would track this enemy all the way back to the battle site by the Yellowstone River, and join his comrades again for the ride home. Precious time would be lost, and he too did not trust Crooked Claws to justly share the war prizes. There would be much wrangling and discontent when the Bulls finally got home, he thought, but he would be sure he was not cheated. He led a steady but not swift pace up the mountain, and soon found himself climbing under a rock outcropping about twenty feet tall, on a narrow trail.

He heard the whir and thud as the arrow drove downward through Shining Crow's chest. Jerking his head up, Red Horses saw the Shoshone standing above him on the rock outcropping, already fitting another arrow into his bow. He dove off his horse while simultaneously throwing his warclub in the general direction of the enemy. An arrow just missed him, and he hit the ground hard, rolling away, and then came up, scrambling up the mountain on his hands and feet, trying to close the distance with the Shoshone while securing the first cover he could make. He needed about three more feet up the trail when he felt the arrow smash into his lower left leg, but his adrenaline kept him going up the steep ascent. The Shoshone was closing fast on him with his own war club as he pulled his hunting knife out.

WHEN LAME ELK saw the big Blackfoot warrior swiftly climbing up the trail toward him, he dropped his bow and grabbed his club. He still had the advantage of higher ground as he leapt off his rock perch and swung the club downward toward the big warrior, but the Blackfoot warrior rolled away again, and he missed. He pulled out his knife and jumped on top of Red Horses, unaware that he was screaming wildly. When he crashed into Red Horses, and they grappled momentarily, Lame Elk instinctively sensed that he was outmatched in strength and skill, so he broke free and immediately rolled over and up on his feet. The two protagonists glared at each other, knives extended, and it was then that Lame Elk saw Red Horses could not stand on his left leg. His arrow had smashed the Blackfoot's shinbone. Lame Elk stepped back, and Red Horses swayed on one leg, holding the useless one gingerly above the ground. Slowly and carefully, Lame Elk circled back to his bow and picked it up.

IN RESIGNATION RED Horses began his Death Chant. He dropped to both knees, dropped his knife, and picked up some dirt. He let it fall through his fingers as he sang and prepared to die. A minute later, Red Horses wondered why the Shoshone had not killed him and stopped his chant to turn and look. The Black Hand of Death was gone.

Red Horses struggled up to his feet with the help of a small log, and after an exhausting effort, was able to grab hold of Shining Crow's pony. His own horse was limping badly. Sitting sidesaddle, he removed the broken remains of the arrow shaft stuck in his leg, but he knew he couldn't get to the head, buried deep in his busted shinbone. He applied the poultice he carried for cuts, and wrapped the leg as tightly as he could, but he knew he needed help. He felt he could ride back to the Blackfoot camp without much danger, but the humiliation of facing Crooked Claws and the families of Shining Crow and Stone Bear set his mind to the much more courageous option of riding to join the Bulls to avenge this new loss. Should he die in the venture, his honor would be great. If he were to be crippled, he wouldn't be the cripple that lost and ran home. The pain from his wound was severe as he swung his good leg over the pony and headed down the mountain to the South. He would return to honor Shining Crow if and when he was able.

When he eventually reached flat ground at the bottom of the mountain, he kicked with his one leg and urged the pony into a steady trot. Each bounce made him wince with pain, and his leg continued to bleed, dry, and bleed more. He stayed out in open country as much as possible to shorten the ride and ease the riding conditions. At first he felt very good about his decision, and envisioned a great story would come from his effort. He knew it was important to continue to drink as much as he could, and since his thirst seemed to be with him all the time, he drank and provisioned himself with as much water as he could carry by riding into a deep pool of water he passed. Each hour the pace got a little slower, so he kept moving on through the night at a walk. When the sun came up, he ate a little and drank some more, which made him feel better. His leg was now numb and didn't hurt as badly, but it had swollen up and was very ugly. He had lost a lot of blood. Mile after mile slowly went by, and he could not increase the pace for fear of falling off. That night he slept on his pony. By the third day he realized that he was getting steadily weaker and would probably die. He could no longer consider dismounting, and expect to get back up. He had time to reflect on his life. He tried to remember his childhood, his parents, his battles, and his wife. He felt pride in his accomplishments and his ascension into the Bulls. He relived his greatest triumph again, when he had counted coup on the Cree war chief. About to slip off the pony, he stopped to make an adjustment, tying his legs as well as he could to the horse, and then he set off again, not aware this had started his leg bleeding again. He rode the pony at a walk now; afraid he would fall off if he moved any faster. He was beginning to dream with his eyes open, and at one point, he thought he was in trouble with his father for not watching the band's horses as he had been instructed to do many years earlier.

Red Horses woke up sitting on his pony. He didn't know how long he had been asleep. It was late afternoon, and he was very cold and very weak. He thought he saw a warrior watching him by a large oak tree, but concentrating was difficult to do, and he soon forgot what he was looking for. He kicked the pony to move, but it didn't move, and he realized he really hadn't been able to kick the pony. He was very tired and wished to sleep, but his desire to join the Bulls pushed him on. He raised his arms into the air and called on his ancestors to give him the strength to accomplish this last mission, and then slumped forward dead.

Lame Elk waited a while longer and then rode over to the Blackfoot warrior. Even in death, this was an imposing figure. Lame Elk had figured out some time ago that the warrior was riding to meet his comrades, and with the direction of the ride, it became obvious that the Blackfoot were headed back to the Yellowstone, where he presumed they intended to surprise and kill him. He leaned over and tied the tired Blackfoot pony to his own, and led the warrior forward toward the Yellowstone.

Riding with the dead Red Horses, now secured to his pony, Lame Elk's thirst for revenge was ended. He admired the man he had fortunately killed with a lucky shot in his leg. This man had ridden to his death, probably knowing it was a lost cause. The events of the last several weeks were beginning to leave their mark on Lame Elk. The rage and sorrow, while still constantly with him, were more intermittent, and an understanding, albeit a vague one, was beginning to form in his thoughts. Was he the man who had truly killed all those Blackfoot? No one including himself would have thought him capable of so much carnage. He had gained confidence but not pride in his deadly work. In fact, now that the reality of what he had done was setting in, he knew that killing more was something he could do, but wouldn't want to do. This Blackfoot warrior riding dead next to him had undoubtedly left loved ones who would rightfully mourn for him. How much sorrow had he triggered that he would never know? His grandfather's image came back to him: a picture in his mind of the two of them climbing through the forest, his grandfather teaching him the great ways of the People, and the balance of all living things. Swiftsnake would say that it was time to move on with life and make peace in his mind. Lame Elk thought the dead warrior might help him to do so. He was entering the fringes of his people's old territory, and he swung even farther South to circle it and approach from the West, just as he had the awful day of the Blackfoot attack.

SOMETHING WAS OUT there. It was a very dark and cold night, with the usual animal noises, but out in the clearing by the river, Blue Heron could hear a large animal moving slowly about. It had been several nights now that he had hidden under this big dead tree. Lying in the dark with all the dead spirits of the Shoshone so close by was an unnerving experience. Knowing that the great warrior Blackhand was probably approaching didn't help. Blue Heron carefully worked his way over to Long Bow's position to relay his concerns.

"You were almost one dead warrior," Long Bow whispered as Blue Heron slid down the small bank into Long Bow's hiding place.

"There is something down by the river near my guard spot," hissed Blue Heron. "It will be light soon. You should come with me to see what it is."

"It is your mother-in-law wishing to sleep with you again," Long Bow said with a grin, but he slowly snaked his way back to Blue Heron's post, and was glad for the company.

As the night slowly lifted, there was a fog over the valley floor, especially down by the river. Still they could occasionally hear the heavy thump from some large animal, and eventually a form came into view. A rider on a horse stood alongside the river. The Blackfoot warriors relayed the sighting and began to close in on the area. As the fog began to lift, they were surprised to recognize Red Horses sitting on Shining Crow's pony. His head hung down, but his body was straight.

Two Horns broke cover and walked out into the open toward the warrior. The other Blackfoot followed him. Two Horns sensed that Red Horses was dead, and as he drew near, he could see that the warrior was propped up on the horse. The great Blackfoot warrior Red Horses was cut loose and lowered to the ground. His only wound was his left leg, and he held a broken arrow with Blackhand's markings between his hard, cold fingers. Two Horns understood. The Shoshone warrior was calling off his campaign. Blackhand was watching them for their response. Three of the elite Bulls, along with over twenty others, had been slain by this elusive killer, and now they were on his ground. Blackhand's message of peace was one that also spoke volumes should the Blackfoot not accept. The Shoshone had somehow delivered one of their best back to them, springing their own trap. Two Horns could see that his fellow warriors were shaken by the great magic this Shoshone Blackhand possessed. He instructed the others to wrap Red Horses up in two buffalo robes tightly, and then, assuming the mantle of command totally for the first time, he strode out into the open away from the group of warriors, raised his heavy lance above his head with both hands, and yelled his best war cry. A second later the lance came crashing down on his knee and broke in half. He then raised the broken lance over his head and yelled again.

Somewhere up the mountainside the Blackfoot warriors heard a distant answering war cry. In the early morning mist, it sounded unworldly as it reverberated across the valley. Lame Elk climbed on his new horse, and looked down into the valley of the Yellowstone where he had lived for so long. The big Blackfoot warrior who had accepted his peace offering was climbing on the Whiteman's big black horse. Too bad; he would have liked to have that horse back. He started to climb a little further up the mountain. He would stay in the area for another year alone, mourning the loss of his mother, wife, and son. Unknown to him, his fame was about to spread, as some of the captured Shoshone escaped or were traded to other tribes, and the Blackfoot themselves elevated his exploits to mystical proportions.

Down on the valley floor, Two Horns organized his fellow Bulls for the ride back to the North and the Blackfoot camp. Filled with sorrow and anger, Two Horns went to face Crooked Claws. He did not think the Blackfoot would be coming to live in this strange Shoshone land of hot springs and geysers.

II

CHARLES LOUCHEUR SLUMPED IN his chair, his stomach churning. He had the proof he had hoped he would never find. Slowly his devastation began to turn to anger. This common conman DuPort had defiled his home and honor. His lovely Gabrielle was now tarnished in his eyes, and his shame would be incredible should any of this come out. Mr. Fitch had been paid well enough, and came with certain recommendations that Charles did not worry about him. He would stay silent and continue his lucrative trade in New Orleans. Charles had to decide what to do about Gabrielle first and foremost; then he would deal decisively with this riffraff, DuPort.

He banged his fist on the table, giving in to his frustration, as mad at himself for allowing all of this to happen as anyone. How fickle life could be. Just when he felt everything was working the way he wanted, suddenly his fortune reversed, and he sat with this mess in his lap. Of course he had been too permissive with a young and beautiful wife. He had enjoyed indulging her. He had in fact encouraged her wanton spending and exaggerated social life. It had played to his own vanity that she could afford to do as she wished and was prominently on display around the city as his prize. This city had contributed too. He was aware of many such scandals, and many more hinted at. Some of the matrons he knew seemed to have an endless supply of such gossip, and at times it had alternately annoyed and amused him to hear their banter.

Well, since this was his mess, he would begin to clean it up, as he always had. Charles prided himself on his fortitude to face all challenges head-on. He knew that the bottomland he had purchased could be resold fairly quickly, if he was deft enough, at a small profit. That would end his overextension for the moment. As much as he would have liked to keep the rich parcel, he was pragmatic enough to cut his potential losses and extricate himself from growing problems. He had already accepted the fact that he would keep Gabrielle, just not in the fashion she had lately enjoyed. He was not a young man anymore, and he did not wish to live out his remaining years alone. She was not much more than a child in his eyes, and his own behavior had led to her disgrace as much as she had. That would not shield her from his wrath however. The Loucheur name had been greatly compromised. Tidbits of the harangue he would administer to his wife ran through his head. She would bend under his will, and he would control every penny henceforth. She would still have a good life, but she would carry the great burden of guilt with her from now on. Perhaps there was a silver lining in here somewhere. He was very mad, and things were about to change, but he didn't wish to destroy her, or even break her. He would temper his rage just enough to control her.

As concerns the duplicitous Zachary DuPort, Charles needed a more permanent solution. It was time to meet with Jean Paul and deal with their mutual problem in the most fortuitous fashion possible. A new thought entered his mind, and he smiled. If everything went well, maybe he could even keep that piece of bottomland.

AFTER A LATE morning of shopping, followed by a visit to her preferred dressmaker, Gabrielle arrived at the entrance to La Vie en Rose, her favorite restaurant, appropriately late to meet Rochelle and Daubert for an afternoon aperitif and maybe some raw oysters. She was still reminiscing about her amorous appointment the previous week with Zach. He was always solicitous of her comfort, but he had a rough and urgent manner to him that, in limited doses, she found very exciting. If Daubert could imagine the pictures she had in her mind from her activities with Monsieur DuPort, he would be shocked. The Beauvais family, like others in the well-established New Orleans high society, was the picture of refinement and culture. Should she ever capture an afternoon with Daubert, it would be after a long and elaborate play, with extreme and extensive innuendo, carefully crafted to maximize safety first. It was refreshing to know that Zach was not so concerned with such amenities. Gabrielle had not totally accomplished her mission yesterday, leaving the door still slightly open for more possible rendezvous with Monsieur DuPort. She was aware that her life had taken some dangerous turns of late, and she was determined to right her ship soon, but...

Daubert rose as she was escorted to the table by the majordomo. Rochelle leaned over for a touch kiss, and she was seated in the third chair at the table. After the obligatory greetings and ordering were done, Gabrielle finally took some time to inspect Daubert. Of course he was inspecting her too, and the afternoon was progressing splendidly when the waiter brought over a note for her to read. It was from Charles. After a deep blush and quick apologies, Gabrielle headed for her coach and home directly.

ACROSS TOWN ZEKE Bridges, alias Zachary DuPort, was sitting next to his lawyer, Matthew Hinds, at the law offices of J. Pierpoint Buchanon, Esq., in the trendy financial district. Five of his former partners from the failed shipping business were also there. Matthew Hinds had been quietly reading a stack of legal documents for the past twenty minutes while the rest of the room assumed a frosty but cordial air while not engaging one another in light conversation. This was a realm that was completely new to Zeke, but he knew an old-fashioned muscle game when he saw it. Matthew had reassured him prior to their arrival that his risk was limited, and a strong bluff would likely be the tactic applied. Zeke put on his best tired and bored face, and thought about Monsieur Loucheur's lovely wife. He couldn't help but smile at Charles Loucheur and was a bit surprised to see Charles smile right back at him. It certainly wasn't a friendly smile, and Charles's eyes sent a chill through his spine.

"I'd like a private moment with my client, please," Matthew Hinds finally intoned.

A few moments later when alone, Matthew asked Zeke, "Zachary, is there more than what you and I have discussed that I need to know about?"

"No, what are you trying to tell me?"

"Well, to start off," Matthew said, "these men are after more than their losses from the business venture. They are out to ruin you. There are claims of all natures in here on a wide variety of supposed agreements you have defaulted on."

"I've only had this one arrangement with these gentlemen. Show me what you are talking about."

Another ten minutes of leafing through the pages took place.

"This is utterly ridiculous," fumed Zeke. "None of this is true or in any way provable."

"Well, then I assume they wish to extort you into a settlement, or possibly just hassle you or tarnish your name. We can defend you and win if these are fraudulent claims, but it will be time-consuming and expensive. If you don't defend yourself, you are liable to lose a great deal."

"Can't I hit back somehow?" a frustrated Zeke exclaimed.

"Yes, you can sue them for slander and fraud, provided it is slander and fraud."

"Call those bastards back in the room and let them know they're in a fight with a dog that has some teeth. I'll be damned if they think they can bully me into rolling over."

"I agree that under these circumstances a strong response is the appropriate one," Matthew responded.

Some twenty minutes later, after the two legal sides had performed their various parts, Zeke and Matthew Hinds stepped outside the law office. It was a sunny day, and the street was busy. About the time they reached the little gate in front of the building, a small, dapper gentleman in a gray topcoat blocked their path.

"Monsieur Zachary DuPort, I, Monsieur Gaspard LeMond, demand satisfaction for your barbarous behavior and insults." The little man then slapped Zeke twice across the face with his fine gray kid gloves, turned, and strode away. As he walked off, he said over his shoulder, "My seconds will be contacting you for an appropriate time and place for our meeting."

Zeke didn't move. He was both surprised and confused. "Hey, you," he finally managed, "who the hell are you?"

The shorter man turned around and calmly answered, "I told you, I am Gaspard LeMond." He then continued his walk down the street.

Zeke turned to Matthew Hinds, who was white-faced, with a questioning look.

"Monsieur LeMond is the finest duelist in New Orleans. Pistols, swords, knives, it doesn't matter," Matthew Hinds muttered.

Zeke turned around to see Charles Loucheur, who had exited the building behind him, smiling at him again, standing next to Monsieur Mirabeau.

TEN DAYS LATER, Charles was sipping his morning coffee, feeling rather well. Tomorrow, he would witness the death of Zachary DuPort, and then begin his legal process to steal whatever assets the rogue had left behind. His scheme had worked out flawlessly. A dead DuPort could not dispute the legal claims, nor could a coward who ran, if that worked out to be the case. DuPort's property on the river would turn a handsome profit. He flipped to the society page and casually glanced across the headlines.

"Madame Loucheur, La Comtesse de Larousseau, will be traveling abroad this year, with planned stops in London, Paris—"

Charles spilled his coffee on the table as he grabbed the paper in shock and disbelief to read further.

PIERRE DU MONTFORT, Le Comte de Larousseau, had lived an interesting and well-traveled life. A soldier of fortune, who had inherited a fortune as a young man, Pierre had been the typical well-bred man of leisure in France. He had served in his country's army, having purchased a commission, and found he enjoyed the experiences his travels presented. However, a restless spirit and a weakness for young wives had prompted him to leave his ancestral home to travel to the New World where he ended up in New Orleans, the home of his lifelong friend and school chum, Henri Seurat. Naturally talented, with economic resources, he quickly became one of the city's leading businessmen, with Henri's help, and a known character as well. Late in life he had married the most energetic and beautiful woman he had ever met, and Gabrielle was the result of that union. His wife had died of cholera, still a young woman, and Pierre, who was already extremely fond of Gabrielle, began to dote on his daughter thereafter. The older man and his young charge were inseparable, as Pierre insisted on taking her everywhere with him. Many a code of etiquette was broken to accommodate the young girl at strictly men-only events. She became a favorite among the friends of Pierre, and was graciously tolerated elsewhere, due to his influence. She learned to ride and shoot, she tutored with Henri Seurat, who handled some of the accounting and personal affairs of her father, and learned at her father's side the lessons he felt she needed in this New World. Shortly before he died they had traveled back to France together to deal with family business, and she had learned of the very large family fortune in her name that he had willed to her. One of the lessons he had instilled was the financial control of her life. Should she ever marry, she would not ever relinquish control of her fortune, or, for that matter, even reveal the extent of it.

When her father had died, Gabrielle had been pursued by every eligible bachelor in New Orleans. Most wanted to control her father's known business interests. Charles Loucheur had not been interested in the money at the time, and had been a friend of her father's. Their marriage had been a comfortable arrangement for each, and Gabrielle was overcoming the loss of her father with Charles's affection.

When Gabrielle had sorted through her own guilt and had also learned of Charles's hand in the death plot for Zachary DuPort, her father's training began to kick in. She dispassionately assessed her marriage to Charles, and concluded it was ended. She did not wish to live a false life of pretense, nor did she plan to live in remorse under Charles's thumb, and she had her father's zest for adventure. She decided to employ Daubert Justin Beauvais as her business representative in New Orleans, along with the venerable old friend of her father's, Monsieur Seurat, who had long handled her lesser-known high finances, just as he had for her father. It was time to take action.

Everyone had heard of the annexation of California and the fact that gold was just discovered there. It was said that fortunes were being made there, and the promises of a new land were intoxicating, Gabrielle had Monsieur Seurat draw up letters of credit with her various banks to take with her to San Francisco. She also arranged to buy a large commercial safe in which she placed reputable bank notes and gold coins. Apparently, according to Monsieur Seurat, there was no commercial bank in San Francisco as yet, and therefore no place to put her money other than in her own safe. She then booked a stateroom for passage on the first acceptable ship going that way. She even helped Zachary delay his duel while he extricated as much of his holdings as he could, and booked him a separate room on her ship to San Francisco. Angelina, her old nanny and now personal assistant, along with Barton, her personal driver/bodyguard, both longtime family employees who were devoted to her, would travel with her. Next she planted the news story, of her sail to Europe, including the ship she had supposedly sailed on, and instructed Daubert to dispose of the personal belongings she would be leaving behind once she had departed. She also made it clear to Daubert and Monsieur Seurat that she did not wish to disclose her destination to her husband or anyone else.

Now she stood by the rail of the ship as it sailed through the Gulf of Mexico. The evening sky was overcast, and a cool wind whipped through her hair. Angelina had tried to get her to come inside, but Gabrielle was enjoying the sense of adventure, a feeling of being alive, and a new start. The sky seemed enormous out at sea. The American West was in front of her. She felt the presence of her father, as if he too stood by the rail. Indeed, Pierre would have relished the trip. La Comtesse was sailing as Madame G. Montfort, of Charleston, South Carolina, at least until she was clear of Charles. Barton made sure she wasn't disturbed in her reflections. It would be several months to reach the city of San Francisco. By the time they would arrive, Zachary DuPort would be in love with Gabrielle. However, La Comtesse would discover she had a growing aversion to this man of weak character and presumption. Barton would deliver several "personal warnings" to Monsieur DuPort to respect La Comtesse's privacy. Gabrielle did in fact feel a little sympathy and responsibility for Zachary, but that was all. She knew her father would have disapproved of Monsieur DuPort, and she knew she wished to distance herself from him once they debarked in San Francisco. As far as she was concerned, having helped him escape cleaned the slate between them, and they should go their separate ways. Gabrielle was also determined to make her departed father proud with her newfound resolve to make an honorable and profitable life out West. The scandal in New Orleans had finally awakened her to the frivolous and self-absorbed existence she had fallen prey to, and she was filled with self-reproach. Her father would have expected far better of her, and she knew she would begin to apply the many lessons he had so often drilled into her to build her own empire, whatever that would entail. She shut her eyes and breathed in the sea air again. Exhaling, she opened her eyes and looked out at the distant horizon. Instead of the concerns she had worried about earlier in the day, leaving her home and acquaintances for an unknown and potentially dangerous future, she now reveled in a remarkable sense of calm. This felt right. The lap of the water against the ship's side was a stimulating but simultaneously soothing sound.

12

His name was Juan Drego de Santarosilla, and he was the bastard son of a wealthy landowner down by Tucson, Mexico. His father had treated him well, but his father's wife had her own child. For several years as a very young man, he had ridden with bad company, picked up bad habits, and paid for both. He favored fancy black clothes, along with his black sombrero, and a long blade with a black inlaid handle. He wore his black hair long, and occasionally pulled it back in a ponytail, but, more often, he just let it hang down to his shoulders. A well-maintained mustache drooped down the sides of his mouth, and he spoke with a big voice. Though he only stood five foot five, he had a barrel of a chest and muscular arms, and he liked to say, "Drego ees the brother of the great bear of California. Be careful, or I will eat you up," to the Indian children. They would run and scream and come back for more.

He had been in Oregon for about a year. His travels had brought him up through the new Mexican territory of California, ceded from Spain some twenty-five years earlier, which had just been wrestled away again by the United States of America. With Americans arriving by the boatload, Drego had been planning on moving farther South, about the time he made acquaintances with Corby and Donovan.

"Theese reever, she will take you to the ocean and El Camino Real," drawled Drego.

"What's that?" Corby asked.

"El Camino Real? Eet ees the road to Old México. The way I return home, amigo," said the Mexican. He flipped the salmon steak in his frying pan and added some sort of spice to the other side, and sat it back down again over the fire. "Eet really ends een Yerba Bueno, San Francisco to you, but Drego has extended his own road north to here."

"Well, we both want to see that ocean, come as far as we have," said Donovan as he inhaled the smell of the frying fish.

"*Tres días*, three days, more or less, and I will cook for you my famous paella, eef we can find the good clams and crab."

All three were ready to eat the wonderful-smelling fish in the pan. The Indian children were back and also had an eye on the food. Fortunately one of Indian women called the children to come away, realizing that the men were about to eat. Drego waved his thanks, and the women smiled back at him before shooing the children up the rocky river beach to the main encampment.

"Friendliest Injuns I've ever met," Donovan said. Corby agreed, remembering the horse he had lost last Fall. "Nobody to bother them yet, I guess," he said, finishing his own thought.

"Americanos, they are coming," Drego answered. "You see some tomorrow down river, and more as we get close to the coast. *Cómo se dice…* cows? And sheep. Farmers. These indios will be pushed out, no?" He frowned and placed large pieces of the salmon steak onto each of their tin plates. "Enjoy, *la salmón de la Drego*," he grinned and began eating. The fish melted in the men's mouths.

Later he told them about the territory, as Donovan was interested in where he might settle down. Apparently a little farther down river, another branch merged with this one and the river doubled in volume. Still it was tame compared to its springtime burden, when it spilled its banks in some areas.

There was a long rainy season soon to start in the Fall, but rarely did it snow down in the valley. Obviously this was timber country. The trees were enormous, and Drego told of trees down in California as wide as a house. But here in Oregon, the forest stretched on forever. There were rivers to the sea every twenty miles or so, due to the snow melt of the Cascades and the wet climate of the valleys. Another smaller coastal range of mountains ran on the western side of the valleys, but traveling along the riverside was fairly easy, especially in late summer with the river at its low ebb. Osprey and eagles were everywhere, as testament to the good fishing, and Drego told them to watch out for bear, which were fishing this time of year too. A small settlement was at the river branch merge, but Drego didn't know if it had a name. Deer and elk thrived in this area from the ocean to the Cascade Range, so hunting was plentiful. There were small box canyons with streams coming out of them, feeding the river. The canyons were steep enough that a lone stretch of fencing at the mouth of one would serve to keep any livestock in the canyon, making homesteading a lot easier

Donovan began planning as he listened to Drego. Water certainly was no problem, with little lakes everywhere and the ability to dam numerous streams. The waterfowl obviously migrated through here by the thousands, so Christmas dinner was assured. There was no shortage in building materials, as granite and shale protruded from the sides of the canyons and lumber was going to have to be cut, just to clear some land for grazing or planting. A snug cabin with a good rock fireplace next to a nice stream began to form as a picture in Donovan's head. Maybe a corral of a dozen good breeding horses, some chickens and ducks...

As they rode on, Drego talked more about California, its sunny climate, more open pastureland, and growing communities. As much as Donovan admired the Oregon country, it really wasn't horse country, and getting breeding stock up here would be hard. And whom would he be able to sell his horses to, the few farmers and Indians around? He asked Drego about the hunting and fishing in California.

Three days later they reached the end of the Umpqua River and looked out on the Pacific Ocean. It was a sunny early September day, and the ocean sparkled like so many jewels. Neither Donovan nor Corby could quite comprehend the vastness of the ocean. Small seals basked on sandy islands in the river's wide mouth. A few buildings were loosely scattered on the south side of the river on a low bluff, and they could see a few more structures farther on to the South. A dock ran out a few feet into the river. Drego led the men up to a tavern and dismounted.

"Friends of mine. Pirates," he said, and walked in to the rough-hewn structure. Corby and Donovan looked at each other and Donovan double-tied the horses and mules before following Drego in.

The room was dark, and it took a second to adjust their eyesight. The bright afternoon sunlight streamed through the door behind them, but didn't spill into the rest of the closed-windowed room. There was a trading post on one side of the room and a bar/cantina with two tables and chairs on the other side. A stair ran up the far wall to what probably was living quarters, or maybe a room for rent. Two men, who had been playing cards with a very worn-looking deck, were now talking to Drego in Spanish. One was a very large man in a short-sleeved shirt and suspenders, and the other was a slender Mexican in high boots and a puffy style of pants. Neither looked too clean. The big man came over to Corby and Donovan and stuck out his hand. "Welcome to Big Jake's place," he said. "I'm Big Jake."

Donovan shook his hand, and introduced the two as prospective ranchers. Drego came over and said, "Big Jake can help you with whatever supplies you need... for a price," and he raised his hand to indicate the price would be high.

Big Jake laughed and said, "That's true. But things are sometimes hard to get up here. We ain't in St. Louie. Excuse me for saying so, but you boys don't exactly look like settlers."

Before Corby could talk, Donovan quickly jumped in and said, "Everybody changes occupations out here, don't they?" He smiled a conspiratorial smile at Big Jake.

Big Jake laughed again, and offered to buy them their first drink. He walked over to the bar to get a bottle and glasses.

Just then a group of three walked in: a tall, mean-looking Indian with a scar on his cheek and a detached look in his eyes, a heavy, red-bearded man in a long coat, and another mean-looking, dark-skinned man wearing fancy holsters and guns and a weathered, wide-brimmed western hat with an eagle feather stuck in its band. Donovan sized them up immediately as trouble, and moved to his left slowly and carefully, to optimize the use of the bright light coming in the door, keeping himself in the shadows. Corby sensed Donovan's move and edged over by him. Drego stood by Big Jake at the bar and straightened up, while the slender Mexican nearly disappeared in a corner chair.

"Jake," the heavyset man boomed, "who owns those fine mules out front?"

Drego said, "Those mules are not for sale, Señor Targon. They belong to my compadres, Señores Donovan and Corby."

The red-bearded man turned to Drego with a contemptuous look and sneered, "Ah, Drego, you're back. Well, go tell your friends that I want to buy their animals." The dark-skinned man grinned at Drego, while the Indian continued to scowl.

"Drego's right," Donovan said in a low voice. "Not interested in selling the mules."

The three men were startled by the voice, and turned to their right, squinting into the darkness to see who had spoken. They were unable to see well, but now they were aware that there were two men standing in the darkness.

"Well now, mister, you ain't heard my best offer yet."

"Appreciate the interest, but I need those mules. Sorry," Donovan drawled good naturedly as he kept a keen eye on the dark-skinned man with the revolvers.

The gunman now spoke up. "You should listen to Mr. Targon's offer. Come on out here where we can see you. No need to hide in the dark, boys." He grinned his evil grin again.

Corby felt his blood boil at the taunt and began to step forward, but Donovan reached over and grabbed the back of his shirt before he could take a step.

"We're fine right here, thank you. Big Jake, you bringing those drinks?" Donovan asked. The tense moment seemed to diffuse. Targon and his men turned on their heels and walked out the door.

Drego and Big Jake walked over to the table, and the slender Mexican also appeared again and came over too.

"That ees Jimbo Fisher, the deadly pistolero." Drego exhaled.

"You boys better keep your eyes wide open and do your best to avoid running into him again," said Big Jake. "He hasn't been up this way for awhile. Wonder what Targon is up to this time. Sure as hell someone is going to find out the hard way."

"Where's your lawman?" Corby asked.

Big Jake laughed, but it was an ugly laugh. "No one is going to be a lawman in these parts with the likes of Targon and his crew running around. Fisher is as bad as they come, and I've seen bad. They pretty much control the coastal settlements north of San Francisco. I used to run with them myself, until I got enough together to build me this place. Couldn't wait to get away from them, and I'm no angel. If there is money in it, Targon is in it. Doesn't care a lick who gets hurt. The Indian they call Ishka does nasty things with his knife, and Fisher is a pure killer. Enjoys it. Targon has maybe twenty hands on board his ship. I think he has three ships now. Smuggler, pirate, tied in with big money down in San Francisco, preys on the whalers, sealers, immigrants, anyone who has something he can take away from them. Must have rode up here from Coos Bay with a few of his boys. I'd secure them mules real good tonight if you're staying around here."

Big Jake and the Mexican went back to their card game on the other side of the room. The three traveling companions sat and discussed their next move. They decided they would get some supplies and start down the coast for California, keeping an eye out for both Targon's men and a future home for Donovan. Drego was very pleased to have company on his ride South, and promised Donovan that he would not be sorry he took a look at California. Drego was also nervous about the three men Big Jake had just detailed for them and wanted to get moving. So after buying some provisions from Big Jake, they went outside to load up their stocks and get out of town for the night. The sun was beginning to set as they packed the animals.

"Hey you, mule man!"

The three turned around to see Fisher and two others walking up the hill toward them.

"You ain't from around here, so maybe you don't understand how things work," Fisher pronounced. This time he had the sun to his back, and his two helpers fanned out on either side of him. "Targon wants them mules, so you best sell them to me now. I'll give you ten U.S. dollars for each."

Donovan moved a little away from the mules and said, "You know they are worth a lot more than that, and I told you I'm not interested in selling them."

He tried to get a little closer to the man, but Fisher stopped him cold by spitting at his feet and saying, "Some dumb sodbusters just don't know when to cut and run."

It was obvious that Fisher was intending to just take the mules. All six men squared off, and Fisher said, "Go for your gun anytime, big man," looking up at Donovan.

Donovan went for his gun first, but true to his reputation, Fisher was a lot faster, and would have gunned him down, when Corby's bullet slammed into Fisher's left shoulder, spinning him around and knocking him down. Corby's draw was so fast that no one else had even cleared their holsters. The other two gunmen with Fisher let their hands drop off of their gun handles and backed away. They then slowly picked up Fisher, who was screaming curses at Corby, and helped him stumble away.

Drego was dumbfounded. "*Madre de Dios*! Did you see that? No, you couldn't; eet was too rapido." He then went over to tell Big Jake what had happened, as he had come outside when he had heard the gunshot.

Donovan shook his head in disbelief. "Seems like you were holding out on me, son. I've never seen anyone half that fast."

Corby was in shock himself. He faltered and then said, "I wasn't aiming for his shoulder."

"So what, with a draw like that you could have put two more bullets in him." Donovan then realized that Corby was shaken. "Look, Corby, that son of a bitch was going to kill us and take our animals. I was a goner. Too bad you didn't kill him."

"How do you suppose...?" Corby was still not sure he was that fast.

"Sometimes people get pumped up when in danger. I figure you get that speed from the excitement. Seen it before." Donovan tried to explain, "We can keep working on the delivery, so the next time you can shoot him anywhere you want. Right now, I'm damn happy the way things turned out. I intend to tell anyone who asks that you shot him right where you meant to. C'mon, kid, I could use another drink."

Just the same, the trio left town shortly thereafter, skirting to the East on their way South.

13

ANOTHER SUMMER AND WINTER had come and gone in the Yellowstone country. Spring was breaking out in the mountains, as the fast-rushing streams delivered their snowmelt down to the lower elevations and the river. The elk were beginning to move up the mountains with the warmer weather, and Lame Elk felt the urge to move too. He had not seen a single person for over a year now, but his thoughts were still conflicted about rejoining the People. He was now comfortable with his own company, and did not wish to repeat the devastation of losing another loved one. Still he felt an obligation to his tribe and thought he should tell them that they could return to the Yellowstone if they wished. It was such a magnificent area, and he knew the People would be living on harsher lands like some of the other Shoshone tribes did.

Lame Elk had been changed from his experiences. He was more reflective by nature than ever before, wondering the origins and causes of the world he lived in. He was braver, first from not caring about what could happen to himself in his time of grief, and then from discovering he could survive much better than he had previously imagined. When challenged by the forces of nature, he wanted to persevere, to prove to himself that he was now the master of his own destiny, to never feel helpless again. He had grown stronger from his self-imposed isolation, both physically and mentally, shaped by the self-reliance it took to survive alone in the wilderness. Cleansed of all personal responsibilities, he was developing a new value system that did not include anyone else. He felt no need to explain the last year, or even to remember it.

The Blackfoot warrior who had ridden to his death revisited his thoughts from time to time. He had a new understanding for the warrior cult of his enemies, even a small admiration for the heroic and selfless nature it inspired, but he did not believe in the never-ending belligerence he thought came with it.

He wandered around the floor of the valley and followed the river to its entry into the gorges, and then reluctantly turned and climbed out of the basin, riding to the Southwest in search of his people. Even if his people did not return to the Yellowstone, Lame Elk knew he would. His connection to the area had taken on a spiritual nature, as he felt a part of the ancestral lifeline. It was where he was supposed to be.

THE BLACKFOOT WARRIOR Two Horns also had trouble with the warlike posture his people always seemed to be in. When he had returned home with Red Horses's body, the camp seemed to care more about the failed campaign to kill a lone enemy than the loss of three of his best friends in the effort. Perhaps the sneak attack and easy defeat of the Shoshones, and the riches garnered, had temporarily warped an otherwise sane and intelligent people. Just as he was presenting the killed warrior to his family, two of the council members and then Crooked Claws had come over to demand an explanation for the failed expedition. Two Horns had tried to ignore them as he continued to address the family of Red Horses, praising his friend and trying to console them, but Crooked Claws was not to be denied, and grabbed his arm, turning him away from the elderly father of Red Horses. The anger in Two Horns had been building for days as he had ridden back to the camp, and now the dishonorable and disgraceful behavior of Crooked Claws was too much. Two Horns thrust his left hand up to squeeze Crooked Claws's throat. Crooked Claws face turned black with anger at the insult and he reached for his knife. As his right hand was trying to pull Two Horns's viselike grip off of his throat, he elected to draw his blade with his left hand. Killing a fellow Blackfoot was strictly forbidden and could mean death by the tribe. But this would be a fight to the finish. Sensing as much as seeing the unsheathed knife in Crooked Claws's hand, Two Horns grabbed the war chief's wrist with his free hand before Crooked Claws could raise his arm, and twisted Crooked Claws's arm down and then behind his back. Then releasing Crooked Claws by the throat, he drew his own hunting knife and drove it deep into the war chief's belly with his left hand. Still holding Crooked Claws in an armlock, he pushed the knife as far up his belly as it would go, piercing his heart. The vengeful look of rage was still there in Two Horns's face as Crooked Claws slumped in his grip. Then, realizing the war chief was mortally wounded, Two Horns dropped him in the dirt, and turned on the two council members who had also shown the lack of proper respect to the dead warriors and their families.

"Are these the mighty Blackfoot of my ancestors?" he shouted. "Do a few stolen ponies cloud the vision of a once proud nation? Have we no better example of leadership for our children than this piece of dog dung dying at my feet? Many good warriors were killed in order to take the Shoshones' land from them. The Yellowstone Shoshone had lived with us in peace for many generations, until we in cowardice slaughtered them from ambush."

Taking a deep breath as the anger and frustration began to dissipate, Two Horns continued in a softer and sadder voice. "You, the old men of the Council, shamed us by joining Crooked Claws in his greed. You shame yourselves now in not honoring the brave warriors who have just died for you. Go away, and leave these poor families in peace before I slit your throats as I did Crooked Claws's belly." With his bloody knife and arm punctuating each sentence and the remaining Bulls looking like they too were ready for mayhem, the crowd quickly split up. Crooked Claws twitched one last time on the ground, his eyes wide open, before succumbing to death.

The sentiment of the camp was clearly with the Bulls, as Crooked Claws was feared and unpopular. The Council of Elders, relieved of their burden of Crooked Claws, quickly moved to disavow the two unfortunate council members who had accosted Two Horns, and unanimously supported the demise of the past war chief in a fair fight, citing heretofore unknown differences they had had with Crooked Claws. Soon after, the camp finally broke up for the winter, and the smaller bands returned to their nomadic ways. Most prominent among the Blackfoot of the Gray Woman Mountain tribe now was Two Horns, but it was an unsettled and uncertain people that left the campground.

The following year when the Blackfoot gathered by the lake for their summer camp, Two Horns, the remaining Bulls, and all their families did not join the larger group. The Council of Elders fearfully sent out four riders to find the missing tribesmen and request their attendance at the camp. The riders came back having visited the breakoff group, to report that the Bulls would think about it next year. Several more families left to join the Bull encampment on hearing the news, and the Blackfoot camp by the lake spent a summer of discontent, wondering what the next year would bring. By Fall, the Council of Elders was resigned to offering Two Horns leadership of the tribe, if they could find him to make the offer.

SOME DISTANCE AWAY, Lame Elk climbed to the top of the encircling mountain to the West of the Yellowstone valley. He had postponed his search for the People one more summer. This time as he crested the last rise to exit the valley he would finally leave. He looked back down one last time to the campsite of his childhood. It was from here he had seen the attacking Blackfoot, and it was from here he had led the dead warrior down to end his personal war. It was also from here that he had paused with the Whiteman's big black horse, rejoicing in finally returning to his people. Now turning to face the other way, he would try to find the remnants of his tribe before returning to his solitary travels. He gave out one last war cry, which dispersed into the silence around him, and then headed his pony down the other side of the mountain, away from the Yellowstone valley.

TWO HORNS HAD kept the tall black horse that Blackhand, the Shoshone killer, had left in his escape from the Blackfoot. Its hooves had toughened over time and it was a prize that the other warriors often wondered about. There was no horse in the Blackfoot camps that resembled this breed. It was thicker, stronger, and heavier than the Indian ponies, and Two Horns sat well above the others when riding. It was indeed a fitting horse for a chief to ride. It had a stamina the smaller ponies didn't, but it wasn't as fast until it finally got into a full gallop, and then it just ate up ground. It had a proud manner to it, and it took almost a year before the two were a match.

Now lying on his stomach, peering over the hill at the buffalo below him, he sensed the big black horse's excitement, as it pawed the ground behind him with the others. The black had been on numerous hunts now, and clearly enjoyed them. He had also established himself as the dominant male stallion in the band. Two Horns felt this gift from the Sun God would someday be explained to him in a vision, and he would be instructed on some important mission. Such a horse did not come to you by mistake. He lavished great attention on this animal he now called Messenger, as in the Creator Sun God's messenger to the Blackfoot.

Slithering back down the hill, he informed the four other hunters that the small herd was still coming to them, and to remain quiet. The biggest concerns were always smell and noise when hunting buffalo. They were blessed with a calm day, so the buffalo shouldn't be able to smell them until it was too late. But the beasts were also keen in their hearing, and the Blackfoot had to have trained horses that kept still. One lone buffalo spooked would trigger a stampede, and buffalo could run a long way. The hunters waited patiently for the slow-moving herd to come within range.

It started with a low thunder, and the hunters knew the herd was beginning to run. They jumped on their horses and flashed up over the hill to see the herd moving together on the run. There, also, were the Crows, giving chase. Two Horns counted six braves in full pursuit, riding on the opposite side and behind the small herd of maybe two hundred buffalo. The Crow were well spread out. Intent on their hunt, they probably had not seen the rival band of Blackfoot yet. This was no-man's-land, claimed by many tribes and controlled by none. It was too far out in the sea of grass to be a permanent home to anyone. Out here the weather was too dramatic and dangerous, with no shelter, and water often in short supply. But this is where the tribes could always find some buffalo, so they often had brushes with each other.

While the two tribes were avowed enemies, this was a buffalo hunt, and both bands needed the meat. The herd was going to run right past their position, so Two Horns decided they would try to hunt with the Crow, and see what might happen later. So he signaled his hunters to start in on their side of the herd but to keep an eye out for each other, and off they rode.

This was a food hunt, so they singled out animals that were no more than five years old for the best meat, and they would only need three. Like all plains Indians, the Blackfoot killed only what they needed, and used the entire animal. To the Blackfoot, who believed the buffalo was a gift from the Creator, to waste any would also be sacrilegious. So the hunt was over very quickly, and the two bands of hunters regrouped to stare at each other and decide what to do. Normally, the women and children would follow the hunters and do the skinning and butchering, but with the potential enemy so close, that was out of the question.

The kills were strewn out over about a two-mile span, with the Crows having killed four buffalo, and the Blackfoot, their intended three. Riding out alone on his big black horse, Two Horns waved in an acknowledging fashion to the Crows, and rode over to one of the Blackfoot kills to start the butchering job. The other three Blackfoot rode over to join him. They kept an eye on the clustered Crows, who apparently were still mulling over their options. After a long moment the Crows rode in an indifferent manner over to their first two kills and began the skinning and butchering process. Neither group let their guard down the rest of the day, until the Crows, who finished first, rode away to the southeast. The Blackfoot continued their work until they could no longer see the Crows, and then Two Horns set a sentry on the highest hill in case the Crows tried to double back to steal the Blackfoot's day's work. The finishing work was done as quickly as possible. The Crows had not seriously fought the Blackfoot for a few years, but they were generally considered enemies nonetheless. Two Horns decided he should move the band back to the northwest some more after the meat and hides were tended to at the Bulls' camp. Tonight, they would post a double guard, and tomorrow they would scout out the Crow camp to see what they were up against.

The Blackfoot camp sprang into action when the hunters finally came back with the partially butchered buffalo. The women and children fell to their tasks of dissecting the buffalo further. The men immediately sat in council to decide what was best to do. They ate while they conferred, and they decided to scout the Crows immediately, in case there was a larger than normal risk. Howling Wolf and Buffalo Lance were dispatched to search out the Crow camp and report back by nightfall. It was believed that the Crow camp would have to be fairly close by to be hunting the same herd.

The two warriors grabbed their weapons and rode out of camp to the southeast. Two Horns posted extra guards and informed everyone they could be moving depending on the information brought back by the scouts. The late afternoon sun was still hot out on the plains, and the band made sure the horses were well watered. The whole camp became alert to any danger sign. The band was now some fifty strong and larger than most, due to the politics of the previous year, including fifteen warriors, and another ten able-bodied women and boys that were capable of fighting. The balance of the band consisted of the rest of the women and children, and a few elderly. Like many such bands, there were more women than men, as the Blackfoot males had a high mortality rate.

Afternoon shadows were lengthening when Buffalo Lance rode back hard into camp, wounded and alone. After he was pulled from his horse, and as the band's Shaman attended his wounds, he gave his report.

"We were discovered from behind as we crept forward to spy, and had to fight on foot against three Crows on horses. After their first pass, we were able to mount, but we were wounded. Howling Wolf was barely able to sit on his pony, but he ordered me to ride to report. He stayed to fight," groaned Buffalo Lance. "One Crow chased me to within sight of the camp." He pointed vaguely in the direction he had ridden in from. "We must ride back now," he said trying to rise.

"We will ride, but tell me of what you saw," Two Horns said quietly.

"Crow camp, maybe three hands full," said Buffalo Lance. "They will try to get away. We must go."

Two Horns calculated that meant a fighting force of perhaps seven or eight Crows. The Crow would know that the larger camp was the Blackfoot, from what Buffalo Lance had said about being chased back. Two Horns had no interest in starting a war. A measured response was required. His warriors had been unfortunate in being discovered spying on the Crows, and of course as longtime enemies, the Crows had predictably reacted. The Blackfoot would now kill a couple of Crows to show them the error of their ways, and chase the rest in disgrace a few miles. Perhaps both sides would count some coup, to put a positive memory on an unfortunate event.

As Two Horns stood up, the warriors surrounded him. He had five Bulls left including himself, as Buffalo Lance was in no condition to ride again today. He had seven other fighting men that had joined his band with their families, so the clear advantage was with the Blackfoot. Howling Wolf's young wife, Moon in the Daylight, demanded to go with the war party, to avenge her husband's death. No one considered the possibility that Howling Wolf would still be alive. Two Horns acknowledged her right to come, but asked her to listen to him in battle, and to pull back when he said to pull back. Moon in the Daylight nodded her agreement. The war party of thirteen then set off at a canter to administer justice, Blackfoot style.

About a half an hour later the Blackfoot war party stood on a small hill looking down at a retreating band of Crows. The women, elderly, and children were pulling travois with their possessions behind their horses, and a rearguard of nine warriors and boys trailed the procession. The sun was starting to set on the long summer day, bringing a light and refreshing breeze with it.

When the Crows spotted the Blackfoot, the rearguard wheeled around to face the attackers. Two Horns recognized the six hunters from earlier in the day. A large Crow with a feather bonnet now waved his lance above his head and began yelling taunts at the Blackfoot. His fellow braves took up the chorus and looked very intimidating in their defiance. The Crow line stood firm as the families put as much distance between the combatants-to-be as possible.

Clearly the Crows, who had some guns, were trying to provoke a charge by the Blackfoot, believing they could injure the oncoming warriors with a barrage of missiles and shot as they grew closer. As Two Horns had no interest in the fleeing families, he elected to send out half of his party in a feint to draw the Crows' fire but stay somewhat out of effective range. Running Wolf Leaps led the group at a charge to within thirty yards of the Crows, where they reined in sharply and let fly their lances and assorted other weapons. The Crows had no choice but to throw their weapons and shoot their guns in response. Both groups stayed apart, yelling and dodging the deadly weapons, and working to control their now spirited horses. Little damage was done on either side. About the time that Running Wolf Leaps's warriors were about to pull up from their charge down to the Crows, Two Horns and his second group started down behind them. So shortly after the first exchange of flying weapons hit the ground, Two Horns and the second group charged past the first group of Blackfoot on the full gallop into the Crows. Two Horns headed straight for the Crow chief, and Messenger slammed into the smaller horse, causing the Crow chief to have to grab hold of his horse with both hands or fall to the turf. The collision surprised Two Horns, too, as he was not used to such an advantage. Before he could swing his war club and strike the struggling Crow chief, Moon in the Daylight, who had ridden next to him, ran her lance into the big warrior's side. Surprised and dismayed, the big Crow just looked at her as Two Horns finally dispatched him with his belated swing. The advantage in numbers for the Blackfoot, along with the sudden fall of the Crow chief, ended the battle as quickly as it had started. The Crow line broke and retreated. Moon in the Daylight let out a bloodcurdling war scream, which unnerved everyone, and Two Horns called off the beginning pursuit of the fleeing Crows. Besides the Crow chief, another warrior and a boy lay dead, while the Blackfoot barely had any scratches to show for the brief encounter. Satisfied, and with three new Crow ponies, the Blackfoot turned around and rode through the early evening back to the camp reliving the victorious battle in detail. Two Horns told them of the revenge taken by Moon in the Daylight. Clearly this was a woman worth considering taking as another wife. The next day, Two Horns prudently moved the camp back to the northwest, until he felt he was well within accepted Blackfoot home range and the Crows would not know where he was. The sea of grass, as always, helped to swallow up the departing Blackfoot.

14

AS THEY TRAVELED SOUTH, the three companions saw more settlements, and the forest began to open up. The shoreline was dramatic with its huge boulders and crashing waves. There was often a morning mist so thick that the men were forced to move slowly and stay close together. Drego pointed out the huge Redwood and Sequoia trees, stating his people believed that they were hundreds of years old. Both Donovan and Corby had no doubt that it must have taken a long, long time to grow trees to these towering heights. When in the old redwood forests, the travel was easier, due to less ground cover, from the massive canopy, though somewhat of a zigzag due to riding around the ponderous trees that had fallen. Drego said it felt like a church in the forest, and both Corby and Donovan had to agree again. Many of the trees out on the coastline itself were twisted and windswept to exaggerated degrees, and some trees seemed to be growing right out of the rock cliffs. As beautiful as the scenery was, following the coastline was not a good way to travel for long, as the many rivers to ford and the coastal range of low mountains made for little daily progress. Besides that, the men did not wish to run into the pirates again, so Drego led them back inland after a few days to a road he said would run along a south-flowing river all the way to the great bay of San Francisco.

As they moved inland and south, the land started to lose its lushness, with more pine and then oak groves. The sunnier climate was a welcome change for the travelers. The land was still largely undisturbed and teeming with game. Now more deer and birdlife appeared and watched as the small caravan passed by. Corby realized he was as happy as he had ever been, in this new land of unknown sights, with two men he trusted. They enjoyed each other's company, and Drego could make them laugh with his wild stories and prognostications. Life didn't have to be a guarded and bitter experience, as it usually was for him. Perhaps he could build a life out here that brought him a daily happiness like the happiness he now felt. Corby found himself expressing thoughts to Donovan and Drego freely and without concern of how they were received. He even found a sense of humor, a wit that the others said was quick and funny.

As Donovan had promised, at each campsite he worked with Corby on his draw and aim. Drego was included in all their discussions, and after getting over the shock of traveling with an ex-lawman, he began to have a great deal of fun reinventing each of their histories and futures. Drego showed the men how to throw his knife, and while all of this training and practicing was going on in an almost playful mood, the three men were honing their deadly skills.

Donovan became a little concerned with where this dedication to weapons training might lead his young friends. Where he enjoyed Drego as much as Corby did, Donovan knew that Drego was set on a different path, and someday would probably return to the other side of the law. Well, it wouldn't be his problem when that happened. At least he hoped it wouldn't. Meanwhile, Drego was a good guide and allied to the two of them. But unlike Corby, Donovan was far from willing to trust Drego. The lessons of a lifetime had taught him a caution and given him an instinct that had saved his life many times before. That instinct and caution told him to keep an eye on Drego.

Now as they came down into the foothill country of northern California, they began to see more people and activity. The Gold Rush was in full swing, since the discovery at Sutter's Mill in the Sacramento Valley. Drego had panned for about six months himself before giving up, explaining that the gold sickness he had witnessed firsthand was as close to insanity as anything he had ever seen. People were killing each other over paranoid suspicions, and the real criminals in the towns and cities were allowed to run unchecked, in wholesale extortion and graft. The rise of organized crime was enough to chase an honest bandido like himself right out of California.

Donovan had seen similar performances in greed, and wanted nothing to do with the area. They would re-provision at the fort, and then travel on to San Francisco. Donovan was already sensing that he had traveled through the more appealing territories of the West Coast, and would likely head back to the North to find his homestead. But seeing San Francisco would be a worthwhile excursion, and he could tell that Corby was very excited about getting there. So they rode on through the small camps and towns catering to the miners, until they reached Sutter's Fort.

The sight of the impoverished and largely unhappy miners was a shock to Corby. This was nothing like the stories that had come back to the rest of the country, of overnight millionaires, and riches lying around just waiting to be picked up. These people looked haggard and wretched, even by Western standards. At the fort, the conversations were about played-out veins and outrageous supply costs. Miners were leaving as fast as miners were still coming to the goldfields. It was said that John Sutter's properties had been trampled over, his cattle killed, and his businesses looted. He had given up trying to stop the hordes of locust that had descended upon him, and was now a broken man. The government had not helped him defend his claims and property, and now it was gone.

After finding a stable to put up all their animals, the men found a clean room for the night and dumped most of their baggage. Then they set out to look at the town. There was one long front street, and about four side streets running out of it, and the small town seemed very busy indeed. The fort itself was at one end of the long street. A scattering of houses and outlying buildings could be seen behind the main traffic areas. After buying a few personal items at the mercantile store, they crossed over to a bar called the Lucky Lady. Donovan commented on this being about the fifth Lucky Lady he had encountered. This Lucky Lady was one large room with two long bars and a handful of tables. Sitting down at the only empty table with a miner who called himself Silverquick Sam, the three travelers picked up on the latest news and sought more information on San Francisco. Silverquick Sam told them to watch their pockets if they were going to San Francisco. The goldfields were a church social compared to the city. Gangs of robbers roamed the streets at night, and people simply disappeared, believed to be shanghaied to ships plying the northwest trade. The law was bought and paid for by the big money players who owned the saloons and gambling halls, along with most everything else. The new governor had repeatedly asked for federal troops to begin to control the streets, but so far, there was only a little fort to guard the bay. So said Silverquick Sam, but the trio took the gossip with a grain of salt, feeling that no one would live in such a place as was being described, and they knew from all accounts that San Francisco was thriving. Still, such an ominous warning had to have some truth attached, and perhaps it was good to hear it prior to arriving in the city.

Certainly, after many months in the wilderness, their first night back in civilization made Donovan wonder why people wanted to live together at all. The saloon was overcrowded with an assortment of characters that would never be welcome in Donovan's new home-to-be. The noise level was too shrill and the shared air was downright smelly. So when Donovan suggested that they find a quieter spot to eat, there was no argument. Silverquick Sam said they could find him right there at the bar until morning. The three left to look for a dinner somewhere else in town.

After a brief conversation outside a restaurant run by Mexicans, Drego gave his stamp of approval and told the other two that they would feast on the good food from Guadalajara, and then explained that meant a region in Mexico, famous for particular seafood dishes, which this restaurant didn't have. Shrugging his shoulders, he said, "At least the price will be reasonable."

Actually, the restaurant served up a fair steak, and the men were enjoying a beer when the gunshots and hollering started. Looking around, they noticed that no one else seemed to notice. When the waiter came by, urged by his friends, Drego asked about the commotion down the street, and was told that the noise would go on most of the night, and that a few gunshots were quite normal. The waiter suggested they look in on the Golden Bucket, where the prettiest girls were working, but to look out for drunks and gamblers. The men decided to take a look, and after dinner, a short walk brought them to the Golden Bucket as night fell on Sutter's Fort.

Men were crowding around various gambling tables and the long bar when the trio entered the Golden Bucket. There was some kind of music being played, but the place was so loud with talking and yelling that it was indistinguishable. The miners were gambling, drinking, and carousing. Two men with shotguns were perched up on very high chairs looking down on the melee. An assortment of ladies was mingling with the crowd, easily picked out by their bright dresses against a drab background of wall-to-wall miners. The three made their way to the bar, and were greeted by a matronly lady with a purple boa around her rather ample neck.

"Well, well, it looks like we have some real men here tonight. My name's Jean. I run the girls here, so when you've made up your mind, come see me. I suggest the whiskey that comes on the top shelf. It costs a little more, but it's worth it. So, what'll it be, boys?" she asked with a big smile.

Drego swept his hat off his head, and gallantly said, "Señorita, *con mucho gusto*, I have been here before, and your top wheeskee ees beyond my humble means. *Particularimente* eef I am to veeseet la señorita Helena."

"Sorry to tell you, sonny, but Helen took off with a minor that got lucky just last month. Headed to San Francisco, and then Philadelphia, I think. But don't you fret none, I've got some mighty nice new girls, just in from the East; a couple of Mex girls too. You'll do just fine."

"Then I would like to buy my compadres a lower-shelf wheeskee, please," he countered.

"Three coming up," she said and reached under the bar for the glasses.

A couple of drinks later, Drego was off to try his hand at the faro table. Donovan took the opportunity to talk to Corby. "That Drego is a real likeable fellow. Good travel companion."

Corby smiled at Donovan and said, "But you think he might be dangerous company here in town, right?"

Donovan had to laugh, and put his drink down. "You saw me coming that far away, did you? Yeah, Drego's off to see the circus. Ain't nothing going to stop him from what he wants to do tonight. Usually not a good idea to tag along with a fellow that hell-bent."

"Then how about you show me how a famous lawman plays poker?" Corby suggested, nodding toward a table.

Donovan winced and looked around to see if anyone had heard the comment, and then waved Corby on to the table. He would have to instruct the kid on keeping mum about his past vocation. Being known as an ex-lawman would serve only to invite unwanted problems in a town like this. There was much he needed yet to teach his young companion.

It took a while before both could get in the game, but eventually they did, and Donovan indeed was showing Corby how to win at cards. Being around saloons most of his adult life had taught Donovan a thing or two about cards, and just as he was a reader of potential hardcases, he was a fair reader of poor card players. That, and patience, were enough to make him the winner at this table. Corby was holding his own, and several chairs had exchanged ownership a couple of hours later. As men were standing around all the tables watching, Donovan didn't notice at first when several men came over and were looking at Corby and talking in whispers. Finally one spoke loudly and said, " Some Mex is saying you're the man that drew down Jimbo Fisher. Is that right, mister?'

The area grew suddenly quiet, and Corby looked over to Donovan.

Donovan laughed and said, " My partner? A gunfighter? Was this a sober Mex?"

A few people laughed, but the man persisted. "They say the man who shot Jimbo Fisher could have killed him and all six of his gunhands if he wanted to. You saying you ain't that man, mister?"

Corby wanted to say, first off, there were only three men, not seven, and Fisher was looking to shoot the Marshal, not me, and finally I shot him in the arm when I was aiming for his stomach, but instead, he said, "That's right, you've got the wrong man. I'm just an average draw, and a worse poker player."

That drew a few laughs and seemed to satisfy the man asking the questions, who said, "Don't really believe anyone is that fast. Fisher ain't that fast to start with."

"Not as fast as you, Clay," his friend said. "Let's go find that lying Mex."

The two men turned and left, followed by most of the men standing around the table.

"Cash me in," said Donovan. "Sounds like it might get a little too hot around here for an old cowboy."

Corby and Donovan abruptly left the premises, and melted into the shadows across the street.

"Shouldn't we go get Drego?" Corby asked.

"And confirm to every drunk with a gun that you are the 'deadliest pistolero west of the Mississippi'?" Donovan shook his head. "No, Drego will have to get himself out of this. I'm sure he will find a way to weasel around any real trouble. That is until he sees me." The men wandered down the street and looked in on the Lucky Lady for a nightcap.

The next morning the two left town on the road to San Francisco. About midmorning Drego caught up to them on the trail, looking none the worse for wear.

15

*T*HE YOUNG CROW WARRIOR had returned to the side of his dead brother. He sat down next to him and remembered the eventful day. Loud Thunder had always looked up to his older brother, Proud Eagle, and why not? Proud Eagle was a leader among the Crow. Some said he would be a major chief soon. For Loud Thunder, he had been a father as much as a brother after the death of their father in a raid on the Lakota some years back. It had been Proud Eagle that had taught Loud Thunder how to fight, and it was Proud Eagle that had provided for him and their mother over the years as Loud Thunder grew into a man.

This had been something of a belated honeymoon for Loud Thunder, who had just taken his first wife. Proud Eagle had asked the young couple if they would like to join his extended family band for a small hunt. Loud Thunder had expected to stay with his family band anyway, but the formal question had been another sign of respect his older brother had given him as a new husband of his own family now. Three other families had joined with Proud Eagle on this buffalo hunt.

That morning they had snuck up on the small herd they had spotted the day before and begun the hunt. It was then that the hated Blackfoot had joined in to also hunt the buffalo. Loud Thunder had encouraged his brother to drive off the Blackfoot, who had four hunters to the Crows' six, but Proud Eagle had watched the Blackfoot leader ride out after the hunt waving a peaceful gesture to begin the skinning, and had decided to ignore their intrusion into the fringe of Crow territory. Proud Eagle had said that the families had to be fed first, and the buffalo was a gift to all the Plains Indians. He had said that they would keep an eye on the Blackfoot, and if they tried anything, then Loud Thunder would have his chance to kill a Blackfoot.

Later that afternoon they had indeed caught the thieving Blackfoot trying to sneak up on their camp. Loud Thunder had helped to dispatch the Blackfoot warrior that could not escape. But news came that the Blackfoot camp was a larger camp than the Crows', and Proud Eagle became worried for the women and children. They had been retreating when the cowardly Blackfoot had attacked with more than twice the Crows' number. Loud Thunder had fought with his brother, and watched as the Blackfoot leader on the large black horse had crashed into his brother's mount, allowing a warrior woman to run her lance through Proud Eagle's side. Overwhelmed, the Crows had been forced to run, leaving the dead and dying while hearing the jeers of their enemy. Loud Thunder had wanted to continue fighting, but Strong Bear, who had assumed leadership, as was his right when Proud Eagle fell, reminded him of his responsibilities to the others, and they had left the battle scene.

Now Loud Thunder rose with his brother in his arms and put him on the pony he had brought to carry him. The other dead were also collected and taken back to the tribe to prepare them for burial. As per his agreement with Strong Bear, Loud Thunder now swung himself up on his pony and headed toward the Blackfoot camp. He would track them for the next two months until they rejoined the main tribe by a lake in the foothills of the Western mountains. Loud Thunder would remember the Blackfoot chief and his band, and he would scout the surrounding area thoroughly to know the terrain for when he would come to exact his revenge on the Blackfoot. It would turn out to be several years before that opportunity would arise. Loud Thunder had that time to nurture his hatred.

16

S o *THIS IS CALIFORNIA.* Gabrielle had been watching the coastline for several days as the ship drew closer to her new home. The wild shore-line triggered her imagination, with its beautiful beaches and rocky cliffs. As they had neared San Francisco, the weather had changed dramati-cally, and the greenery had intensified. The captain explained that the city often had a fog bank on it in the summer, and light rain in the winter, but sunshine was a short ride away to the South and East. He said that even in the massive bay, one side was often overcast and the other sunny. They were now waiting for the tide to change, as the wind was insufficient to overcome the riptide pouring out into the ocean from the bay. The city opened up on the bay side, with its docks and warehouses, and climbed up the hills into a small coastal range of mountains. There was relatively little to see from the seaside, except an occasional boat or ship coming out with the tide. The mouth to the bay was wide, but the captain said the bay inside was huge, draining a vast area of wetlands to the North, East, and South. Millions of birds migrated through the area, often filling the sky. The captain believed that someday San Francisco, due to its natural harbor and West Coast loca-tion, would be as important as Boston or Baltimore. However, at this time, it was no place for a lady, and until the Countess had obtained appropriate local protection, the captain had insisted on assigning two of his men to accompany her entourage for a few days. Gabrielle had graciously accepted the offer.

When the tides turned and the ship sailed into the bay, San Francisco's bustling prosperity became evident. It was as if everything was being built simultaneously. New piers for the maritime traffic, new businesses, and new homes were all under construction. Whalers, fishing boats, packet ships, and others she couldn't identify were anchored due to lack of mooring facilities. What she could see of the city was unattractive but busy. There were no flowered cafes and restaurants like in New Orleans. The streets were mostly dirt, and the people were scruffy looking. But the energy coming off those streets was intoxicating, and Gabrielle was anxious to get ashore after all these months at sea and take a closer look.

A shuttle boat came to pick up the mail and those wishing to come ashore. Gabrielle and Barton, along with the two sailors and Zachary DuPort, were among the first to climb down to the transport. Once ashore, Gabrielle wished to first find the newly established Bank of San Francisco she had heard just opened. Zachary decided to inspect the businesses on Portsmouth Square, the gambling district. Guided to Market Street, Gabrielle found the bank just where the street ended at the foot of a large sand hill. An unimpressive building, of newly cut timber, it had a plank sidewalk in front of it, partially covered with blown sand. Upon entering the building, business literally came to a stop. Few women of high standing were in the city, and none as stately or attractive as Gabrielle. The bank's owner came over to greet her and usher her into his office.

"I am Thomas James, the proprietor of the Bank of San Francisco. How may I help you, Miss...?"

"May I introduce Madame Loucheur, La Comtesse de Larousseau, of the Montfort family of New Orleans," Barton barked out.

"Comtesse? A real countess?" Mr. James fumbled.

"Please sit down, Mr. James," Gabrielle said, smiling. "I have some letters of credit to show you, and I would like to see your security arrangements, if you would be so kind."

Mr. James yelled out the door, "Ferguson and Jacobs, come in here and help me with the Countess."

Within minutes, the word was spreading that a real live countess was in the business district, and shortly thereafter, a small crowd had amassed to do fictional business and get a look.

After examining her letters, Mr. James realized that Gabrielle had many more assets than did all of the combined customers in his bank, and he had a good share of the business of San Francisco. Any way he could do business with the Countess would enhance his growing enterprise. He sent a runner to the nearby land office of Prannel & Stouts, to show the Countess the best homes available in the area. He promised to find her suitable servants and security for her new home. After a tour that consisted mainly of the new vault and the wall of safety deposit boxes behind a barred wall of bricks, he opened an account with extensive credit for her at the bank, and promised to introduce her to the prominent citizens of San Francisco. Hell, he wasn't about to let anyone else introduce her.

When Gabrielle got up to leave the bank, she first had to work her way through a dozen introductions with businessmen in the bank, before escaping with her sailors and Barton. She was escorted to the Benson House, then considered the most appropriate hotel, where she sent for Angelina and the bulk of her baggage, including the large safe, which was disguised in a crate.

As she reviewed the conversations she had with the banker, several thoughts stood out. Personal security led the list. The town was flush with gamblers and thieves, and she would make a prime target without adequate help. Second, cash was king in the city, and since she probably had the most, there was no reason she shouldn't prosper. Third, the town seemed to have a curse of large fires, so whatever ventures she was going to get involved in had to be picked not just for their potential, but also by their location, or more precisely, their lack of location contingent to other buildings that might burn down. It was clear that there were great opportunities in this fast-developing city, but also great dangers. The hotel she now sat in was a good example of the opportunities. This was not even a second-class hotel in New Orleans. The idea of running a grand hotel was especially appealing to her, as it would allow her the opportunity to build a small piece of her old world around her. She would get to know the city well enough first to know where the prime future location of such a hotel should stand, and then she would build the finest hotel in the West.

But first she needed a home and security. The local real estate people were due to pick her up in the morning for a tour of some properties. It would be good to know the local opinions on these properties, from Mr. James and others. She would be dining with Mr. James and his friends this evening.

ZACHARY DUPORT ALSO saw opportunities in this city. Gold dust was being measured by the ounce on a variety of different scales. It was clear to the discerning eye that different amounts of monies were being exchanged at each gambling house he entered. Some of the houses that had been put up looked like they might fall down, but business was brisk everywhere. Even the bigger and fancier saloons and hotels had gambling areas. Zachary noticed the professional gamblers in these relatively nicer buildings, men who had the cold and bored look of long hours at the tables. He recognized the games of roulette, monte, and faro, and was told of others named vingt-et-un, rouge et noir, and rondo. All were fast ways to win or lose money. After seeing the fine establishments of St. Louis and New Orleans, these rickety buildings were a big step down in style and comfort, but no one could deny the amount of money passing through them. Zeke started asking questions about how much the gambling halls cost. He realized that he could own his own, nothing too ritzy at first, but with a little luck or maybe a loan from Gabrielle, he could build up his business and make his life back in the West a very good one. It was time to sell the rest of his Mormon loot, and cash in on the gambling craze in this wild new city. Maybe he could interest Gabrielle in his gemstones, as he was getting the idea that selling them for fair value, whatever that was, would be a difficult job in a city like this. His own business meant he wouldn't be dependant on investors, as he was in New Orleans. The idea took on more and more appeal as he thought about it. True to himself, he celebrated his newfound enterprise-to-be by buying a new suit and the best dinner he could find. San Francisco was going to work out just fine.

"WE REPRESENT THE future of this fine city. Between the five of us," Bertram gestured with a wave of his hand at his fellow diners, "we control the vote on the City Council, Countess. We intend to clean up the old shanties, the fire hazards, and the scoundrels that are now so prevalent in the city. Commerce from the expanding shipping, forestry, and mining operations are enough to gain control of the more exotic industries and reshape a solid and respectable future here."

"Someone such as you will be very useful in promoting the new, emerging San Francisco, Countess," a man named Morley added. "Particularly if you are an investor, as Mr. James has indicated to us."

Gabrielle pointedly looked at Mr. James to make sure he understood that her business was not something she wished for him to discuss. Mr. James immediately added, "Whatever those investments might eventually turn out to be."

"And when would we expect the Count to join you?" asked a tall, well-dressed man named Paul Logan.

"My husband does not bear the title of Count; only through bloodline, gentlemen, and it would be hard to ascertain when he might visit. Family business, as you can see, tends to take us far afield."

"Then may I extend the welcome of the city to you, and offer my personal assistance until your husband does visit," Mr. Logan suggested.

"How very kind. I shall let you know if that becomes necessary," Gabrielle said, taking a moment to appraise the gentleman. Her first instinct told her that Mr. Logan was not the gentleman he proposed to be this evening. The feeling of being a fly seated next to a spider came into her mind, and she smiled and looked back at Mr. Bertram again. "Tomorrow, I will be looking for a home to purchase. A Mr. Prannel is to show me a few properties."

Bertram grunted. "That old highway robber will try to sell you the most overpriced outhouse in San Francisco." That brought a laugh and they then discussed what she was looking for.

"The old Dominguez ranch!" blurted out the less talkative Mr. Stevenson. "It has a fine old hacienda. Maybe a lot more land than you may like, but it sits as the finest spread in the area, and right on top of the city. Too rich for any of us."

"I'm sure the Countess wouldn't be interested in that old thing," Mr. Logan asserted. "Too much upkeep—cattle, fences, and ranch crew. I'm sure you would be much more comfortable here in the city, say a fine house overlooking the city and the bay."

"No, no, Stevenson is right," said Mr. Bertram, "if you can find the right men to help you, the Dominquez place is the best value in California. Excellent water, forested, runs to the ocean. Those old Dons knew how to live. I think it has its own little church. Magnificent property! But very big."

"Too big, my dear," Logan tried again shaking his head. Gabrielle then marked Logan as a potential rival, and moved on to other subjects. She would be sure to travel out to the Dominguez Ranch in the morning.

Mr. James, the banker, then said, " I think I may have found you a good man, for awhile at least, on your security need. Just got into town, says he wants to find his own place, but running an operation like yours could put the extra money in his pockets he might need. I made him promise to see you tomorrow, perhaps after you return from your property tour. An ex–U.S. marshal, from Missouri and the Oregon territories. Tough as they come by the looks of him, but I judge him to be honest and smart. The kind of man that could oversee a few diverse responsibilities."

"Didn't think you could clean up that good," drawled Corby. Donovan had on a fresh shirt with his new hat and silver buckle. Freshly shaved, he wasn't a bad-looking man. Then you looked into his eyes and knew he had seen his share of the world. Hopefully you wouldn't get "the look" as Corby described it. The look happened when Donovan wasn't happy with what he saw, and his face turned to stone. Looking into his eyes then, he could tell there wasn't a shred of doubt, or a scintilla of fear; this man was going to do whatever he had decided must be done, regardless of the fallout. The look could suddenly show up for the smallest infractions, sending a clerk scurrying away for interrupting, or causing a waiter to fear for his health for bringing a cold cup of coffee. Donovan wasn't even aware most of the time as to how his persona would intimidate people around him. It was a physical presence that read, "I am going to stomp on you." No one that saw it doubted the sincerity of the expression.

"The bank man says this is a real French-type countess. I always clean up good for countesses," Donovan retorted. "Someday you may have social connections like mine, and have to take a bath."

Corby smirked and asked, "You think Drego and I might get some work out of this?"

"Don't know, but I wouldn't be surprised, the way this woman was described to me. Rolling in money."

"We sure could use some honest work. This city is damn expensive. But working for a woman? What do you think?" Corby asked.

"I've worked for good men and bad men, most of them idiots. She pays on time, she could be the devil himself. No problem here," Donovan said as he pulled on his shined-up boots. "You want to stay in this dump because your boss might wear a dress, is up to you. I figure she has got to smell better than any boss I've probably ever had before. Now I've got to go, so please open the door for me, being as I associate with countesses and the like."

Corby smiled and pretended to kick Donovan in the pants on his way out. It was good to see Donovan in such a good mood. The prospect of not shelling out any more of his hard-earned savings for a while had lifted Donovan's spirits. It felt good to be recognized as a professional again too. The banker had been impressed with his history and very insistent on his talking with this countess. If he could earn enough to pay for their time in San Francisco, he would have that much more to use when he found his homestead.

Crossing the street to the bank where he was to meet the Countess with the banker, Donovan grew a little concerned by the group of people standing around outside. As he started to go in the bank, a man said to him, "There's a countess from France in there."

"Damn, they told me it was Napoleon!" Donovan answered as he entered.

"Marshal Donovan," Mr. James called out, "over here." He was standing by his office door. Two sailors were almost at attention outside the door, and a gentleman and a lady with her back to him were seated inside the office.

As Donovan walked over to Mr. James, he studied the back of the Countess's head. Her hair was a deep auburn color, with copper highlights in it, and yes, she did smell nice as he passed her to sit down in the chair indicated across from her in Mr. James's office. That was when he got his biggest surprise. This was a very young and beautiful woman. He placed her at not more than twenty years old, maybe less. But then she started talking, and he was surprised again at her poise and command. He started listening, besides looking.

"What I need is someone to appraise the property from an operational point of view," she was saying. "Apparently, it is owned by the government now, and there are leases for grazing and timber on it, along with some necessary repair work. Also, if I live there, I would like to know that I am secure from both man and beast. I would need an assessment of what kind of household I might need, and someone who could pick out good, honest employees and run them. Then there is the issue of my businesses in town, and—"

"Whoa, now slow down, Missy...er...Countess; let's take these one at a time," Donovan said, smiling.

"Please excuse me," Gabrielle said. "Call me Gabrielle." She was surprised by what she had just said, but she felt at ease with this westerner, as if she could trust him and learn from him. "As you can see, I really do have to find some help on a variety of issues. Would you assist me, Marshal Donovan?"

"Well, I reckon I never left a damsel in distress before, so why start now? Let's start with a look at this government property and take it from there. You have a buggy, or perhaps you would like to ride?"

"Told you, you should have taken a bath, Corby," Donovan said, but he wasn't kidding this time. "You and me are going to go riding with the Countess and her...whatever he is. Put on your cleanest clothes and try to stay downwind. Where's Drego?"

"Haven't seen him since last night."

"Probably just as well. He would be as bowled over as you are going to be when you see this gal." Donovan groaned.

"She's pretty?" Corby smiled.

"Pretty don't cover the territory with this gal. You remember she's a countess and our meal ticket, and mind your manners."

Corby sniffed around himself and decided maybe a quick birdbath with some soap was in order. As he washed and changed, Donovan went over to the stables and got their horses and two others saddled up. An hour after leaving the Countess, he and Corby showed up at the Benson House to take her and Barton out to the Dominguez Ranch for an afternoon of looking the place over. A vaquero named Paco would be acting as their guide, provided by the bank. He was waiting in the street when they got there. Donovan went inside to let the Countess know that they were there on time. She was waiting in the lobby with Barton. Dressed in riding pants and boots, she was even lovelier that Donovan had first surmised. Just keeping the wolves away would be a full-time job. But he guessed that was a large part of Barton's work. He hoped Barton knew the rules were different out West.

Gabrielle had leaped at the idea of riding western-style out in the California wilderness. Not since she was a girl had she had a chance to ride that way. New Orleans meant sidesaddle, if at all, and she missed really hanging on and riding as men do. Also, when she had looked at the property from the buggy with Mr. Prannel, she knew she wasn't seeing nearly enough. By horseback was the only way to tour a ranch. She was looking at her watch in anticipation when Donovan strode in to the lobby.

"Ready, ma'am?" Donovan asked with a little nod of his hat.

"Marshal Donovan, of that you may rest assured."

Stepping out into the sun, Donovan led her over to a nice bay mare, which the stable had recommended. She shook her head and took the feistier two-year-old paint. "It's an Indian pony, isn't it?" she asked.

"Yes, ma'am, and it has a little spirit too," Donovan warned.

"Oh, I think you will be able to keep up," she teased as Barton helped her up into the saddle. The horse wheeled halfway around before she got the reins pulled in.

"Ma'am," said Corby as he suddenly found himself knee to knee in the saddle across from her. The silhouette of the cowboy now changed into a face with the sun behind her. He was young and handsome in the rugged Western way. She could tell he was strong, and he had the most beautiful blue eyes she had ever seen on a man. Strikingly blue.

"That there is Corby, Countess. He is my protection in these wild parts," Donovan joked. "Kind of picked him up like a stray dog, and can't get rid of him. Good story there; I'll tell you sometime. Paco, why don't you lead us out?"

The five riders started out of the city to the South. " Is this here the Camino Real, Paco?" Donovan asked.

Pleased and surprised, Paco said, "Sí, señor, the King's Road. It will take us straight to the Don's rancho."

"What can you tell us about the ranch?"

"Me? OK, well I used to live on it. The Don was the governor of northern California when España, she ruled here. Then the Mexican government took control, and their governor lived there too. Since the war it has been deserted," Paco explained. "It was the Spanish who built it and ran it. The hacienda looks over the whole valley and bay, and a short ride will take you to see the ocean. It is protected from the ocean storms, built into the rock ground like a fort. The timbers are *gigante*, from the old redwood trees. The cattle are now wild, some horses too. The only fencing is on this side of the mountains, because the rancho runs up over the mountains and all the way down to the sea. The best grazing is in the valleys on top and over on this side of the mountains. The southern end is very wild. The Don planted orchards in the valley below the hacienda, but they are now overgrown, and eaten by the birds and deer. There are many wells for the cattle, which need to be found, unplugged, and cleared of brush. Of course the hacienda itself hasn't been cared for in some time. But when it was a working rancho, there was none finer. And game ... turkeys, geese, quail, deer, elk, bear ..." Paco paused, fearing he had rambled on too much.

They were out in the countryside now on the main road heading south. Much of the peninsula was treed, but there had been some clearing along the road, with an occasional adobe or log home sprinkled around.

"Why aren't there brick homes out here?" Gabrielle asked. "I understand there have been a lot of fires in the city."

"The Spaniards built mostly with wood frame on adobe, like in Mexico, and they withstand most fires well. The Americanos are interested in building very fast and cheap, and with trees like these," Paco swept his hand across the forest, "they can do that."

Another road right angled to the West, and Paco turned his horse on to it.

"You are now on the Dominguez Rancho," he said.

Donovan swung around in his saddle looking for some kind of marker or fenceline, but saw none. "One thing you are sure gonna want is a surveyor, Countess. No indication of where this begins or ends."

He noticed a group of five riders coming up the main road at a fairly good clip, and motioned to Corby. If they turned on to the ranch road behind them, it could spell trouble. The group continued their leisurely pace, as Donovan kept a rear view on the approaching riders. When the riders turned on to the road behind them, Donovan took precautionary action.

"Look, Countess, there are five riders coming up on us. Probably is nothing, but in case it is some sort of trouble, I'd like you to stand your horse behind me. Let's get off the road to the left over here, to let them pass. Corby, you stay to the far right as we face them. Paco, you and Barton curve around a bit to the left. If they mean trouble, ease out a bit more to the left, try to bunch them in front of us, got it?"

"You mean these men could be bandits?" Gabrielle asked.

"We'll find out real soon. That's why you hired me."

The riders began to slow down when they saw that Donovan's party was waiting off the road for them. It was no coincidence that the afternoon sun slanted over the backs of the waiting party. When the group arrived, the leader pulled up in front of Donovan and said, "My my, what do we have here?"

Donovan then recognized the rider, and said in a mocking voice," Aren't you that famous fast draw, desperado Jimbo something or other?"

Jimbo Fisher squinted a bit and then recognized Donovan too. Next he swung his head around to find Corby, who was sitting with the sun most directly behind him as Donovan had instructed him to do.

Donovan continued. "Oh yes, he's here too. How's that shoulder of yours doing? They can hurt like a son of a bitch if it nicks the bone."

"It's them Oregon fellas," one of Jimbo Fisher's men said excitedly.

Another then chimed in. "Then let's drill 'em, Jimbo."

Jimbo Fisher's face was a contortion of rage. He wanted to kill in the worst way, but he also knew fear. The battle raged on inside him as everyone waited for the decision. Donovan read the decision first, and drew first, but again it was Corby's bullet that knocked Jimbo Fisher from his saddle, gun still in his hand. Even Donovan hadn't gotten off a shot, but at least his gun was drawn and pointing. This time Jimbo Fisher didn't move, as the shot had killed him. A couple of horses jumped and had to be restrained. Barton slowly pulled out his small revolver and pointed it too. Then Paco did the same.

The man who had identified them as the "Oregon fellas" said, "Everybody stay cool. This here ain't a fight we want. You got no cause to murder us. That was Fisher's play. Boys, back up slow now."

The remaining four riders backed their horses up onto the road, turned, and started to ride away. One of them yelled back. " This ain't over yet, Oregon. Targon will have his Injun skin you alive!"

It had all happened so fast that Gabrielle wasn't totally sure what had happened.

"Did that man try to shoot you, Marshal Donovan?" she timidly asked.

"No, ma'am, I think he was trying to get the jump on Corby there. Not real sure what they were sent to do, but it weren't to exchange pleasantries. Poor old Fisher was some out of sorts when he realized he had stumbled into a bee hive."

"Excuse me, Marshal Donovan?"

"I figure those boys are used to taking pretty much whatever they want, and they saw a group of city folk out for a ride. Fisher sure wasn't planning on facing down Corby again," Donovan tried to explain. He went on to tell what had happened in Oregon and who Targon and Fisher were.

"These are just the men the City Council is trying to get rid of," she exclaimed. She felt a chill run up her spine. This certainly was not New Orleans. She looked over at the handsome, quiet face of Corby, stoically sitting on his horse. These westerners were more than what met the eye. A man lay dead right in front of her.

"I'm sure they are, Countess, but there are always moneymen pulling their strings too," Donovan commented. "Now I'm afraid our tour has been cut short, as we will have to take Fisher back to town to the authorities."

"Of course, of course," Gabrielle muttered, as it was just sinking in that she may have been seriously hurt. What would have happened if Corby and Donovan had not been with her? She shuddered again as the ugly images appeared in her mind. A lesson learned; she was very fortunate to have learned it this way.

Corby looked down at the second man he had killed in his young life, and a shiver ran up his spine too. He suddenly felt very tired and a bit nauseous.

17

THE TWO MEN SAT alone in the dimly lit room with a bottle and two glasses between them. The room had no windows, and the door was shut, so there was a stuffy atmosphere that made Paul Logan even more uncomfortable. Eventually he would have to end the relationship, once he had enough money to afford to do so. Until then, underwriting the activities of Günter Targon was making him a great deal of money. He had no doubt that Targon was cheating him most of the time, but it was nickel and dime, compared to what Logan reaped on his end. The contracts for supplies and transport up and down the West Coast that Targon enforced for him at inflated prices were instrumental in his capitalizing of the gaming houses and other legitimate businesses in San Francisco and the goldfields. The elimination of competition was a cash bonus for Targon and his pirates. Logan understood that the goldfields wouldn't last much longer, and that civilization would continue its advance West, with so many more people coming to the area. He had a handful of years to convert his illegal gains into legitimate enterprises, and sweep the tracks behind him. The trick would be to keep Targon happy and oblivious until that day. The recent high-profile death of Jimbo Fisher had thrown a wrench into his well-oiled machinery. The account of the broad daylight attack on the city's newly arrived symbol of prosperity, the Countess de Larousseau, had invoked a veritable crusade to clean up the corruption by the good citizens of San Francisco. How could they ever develop into the fine and important city and state they wanted to be when ruffians and thugs were openly terrorizing anyone and everyone?

"Let them concentrate on the Barkley gang and the low-end gambling dives for a month or so. Then you can come back and pick up the pieces. If we play this right, I can direct the Council to some of our gambling and brothel competition, and then we can step into the void. This will die down soon enough." Logan looked across the table at the big German to see if he understood the situation.

Günter Targon was not a stupid man by any measure. A sea captain by trade, he had experienced a mean world from the day he was born. So he had grown up tougher and meaner than those around him. Those who had never seen Günter in action, might perhaps think he was too heavy and slow to be formidable. They would be wrong. He was a mass of muscle, underneath an armor of fat. He had lost count of the number of scars marking his numerous brushes with rivals and death. Like the great bear of the northwest, a single bullet would only cause to enrage him. If Günter himself didn't get you, he could count on the likes of his employed killers, like the late gunman Jimbo Fisher, or worse yet, the Indian assassin Ishka.

He now studied the man who had been his partner the last four years. Paul Logan had helped to establish Günter as the scourge of the West that he was. But Günter was well aware that it was Günter that had faced the dangers, while Logan had gotten richer and richer, living a life of ease and influence. Günter didn't resent their roles. He had no interest in living anywhere but on the deck of one of his ships, but he expected to get every cent that was due him, and whatever else he could carry off. He also knew that the days of buccaneering on the West Coast would end sometime, and he would then need to sail off to new hunting grounds. It would take a sense of timing on when he would need to plunder what he could, perhaps from Paul Logan, and set sail. Right now he understood that a short hiatus from the Bay Area probably was a good business move, but he wanted to be paid to do anything, if only to reinforce his end of the relationship.

"We just got back from a summer of sailing the northwest and the whaling routes. My boys are tired and need some time for fun. And I've got a score to settle over Fisher." Targon replied. "Besides, two of our ships haven't even made port yet for the winter."

"I've been thinking about that," Logan said. "We have been ceding the southern half of California because it's just a few Mexicans, but now that it is U.S. territory, Americans will start showing up down there, too. Getting our foot in now may pay off well down the road. If we invest a couple of month's extra pay for the crews, plus whatever you find on your own, your men may enjoy wintering this year in Los Angeles. Meanwhile you can scope out the opportunities, and next Spring we can discuss where we stand, after this local huff has blown over."

"Make it five months pay, and we keep anything we find, and I think I can sell it."

"Four months pay. And you sail back here by April, to help refit the whaler crews. Meanwhile, you will be pleased to know that we will be opening a bank soon. That should allow us to make a higher return on some of the merchandise you come across. And forget about Fisher. I told you we don't want that kind of visibility. It's a blessing he's gone," Logan countered.

"Four months it is then, in advance," Targon poured a drink for himself and drank to the agreement without offering Logan one. "But I will get my revenge for Fisher when I return, and I will determine who I need in my services. We will sail tomorrow with the three ships here, and you will direct the other two South when they arrive. I will take their money with me too. Helps to keep them in line. Send the money in the morning."

Targon then got up, took the bottle, and walked out the back door without another word. Logan continued to sit awhile, reflecting on the conversation. In his line of work, a four month window allowed him now to put Targon on a back burner and deal with other pressing matters, such as the lovely Countess and all her money.

Life was complicated for Paul Logan, but that was just the way he liked it. Thomas James was making a killing with his bank. Logan thought he could be doing the same, while developing a perfect vehicle to convert his illegitimate funds into working capital. One's own bank, run by one's own rules. What could be better? Now, how could he get his hands on the Countess and her money?

18

CHRISTMAS EVE 1849, A major fire again threatened San Francisco, and was only put out by blowing up surrounding buildings. Even though it was the wet season and muddy, the city had scarce water reserves and fire fighting assets to deal with the blaze. However, when the danger had passed, once again the quick profit mentality came into play, and buildings of similar materials and questionable engineering were immediately built in their place. So when two young Polish brothers approached Gabrielle about starting a brick factory, she jumped at the idea. She would need those bricks herself, to build the St. Montfort Hotel. On a property high above the growing city, with a view of both the city below to the East, and the bay stretching around to the north, Gabrielle began the major construction of the hotel she had envisioned on the long trip West. A monthly steamer now left San Francisco, and Gabrielle had sent orders back East for a wide variety of furniture and decorations she would need in her grand hotel. Realizing that this would take several years to fully complete, she had concentrated her plans on the main lobby and a handful of elegant suites to begin. The structure would be constructed as to allow future stories to be built above it and around it. She saw a long-term project that would eventually have gardens, a ballroom, meeting rooms, and the like. She would blend Old World elegance and New World openness into the premier hotel in America. Perhaps she wouldn't be hosting presidents and kings in this frontier, but she could if they came.

Several of the orders she had sent back East were for her new home in the high hills, the former residence of the Spanish governor. After buying the ranch, she had installed a working crew, supervised at the moment by Marshal Donovan. He had complained that this was not his calling, but had so far done an admirable job of cleaning up the old hacienda and repairing ranch buildings and fences. Along with the former old ranch hand Paco, the two had found a good crew of vaqueros who were happy to restore the ranch to working order. The silent gunman Corby was part of the crew. Marshal Donovan had insisted that Corby live out on the ranch, she surmised, to protect him from the instant and dubious fame he had attained by killing the outlaw Jimbo Fisher. A sadness had taken over the cowboy, and Gabrielle, as was her want, felt a sense of responsibility. Clearly the outlaws had intended her as their victim, to whatever extent that may have gone. Both Marshal Donovan and Barton had assured her that Corby's ability with his gun was probably the sole reason she had escaped untouched that day. As busy as she was, she would find time to thank the man and perhaps help him through whatever demons he was fighting. Clearly Marshal Donovan was worried about his friend, and Marshal Donovan was someone who was becoming increasingly indispensable to her.

The City Council had found a new seat for their stylish and rich new citizen. In a city composed of five men to every woman, many still living in tents and ramshackle housing, Gabrielle stood out like a rose among thorns. She was seen to be everywhere as she canvassed the city for opportunities and real estate. Gabrielle added the responsibility of the governing council to her growing list of activities. Between the shock of the Christmas fire and the fear of the criminal element, as showcased with the incident with Gabrielle, the Council had a wave of citizen concern and support to address the twin problems plaguing the city. A raft of new ordinances and committees were put together to stem the tide. A fire department was formed, and work began on a number of new wells and reservoirs to furnish the city's water needs. Property owners were assessed to make street improvements, including some sewers, and some of the sand hills were removed from the downtown districts for faster access around the city streets. Firewalls were mandated for city buildings, which helped to expand the use of more brick in building. But crime continued to be the biggest hill to climb. Many of the businessmen in town had ties to the quick riches and vices attached to the goldfields, and were reluctant to crack down too hard on the establishments that lured the cash to the city. The general agreement of the Council was that the law enforcement was corrupt at best and unsalvageable at worst. A clean start would be needed when they could garner enough support to do so. In the meantime, it was best to lock your doors at night and travel with appropriate company.

Still, it was an exciting time for the city, and business opportunities were everywhere for those willing to take risks. Gabrielle had in a few short months found an exciting new life that fully engaged her. She had no regrets about her sudden move to California.

SITTING ON A big rock eating his lunch, Corby saw Donovan riding out to see how the new water hole was going. Corby had been working on hammering a pipeline into the seeping hillside to create a dependable water source for the cattle that would soon be purchased and released. He had already built a circular wooden tank to collect the spring water once it began to flow. The small ravine had been widened to allow the cattle to surround the tank to drink, and the surrounding trees meant they would probably stay in the area on hot afternoons. This was a part of the ranch that had oak groves and grass hills. The deer were particularly fond of the acorns in the winter.

A month of hard labor had had a beneficial effect on Corby. He was smiling again, and enjoying the bunkhouse camaraderie. Donovan's search for a new home had taken a serious postponement, and Corby could tell that Donovan was relishing his new duties. Even though Donovan was now technically his boss, Donovan still treated him as his friend. The world was expanding for Corby, in that he saw the groundwork being laid for an empire by the Countess through Donovan's eyes. It wasn't just about money. It was like watching the pieces of a large puzzle come together. The Countess had a finger on the pulse of everything, often using Donovan to obtain information or make initial contacts. Donovan was amazed at the doors he could now walk through and feel comfortable. Never one to be intimidated, Donovan was however experienced enough to know where he wasn't experienced enough. With the Countess's cachet, he was surprised by how quickly he could bridge that knowledge gap. Access to information had its many rewards. Corby knew Donovan was trying to pull him into that world of opportunity too.

When Donovan climbed down from his horse, Corby handed him a tortilla that had been packed from the ranch kitchen. Drego had been exposing Corby to more and more Mexican food, and he liked it. Donovan looked at the somewhat squished offering with some skepticism.

"Just eat it, fancy pants. That's as good as it gets when you mingle with the peons," Corby teased.

Donovan sat down on the rock and took a bite. "Looks like you will be done here today," he said, surveying the work. "That will make five new holes to go along with the ten ... twelve? ... old ones. Fencing isn't done. A few more gates to build. But it's starting to look like a ranch."

"Never saw a better crew than Paco's," Corby said between bites. In fact, the now thirty vaqueros had taken to building up the ranch as if it were a religious calling, and in some ways it was. Now the outsiders in what had been theirs since it was claimed in the 1500s, these descendants of the New World Spain were happy for the good jobs and proud to be working on what would become again the most important ranch in northern California. "La Condesa," as they called Gabrielle, added stature to their employment. They worked very hard.

"I want you to come to the city and help me with the hotel construction," Donovan said.

Looking up, Corby asked, "I thought you wanted me safe and sound out here in God's country?"

"Change of plans. We are having a rough time coordinating all the contractors and materials. The architect is a head case, and the Countess is overpaying for what she is getting. I'm spread too thin, and I can't trust any of these businessmen. Give me a hand, will you? I need someone to organize and control who does what and when, that has the Countess's interest at heart."

Corby was about to explain that he had no idea how to do that when Donovan cut him off saying, "She needs some more protection too. You just use your head. You will see when things don't make sense. In a month you will be an expert. OK, maybe a few months. Meantime, the Countess is safer."

"You getting attached to this gal, Donovan?" Corby queried.

Donovan thought for a moment and then said, "She's a nice lady, but kind of a loose cannon like you. She grows on you, I guess, like a kid you never had. Now I got me a boy and a girl." He added grinning.

"OK, Pop," said Corby, "I'll give it a try. But don't blame me if the hotel falls over someday." Corby definitely had some misgivings about Donovan's idea.

19

"WHERE WILL YOU GO, warrior?" asked Small Hand. The old man was stirring his pot, and then offered some stew to Lame Elk. Lame Elk tasted the food, and remembered what a poor cook Small Hand had always been. Seeing the expression on Lame Elk's face, Small Hand added, "I miss my wife."

The People had been overjoyed when Lame Elk had finally caught up to them. They had called him Blackhand, and reveled in the tales of revenge they had heard repeated by the Blackfoot captives who had returned. Lame Elk, however, did not wish to be called Blackhand, but the stories continued. Barely a hundred had survived the massacre. The Yellowstone Shoshone had drifted to the southwestern corner of their previous home range, where high plains and desert bordered the mountains. Lame Elk had been unable to convince the People that they could return to the Yellowstone. He understood their reluctance in their weakened posture. So they had camped on the edge of the dry forests, still in the mountains, but now closer to the Whitemen's settlements along the Snake River. He had been happy to find out that three surviving captives of the Flathead Indians had also found their way home. But over 150 of the People had been killed or were still missing. It would be many years before the Yellowstone Shoshone would stand tall again. Lame Elk could see the visible mark of fear and uncertainty in their eyes, left from their ordeal.

As the most prominent warrior left, the People had wanted Lame Elk to stay and lead them, and for a while he did. But his life with the People had changed too much, and his sadness returned when he saw the children play. He decided he should go on a quest. No vision had appeared to him, but his curiosity about his ancestors, combined with his daily burden of loss, compelled him to search for a peace somewhere out there alone. In truth, he was uncomfortable with the high status the People had placed on him, knowing too, that they had unrealistic hopes that their lives would return to normal soon.

"I will go where the spirits call to me," replied Lame Elk. "I will start near where the great black horse was provided to me, deep in the mountains, at the highest peaks. It would seem a good place to seek a Living Spirit."

Once he had decided, he was anxious to go. He had called the People together and told them of his need for a quest. A common occurrence for the People, they seemed to understand, but also expected him to return when it was over. Lame Elk was not so sure that would happen, but he did not mention that to the People. He felt a need to give a small speech about the great heritage of his people, and the wisdom of the Ancients. It was these ancient spirits he wished to commune with to give him guidance in a troubled life. Old Leaning Tree, a friend of his mother, had given him a benediction of sorts, as they had no head Shaman at the time. He had looked over the tribe, memorizing the scene, sensing that this might be the last time he would see them. Sadness welled up in his chest as he recounted the faces he could no longer see.

The next day as he swung up on his pony and walked it out of the camp, he was overcome by emotion as the People lined up to say goodbye to him. The children ran along beside his horse, and the women hugged his legs as he passed. The men were in full battle gear on their ponies, saluting him and yelling out Shoshone war chants. When he had cleared the camp, he turned back and raised his bow above his head. Everyone yelled together, and then he was gone.

For three days he rode northwest, and on the fourth day, he crossed over the Salmon River. He was now back in no-man's-land, deep in the mountains. To the North and East of his present position were the now-hated Blackfoot; farther to the northwest lay the lands of the Nez Perce. But these rugged mountains were a shared boundary, helping to keep a little peace. It was here he had traveled as a boy with his father and later his grandfather to learn the ways of the Shoshone. It was here he had slipped off as a young man to test his skills as a hunter and a tracker, and it was here he had felt the presence of the spirits and found the ancient sites of the People. Lame Elk wished to find a new ancient site of the People, and see if he could have a vision, a place where he could talk to the Living Spirits of his ancestors, and ask them why the Creator had brought them to this hard time. In dreams revealed by others, communications with the Creator directly were always open to interpretation. But his grandfather Swiftsnake had always said that the Living Spirits would guide him when most he needed them. So he climbed the highest, most remote peaks probing for a sense, a sign, and a contact of some sort.

Three months passed. He had found some artifacts, caves and the like, but could not sense anything else. He began to doubt that his quest would be successful. One night he was awakened by a violent storm. He had been exploring another cave high up on the mountainside. The lightning cracked, and the wind blew and swirled. He stood up to address the Creator.

"I am Lame Elk, of the Yellowstone Shoshone, the son of Yellow Elk, who was the son of Swiftsnake. You have allowed the Blackfoot to murder my wife and son, and chase the People out of our home by the Yellowstone River. Why have you done this, Father Creator?" Lame Elk yelled into the teeth of the storm, slowly turning as he spoke, looking to the sky overhead. Getting no answer, he continued, "We have been taught to be strong, to endure and to seek out wisdom. Where is the wisdom in this?" he demanded.

The night sky crackled with electricity, and the rain came down in a sudden torrent. A strong wind pushed Lame Elk a step sideways. "So, you are not pleased with me. Maybe you are not pleased with what I have to say," Lame Elk persisted as the storm picked up intensity. A great bolt of lightning lit up the night, splintering into five branches, and the rain stopped as suddenly as it had started. The wind continued to blow. Lame Elk walked over to the small cave as more lightning broke behind him. The shadows around the cave took on many shapes, but still he could discern no message. He lay down to sleep again, and shut out the noise of the storm.

Then he had his dream. The Creator was trying to tell him something. He saw his son, Beaver on the Rock, and his wife, Dancing Cloud, laughing and running. They were calling to him, but he could not understand what they were saying. Then a storm suddenly came and the Creator reached down with his hand like the five fingers of lightning he had just seen, and there was nothing but darkness, and then the storm ended. The sun came out and several children he did not know came out to play. A small girl reached out her hand to him, just as the Creator had done. Then on a nearby hill, the Whiteman's big black horse whinnied to him, tossed its mane and ran across a meadow. Lame Elk was happy and running. He could feel the warmth of the sun upon his face.

Then he woke up. He was sweating and trembling. This had been his first ever vision. He could recall every detail in the dream. It ran over and over in his mind. But what did it mean? He could not decipher the riddle handed to him. Looking outside, the storm had broken and the morning was sunny. As he stood up, he felt a sense of purpose, but did not know what it was. But, he had had a vision. It was enough for the moment to lift his spirits. The Creator had sent him a message. He had awakened to a beautiful morning in the mountains, and he remembered Swiftsnake admonishing him as a boy to appreciate the beauty around him. This morning he did so, for the first time in over two years. Now his quest would continue, as he would work to understand the message from above.

He felt drawn to the setting sun and began an extended march in that direction that eventually brought him to the Snake River. A late-afternoon sun was streaking through the trees along the river. The surrounding hills on the far side were rather bare, so Lame Elk decided to stay close to the river until he could pick up more cover. There were many places to cross in the late summer, but the banks were rather steep and finding a good path down to the river was not so easy. Eventually he got down to the river and dismounted, allowing his horse to drink at leisure. He squatted down by the river to fill his waterskin, and listened to the animal sounds, mixed in with the water lapping against the rocks.

Instinctively, he froze as he heard something coming down the bank through the trees on the other side of the river. It might be a bear, as it made its presence known with each step. Then out of the trees stepped a little white girl, with a dirty blue dress and copper-colored hair, dragging a large bucket. She was intent on filling the bucket, and didn't see Lame Elk and his horse some fifty yards away down stream. Lame Elk was startled at first, but then he simply enjoyed watching the little child struggling with the bucket. Once she had filled part of the bucket, she tried to pick it up. It was too heavy, so she began to pour a little of the water out. Lame Elk's horse shifted its feet in the gravel, and the girl glanced downstream. A look of surprise was quickly replaced by a look of terror. The little girl turned and ran up the bank, leaving her bucket behind.

Lame Elk decided it would be prudent to change positions in case other Whitemen with rifles came to see what the matter was, so he swung back up on the pony and crossed over to the girl's side, expecting any pursuers instead would figure him to retreat upon being discovered. He sat quietly in a thick grove of cottonwoods listening for any approach. No one came. Night fell. He led his horse slowly and quietly in the direction the child had run. He smelled the fire before he saw it. Tying the horse loosely on a bush, he crept forward until he could see a lone wagon, one horse and a woman wrapped up and lying down by the fire. Then the little girl, who he judged to be around four years old, climbed out of the wagon and went over to the woman, sat down next to her, and started to feed her. He could not understand their language, but he could plainly see that the woman was sick, and her child was too young to take care of her. He looked for the Whiteman's gun, and saw it beside the woman. The woman was now holding the child and stroking her hair. Lame Elk realized the fear this woman must have for her child. He watched until they both fell asleep. Then he went down to the river and brought up the bucket of water. After securing the rifle, he knelt over the woman with a cold, wet rag and placed it on her forehead. She did not wake. He threw a blanket from the wagon over the little girl and began to cook some food. Then he sprinkled in some herbs the People used for the coughing sickness from his pouch, and filled a cup of water. Next he pulled a log over next to the woman so he could feed her. Finally he woke her. When she was awake enough to realize an Indian was sitting in front of her, the woman clearly panicked, but Lame Elk's look of equal fear kept her from screaming at that instant. Lame Elk was frantically waving his hands to show he meant her no harm, while pointing to the food and water. Too weak to do anything about it anyway, the woman gradually relaxed, and accepted the cup of water. All this had happened in a few seconds and, miraculously, without a word being uttered. The little girl slept on. Lame Elk urged the mother to eat his pemmican brew. He then put a fresh wet compress on her head and indicated to her she should sleep. Finally he put another blanket on her and then caught a little sleep himself. He dreamed his dream again.

When the woman awoke, Lame Elk was rebuilding the fire. Her daughter was helping. It was probably about noon, and she felt a little better. Lame Elk came over with more cold water for her to drink. She could study the Indian a little more. He was an average size man, though muscular, with long black hair and a shiny, reddish brown skin. He had intelligent eyes, and a quiet, kind manner. This was not what she had expected in her first wild Indian. Although they didn't speak the same language, she noticed that the Indian and her little Katy were talking to each other. Katy seemed to be explaining that the other horse had run off, and the Indian was nodding to acknowledge he understood. He then came back over and explained to her with his hands that he would go and try to find the horse, and then he gave her the rifle. An uneasy moment dragged on, until it dawned on her that he was wondering if she would now shoot him. She smiled and shook her head as she lay down the rifle. He smiled back and then motioned to the girl to watch her mother until he came back. Then jumping up on his pony, he left the camp.

"Mama," the little girl said, "do you like my Injun?"

"Yes, Katy, he is a fine Indian. We should try and make friends with him," she said as she drank some more water.

Finding the missing horse was fairly easy, as it had not wandered too far away. As he eased a rope around the animal's neck to bring it back, Lame Elk wondered what he should do with these helpless travelers. He couldn't help but feel that they were part of the message he had received in his dream. The dream had shown a girl reaching out to him. Couldn't it be this little girl? What did the Creator expect him to do? He knew he would try to nurse the woman back to health and take care of the child until an answer came to him.

On the way back to the camp he noticed a road, more like a path where wagon wheels had left the ground scarred. This must have been the trail the Whitewoman had been on before becoming sick. And where was the man?

He did not believe the woman and girl would have been traveling alone. Maybe he would scout the area to see if more wagons were around, or other Whitemen settlements.

20

EVER SINCE ZEKE HAD heard that Donovan and Corby were in San Francisco—and who hadn't?—he had kept a low profile. He couldn't believe the incredible bad luck. How in the world could they have been here? Clearly his story of the posse chase had unraveled completely. If either recognized him, he would be on his way to prison. There would be a warrant out for the murder of that Quaid fellow, and they would probably try to lay the murder of old Luther on him too. Of course, abandoning a U.S. marshal for dead was not a mark in his favor either. It was also possible that Corby, being a gunfighter now, would just shoot him, and he couldn't put that past Donovan either. In fact, as he thought about it, Donovan had a lot more reason to be sore than Corby did.

Taking the unlikely appearance of Donovan and Corby, together no less, and then the inconceivable chance that they would then go to work for Gabrielle … it was enough to make a man believe in the devil! Not a day had gone by in the last six months that Zachary DuPort had not cursed the heavens for the cards he had been dealt. He had always deserved better than he had received. His high-profile plans would have to take a backseat for the moment until he could figure out how all this should be handled.

But not all was bad. San Francisco was a gambler's dream come true. His small gambling house was making a good profit, and he was ready to open another. Exchanging the gemstones for bank notes had been easier than he had first thought. Not only had there been no questions asked, but he had the luxury of getting three appraisals before selling them. With the successful opening of his first venture, the big money in town had recognized his talent, and only last Tuesday, Paul Logan himself had suggested they go into business together. He had a proposal tucked in his breast pocket whereby Logan would go partners with him in his existing business and fund him in the next one. Zachary would be the operating partner and run the day-to-day business. But the ability to get some of his cash out was what sold him on the idea. He had signed a letter of intent, but had purposely not completed a final agreement, to see if he could make it a little sweeter. Maybe having some powerful new friends could solve his potential new legal problem. Then also, not being able to see Gabrielle was something he had to resolve. He was sure he could convince her to resume their affair and possibly marry him if he could spend time with her. Clearly she had a great deal more money than he had ever realized. They could own this city if he could leverage her money into the right investments. He had seen her moving about the city on numerous occasions, but busy business people always surrounded her, or Donovan had been with her. He had sent her several notes, but she had not written back as yet. Well, soon he would have enough money to be moving in the same circles with her again.

It was time to get some dinner, and he left his gambling house after checking the largest table's play. All seemed to be going well, so he signaled to his floor manager that he was going out for an hour, and stepped out into the San Franciscan night. It was quite cool, and he pulled his suit collar up around his neck, and strode up the street toward the variety of diners on Grant Street. As he rounded the first corner to start his small climb up to dinner, he was aware of a shuffling sound behind him.

Approximately one hour later, Zachary DuPort woke up with a severe headache. He tried to raise his hand to his head but couldn't. He was chained to the floor. A rising panic gripped him as he tried to organize his thoughts. It was cold and dark but not enough so that he couldn't tell that he was on a ship.

A voice in the dark said, "Coming to, are we?"

"Who, what …?" Zeke stammered.

"Been here two days myself," the voice said. "Oh, I'm Shug O'Brien. It would seem we are set to go whaling."

That brought Zeke fully awake. "There's been a big mistake. I have money and a business. Captain, Captain!" he yelled.

"Quiet down, or you will get another bonk on the head, maybe get me one too," said Shug. "No one here but the deckwatch at this hour. You can talk to someone in the morning maybe."

But Shug was wrong, and a man came down the ladder into the hold with a lantern.

"Sounds like my new crew member is shaking the cobwebs out," the man said, standing over Zeke with the light. "Things will go along a whole lot better if you just reconcile yourself to the fact that you're here to stay for awhile. Sorry bit of luck, that. I'll take them irons off once we are well out to sea."

Trying to sound in command, Zeke said, "Look here, mister, I'm Zachary DuPort, and I'm sure there has been a terrible mistake. I could certainly make it well worth your while if you were to release me immediately."

"I'm sure you could, Mr. DuPort, but from now on I'll just call you Zach, OK? This here is a whaler, and after I get two more volunteers, we will be heading South, toward Mexico, to find us some gray whales, and then come Summer, we will be back off to Alaska looking for humpback, bowhead, and right whales. If you work hard, you get a share, and maybe, in a couple of years, you can come back and try to settle scores. If you don't work hard, the sea will take you, understand?" the man asked.

Desperately grasping at straws, Zeke proclaimed, "I'm sorry, but it is you that doesn't understand. I'm the partner of Paul Logan, one of the most important men in the city."

The man slowly shook his head and said, "Is it possible, Zach, that this Mr. Logan has too many partners?"

HAVING SENT THE remaining two privateers South to join Targon for the winter, Paul Logan couldn't resist first arranging with them for the shanghai of the young DuPort, who had proven too greedy and competitive for Logan's taste. Paul would talk to the landlord of DuPort's enterprise and step in as the new business tenant before the news got out that DuPort had disappeared. It wasn't the cheapest way to gain the business, but Logan drew a line at murder. Targon's men had received the normal fee for shanghai services, such as they got when many of the whalers were in need of help.

Boldly walking through his soon-to-be business, and looking through the personal effects of this DuPort fellow, having obtained Zachary's keys and wallet, he saw raw talent, but as yet unsophisticated. The clothes were too flashy, if well made, like the gaming clientele here, which were primarily the lower half of the gambling population. He did find a nice old Walker Colt that he decided to keep before having the other personal belongings disposed of. He had always heard about the gun but had never had one.

It was going to be a great Winter. He would start construction on his bank in the Spring, and Günter Targon would return only briefly before summer duties would send him sailing away again. Logan thought it was nice not to have the man around, as he had been the last four winters, grousing, and posturing, demanding time Logan didn't want to spend.

It was becoming increasingly obvious that the young Countess was not expecting her husband to show up in California. Someone would need to squire the woman. Set aside her wealth, she was the most attractive woman of good standing in California. Her assets just made her that much more attractive. This winter Paul Logan would kill two birds with one stone if he took Gabrielle as his mistress. Why not? Who better?

21

THE WOMAN WAS GETTING better. She could stand for short spells, and tried to clean herself and her daughter. Lame Elk and Katy had developed a working relationship, dividing the few daily chores between them. When they weren't working, they fished a lot. The late summer was perfect for salmon on the Snake River. Chinook, coho, sockeye, and steelhead had been feeding the local tribes for centuries, swimming up to a thousand miles inland to spawn, along the mighty Columbia River and its many tributaries. Lame Elk showed Katy how to cut a good spear, and catch a great meal. The little girl loved the taste of the fresh and meaty fish as much as the fun of catching them, though she seldom returned from the river dry. The fish were helpful in the recovery of Valerie, the mother, providing the nutrition she needed badly. The wild game, fish, and berries diet, along with the contents of Lame Elk's herbal pouch, were working their wonders.

Their limited conversations nonetheless got them to an understanding that the three would travel back to Fort Hall, upriver. It would take them perhaps two weeks to retrace the route. Lame Elk had seen the grave, where he assumed the man had been buried. Katy was responsible for putting flowers on it every day. Lame Elk was taken with the little girl's spirit, and when she took his hand one day to bring him to the grave, he was touched to the heart.

Valerie watched as Katy lay the flowers down on her father's grave. The wild Indian stood beside her. She thought, "God is in his Heaven after all."

After a difficult time pointing out how to harness the team, Valerie and Lame Elk succeeded, and one morning they turned around to go back East to Fort Hall. In an hour or so, Lame Elk had mastered driving a team. Katy started to sing some songs, and eventually coerced Lame Elk to sing a Shoshone song too. They were a very unique wagon on the Oregon Trail that day.

Almost two weeks to the day, and after a complicated explanation to a reticent wagon going the other way, Lame Elk drove Katy and Valerie into a surprised Fort Hall late one afternoon. There were plenty of Indians around the trading post, as always in the late summer, including members of various Shoshone and Bannock tribes. Word ran through the community quickly about who had just arrived. Lame Elk helped Valerie into the post's doctor's quarters. The white settlers at the fort hurried over to lend assistance. Lame Elk was carefully pushed aside. The doctor shooed everyone outside, including Lame Elk. But Katy went out and took Lame Elk by the hand, and pulled him back into the doctor's office. Valerie had apparently insisted.

When the doctor and Lame Elk finally came out, a crowd of settlers was still waiting to hear what had taken place. Behind them was a crowd of Indians with the same interest.

"Hey, Doc, are they diseased?" someone asked excitedly.

"Is there Injun trouble on the trail?" another wanted to know.

Then a dozen more questions started to fly.

"Quiet down!" yelled the doctor. "Mr. Fuller succumbed to pneumonia. He had come West with a case of emphysema. You all know how hard that can be. Unfortunately, he also contracted a case of influenza, and as weakened as he was from the emphysema, it became pneumonia and killed him. I know this because Mrs. Fuller still has a mild case of influenza. She will recover in a few weeks. This Indian apparently came along and nursed her back to traveling health and then brought her here. Probably saved her and the girl. Someone find me Fournier. I want to talk to this Indian about what he gave her for medicine. The rest of you can go about your business. Nothing here to concern you."

He then turned and went back into the building. Lame Elk looked around as the crowd of settlers dispersed. Then the Indians moved forward. Lame Elk recognized a cousin with the Lemhi Shoshone, who lived in the area and shared the mountains he had gone to for his vision.

"I have told the People that you are Lame Elk, Chief of the Yellowstone Shoshone, known as Blackhand by our enemies the Blackfoot," Waushaute said. "It has been many years since the Yellowstone Shoshone have joined us for rendezvous in Round Valley."

"I know you, Waushaute. As a boy you ran like the wind. No one was faster. As a hunter, you are keen of sight and true with your arrow. Yes, it has been many years since last the Yellowstone People and the Lemhi People of Round Valley have gathered together," answered Lame Elk.

The Indians moved in closer to listen to the two men.

"The Blackfoot are cowards and dogs with no honor," spat Waushaute, "but they learned what a great Shoshone warrior can do alone."

A couple of the listening Indians echoed the sentiment.

"Come, let us smoke and eat together," Waushaute gestured. Lame Elk untied his pony and accompanied the Indians out of the fort to their camp-ground by the river.

It wasn't long, however, before Katy, accompanied by an old trapper named Fournier, ferreted him out. It was Katy's first visit to a teepee, and she made herself at home right away.

22

THE REDUCTION FROM TEN members to six over the last two years had weakened the Bulls battle strength and morale. Buffalo Lance was still recovering from his wounds. It would be necessary to replace the four departed members. Red Horses in particular was sorely missed. Each member had earned their way in, but as in all clubs or societies, a base chemistry was also needed. Red Horses had exuded the warriors' personality, at the same time providing a constant energy and optimism that charged the group and helped in their bonding. No one missed him more than Two Horns. They had been companions since boyhood, Red Horses always creating the challenges, taking the chances, and pulling Two Horns into his chaos. As a pair they had pushed and prodded each other to evolve into the superior warriors they had become. Now Two Horns didn't have his daily companion to talk to and plan with. The Bulls were without their sparkplug and drill sergeant. Life had changed again. The spirits of Red Horses, Stone Bear, Shining Crow, and now Howling Wolf however would stay with Two Horns and be honored there.

When the band had returned to the larger tribe at the lake campsite the next summer, Two Horns had not sought out the leadership role that everyone else was sure he would assume. He seemed lethargic and disinterested in the politics and needs of the tribe. What he did seem interested in was Moon in the Daylight. Her aptitude as a warrior was obvious, and it was not unheard of for a woman to excel as one. The inclusion of Moon in the Daylight in the men's activities had clearly brought on a more confident and attractive side to her. She showed a strong interest in improving herself as a horsewoman, hunter, and warrior. Two Horns took on the primary task in those regards. Both knew where this would ultimately lead, and in due course, Two Horns took her as his second wife. Now Moon in the Daylight's mission was to protect her husband. She was a weapon guarding his back, another pair of eyes and ears on a single entity. And she was becoming his new best friend.

It was ultimately Moon in the Daylight that made Two Horns turn his attention to the Blackfoot's leadership vacuum. She was the one who told him of the Council of Elders' rulings and the petty fights among the families. It was Moon in the Daylight that shoved Two Horns out of their teepee to attend a Council meeting to see for himself.

"We are pleased to have Two Horns join us in council, though there are few important matters to discuss tonight," said Buffalo Robe, one of the Council Elders, as Two Horns entered the large Council teepee to sit and listen. "Is there something you have come to say?" he then asked.

Two Horns shook his head and sat down, crossing his legs. However, within five minutes, he had become very vocal, asking many questions and becoming more agitated as the meeting continued. Trying not to be disrespectful of the Elders, he held back his strongest opinions, but everyone could sense that Two Horns was not happy with the Council proceedings. When the meeting finally ended, Buffalo Robe asked Two Horns to walk with him. They strolled down by the lake. It was a clear night with many stars out.

"Why doesn't the Council act on all these arguments among the people?" asked Two Horns in obvious frustration.

"Because the Council no longer has power with the people," explained the soft-spoken old man. "When you killed Crooked Claws, you opened a dam. You are responsible for the rush of water that followed." Buffalo Robe spoke as he gazed up into the sky. "The Blackfoot are no different than any other people. They need to know that their leaders are strong and looking out for them. They need to respect those leaders. There is no one of strength to lead now. The Council is full of old men like me. Old men look to the setting sun; the Blackfoot must always look to the rising sun. That takes the energy and optimism of a young man. You must rebuild the dam."

"But Crooked Claws was despised by the people. He bullied with his strength," Two Horns responded.

"You must lead with a different strength. You must lead for the Blackfoot. Crooked Claws never understood or didn't care that the needs of the tribe come first. It is not an easy thing. The Council will be a thorn in your side, and the people will always complain, but to make a difference is a great reward."

Two Horns thought it over and walked some more. "Crooked Claws was war chief. I do not think we should be at war all the time," he said.

"Well, that's a relief," Buffalo Robe said smiling. "The elders are in agreement that we need a new leader, and you are the obvious choice. Will you be Chief of the Gray Woman Mountain Blackfoot?"

Book 2

1852

23

DAWN BROKE A STEEL gray, with low cloud coverage. There was a small chop on the water, and a fair southwesterly wind blowing. The creaks and groans of rope, canvas, wood, and iron sang choir to the steady background beat of the waves of the Pacific Ocean as they rhythmically splashed against the hull of the *Mary Jane*. True to his word, Captain Harden was sailing back to San Francisco after a little over two years of successful whale hunting. Zachary DuPort was to be set free, with a full share of the voyages' profits.

Two years at sea had left their mark on Zach, both literally and figuratively. No longer a man of leisure, he had gained a good ten pounds of muscle. His face had filled out, and he had a scar that cut through his left eyebrow from a hard fall on the deck during bad weather. He had taken to wearing shorter hair and longer sideburns. He both looked and walked like a seaman. More significantly, he had plenty of time while at sea to decide what was important to him. Some growing up had taken place as well. He held no grudge with Captain Harden, despite being kidnapped. The captain was not the one that had sold him into bondage. He was smart enough to know that despite not wanting to go to sea, he had benefitted as a man. His confidence in his abilities had actually grown, as he had been able to hold his own with the rough crew of the whaler. What had previously passed unobserved, such as a good, hot cup of coffee after a cold morning of hard work, was now appreciated and savored. He took pride in his newfound strength, and even enjoyed the feel of being part of a team. None of which could erase the daily anger and resentment he had for whomever had arranged for his little excursion.

As he leaned against the rail watching the approaching coastline, breathing in the salt air, Shug O'Brien joined him.

"Landfall has a whole different meaning this morning, hey, mate?" Shug said.

Zachary continued to stare ahead. Now that his freedom was about to happen, he wanted to think carefully through his next moves. Anything too rash could land him back where he was or worse. Someone, possibly Paul Logan, would not be happy to see him again. Captain Harden had revealed that his service was not a random act. The middleman had explicit instructions to ship off Zachary DuPort. Logan was the most logical candidate to gain from his absence. But two years of thinking about it had convinced him that he had to know for sure, and to do that, it would be easier if no one knew he was back for a while. Zachary knew that people rarely kept a secret, and one like his was probably not unique. If he could find out who was behind the shanghai trade in San Francisco, he would probably find his answer. Shug O'Brien would lend him additional muscle—something he should have had before. Shug had attached himself to Zach for lack of many other options, but now the man's presence would serve as a welcome strength in times to come. As strong as an ox, Shug had no ambition in him. He wasn't slow of mind, or quick for that matter, but content with whatever life threw his way. Zach had given up trying to ignite a spark of hunger or a semblance of a dream in him.

The way Shug saw it, Zach was smart, and that meant a better meal ticket than being on his own, and staying on the boat was too much work. He would tag with Zach, to get their revenge, and then maybe Zach would keep him around in his next business, like they had talked about. He leaned over the rail next to Zach, and the two of them stared out at land together.

An offshore breeze reached the ship with its pungent smell of plants and decay. It was quickly replaced by another fresh wind from the sea, and Zachary felt a strange sense of loss at the close of this chapter in his life, without fully understanding why.

24

TWO MORE MAJOR FIRES had devastated San Francisco since Zachary Du-Port had departed the city. Finally some citizens were rebuilding with brick, and the City Council and mayor had imposed some building codes for safety and fire control. The speed with which the city was growing demanded an attempt at planning the future.

The fledgling California Territory, wrestled from Mexico in 1846, had been quickly adjoined as a state of the Union in 1850. Like an island in the West, bordered by ocean and largely untamed, vast territories, California, with its burgeoning population, was a beacon to the nation. The race West continued unabated through Indian lands. The northern route—the Oregon Trail, which ran along the great rivers, the Platte, the Snake, and the Columbia—with its cutoffs southwest to the goldfields, the Cherokee/Overland Trail and the California Trail, were opening up the Pacific Coast. In the newly established Utah Territory (1850) and New Mexico Territory (1850), the southern route to California was along the Sante Fe Trail, and then the Old Spanish Trail into Los Angeles over the inhospitable deserts of the Southwest.

But more than Americans were flocking to California. The Gold Rush brought people from all over the world, tripling the population of the state in a mere five years to over eighty thousand by 1852. San Francisco was the center of that onslaught, with a population of over thirty thousand. It was the preeminent city of the West almost literally overnight. Needless to say, the founding fathers were in great position to take advantage of the boom. The St. Montfort Hotel, though still under continuous construction, was the grand hotel of San Francisco, and the meeting place of most of the important decisions being made of the day. Gabrielle had imposed herself right into the middle of all of it. An established member of the City Council, the Mayor's Council, the Port Authority, and the Board of Regulators for the Water Commission, she effectively had a say in a majority of civic decisions. She was also a major entrepreneur as owner and proprietor of the St. Montfort Hotel, the

Montara Ranch (renamed for the small mountain range of the same name on the ranch), and assorted other business ventures. Her investment in bricks was paying off handsomely, and had she the time, she could have been involved with just about any industry she would like to choose.

A new steamship company was being proposed with several key investors, including Paul Logan, Thomas James, her banker, and Stewart Bertram, a fellow Council member.

Stewart Bertram had found a middle-management executive from the Vanderbilt Lines that was eager to run a western-based steamship line. The costs were enormous, but the regular transport by ship was a lifeline to the city. Gabrielle had her doubts, as her proposed partners were extremely anxious to have her name and money associated with the line. Bertram went as far as proposing they name the line the Countess Steamship Company. It had a ring to it, and with a real countess as a principle investor, it would perhaps have an appeal to those wishing to travel in comfort. Still, Gabrielle was hesitant, as she researched ship losses, from storms and fires, the enormous distances to travel, and the inexperience of her fellow investors, herself included, in such a business. The shipyard by itself would cost a fortune, before the first ship was ever launched. Then there was the ever-present dialogue about a transcontinental railroad. Still years off, it would eventually be serious competition for the shipping business. But most concerning to Gabrielle was her total lack of control as one of several partners in the business. She could influence James and perhaps some of the minor investors, but Logan and Bertram would be another matter entirely. They were asking for a lot of trust that Gabrielle didn't have.

When the City Council had last met, evidence of Logan's self-interest was apparent. They had petitioned the new governor once again to help provide troops or other assistance to combat the lawlessness that still plagued the city. At the meeting with the Presidio captain and the governor, Paul Logan had launched into a fervent speech targeting the organized crime in the gambling district, demanding federal and state help to eradicate the gangs and businesses operating there. He was unconcerned about the waterfront problems, or the robberies in broad daylight along Mission Street. He was uninterested in creating a police force substantial enough to have an ongoing control over illegal acts. Clearly to all who knew about his personal holdings, he was trying to direct the city's need to crackdown on crime against his major competitors in the gaming business. Gabrielle had added another caveat to dealing with Paul Logan.

Then there was Stewart Bertram, who believed in Stewart Bertram. He was one of those rags-to-riches stories so prevalent of the times, making his money first as an architect, and then later as a contractor. Gabrielle had heard his litany over and over again, that anyone could do anything in America if they just worked at it. He was convinced that there wasn't a challenge he could not overcome, and that worried her. She remembered her father talking to his business partners on many occasions about how someone had gone "too far afield" and lost their investment by not understanding fully what they were getting into. That also brought to mind her husband's investment with Zachary DuPort. Another lesson: Zachary himself had disappeared under suspicious circumstances, probably running afoul of some of these violent criminals out West. More proof to stay where she understood the playing field.

So, slowly and deductively, Gabrielle had decided to not go into the steamship business with her peers on the City Council. She would let Stewart know tonight when he came for dinner at the hotel, as he did every Saturday night. They needed to talk about the proposed Coalition Against Crime Force that they had agreed to try setting up under the authority of the governor. Without proper direction, it could be a waiting disaster. All these thoughts ran through her head as she dressed for the evening, including her escort, the enigmatic Mr. Corby.

Since Donovan had insisted on her having constant protection, Barton or Corby was always nearby. Sometimes a couple of other handpicked employees would fill in, but the majority of the time it was Barton or Corby. Barton was usually with her at night and around her hotel. He had been at it for so long that Gabrielle barely noticed him most of the time. He fit the part, with his New Orleans style and manner.

With Corby, it was a project in the making. Donovan had insisted that he must improve his education. She understood that he had been going to school for the last two years at night. At first he had acted as a courier of sorts during the working day, relaying Gabrielle's instructions to various contractors as she built her hotel. Then he started to assume some small overseer roles as he began to understand the concepts and standards she was wanting. Recently he had been supervising the construction of the latest guest wing by himself, and she was getting very good reports. He apparently wasn't about to allow anyone to fail in his or her obligations. And it didn't hurt that he was recognized as a gunman; that seemed to spur the contractors on. He clearly was intelligent, but difficult to draw out. They had very few real conversations, and he always seemed to remember he had to be off to somewhere once one was started.

Through Donovan, however, Gabrielle had dressed the man up. She was uncomfortable suggesting anything personal to him, and he seemed to have the same problem. Aside from the leg iron he always wore, he could be walking down the street in any business district in the country now and fit in, at least in the clothes he wore. But she knew he was more comfortable in his Western wear and always looked forward to visiting the ranch. Gabrielle was annoyed with herself. She was thinking about this employee too much. But was he thinking about her? If so, it sure didn't show. Every man in San Francisco reveled in her company. Now twenty-five, she was an unparalleled beauty, highly successful and with a title no less. Why wouldn't any man wish to be with her? Maybe there was something wrong with this man. But she had seen him flirting with a cute little Mexican girl.

She put on a particularly striking red gown that showed off her figure well. Saturday night guests expected to see her in the hotel. Corby would see how the men couldn't keep their eyes off of her tonight. Perhaps a new intriguing visitor would also be downstairs tonight. "All work and no play," as they say...

"Angelina, let's wear the diamonds tonight...offset all this red," Gabrielle said to her old nanny, and now, confidant. "The necklace, and Montfort ring, and that small silver and diamond tiara."

The elderly lady grumbled something incomprehensible and went to the built-in wall safe to pull out the asked-for pieces. Upon returning she reminded Gabrielle that she was already thirty minutes late from the time she had asked Mr. Corby to meet her in the Grand Lobby.

STANDING AT THE bar adjacent to the lobby, Corby fidgeted in his new suit. Made of a fine gray weave, he had on a log top jacket cut to midthigh that hid his gun. A ruffled shirt and cravat were the most uncomfortable. Donovan had made him leave his cowboy hat at the reception desk.

"I feel like a damn peacock!" he complained.

"You do look rather prissy at that," Donovan said with a straight face. "Now remember to compliment her when you see her, and don't spill anything on anybody." He then leaned over to sniff at Corby. "Good."

"Now I know you are sliding downhill, old man. Once a man among men, a decorated U.S. marshal, reduced to sniffing for bad odors." Corby ran his hand through the air like it was a newspaper story. "I don't see why I need to spruce up and eat at a fancy restaurant anyway."

"The prosecution rests. When you do see why, it won't be a problem anymore," retorted Donovan. "Come on, Corby, you've got to finish off your education, and that means being able to sit down with the movers and shakers without wanting to turn tail and run. How many people get the chance to learn while sitting beside a beautiful countess?"

"She makes me feel so...inadequate."

Donovan looked at his friend and said, "I've never seen her be mean to you."

"I didn't mean it like that. It's just that we are about the same age, and she can do so many things, and she's a girl, and..." Corby tried to explain.

"She's a countess. She's had special training since she was two, probably. You are just as intelligent, and you are getting educated. Take her out of San Francisco and into Indian country, and she would probably feel about you the way you do about her," reasoned Donovan. "Besides, she is a nice woman who has been very good to us. You can do this, and be a better man for it. Now drink up, because here she comes."

The Countess was descending the stairs as the whole lobby stopped to watch. She could have been the Queen of Sheba for her striking beauty, or Queen Victoria for her regal stateliness. Corby swallowed hard and walked over to the bottom of the stairs.

"Good evening, Countess," he managed. "You look...well tonight."

"Why thank you, Mr. Corby. Such extravagant praise could turn a girl's head. You look...well yourself. Good evening, Marshal. I'm sorry to have given you such short notice, but I thought you should be with me when I discuss this police force with Mr. Bertram. You are the expert." She reached over and took Corby's extended arm, and stepped down the last step to the lobby floor. "Maybe we should reach our own decision before meeting with Bertram. Would you gentlemen accompany me to the salon for an aperitif?"

Noticing the blank look on both men's faces, she added, "A whiskey."

When they had seated themselves and ordered their drinks, Gabrielle filled them in on the Council meeting with the governor.

"Bertram and the others want you to lead up the force, Marshal. The governor will give you the legal status to round up whatever criminals we can identify. Mr. Corby...Oh for God's sakes, it's been over two years now. What is your first name anyway?" she asked in mock anger.

Corby smiled and said, "You may use Corby as a first or last name, Countess, however you please."

Gabrielle frowned and looked over at Donovan. He shrugged as if to say it didn't bother him.

"You westerners are steeped in mystery I see." She gave in. "Corby it is...for now. Well, Corby, you were mentioned by name too as being a resource the force should have."

Donovan said, "Countess, I'm flattered that they would want me to do this, governor and all, but from what you just told us, this sounds like a vigilante party, with Logan's guest list. You need a full time officer that's done his homework and stands apart from the business leaders. I've seen this kind of thing before, and innocent people get hurt. There are no short-term solutions to long-term problems." Donovan shook his head.

"Corby?" Gabrielle asked.

He thought a moment and then said, "Back in Idaho a fellow who was drunk drew on me. I killed him to defend myself. His dad, who wasn't there, decided to hunt me down as a killer. I was a stranger in the town. I had to ride." His eyes had that sad, haunting look she had seen before. "If the Marshal is worried about political justice…"

"OK then. Bertram will get a double dose of bad news tonight. No Marshal and no Corby, plus no ship deal. Who's ready for a fun dinner?"

"I'VE MADE HUGE commitments to this project, and collected substantial monies from investors who thought you were in on this. I can't believe you are pulling out at this point!" Stewart Bertram almost bellowed at Gabrielle.

"Why did you do that? I told you I would consider the deal and let you know. I never indicated I was on board," replied Gabrielle.

"But the potential is incredible! You can't fail to see how this will be a great success. Paul and I naturally assumed that you were on board!"

"I'm sorry, Stewart, but the answer is no. I wish you and your partners the best," she said with a finality that ended any chance of further persuasion.

Stewart Bertram rose from the table, his face beet red. "We let you into the center of power in this city. We didn't need you or your money to build San Francisco. The town was booming. You have done very well in your short time here, and this is the thanks we get?"

Corby and Donovan rose simultaneously. "Bertram, you're out of line," Donovan growled.

"So now you are going to turn your guns loose on me?" Bertram spat out. "Well understand this, Miss High and Mighty, Logan and I will complete this shipping line without your help, and you will rue the day you turned against us."

"I didn't turn against you, Stewart. I just don't want to invest in this business with you." Gabrielle tried to soften the escalating confrontation.

Bertram calmed down and quietly glared at Gabrielle and said, "Maybe so, but our investors will see it as a slap in the face, as I do." Then he spun around and left the hotel.

"He had a little too much to drink. He will reason through it and feel differently in the morning," Gabrielle said as if to convince herself.

The evening was definitely not what she had envisioned. A waiter brought a note over to Corby.

"Excuse me," he said. "There is someone I should see out front for a moment." He rose and left the table.

"Listen, Princess." It was a name Donovan had been calling Gabrielle when they were alone since they had first become friends, and only Donovan could get away with it. "This is a tough town, and if that was any indication of what having them as partners would be like, you just saved yourself a lot of grief."

Gabrielle smiled and said, "Thanks, I needed to hear that. Would a handsome, distinguished gentleman buy me a drink until my 'escort' deigns to return?"

"If you mean, can you charm a broken-down old cowboy out of his hard-earned money for a whiskey, that's a given." Donovan smiled. "Now this 'deign' business is beyond me, but I figure Corby will be back like he said."

Out in front of the hotel, Corby walked over to Drego and asked, "Que pasa, amigo?"

"I thought you would like to know that Targon and his Tlingit Indian are back een town and looking for you."

25

"OUR ELDERS WERE WISE to keep the Whitemen out of Blackfoot lands. They have brought disease and death wherever they go. They have no honor, and they lie and cheat. They trade with our enemies, and this is a problem they now bring on us. The Lakota tell us that the Crows now have many of the Whitemen's guns. So do the Shoshone. The Americans have taken over the British and French trading posts, except in the Cree lands. Our enemies camp outside the posts and trade with the Whitemen. The wagon trails through Sioux and Shoshone lands bring more Whitemen on their way to the Great Water. Our enemies will trade for even more guns. With these guns, the Crows have attacked the Lakota in smaller numbers successfully," Two Horns explained to the Council.

"What have the Lakota done about these incursions?" asked Tall Bull.

Blue Heron, who had been sent to speak with the Lakota Sioux, answered, "The Lakota are stealing and trading to get more guns too. They will make war on the Crows when they are ready."

"This is good," said Buffalo Robe. "The Crows will have to turn their attention elsewhere."

"Yes, this is good," countered Two Horns, "but we also must have more guns. The Shoshone Chief Blackhand has become a more powerful leader since the Shoshone bands have begun camping together in summer rendezvous at Fort Hall. If all the surrounding tribes have more guns, which one may decide to test the Blackfoot soon?"

The mention of the Shoshone chief made its impression on the Council, and many nodded their heads in agreement and concern. The Council had been called after receiving news from the Lakota of their increasing conflicts with the Crow Indians, a shared enemy of the Blackfoot. The Blackfoot too had seen more hostilities of late with the Crow.

Two Horns said, "I will send out a war party of about thirty of our best warriors under Blue Heron, to raid the Crow camps closest to our territory and take some of these guns for the Blackfoot. If they run into any of the

Whitemen, or journey far enough South to cross the wagon trails, they should take their guns too."

There was a general murmur of approval. Buffalo Robe then said, "We should send a messenger to the Lakota saying that we are assisting them in their fight with the Crows." He shrugged and added, "Maybe they will believe it."

MOON IN THE Daylight had insisted in being part of the war party. She was a Blackfoot warrior, and a good one. Two Horns of course didn't like the idea, but there was little he could argue against it, so she joined the warriors. Blue Heron, Long Bow, Buffalo Lance, and many others were eager to get started. Stealing guns would be a major accomplishment and would reflect great honor on the successful warrior. The last two years had not provided too many opportunities for advancement as a warrior. This foray should allow the warriors to be exposed to great personal danger, the ideal way to prove their courage and worth. The warriors gathered in front of Two Horns's teepee, where he gave them instructions. They were to swing out to the East and South in a half circle, being as stealthy as they could. Their objective was to steal guns, powder, caps, and horses, in that order. They were not to run from a fight if they came across one, but should remember to bring back the guns as their main objective. If Blue Heron were to be killed, then Buffalo Lance would be in command. They would return no later than one full moon's time.

Pulling Blue Heron aside, Two Horns gave a few more instructions, as a more senior warrior and leader of the raid.

"Move as swiftly as you can from place to place, but not in the middle of the day. The more country you cross, the less chance you have of being pursued and caught. Do not travel in a straight line, and use many scouts. You may not find anything for days, or you may see much to do in a short time. Plan for both with your supplies. Let each warrior have the opportunity to show his courage. If you are successful, we will probably need those guns. Stay away from the Shoshone Chief Blackhand's camp. That should be easy if you stay enough to the East and South. We do not wish to fight the Shoshone while we are dealing with the Crow."

"I will bring honor to the Blackfoot and the Bulls, Two Horns, and I will watch over Moon in the Daylight," said Blue Heron.

"Thank you, my friend," said Two Horns, "but she is a warrior who must take her chances with the others. Now go and bring back many stories to tell over the campfires."

WHEN THE RAIDING party arrived at the edge of the Blackfoot range, it was spoiling for a fight. The day before, they had discovered that a Blackfoot burial site, among the cottonwoods along one of the well-traveled creeks, leading out into the sea of grass, had been violated. The Crows had pulled down the scaffolds of the four dead Blackfoot up in the trees. They had crushed and scattered the bones and left their markings on the tree trunks to show who had done this act. As some time had obviously gone by since this heinous crime had been perpetrated, the Blackfoot could not tell how many Crow had done this, or where they had then gone. The raid for guns was now a raid for revenge.

After crossing the Missouri River in early morning, the raiding party followed it South toward its headwaters along the valley floor, where they expected to find small bands of Crows. Using advance scouts, the main band followed behind at a trot in the heavy morning mist along the eastern banks. Other than the slight sound of many horses' hooves, the band maintained an eerie silence in the drifting fog patches. Blue Heron strained to hear any signal his scouts might be trying to send. An antelope jumped out of the bushes and ran away into the fog. The band moved on until, instead of the agreed-upon signal, the party rode up to the awaiting scouts in the fog.

"A Crow raiding party just crossed the river and went South," Buffalo Lance reported. "We did not want to alert them by signaling, as they were already on horses and close."

"Good," smiled Blue Heron with a malicious grin. "We will kill these dogs, and take their weapons. Did you see any guns?"

The scouts indicated that there were some guns, but it was hard to tell how many. The Crow raiding party had ten warriors and two extra horses. It was decided they would try to surprise the Crows to maximize their numerical advantage and minimize potential injuries this early on the raid. How that was to be done was not yet certain, so they would trail the band and look for the opening. Clearly the Crows were heading for Shoshone territory to do their raid. It would be better not to get too far West, as instructed by Two Horns, but the opportunity to wreak havoc on the Crows in a pitched battle for honor was a good one. The chance of finding guns had improved too.

Four more scouts were dispatched to cross the river and resume the track, but from higher up the valley floor and farther back. The main body would try to stay a little closer to a pair of lag scouts that could relay hand signals from the advanced scouts. It would mean a very careful stalk, and no mistakes, but if the Crows were intent on their mission, it could be done, and the surprise attack pulled off.

As the morning dragged on, the fog receded and then disappeared, making the tracking easier. The Crows very confidently stayed together as a group maintaining a steady pace. Blue Heron figured the Crows had scouted their target previously and would slow as they came closer to it. That gave him the idea he had been searching for. What if he allowed the Crows to attack the Shoshones? Hopefully the Shoshone and the Crow would kill each other. Then, when the Crows were jubilant in their victory and collecting their spoils, the Blackfoot would sweep in and destroy the remaining enemy. Yes, that would work well. He passed his plan around quietly to the warriors as they rode. The Blackfoot warriors were smiling in appreciation with the battle plan. Now if only it could happen that way.

They trailed the Crows all day. By late afternoon the Crows started to slow down. They sent scouts ahead, and kept to cover more in the surrounding forest. An hour later, they stopped altogether. They made final preparations for their raid; some body and facial painting, weapons sharpening, and eating was done. The Crows then remounted as the sun began to set and light faded. Slowly and quietly they advanced in a classic pincer movement, until they were about a hundred yards out from the Shoshone camp, still in the trees.

The Shoshone camp was a small one of what looked like four hunters, cooking some trout they had caught for dinner. Some beaver skins were stretching on an improvised rack. The camp appeared to have been in use for a number of weeks, from the clutter and garbage around the fire. These men were trapping furs to trade, probably at Fort Hall.

The Crow now started forward, first firing their guns, and then rushing the camp. Three of the four Shoshones survived the rifle assault and ran behind some large rocks where they began to fire their own guns and arrows at the now interrupted Crow offensive. In standard coup counting fashion, the Crows now started to individually charge the Shoshone position, taunting as they came, shooting or throwing their weapons, and then whirling and retreating, showing their courage in a cat-and-mouse game. However the Shoshones weren't giving up. They injured several of the Crows as they came forward. Eventually all knew the demonstrations of bravery would end and the real blood work would begin.

Meanwhile, once the action had started, the Blackfoot also moved forward. They watched the Crows prancing their horses, shooting forward and retreating, enjoying their inevitable victory. The Shoshone, who knew they would die, now taunted back, and the Crow massed for a decisive charge.

It was then as the Crows massed that Blue Heron saw his best advantage, and the Blackfoot swooped down on the startled Crows yelling with all their might. The force of their attack took the Blackfoot right through the Crows milling around, who had barely enough time to turn their mounts in the direction of the sudden danger. Now forty warriors swirled around in hand-to-hand combat on their horses, war clubs, knives, and lances flashing. The Crows had not reloaded their single-shot guns, but desperately fought, as they knew their lives depended upon it. Long Bow found himself off balance as the horses jockeyed about in his fight with one of the Crows. Before the Crow warrior could take advantage, Moon in the Daylight jumped on to the Crow's back from her horse, knife flailing at his lower back. Blood spurted all over her as the Crow warrior slid off of his pony. Meanwhile Buffalo Lance swung his war club in a large circle, nearly hitting a fellow Blackfoot before connecting with a Crow warrior with a sickening thud. Badly outmanned, three Crows broke free of the fight and rushed off into the fading light. The rest were overwhelmed and beaten badly before being killed.

The three Shoshone also took the opportunity to disappear on foot, leaving behind their weeks of work and the one killed by the Crows. After some postdeath mutilation, Blue Heron assessed the scene. He had one badly hurt warrior and several minor injuries to others. Six guns were collected, along with some powder caps and balls, eight Crow ponies and four Shoshone ponies, and the furs. He calculated he was missing one pony that had probably run off into the night unnoticed. The seven dead Crows and the one dead Shoshone were left where they were.

Most of the warriors did not have their own guns, so they drew lots to see who would get the new guns. In the morning the badly injured Blackfoot warrior was sent with three others, and the excess horses and furs back to report the first victory of the extended raid to the Blackfoot camp. The remaining twenty-six warriors were in very high spirits, and pushed on to the East again. The detour to follow the Crows had taken them farther West than was originally planned, and as they started to correct their course, they passed through part of the Yellowstone territory some of them had raided a few years before. As they rode by the bubbling clay pits and geysers, the talk turned to Blackhand and the haunted lands they were skirting. The pace quickened to the East, ostensibly to find more Crows, but privately each of the Blackfoot were spooked by the living legend and his unnatural homeland.

26

INDING WORK AROUND THE loading docks in San Francisco had been harder than Zach had imagined. Jobs were in short supply as the immigrants kept coming. However, his recent experience at sea helped him finally get jobs for himself and Shug as longshoremen. The work was hard, and neither really wanted to do it, but it kept them close to the activities around the piers, and Zach concluded that was the best way to gather information. He had already learned that his business had burned down about six months after he had been shanghaied. The land had reverted back to the property owner after that. Now a new and larger brick building was in its place. He opened a new account with his whaling money at a different bank, under the name of Zachary Bridges. The former Zeke Bridges/Zachary DuPort, now Zach Bridges, played the role of a laborer/drifter willing to bend the rules for money. It wasn't long before one of his fellow workers invited him to help steal some cargo off of one of the ships they were unloading.

"We do it all the time," Boston Bob said. "We get a 10 percent cut after the goods have been sold. Usually only takes a week."

"And if you get caught?" asked Zach.

"We're just dumb workers doing what we been told," he grinned. "The German, he has men right on the docks with wagons, and the warehouses have a piece of the action. We simply put some of the cargo on the wrong wagons instead of in the warehouse when we get the signal. Since we don't leave with nothin' ourselves, we don't get caught."

"Who's the German," Zach asked.

Boston Bob laughed and said, "You are new here, ain't ya? The big German, Targon, runs everything around here. It can be a sweet deal if you keep your mouth shut. Don't want to mess with Targon though. He'll cut you into fishbait as soon as spit at ya."

So Zach and Shug started stealing for the German, as Zach weighed his next move to gain the confidence of this underworld character.

A FEW WEEKS later, the newest crime crackdown in San Francisco got underway. Guided by prominent citizens, the task force began to make numerous arrests. The Baker brothers, who ran hijack and extortion rings as well as gambling parlors, were arrested along with their key underlings. Their assets were confiscated and held under the governor's authority. A number of petty criminals were picked up and jailed. A curfew was placed on the Chinese and Mexican sections of town of 12 o'clock midnight, and many stories were written in the local newspapers of the long overdue and impressive campaign against crime. City Council members Paul Logan and Stewart Bertram were each interviewed, and spoke of the city's improved order and image.

Günter Targon sat reading his newspaper as he waited for his partner Paul Logan to arrive. He had to admit that Logan's task force had indeed improved business. As quickly as the Bakers were removed, Günter had moved in and taken over. Another story in the paper however had him less amused. It was about the building of the San Francisco Steamship Company by community leaders, one of which was Paul Logan. It was time to delve further into what Logan was keeping for himself. The pattern was a clear one. Paul Logan was building firewalls against his past. The systematic distancing of activities, and even profits by activities, suggested to Günter that Paul Logan was making enough money now in legitimate businesses that one day he could afford to walk away from the association. Where this was good for Günter's pocket now, it was easy to see that someday, Logan would wish to totally bury his past, and that meant turning on Günter.

Günter had been there before. His previous partnership with the Russian privateers had ended with their captain impaled to his mast by his Tlingit assassin Ishka. Günter decided to have Ishka join him in his meeting with Logan to send a message that Logan could not misinterpret.

Ishkahittaan (of the Raven Clan) had been with Targon for over fifteen years. Believed to be cursed by evil spirits the Shamans could not drive away, he had wandered without family until shipping aboard with Targon one summer out of Sitka, Alaska. The two formed a mutual respect for each other, as Ishka, shortened for Günter's benefit, developed his love for knife work in what apparently was a dark and bitter life for the Indian. The Tlingit Indian became synonymous for an ugly exit from this world should you cross Targon. Dark of skin and black of hair, the Indian was wiry and muscular at the same time. His eyes had a dead and ominous look to them, and he rarely spoke. A two-sided copper blade with a bone handle hung around his neck. An ivory blade was sheathed by his side, and he carried a Kentucky long rifle with many carvings on its stock of what appeared to be native animals. He wore buckskins and moccasins. The shirt had a once brightly colored weave on its chest of a stylized raven head like would be seen on a totem pole. He stood leaning against a corner in the small room, with his hands folded over the top end of his rifle barrel, the butt of the gun on the floor.

Fashionably late, Paul Logan breezed into the room accompanied by two bodyguards. Günter looked up and then scanned the two bodyguards. Dressed in black suits, the large men were typical for their trade. They wore sidearms and blank but confidant expressions. Günter then looked back at Paul Logan with an inquiring stare.

"San Francisco is dangerous at night," Logan explained with a small grin. Then indicating Ishka, Logan asked, "What business do we have that would require a butcher?"

Günter folded his paper up, sat up straighter, and looked Logan in the eye. "Do you fear me, Logan, that you now bring protection to our little meeting? Should I wonder if I can trust you now?"

Logan stared right back at him and said in a deadpan voice, "Cut the horseshit, Targon. You have never trusted me, and the feeling has been mutual. That hasn't stopped us from doing very well together."

Günter smiled and replied, "But things change, right, Logan? You are now building steamship lines and tall buildings, while I still break arms and sleep on a ship's bunk."

"I don't know where you keep your money, Targon, but don't try to poor-mouth me. You have got to be one of the richest men in the West," Logan countered. He paused for a second and then said, "But yeah, things always change. It's time to plan an exit strategy, before circumstances plan it for us."

"Those 'circumstances' wouldn't include your police task force, would they, Logan," Günter asked with an edge on his voice.

"That task force is putting more money in our pockets as we speak, Targon. Did I ask for a cut of the Baker brother spoils? Have I pushed for an accounting of your other nefarious dealings that have profited by my redistribution of our thefts? I have practically handed the entire waterfront over to you, without getting a penny."

Now Targon rose to his feet and slammed his hands down on the table. Looking like a mad bull, he shouted, "You live in a fancy home, dress in fancy clothes, and pretend to be a pillar of the community because of me! They were my crews that turned business your way. It was my money that got you started in the gambling businesses. I'm the one that runs the risks outside the law." His temper cooled as quickly as it flared. He sat down. "Do not tell me of the favors you have done for me. Have you offered to let me in on any of your legitimate businesses? Can I eat at a fancy hotel with your friend the Countess? Will I retire to a country home when I get old? No, I don't think so." Then he looked at Logan and nodded. "But you are right, it is time to plan how best to maximize our interests before it is too late. Civilization is coming to California."

"Well then," Paul Logan said, "I will itemize our various ventures and make a proposal on who gets what, what we should sell, and what each of us should keep. It should take me a couple of weeks to complete. It is a wise man that plans for the future, particularly when that future is in flux. The city is indeed becoming civilized. We need to change with it. Is there anything else we should talk about while we are here?"

Günter Targon shook his head no. "Say hello to the Countess for me, hey?"

Logan and his men left. Targon shut the door.

"Ishka, my friend, the time has come. Let us see who can strike the first blow. But first I need to put to sea immediately. Mr. Logan will be sending policemen very soon. Forget about the Corby fellow for now. Scout out Mr. Logan's daily routines and then meet me in two weeks at Half Moon Bay. Here, take this pouch of money to tide you over. I promise you, my friend, when we leave the area, it will be with a piece of Mr. Logan tacked to the mast."

Ishka grinned, took the money, and walked out. Günter Targon reached under the table and pulled up a bottle, and rocked back in his chair to think.

27

THE LAST TWO SUMMERS, the Yellowstone Shoshone had followed their chief to rendezvous at Fort Hall with their cousins the Lemhi Shoshone and the Bannock. They had traded for guns and better knifes, along with blankets and other sundry goods. Many of the Indians traded for alcohol too, and Lame Elk began to preach against it. Some of the Indians would stay year round outside the trading post, buying alcohol whenever they could. Lame Elk could see the slow death it was bringing, and his Yellowstone Shoshone would hide to do their drinking for fear of his wrath. Together with Waushaute of the Lemhi Shoshone, Lame Elk had led two raids in retaliation against the increasingly aggressive Crows. The renewed annual meeting between the tribe branches was very good for mating, and the tribes intermixed heavily during the summers. It was good to have a baby explosion after the disaster with the Blackfoot. The Whitemen at the trading post were generally fair to deal with, and Lame Elk came to trust the doctor and Mr. Fournier who ran the post. Fournier was one of the old mountain men holdovers that ended up behind the counter after a bad experience with a grizzly bear years before. He knew all the dialects and respected the Indian customs.

Then there was Katy. The girl had decided that the chief was her Indian to look after. Now seven years old, she would run and jump up into his arms whenever she saw him. At first he was a little self-conscious about the display of affection in public, but he grew to look forward to her enthusiastic greetings, and the tribes seemed to accept the behavior. Her mother had decided to stay at the fort and had married the doctor last winter. With no children to play with for the most part during the winter, the child looked forward to the Indians coming in the summer as the highlight of her year. Fournier had taught her the basics of the Shoshone language, and she practiced with the Indian children and Lame Elk whenever she could. Lame Elk renamed her Flaming Hair, after her copper colored hair, and then Bouncing Frog, after her way of skipping and jumping, but he settled on Happy Green Eyes, as he had never seen green eyes before. Before long it became shortened to simply

Green Eyes. Of course Katy was very proud of her Indian name, and often introduced herself to passing wagon train children as Green Eyes of the Yellowstone Shoshone.

That summer, a small contingent of U.S. soldiers was visiting the trading post. Fournier brought a Captain Farmer to speak with Lame Elk one afternoon.

"The White Father back East wishes to survey the lands and draw maps indicating where the tribes live," Fournier explained. "They have heard of the hot waters that jump into the sky in the home of the Yellowstone Shoshone. They have heard of the great Chief Lame Elk who is a friend of the Whiteman and enemy to the Blackfoot and Crow. They ask if Lame Elk would show them the Yellowstone River and country?"

"Lame Elk is an enemy of the Blackfoot and the Crow. Also the Nez Perce and the Flathead. We have fought many tribes. We trade with the Whiteman, that is all," replied a reserved Lame Elk. The White soldiers had a reputation of always wanting something.

"We are aware of the services the Shoshone provided for our surveyors in the past and the great friendship of Sacagawea of the Lemhi Shoshone," Captain Farmer added. "We wish only to see the land, draw maps of the headwaters of the River, not to stay. It is said to be very beautiful."

"The Yellowstone country is sacred to the Creator. All who see it must feel his hand upon them," Lame Elk said with pride. He had been promising Katy he would take her there someday. With the guns of the soldiers, perhaps this was the safest way to go. "I will confer with my people and give you an answer tomorrow," he said.

"WHY NOT ALL of us go?" asked Jim Lemmins. Confined as he had been to the settlements along the trail, a couple of weeks riding through what had been described as unique and beautiful country under escort of soldiers and friendly Indians was very appealing. He knew his adopted daughter was busting to go, and Valerie would be put to ease if they all went. He was also interested in spending more time with Lame Elk, talking about native medicines, since the Indian had brought Valerie and Katy back to the fort three years ago.

"Can we, Daddy?" yelled Katy, jumping up and down.

"If it's OK with your mother, I don't see why we can't. I get the impression that Lame Elk isn't interested in going for the soldiers alone. I think it would be a great trip for the family, and safe enough with all the men that are going. Fournier says he wants to go one last time too."

They both looked at Valerie in anticipation. "Won't a small girl and a woman be in the way?" she asked.

"Maybe a little," said Dr. Lemmins, "but a survey crew is pretty slow work, and we shouldn't be too much of a burden. I know Lame Elk would like to show Katy his home, and without Katy going, Lame Elk may decide not to take the soldiers at all. That's Fournier opinion."

"OK, I guess...we'll do it."

Katy hugged her mother, and then flew out the door to go tell Lame Elk.

THE EXPEDITION WAS composed of ten U.S. soldiers, four of which were with the Corps of Engineers, who were to do the surveying, along with Captain Farmer and five escort servicemen, Lame Elk and five of his warriors, and Waushaute and five of his warriors, the Lemmins family, and Fournier. Lame Elk had asked Waushaute to come look at the land with the idea that as a combined tribe they might resettle in the area. He was convinced that his people would not return to their home without sufficient numbers to protect themselves, and he thought he could show Waushaute that the Yellowstone was a far superior region than where his branch of the Lemhi currently lived. Lame Elk was rather excited about showing everyone the wonders of the area.

After an early attempt of trying to ride by herself with the Indians, Katy agreed to sit in front of Lame Elk on his horse. And so the procession started at a walk to the North following the Snake River. After a couple of days of pleasant travel, they crossed over the main branch of the Snake and followed Henry's Branch, continuing North past the abandoned old Fort Henry, the first trading post in the region, the jagged peaks of the Grand Tetons on their right. The march continued, following a smaller river, called Falls River by Fournier, to the northeast, full of cascading waterfalls and began a steady climb up into the higher elevations. Now they sent ahead a pair of scouts and were reduced to single file for much of the climb, then walking. The summer weather was fine, so the trip continued pleasantly. Eventually crossing the Continental Divide after following an even smaller stream bearing North again, they finally dropped down into Yellowstone Basin.

Almost immediately on reaching the valley floor they came across a geyser that shot water high above the treetop level. Everyone but the Yellowstone Shoshone and Fournier jerked in alarm and amazement even though they had been told what to expect. Bubbling sulfuric baths with their bright colors and seeping streams, mixed in with the beautiful forests and rivers and lakes, did indeed give them the sense that this was a unique and spiritual place.

Fournier regaled everyone with tale after tale of the mountain men that had trapped and traded in the region. He was clearly the happiest Dr. Lemmins had ever seen him, reliving his youth through the beauties of the nature around him. It seemed such a magical and peaceful land to Valerie. Lame Elk took them from one marvel to the next as they approached the big lake and the headwaters of the Yellowstone River, not far from where the Shoshone used to summer camp.

His pride in the land was evident to all, so when he suddenly became sad, it was not expected. Fournier told everyone to stay back as they let the Shoshone visit their burial grounds.

It was decided that base camp would be set beside the headwater lake. The surveyors began their work, mapping and measuring from peak to peak. For the next three weeks, the engineers and Indian guides would ride off to different areas expanding their canvass of work.

Lame Elk returned to his prime purpose of showing Waushaute the fishing and hunting opportunities, along with explaining the Indian life to Katy. Dr. Lemmins finally got a day with Lame Elk showing him the natural sources for remedies in the fields and woods. Valerie described the trip as an extended picnic, and reveled in the peaceful and happy nature of the expedition.

One day Lame Elk took Katy, Waushaute, Dr. Lemmins, and Fournier down along the Yellowstone River to a sudden dropoff into a steep canyon. The river plunged over the falls with a thunder, frightening Katy. Lame Elk was concerned and took her hand as they descended down into the canyon, where he had wished to show his friends the large trout that swam in the waters below. Then realizing that he was usurping Dr. Lemmins role as the girl's father, he motioned to the doctor to come take the girl's hand. Dr. Lemmins merely smiled and waved the gesture off. The Indian and the girl continued to hold hands as they climbed down. Just as they had three years before, they fished together, and Katy demonstrated to her father how to spear a fish. Just like three years before, she ended up wet but happy.

Toward the end of their stay, thunderclouds gathered over the Yellowstone Valley. The survey teams began wrapping up their work, and everyone started preparing for the trip home. Waushaute and Lame Elk were seen earnestly talking on numerous occasions, and laughing on others.

For Katy, it was a trip that she would remember all her life...one that would come to change her in the near future.

28

HER HAIR WHIPPED INTO her eyes as she tried to sneak a peak behind her. She dug her knees into the sides of her pony as they raced along the side of the steep streambed looking for a place to cross without sacrificing any speed. Weaving in and out of the trees as they flew by was a dangerous course, but she had no choice if she was to cross the stream. Her pursuers whooped in glee in anticipation of catching her.

Moments before, Moon in the Daylight had been scouting one side of the stream, and Stalking Wolf had been scouting the other, in advance of the Blackfoot raiding party. This was fairly open country, except for trees lining the water's course, amid small rolling hills and scattered brush. Now deep in Crow territory, it was more important than ever to remain stealthy. They had raided to the East for two weeks, killing and stealing from small targets of opportunity. Then they had turned North to begin a circle home, back through the center of Crow territory, knowing they might have to run for home if they were discovered by a large encampment. They had plenty of extra horses in case that was to happen, and had discussed the way they would retreat and switch off riding.

Moon in the Daylight had been alternately scouring the ground for signs of the enemy and glancing up to make sure nothing was ahead of her when she heard the horse snort behind her. Two Crow warriors were trying to sneak up behind her. She had bolted forward when she saw them, and the race began. A third Crow had almost cut her off, and she barely escaped his swinging lance as she slipped by. The Crows were trying to capture her, or she probably would have already been dead. She understood what a capture would mean, and guessed that the Crows were probably confident in their ability to catch her. They had surprised her and nearly trapped her, and now they were forcing her to make a mistake in a deadly race for her freedom and more. She noticed one of the Crows had broken out of the trees to her right into open ground in an attempt to outrace her and cut her off again.

Finally she saw a crossing ahead where the high bank had been trampled down and she could cut across the stream and reverse her direction back to the raiding party. Using all her strength, she slowed her pony down just enough to sharply cut to her left down the sloping embankment, over the shallow stream, and not overrun the path leading up the other side. As her horse dug into the far bank to start climbing out, a lance whistled past her head, and she heard the Crows yelling to each other as they crowded together urging their mounts down the bank behind her. The lance told her that they now wished to kill her if they couldn't capture her.

Not looking back, she gained the top of the opposite bank, broke out of the small corridor of trees, and turned her pony left again to run for the protection of the trailing Blackfoot warriors. Out of the trees burst Stalking Wolf to ride by her side, as the three Crows climbed up the bank in pursuit. All five were yelling now as they pushed their ponies back to full speed. Stalking Wolf twisted on his mount to send his single rifle shot back at the pursuing Crows, causing them to involuntarily swerve for a moment and lose precious seconds. Moon in the Daylight could feel her pony beginning to tire and scooted higher up on its withers, encouraging a smoother gait. She could feel her horse respond, perhaps getting a second wind. The two fleeing Blackfoot warriors angled to the next turn in the streambed, cutting the corner through open grassland. They nearly ran into a prairie dog town, which could have been disastrous, as they pounded away across the plain. As they approached the trees again at the stream bend, they saw Blue Heron and the others come charging out of the trees to their aid. The three chasing Crows split apart immediately in different directions. The closest went down in a hail of arrows, but the other two successfully turned and ran. Before several Blackfoot riders could take up pursuit, Blue Heron called them off. His quick judgment was to use the time to try and distance his band from retaliation, versus being stretched out in two directions on tired horses should they not catch both riders. This was Crow homeland and the clear advantage lay with the escaping Crow riders. Moon in the Daylight and Stalking Wolf mounted fresh horses and the band reversed course back to the West at a full trot. There was no question now that there would be organized pursuit, but from where? They were at a distinct disadvantage not knowing the land, and evasion was now imperative.

The band kept a steady pace through the balance of the afternoon until dark. Selecting a thick copse of cottonwoods and brush on a hilltop at a sharp right angle to their track, Blue Heron had three warriors brush their horse tracks back to the streambed they had intentionally followed the last hours. They would have a cold camp tonight, and double the watch. Looking down from the hill to the creek was a little more than a mile with open space and light brush between. On the other side of the wooded hill were more rolling hills mostly without trees. It would be hard for anyone to pass unobserved.

Later that evening keeping watch, Buffalo Lance studied a coyote slinking along by the trees near the stream. Guessing the spot where he would cross the Indians' trail, he watched for the animal's reaction. The coyote stopped and sniffed around about where Buffalo Lance thought he would, running a few feet out toward the hill before abandoning the scent and moving on down the stream line. This was the second watch and well after midnight. The half moon had moved halfway cross the sky, setting new shadows. Long Bow approached in a crouch to rejoin him. He had just checked on the horses, soothing one who was having a bad dream. They did not want any noises tonight.

"Moon in the Daylight almost was caught," he ventured.

"But she escaped," Buffalo Lance answered.

"I didn't mean she did something wrong," Long Bow said. "She is a good warrior."

"She is getting her experience, just like we did, and she is fierce in battle," said Buffalo Lance.

"She saved me from the Crow at the Shoshone camp battle. I was falling when she jumped on the Crow," Long Bow looked ashamed.

"Ah, so it is the debt to a woman that bothers you," Buffalo Lance said, and then he signaled for quiet and pointed toward the stream. Out of nowhere in the night, a large group of riders appeared moving along the edge of the trees. Buffalo Lance sent Long Bow to quietly alert the camp. He assumed there had been advance scouts, but he had not seen any. They had most likely passed in the trees by the streambed. He started to count and was up to fifty when Blue Heron and several others joined him to watch. The remainder of the Blackfoot warriors were with the horses, to make sure they were quiet. The Crow war party moved by silently and swiftly, following the watercourse. Their steady pace told Blue Heron that they were heading for somewhere specifically, and not hunting per se. Somewhere in front of them, the Crows would gather to spread a net.

As everyone was up, Blue Heron gathered them together to discuss the situation. Six of the most junior warriors kept watch as the other twenty sat down to talk.

"It is possible that the Crows are riding to another camp between us and home, hoping to trap us as we come their way," Blue Heron started. "We were fortunate to see this group pass us in the night."

"They do not know where we are," stated The Badger. Some heads nodded.

Blue Heron smiled, and said, "This is true, but we do not know where we are either." There was a soft laugh and more heads nodded.

"We must go where they do not expect us," offered Running Wolf Leaps.

"The Canadas are too cold," snickered Long Bow. Another laugh.

"No, he is right," Blue Heron said in a more serious tone. "The Crow now believe they have gotten in front of us. We need to pass the net before it is thrown. If we ride hard to the northeast, we may break through before others are alerted of our coming. It is a risk that we will be spotted while on the run, but if we wait, we know they will close their trap." There was a general murmur of agreement. "Does anyone wish to say more?" he asked diplomatically.

"We should feed and water the horses and go while the night still covers us. We may have to ride hard for two days or more," said The Badger.

"Good," said Blue Heron. "Let us show these Crows how a Blackfoot can ride."

Twenty minutes later, after tending to their stock, the raiding party started out at a canter, angling away from the track the Crows had taken to the West, heading west-northwest. They stayed out in open country now, more concerned about making good time and getting back in front of the Crows than being seen. Using the cover of night, they pushed their horses until just before daybreak. An hour of rest and water, and they started out again in the early morning, but only at a trot on their straight-line path. Two advance scouts were sent out on their flanks within sight range, and a point scout was positioned slightly ahead of them. About midmorning, they passed within sight of a small Crow camp and kept going. It was noted that a rider went South from the Crow camp after they passed. Blue Heron decided to change the flight direction to a more westerly course now, and try for more stealth. Signaling in the scouts, the Blackfoot raiders stopped in some trees to discuss the next strategy.

"I think we should be back in front of the Crows now," Blue Heron stated. "Perhaps it is wiser to disappear like the elk now. Let us slow down and look to fool the hunter, starting with walking in the first stream we cross, maybe finding some rock to change direction, a false trail..."

"The Crows could be close behind. Their rider may not have had to go far, and they could be rested," Buffalo Lance warned.

"Yes, they will ride hard to try and overtake us now that we have been spotted," agreed Long Bow.

"We should not disappoint them," said Blue Heron. "Listen to my thoughts." Blue Heron then told them what he was thinking. Once again the

Blackfoot warriors saw the wisdom of the plan and agreed that Two Horns had been wise in selecting Blue Heron to lead the raid.

Since the raiding party now had twelve extra horses, The Badger and Stalking Wolf and three others were assigned to continue on the same west by northwest track as before with the extra horses, switching horses liberally to keep a good pace. With five riders and seventeen horses, they should be able to outdistance any pursuit. The remaining twenty-one Blackfoot warriors would hole up and hopefully escape detection as the Crows chased the fleet decoy to no avail. Blue Heron figured it would be some time if ever that the Crows would notice the difference between seventeen clustered tracks and thirty-six. So they started off again, with the twenty-one Blackfoot trailing the decoy party, who cut close to a stream on their path home. The twenty-one fell off into the stream at that point and brushed their tracks out. They then proceeded down the streambed a mile before exiting out the other side up a small butte into a crop of pine trees and out of sight. Three warriors were sent back on foot to erase their tracks coming out of the stream. They had barely completed their task when Blue Heron saw the large body of Crow warriors appear, following the Blackfoot trail. The Blackfoot again stood beside their mounts to keep the horses silent and watched the approach of the large war party from their hiding place up on the butte. There were now about eighty Crows, following dead on the track left by the Blackfoot. Like the Sioux, the chiefs had full feather bonnets angled back from the tops of their heads. Most of the warriors wore the pompadour hairstyle on top with long braids on each side of their heads, though others had more braids, or other adornments stuck in their hair. Blue Heron was unhappy to see how many guns the Crows were carrying. Two Horns had been right. The Blackfoot had to keep up. The moment was soon to happen when the Crows would pass the point where Blue Heron and the others had split off. There wasn't any hesitation as the Crows continued on at a brisk pace following Buffalo Lance and his horse band. Moon in the Daylight felt herself exhale, not realizing that she had been holding her breath. Several others made derogatory comments about the Crow Indians as they watched them ride away to the northwest. Once they were out of sight, Blue Heron led his band down the far side of the butte in a due West trajectory that would cut through Shoshone territory again before heading North and home. The horses would need a rest. He remembered the big lake in the abandoned Yellowstone country. That would be a safe place to rest a day before completing the trip home.

Later that day, the Crows came within sight of the retreating decoys, and came to a tired and frustrated halt. Ahead, the five Blackfoot yipped and yelled their taunts at the deception, while increasing their pace for safety with the stolen Crow pony string. The Crows stoically turned to begin a long, unhappy ride home. Another log was thrown on the fire of hate burning in the young Crow Chief Loud Thunder.

29

ORKING ON THE MONTARA Ranch provided Drego with monthly spending money, which usually was gone within days of his receiving it. He was strong and a fair hand, and Paco kept him busy. Perhaps Paco felt he needed to keep this one busy to stay out of trouble. Drego liked to play cards and drink, and he loved his women. When he drank, similar to when he didn't drink, he loved to talk. The problem was, when he drank, his talking ran to bragging, which often led to fighting and other trouble. He usually regretted his behavior the next day. However, when paytime came again, he would head for the city with the same intentions as the last time.

It was Saturday night in San Francisco, and Drego had already visited a female friend. Now he felt like trying his hand at Lady Luck. Frequenting the Mexican establishment Un Poco de Suerte, he sat down to a game of five-card draw. As a regular visitor, he was warmly and humorously greeted. As usual, he started to slowly but surely lose, but that did not bother him, as he expected to, and he enjoyed the game. Tonight, however, there was an animated discussion circulating the town. The police had raided the known hangouts for Günter Targon's criminal empire, but all they could find were building guards and a few longshoremen. Everyone else had been warned and had disappeared, including Targon's five ships. It was on the street that Targon felt betrayed and was readying for an attack against those who had tried to have him jailed. Drego kept his mouth shut and his ears open this night, as he knew Targon was no friend of his. Targon's Indian was said to still be in town, and some bigwig's bodyguard had been found butchered and nailed to a tree on the posh side of town. Since warning Corby that Targon was looking for him, the three men who had come down together from Oregon had been very careful in their movements, particularly at night. Still, Drego had hardly stopped enjoying himself. He was just more aware of his surroundings. Perhaps this was good news for Corby, Donovan, and himself, if Targon was occupied elsewhere. On that thought, he drew three of a kind and won the hand. The night was young, and if all went well, maybe he would buy a nice trinket for another lady that crossed his mind. He would remember to tell his friends about the street talk when next he saw them.

The top floor of Paul Logan's best gambling parlor served as both his offices and his home. It looked like it was under siege, with guards everywhere, including dogs. Two men were even stationed on the roof at night. The brutal murder of one of his bodyguards had the effect Targon knew it would. Logan was in fear for his life, day and night. He could not totally explain to anyone that this was a personal vendetta without revealing more than he wished to. However he wasn't merely hunkering down. He had petitioned the governor for warships to track down the "infamous pirate and scoundrel" Targon, who was "terrorizing the citizens of California."

The idea of a navy base out of San Francisco had been on the front burner since it was annexed from Mexico. The United States was in the process of purchasing Mare Island, on the northeast end of the bay, as the future shipbuilding yard for the U.S. Navy. Troubles in Nicaragua and Japan were festering, and a naval presence on the new West Coast was imperative. The traditional route to the Far East from New York was still around the Cape of Good Hope, South Africa, due to poor port facilities and the daunting Pacific Ocean to the West. But Commodore Cornelius Vanderbilt was laying rail in Panama and Nicaragua for shortcuts in trade routes to the West. The race for a competitive advantage to the new West was on. The Gadsden Purchase had just bought the final piece of real estate from Santa Anna's Mexican government, on the United States' southwestern border, largely to complete plans for a Southern-Pacific railroad to connect the East and the West. The strategic importance of a secure West Coast was obvious to all.

Logan could sense the possibilities of being part of a grand empire, such as the so-called robber barons of the East were making for themselves. Targon and his Indian had to be eliminated, and the sooner the better. But it could be years before the U.S. Navy was prepared to address his particular problem. Piracy was a far-flung epidemic circling the Pacific, ranging from the South China Sea, North through Japanese Imperial waters, to the wide-ranging Russian profiteers and their bases in Alaska, along with America's own, and down the coast to the land pirates ambushing goldrushers coming across Central America on their way to California. It was indeed the Wild West, for travelers in particular.

Meanwhile, construction had started on the shipyards for the San Francisco Steamship Company. Starting in 1851, a company called Pacific Mail Steamship Company had begun to capture the Panama to San Francisco packet mail business, bringing small steamships over from the East Coast, and now ten were chugging up and down the West Coast. Logan's San Francisco

Steamship Company had already had to make an adjustment to building a faster, larger, and safer prototype steamship for its fleet-to-be. That meant more money than originally projected, but financing was still easy to acquire. Paul Logan's main concern was his ex-partner, so he began quietly searching for bounty hunters who would understand what a completed job meant. He had no illusions that this was now a fight to the death. He had Targon on the run, but that meant little to a man like Targon, used to perverting the law, and he knew it.

As PREVIOUSLY ARRANGED, Günter Targon sailed into Half Moon Bay to meet his confederate, Ishka, and plot their next move. Günter had plenty of time to consider what he might do, and he came to the realization that Paul Logan could be hurt in many ways without shining a light on himself and drawing more law enforcement his way. Recently he had become aware of a personal grudge, one he had subsequently fanned between Logan and a young man named Zachary DuPort, alias Bridges, who had come into his employ for the sole reason of finding out who had shanghaied him three years before. As luck would have it, it was one time that Günter hadn't been involved and could prove it, as he did by torturing the truth out of another of his employees for DuPort's benefit. Now he would use DuPort as a loaded gun to hurt Logan. DuPort was a smart agent who would be able to pull off some of the schemes Günter was contemplating. He would test DuPort with an arson project to start. The new shipyards Logan was building would be an entertaining choice.

Now he wanted to review Logan's daily activities, with Ishka, to see if he could steal something valuable before he killed the man. Waving from his quarterdeck to his assassin who had just walked up the beach to his dingy at the shore, he would soon figure out the best ways to end this last and longest partnership. Günter was enjoying himself.

SHUG REEKED OF oil, having spilled some on his trousers. Zach was also concerned about how much noise the big man made as they worked their way around the major structures of the large shipyard. Fortunately it was a dark night, and they had seen only one watchman out moving around. Zach had taken the precaution to bring ample amounts of oil and even some gunpowder to guarantee a big, unstoppable blaze. They would know it was arson, but that was what he wanted too. The key was to get it started enough to catch on and still get out of the area without being seen. He did not trust Shug to accomplish that, so when all the combustible materials had been carried in, he sent Shug up the hill and away from the shipyard, instructing him to get rid of the oil-stained pants and the wagon they had used to get there.

Two huge wooden girders stood over his head, supporting a crisscross of other beams. This structure apparently was a bay allowing the workers to get underneath the massive ships they were to build. A couple of unused five foot tresses were nearby, and he dragged them over to where he intended to light his fire, building a giant teepee of wood under the structure. Under his teepee, he poured out his gunpowder and then soaked the piled wood with the oil. Finally, he lit a torch and shoved it into the stack, jumping back a safe distance. The pile flashed from the gunpowder, and a fire began to climb immediately up the woodpile. Zachary ran up the hill and out into the darkness as the fire reached higher and began to light up the area. As he ran away, he could hear someone ringing a fire bell, and several voices yelling in the night. He could tell they weren't going to be putting out this fire for some time. After reaching a road well above the shipyard, he walked away from the blaze on his way back to meet Shug and make sure he had changed his pants.

PAUL LOGAN HURRIED over to Market Street the next day and entered the Oxley building. Stewart Bertram had sent a message over first thing in the morning, asking Paul to join him and Thomas James to discuss the major setback from the shipyard fire. He knew other investors would be very upset, so the three lead investors needed to come up with a good plan immediately. He took the stairs two at a time to the second floor, his two bodyguards just behind and entered the meeting room a minute past 9 o'clock. The door shut behind him, and he was suddenly looking at ten guns leveled at him and his two men.

"Good morning, partner," Günter greeted him in a cheerful voice. Günter's men quickly disarmed the bodyguards, and gagged and bound the three men. "Before we leave for my ship, I'd like you to meet your replacement, my new junior partner."

A well-dressed man came over to stand in front of Logan. There was a look of smug satisfaction on his face. He looked familiar, but Logan had yet to place him.

"It appears we will just miss being partners once again," the man said. "I believe Günter, however, has carved out a special deal for you." He twisted his wrist, imitating a knife cut. Günter laughed, and Paul Logan sagged in the arms of his captors as he finally recognized Zachary DuPort. Zach then swung his fist flush into the side of Paul Logan's head, knocking him out. At the same time the two bodyguards were murdered where they stood with several knife thrusts from Günter Targon's henchmen. The bodies were allowed to slump to the floor where they were left.

"Put the bag on him and take him out back and down to the wagon. I'll meet you back at Half Moon Bay," Targon instructed his men. "Zachary, you and I will need to buy some opium to help poor Paul sign the necessary sale papers. I don't think we will wish to buy his interests in that unfortunate steamship company though." Smiling, the two men exited by the front door on their way to the small but growing Chinese section of town. Günter had a moment of resignation. Having so quickly and easily defeated Paul Logan, he had ended the anticipation and enjoyment of the hunt. Now all that was left was the entertainment Ishka would provide.

30

THE MEXICAN GOVERNMENT HAD been in turmoil since its inception, in 1822. After losing 55 percent of its landmass to the United States with the conclusion of the Mexican War in 1848 (California to Texas), it had been even more cash strapped and reeling. It was not in any position to clarify land grants legally issued decades and even centuries before by the kings and queens of Spain to their faithful servants in the New World. Most of these grants were of a verbal nature to begin with, and rivers or mountains marked the land parcels in very broad terms on ancient and poorly drawn maps, many by the landowners themselves. As such, record keeping in the Mexican capital could be said to be as faltering as the government.

When the United States took over sovereignty of its war gains, they tried to apply a strict legal definition to ownership similar to what was in common usage in the existing states. Proof of ownership was required through providing some documentation, such as a bill of sale, a land grant certificate, anything that said one had legal right to the land. Determining exact borders was even more difficult. Without such legal documentation, the land would be lost to government auction, even if the purported owner had been living there all his life. Many of the huge estates granted to Spanish Mexican families that now fell within the new borders of the United States of America were confiscated and resold in smaller tracts to ranchers and farmers moving West.

Don Sebastián Drego de Santarosilla was in such a predicament. He had a letter from the former Spanish government in Mexico acknowledging the land grant from Spain a hundred years earlier, but no map defining the boundaries precisely. The U.S. government had accepted his new allegiance to become a citizen, as required to retain his ownership of the property, but had not yet ruled on his legal claim to the land. Under the provisions of the transfer, he held the rights to the land until the courts made their decision. Another problem came from a local dispute regarding the San Pedro River, one of the few water supplies in the area. Local American ranchers were encroaching on Don Sebastián's side of the river claiming there was not enough proof that he held title to the land. Outmanned, Don Sebastián had turned to the local authorities, who had referred him to the government in Washington, and nothing had been done. One thing had led to another, and a small range war had broken out. A letter had finally reached Drego in San Francisco, asking him to come home to help his beleaguered father.

"I LIKE HIM too, but this ain't your fight," Donovan argued.

"It's not just that. I don't like being a manservant. I want to see more of the country, I want to take control of my life. I'm not ... happy here," Corby answered.

Donovan's face fell a little at Corby's statement. Corby saw it and immediately said, "It's not that I'm not happy, like I said ... I'm just not making my own life. You and the Countess are building something that you both want. I'm kind of just helping ... You know I don't have any real family, just ... well, you. You know that. I can never repay you for all you have done for me. You have a great new life going for you here. I'm happy about that. It's just not what I want to do, even if it's what I probably should want to do. Does any of this make sense to you?"

Donovan relaxed in his chair, rubbed the side his head with the heel of his hand, and smiled. "Sure, it's really rather natural. Reminds me of me. I wish I were a little younger so I could go too." Leaning back in the chair, he said, "I knew a señorita once. A real tigress, flashing eyes ... But this is just a chapter in the book. No point in throwing the book away, son. Go on down and pull Drego's fat from the fire, and then come back and we will figure out what comes next. OK?"

Corby nodded and smiled, perhaps a little relieved that he could come back.

"So, we are in agreement then? Meanwhile I want you to leave your savings with the Countess to invest in her company. It could really amount to something, and I want you to promise to come right back when it is over. No dawdling about. I'm going to need that hand on the homestead you promised. Hold you to it," Donovan stood up and stuck his hand out to Corby. Corby took it and shook his hand, and then gave him a brief hug. He swallowed hard and stepped back.

"Would you tell the Countess for me?" he asked, not looking up.

"I think you should do that yourself," Donovan said, regaining himself.

"She'll make me feel like I'm making a mistake, and I'm not," Corby explained. "I'd rather not leave on a bad note."

"Who's leaving?" said Gabrielle from the doorway. Donovan's little office was set off of the back of the registration desk, and was a high-traffic area for the hotel employees.

Corby straightened up like a schoolboy who had been caught and was expecting his punishment. "A friend of mine has family problems down by Old Mexico. I have to help him if I can."

Gabrielle stiffened and said, "I see."

Donovan interjected, "It sounds like a dangerous situation. Sure to be lead flying."

Gabrielle's eyes widened a bit, and her anger dissipated immediately. "Can the Marshal or I help? Do you need ... anything? When would you be coming back?"

Corby shook his head to answer the first two questions and shrugged to answer the last.

"You remember how I asked if Corby could buy into the company a little with his savings?" Donovan asked.

"Yes, yes of course," responded Gabrielle, and then she marched across the room, hugged Corby, and kissed him full on the lips. "You better not get shot. I'm not done with you." Spinning on her heels, she quickly left the room.

Corby and Donovan stood in shock, not saying a word. Donovan finally laughed and said, "Geez, kid, you never run out of surprises!" Corby sat down hard.

31

THE SCOUT CAME BACK reporting a strange group of people was camping beside the Shoshone lake at the headwaters of the Yellowstone River. If Blue Heron were to believe it, Blackhand of the Shoshones was camping with white soldiers. This was something he would have to see for himself. Riding on, he led the Blackfoot party out into the open, within sight of the camp. There was a sudden bustle around the camp as they approached.

Waushaute and Lame Elk swung up onto their horses, as did all the Indians in the camp. Captain Farmer assembled his men too. Fournier stood studying the slowly approaching Blackfoot party.

"Big Blackfoot raiding party, but they don't seem to be looking for trouble right now," he said. "Maybe I should go palaver with them, see what they want?"

About then the Blackfoot party stopped, perhaps a half mile out from the camp, and three Blackfoot Indians continued on alone.

Lame Elk indicated that he, Fournier, and Waushaute would ride out to talk. The two groups slowly covered the ground between, and stopped a few feet apart out on the open grass.

The apparent leader of the Blackfoot Indians sat on a brown and white painted pony with a rifle across his lap. He had an intelligent and pleasant face, and clearly was interested in the camp party members who had halted in front of him. Next to him was a female warrior in leggings and shirt of deerskin, which did not hide the fact that she was attractive, though trying to look tough. The third Blackfoot was a big man, very muscular and menacing looking.

"I am Blue Heron, of the Gray Woman Mountain Blackfoot," said the leader. "We are returning from fighting the Crows, and are passing through the land of the Shoshone." He was looking at Lame Elk.

"I am Waushaute, Chief of the Round Valley Lemhi, cousins to the Yellowstone Shoshone. This is Lame Elk, Chief of the Yellowstone Shoshone, whom you may know as Blackhand." Waushaute said, indicating Lame Elk.

"Blackhand is well known by the Blackfoot," Blue Heron said. "Our Chief Two Horns broke the lance for peace with Blackhand not far from where we sit on our horses today." He nodded his head toward the ridges rising above the river mouth. "Two Horns returned from that occasion to kill Crooked Claws, the war chief who had made war on the Shoshone."

"We have heard of that," said Waushaute. "Still, many Shoshone were killed, others captured. What is it you want?"

"The Blackfoot have a great respect for Blackhand, and have stayed out of the Yellowstone and respected the peace for three years now. Our band saved some Shoshone hunters from the Crows just one moon ago. I have news from the Lakota that the Crows are warring against their neighbors. We have been pushing them back. Perhaps the Crows will attack the Shoshone," suggested Blue Heron.

Lame Elk had been studying Blue Heron, and wasn't convinced that the Blackfoot was here to simply warn an old enemy.

"You wish to know why the White soldiers are with the Shoshone," Lame Elk said in a matter-of-fact voice.

The Blackfoot did not answer.

"The Lemhi and Yellowstone Shoshone will be returning to the valley together as one people. The White soldiers wish to make friends with the Shoshone, through many gifts of rifles, and to fight the Shoshones' enemies," said Lame Elk in the same deadpan voice. "We have already driven back the Crow."

Blue Heron was at a small loss as to what to say next.

"Does your Chief Two Horns still have my big black horse?" asked Lame Elk.

Blue Heron nodded, wondering why he had wanted to start this conversation in the first place.

"I would like it back. You may go in peace back to your own lands," Lame Elk said, ending the conversation. Then he asked as an afterthought. "The big warrior that I brought here to you three years ago, what was his name?"

"Red Horses," answered Blue Heron.

"Red Horses...Red Horses was an exceptionally brave warrior," Lame Elk commented, and then turned to ride back to camp. Waushaute and Fournier followed.

The Blackfoot left to the North, looking for another place to lie up and rest. Back at the Shoshone camp, Fournier was telling Captain Farmer and the Lemmins family about the parley. "That Lame Elk put the fear of God in them Blackfoot all right. Never seen the like of it. Guess them stories about him are true to my way of thinking."

Katy looked over at her Indian. He was whittling something with his knife. It was the knife her mother had given him three years ago. He looked up and saw her, and smiled. She walked over to join him by the fire.

32

ITTING IN HIS STUDY, he cleared a space on his desk and reread her letter once again. She certainly had her father in her. Henri leaned back and remembered Pierre Du Montfort, Le Comte de Larousseau. They had been roommates at the Ecole Polytechnique in Paris in 1808. Pierre was the dashing officer-to-be, while Henri had studied to receive his engineering degree. For two years Pierre had pulled Henri around Paris with his circle of friends, from one party to the next. After graduation, Pierre had bought a commission in the French army and been shipped off to Algeria. Henri had found a love of mathematics and studied at the Mathematical Institute at Oxford before trying his luck in America, where he picked up a law degree at Harvard. When the count came to America, it was Henri who greeted him at the dock. And when the count inherited his millions, it was Henri who counseled him on how to manage it. And then, when the count got married, Henri had been the best man. Eventually, much of the fortune of Le Comte de Larousseau ended up under Henri Seurat's direct supervision, making him a rich man too and dictating a profession he had not expected, as financial adviser to the wealthy. He had done well for Pierre, and had become entrenched in the vast investment portfolio of his friend and chief client. But he was now sixty-five, and had been turning away pleas from many of his former clients to continue managing their financial affairs. As godfather to Gabrielle, having promised his best friend Pierre to always look after her, Henri never considered dropping the Countess's accounts. He had bounced her on his knee too many times, and acquiesced to her begging for sweets and other treats. In his mind, as a lifelong bachelor, Gabrielle was his family.

The letter had thanked him for sending the news of her husband's death. Charles Augustus Loucheur had past away in February of 1852, after a sudden illness at the age of sixty. Having a nephew and a sister, Charles had cut Gabrielle out of his will, not that it had amounted to that much anyway, in comparison to her own holdings.

Gabrielle had gone on excitedly about her life in San Francisco and her new businesses, asking several detailed questions regarding contracts and banking as she wrote. Finally, she had pleaded with him to come join her, citing all the reasons she expected he would, understandably, wish to stay in New Orleans, but holding out hope that her "Oncle Henri" would at least visit. It was clear she was not going to come back to New Orleans.

Henri had a very comfortable life in New Orleans, but very comfortable can sometimes seem routine and lacking. The letter made him pause and consider what the rest of his life would be. He found little to inspire him.

Over the next few days he wrestled with the crazy idea of actually going to the "Wild West." One of the things he most admired in his friend Pierre, and now his daughter, Gabrielle, was their absolute lack of fear in tackling new and exciting experiences. He judged he had maybe ten more years, fifteen if he was lucky. Why not get an injection of excitement? The more he thought about it, the more he leaned toward the change, until he had worked the idea from all sides and reached a solid conclusion. Much like his thorough approach to investing, Henri arrived at his decision in a patient and comprehensive manner, weighing all the pluses and minuses. But this decision also included an assessment of the intangibles, those aspects of life that trigger the emotional needs of the human spirit, and they heavily tipped the scale for a move West.

Putting pen to paper, he sent a letter to Gabrielle that he knew would surprise her, informing her of the asset transfers and disengagements he was putting into play to prepare to move the Countess's financial headquarters to San Francisco, concurrent with his own arrival. He signed it as always, "Oncle Henri."

33

SLOWLY THE HAZE IN his mind began to lift as the pain began to increase. He could smell himself, and became aware of his disheveled appearance. Then it clicked in his mind. He was aboard one of Günter's ships and was as good as dead. Paul Logan rolled over on the cot to find he was tied down. His stomach was queasy, and the fear began to mount. He could hear the activity on deck above his head and sensed the ship was out to sea, with its steady dip and rise motions, along with creaks and moans in the timbers. He had no illusions as to how this would end, and he resolved to try and show as little fear as he could, knowing Targon relished the humiliation as much as the victory.

After awhile Targon entered the cabin to look in on his captive. He sat on a sea chest facing the cot.

"It is a fine morning, on a light sea, we have today, Paul. You couldn't have picked a better day to die. Ishka is sharpening his knives, and promises a spectacular show," Targon said as if he were going to a fair.

Summoning up all his courage, Paul Logan tried to sound as normal as he could. "Well, Günter, it would seem you have won the end game. Congratulations. We have come a long way together. We are both rich … I imagine you are now rich and I am not—"

Günter cut in. "Yes, you were so generous in selling me most of your holdings at a fair price." He smiled, enjoying his triumph. In fact, the documents they had written and filed did show Paul Logan had sold his enterprises at a fair price, but since no money was actually given to Logan, "fair" was an unfair word.

Logan began again. "I don't begrudge you your victory, as had I won, I would have enjoyed it too. However, it was a fair fight, and men of honor respect their opponents. I do not deserve to be tortured and killed. I can't hurt you anymore. I ask that you let me off at your next port."

There was a moment of silence as Günter thought about the request. Then he smiled again. "I'm sorry, Paul, but we are not men of honor, and you do deserve to be killed, and Ishka has been so looking forward to this. I cannot disappoint him at this late hour. As weak as you are, however, I fear it will not be much of a show. Try to hang on a little... for Ishka."

Rising to his feet, he called for two deckhands to come down and carry Paul Logan up on deck. After they untied him, one deckhand grabbed his legs while the other reached under his arms to carry him up the short stairs to the open deck. They tried to get him to stand, but he couldn't. Ishka came over to stare at him, and then walked back over to a round barrel where he had an assortment of knives laid out.

"Now, Paul, you've got to do better than this," Günter mocked him as he lay on the deck, "or the men will be so unhappy."

Targon's men began to gather for the ceremony. The sound of Ishka's blades being honed against each other seemed to hold all conversation to a minimum.

Looking about the deck in despair, Logan saw an iron harpoon lying by the near gunnel where someone had been repairing it. Like a wild animal, he surprised everyone, and with a quick burst of energy, he rolled to his feet, ran over the short distance, grabbed the harpoon, and with his last strength, rolled overboard. Holding the heavy harpoon in a death grip, he slowly sank into the depths of the ocean. Targon was sure Logan's face had a smile on it as it disappeared astern, pleased at his last small victory in denying Ishka and Targon their torture.

Ishka was furious, and the deckhands scattered to stay out of his field of vision. Targon kept looking down into the passing ocean, wondering if Paul Logan had the determination and moxie to kill himself. When nothing rose in their wake, he touched his forehead as if in a salute, turned around still smiling, and went forward to enjoy the fine day at sea.

AN ARTICLE APPEARED in one of the weekly papers, suggesting that Paul Logan may have cut and run. Certain facts relating to the sale of profitable enterprises and the abandonment of other debt had led some to speculate that Paul Logan might have taken his money off the table and left California before financial reverses occurred. It was suggested that the recently disclosed sale of his gambling parlors to a company named T.D. & Associates, Inc., coupled with the crippling fire at the San Francisco Steamship Company yards, and the inability to locate Mr. Logan, added up to a possible solid explanation for Mr. Logan's expeditious exit, one step ahead of financial headaches.

A second article followed the next day in the dailies, whereby Mr. Stewart Bertram said Mr. Paul Logan had informed him that he was going to go back

East to shore up new financing for the San Francisco Steamship Company, in order to forge ahead as planned.

A third article ran a week later regarding the cessation of the Coalition Against Crime Force, heralding the success of the governor's effort to crack down on crime in the city, citing the incarceration of the Baker gang and several others, and driving away certain unnamed pirates and scalawags from the area.

Zachary DuPort read the last newspaper article from his new penthouse office and home. He could reemerge as Zachary DuPort again, but decided this time to keep one bank account under the hybrid name he had been using of Zachary Bridges. He had found Donovan's black-handled Colt Walker in Paul Logan's closet, as he had removed the smaller clothes to make room for his own new wardrobe. Many of Logan's underlings had a pretty good guess as to what had happened to their former boss, but that gave them even more reason to keep it to themselves. The new boss had the same old connections, and paid the same wages. Life went on, with T.D. & Associates, Inc. at the helm.

For Zachary DuPort, it was a rebirth. Understanding that he had a deal with the devil, at least this devil preferred to stay at sea. While Targon had also installed two other front men, Dan Williams and Roland Leach, to jointly manage the new holdings, Zachary, due to his past experience, was given operating authority over the gambling parlors, and was given the fancy apartment and office. Still a long way from being rich, it was another promising start, and he could reappear in society, and finally visit Gabrielle. He began to work on his story to best explain his two-and-a-half-year absence.

SITTING WITH HIS legs crossed, Ishka concentrated on sharpening his knives. Once he was satisfied with one, he would almost absentmindedly flick it across the room and stick it in the wall. The lower wall looked like a porcupine's back with all the thin knives sticking out of it. Günter Targon continued to read the newspaper as he waited for his men to report back. A month had passed since he had eliminated Paul Logan, and it was well past time that he should deal with the gunman Corby. Being in the city was always an uncomfortable experience for the two, but more so for Günter, who really only felt at home on a ship's deck. It had been fairly easy to find the whereabouts of the two Oregon men that had killed Jimbo Fisher. Of added interest was this rich Frenchwoman who employed them. Maybe a ransom gambit would deliver a fine fee, but punishing the two Oregon men was the first order of business. Since the killing of Fisher, his men had been wondering when

Günter would exact his revenge. One thing after another had demanded his attention and postponed his revenge, not the least being Logan's all-out war against him with the San Francisco police forces. It was never good to let anyone see a slippage in his propensity toward bloodshed. A capture and torture were called for, especially since Logan had escaped his just dues, and that meant finding out more about the two and where they could be apprehended. Delayed justice was justice nonetheless.

The Tlingit Indian was almost smiling in anticipation of murder. Ishka had a near religious bent when inflicting pain and suffering. It was a balm to his soul to turn the tables of life around and deliver excruciating mental and physical anguish on someone else, such as the Gods had decided to do to him everyday. The look in their eyes, knowing that he would cut them to pieces, and they could not do anything about it, was the best moment. Their screams to their Gods in futile agony were blows against the unholy alliance of man and the Gods that had stripped him of everything including some of his sanity. Years of nightmares and daily injustices, both real and imagined, pushed Ishka, and he lived to kill. He had no other purpose or plan. Targon protected him while allowing him to kill every few months. It was probably the best arraignment the poor Tlingit could have hoped for. Where some fears and obsessions would rightly challenge one to question his sanity, they did not diminish from his native intelligence or natural skills. Ishka could vanish or appear like a phantom. This proved to be an excellent skill in the assassin's trade. His preference for knives lent to a quiet kill when it was necessary, and his lack of other interests meant a willingness to stalk for hours on end with patience akin to the mountain lion. Targon had the perfect weapon for his many needs, and Ishka was the consummate professional when given an assignment.

Eventually the two men sent to spy on the Oregon pair returned to report to Targon. They had established that Donovan lived in the hotel, as did Corby. The young gunman was more active in his travel patterns, often moving around the city with the Countess during the day, or meeting with various contractors working on the hotel. He was known to ride out to the Montara Ranch, but there appeared to be no set schedule on that. The ex-marshal was a little easier to locate, but less inclined to venture out and about. Neither was particularly interested in San Francisco's nightlife, but Corby would sometimes join a Mexican fellow for an hour or two on Friday pay nights. Targon figured that was probably his old acquaintance Drego.

When the men had gone, Ishka got up off the floor, collected his knives, wrapping them one on top of another in a long cloth belt. He looked at Targon.

"It is the young gunman we want. He is the killer. You must track him and look for an opportunity, but do not get killed, my friend. He is obviously very fast. Faster than you can throw your knife or slip away. You must catch him unawares."

The Indian gave another rare grin and slipped out the door, but as fate would have it, Corby and Drego were slightly ahead of their stalker, leaving the city for Tucson, via San Diego.

34

AMUEL JOHNSON DIDN'T THINK Mexicans should be able to hold on to vast lands inherited centuries ago just because some king who had never even seen the land waved his hand and said so. This was the United States of America, destined to become the greatest country in the world. Here people worked for what they got; no one gave it to them. If Mexico had won the war, he doubted they would allow gringos to control big ranches in their country.

His cattle needed more grass and water if he was to continue growing, and this Don Sebastián Drego had land to spare. Hell, he probably hadn't even visited all of the land he had in his lifetime. Sam knew plenty of other folks who felt the same way. More ranchers were encroaching on Don Sebastián Drego's lands all the time, and the law wasn't stopping them.

Whistling and yelling, his three cowboys drove the small herd across the San Pedro River onto Don Sebastián's land to feed for the day. Another hot and dry summer had turned much of the grasslands unusable for grazing purposes. What higher grazing ground there was in the mountains was also on Don Sebastián's land, but so were the Apaches.

THE VAQUEROS WHO worked for Don Sebastián had warned Sam Johnson not to cross the river again, as they had with a variety of other poachers, miners, settlers, and cattlemen. Just patrolling the huge estate was a full-time job, and Don Sebastián had his hands full running a profitable ranch. As of late, the ranch hands had been alerted to certain places on the ranch where it was most likely intruders would crossover. The Don had been trying to stem the tide and meet aggression with aggression. Therefore, as was to be expected, on a standard patrol, one of the vaqueros, Miguel by name, spotted Sam Johnson's incursion onto El Rancho de El Viento del Norte. As instructed, he rode back to the hacienda and informed the foreman what was happening. After a brief meeting with Don Sebastián, the foreman, Julio Sánchez, and fifteen vaqueros rode out to drive the cattle herd back across the river.

Upon arriving at the river, Julio once again told Sam Johnson to drive his cattle back across the river. Sam refused. Riding back to his vaqueros, Julio explained to them that they would now herd the cattle back over themselves, and if the Americanos interfered, they were to protect themselves but still push them off the land.

As the ranch hands rode over to begin driving the cattle back, Sam Johnson drew his pistol and shot over the heads of the advancing vaqueros. Within seconds, everyone with a gun was firing, and the cattle were running in all directions. Two of Sam Johnson's cowboys were wounded, as was Sam Johnson, but incredibly no one was killed. That stopped the shooting. The cattle were rounded up by the vaqueros and driven across the river. Julio dressed the wound of Señor Johnson, shot in a leg, even as Sam cursed at him. Then they retreated to their own side of the river and rode away. It was the third such incident involving guns in a month, and the territory was splitting along ethnic lines, each side hardening as the incidents increased.

In Tucson, as in other towns in the area, the Mexican and American populations were also dividing. Once a well-integrated and cooperative community under Spanish control, the shift in legal authority to the Americans was not working very well. It was merely a matter of time before the killing would start.

STAGECOACH TRAVEL WAS just starting up in California, but only mail riders were making the trip from Tucson to San Diego. The Yaqui and Apache Indians had long been serious problems for the Spaniards living in what had very recently become the southwestern United States. Corby and Drego waited in San Diego to accompany a combined freight- and mail-hauling wagon train across the desert to Tucson. It was the only relatively safe way to cross the hostile southwestern desert.

Further to the East, a new mining rush had started into the New Mexico Territory along the Gila River, maybe one hundred miles to the northeast of Tucson, with the discovery of copper. Of course everyone there was now searching for gold too.

As the minors crossed the southern plains, usually by way of the Santa Fe Trail from Independence, Missouri, they often fell prey to large raiding parties of Comanche, Arapaho, Apache, Ute, and Cheyenne. This also was now hostile Indian country.

Fortunately for Corby and Drego, coming from the other direction, the

Whiteman had not yet made much of an impression, but it was understood that a roving band of Apache or Yaqui warriors would probably kill them if they could. The Colt Navy revolver was now available and popular, particularly in Texas, with its .36 caliber, six-shot percussion trigger. Both Drego and Corby purchased one each in San Diego before heading to Tucson. It was lighter than the previous horse pistols and more manageable as a sidearm. They expected they might have to use the new guns before all was said and done.

As they proceeded to Tucson, Drego began reminiscing about this girl and that girl. It made Corby think about Gabrielle more than he wished. He was still a little in shock about the goodbye that had taken place. How was he to know she had any feelings toward him at all? It certainly made Corby re-examine his own feelings. In many ways this trip was well timed, as he sensed he wouldn't have known what to do next with the Countess. Maybe he would gain some insight as he spent time away, and maybe he could get Donovan to pass along some tidbits on what Gabrielle was really thinking. "Cowards die many deaths…" ran through his head, and he had to smile.

Traveling with Drego was a nonstop exercise in listening, as Drego always had much to say. Fortunately, Drego rarely required Corby to answer back, and catnaps were possible without disrupting the one-sided discourse. Corby through osmosis was receiving a history lesson in bits and pieces. He could tell that the widely held manifest destiny beliefs within the United States were not inclusive of the Mexicans and Indians thought to be standing in the way. There should be some kind of legal settlement that could be applied, but barring an acceptable compromise, this was the West. The strong dominated the weak, or in this case, numbers prevailed.

As they traveled East, the landscape was vast and desolate; mile after mile of inhospitable, bare, rocky terrain and sparsely vegetated desert stretched out before them. There were some fields of flowers and many insects, along with lizards, owls, rabbits, and birds. He even saw some elk in the trees by a riverbank, and was surprised that they lived out here. But for the most part, no one would want to spend too much time out here in the sun-drenched open, to his way of thinking. He had to admit, however, that the unbroken vistas had a majesty to them, perhaps that feeling of a last forbidden frontier. The wagon train had gone from water stop to water stop in a somewhat jagged path East.

Most interesting to Corby were the few rivers that cut through the desert, seeming to come from nowhere. Often the water seemed to simply pass by without nourishing the ground around it. In other places a small greenbelt of hardy trees and grasses flanked the waters, and animal life was apparent. It would be interesting to follow one of these rivers and see what game was hidden from view. The mountains looked to be bare, but Drego said some ranges had beautiful forests high up, with snow. That was hard to imagine with the heat and dust they encountered every day. Corby had a hard time understanding why the United States would want to own such land, compared to the equally vast and rich Oregon Territory. Having made a great journey around the periphery of the American West, Corby felt there was more land here than any country could ever use. The long distances between East and West, and the natural barriers like these deserts and the mountain ranges, would begin to separate two sides of the country by more than geography. The westerner had a different set of ambitions and problems than his brother back East. A reliance on one's own abilities was ingrained from the remoteness and daily obstacles faced in the West, and would shape the personality of conflicts for decades to come. A sense of resolution through action permeated the thinking, and what was right was colored by local opinion and shared need. Sometimes that produced a quick and good justice. Sometimes it did not. But resolution rarely tarried.

By the time Corby and the large wagon train arrived in Tucson, the old pueblo was an armed camp. Not only were the Spanish descendants and Americans at each other's throats, but Apaches were now thrown into the mix, as the minors and settlers began moving into their home ranges. The Jacarillo Apache were currently at war with the United States military in Texas, but the larger and harder to find Chiricahua, and the Mescalero Apache, living in the mountain areas of the new southwest, were now systematically attacking the area residents. Corby had the feeling that he certainly had found a pocket of the country full of adventure. The question was, could too much adventure kill you?

35

"**W**HAT IS IT?" HE asked.

"My guess is that is the largest table for two thousand miles in any direction," Gabrielle answered with a smile. They were standing in the new structure atop the palisades facing North with a view out over the straits of the San Francisco Bay. The building would serve as a home and an office for Henri Seurat. A single massive beam of redwood ran across the center of the ceiling of the room, some thirty feet, with a width of five feet by five feet. The ceiling was fifteen feet high, also planked in redwood, leaving an impression of a mammoth cave facing out to the waters below. A series of french doors, with windows above them, opened out to a large terrace that dropped down with steps like a ship's deck below the room to a railing and wooden platform. Several benches had been cut below into the steep hillside for gardens to be planted. Rooms ran off of either side of the large room, and appeared to wrap around and meet the outside decks. It was all done on an imposing scale.

The little man stood behind the huge table looking out at the sparkling waters well below. Having lived in traditional European-style housing all his life, with many little rooms, the openness and scope of his new home would take some getting used to, but Henri was favorably impressed and touched. When Henri finally turned to say something to Gabrielle, she hugged him and said, "Welcome to our new home, Oncle."

Henri was a little overwhelmed. "Well yes, thank you. Now I should review your accounts with you and we should decide which institutions can best handle your liquid assets out here."

"In good time, Oncle, our first priorities are getting you settled in, and my good friend and associate Marshal Donovan has volunteered to show you around the town and arrange for whatever your needs might be. He is waiting down at the St. Montfort Hotel for us now. I should tell you a little something about the Marshal before you meet him."

"Marshal as in U.S. marshal, a law enforcement officer?" Henri queried.

"Ex, but yes; twenty years in St. Louis, then some Territorial work, and here. An extraordinary man, he has become indispensable to me. Why, he and Corby actually probably saved my life!"

"Corby?" Henri was trying to stay up with the story.

Gabrielle rolled her eyes and said, "That is a discussion for another time. Marshal Donovan is now my operational right arm. He absorbs every little detail about people, and then can get them to do whatever he wishes."

"A Lothario type of man?" Henri asked with genuine concern.

Gabrielle laughed and said, "No, no, just the opposite. People feel that they should be doing as he directs from a sense of fair play and responsibility, and perhaps unwillingness to find out what his displeasure might entail. He is a rather stern father figure, with a hint, I think, of Napoleonic will. But he has the common touch, and everyone can relate to him on a personal level easily. I find myself discussing everything with him, and getting back well-thought-out advice. The employees see him as the one in absolute control, the one that will make the decision for them, the constant in their work."

"This is high praise for I assume a fairly uneducated man?" Henri assessed.

"No one is as educated as you, Oncle, but don't sell Marshal Donovan short on his life's education. He regularly surprises me with his grasp of the intricacies of people and business. He has an insight into motivations that I guess you acquire over years of paying attention. It is a little joke between us, when I have to come back and admit he was right again when we disagree."

"Excellent points, my dear. Business is largely understanding people. Some of the most highly schooled friends of your father's and mine were abject failures because they could not master that critical variable. If this Marshal Donovan is all you say he is, giving him a little financial polish could make him even more invaluable," Henri concluded, as much to himself as to Gabrielle.

The two had walked down the hill toward the spectacular front of the hotel.

"Your father would have been so proud of you, Gabrielle," Henri motioned toward the hotel.

"It is my favorite and most time-consuming activity. Yes, father would have liked the St. Montfort," she smiled in remembrance as they walked into the lobby.

A large, rugged man, with piercing black eyes and black hair with white at the temples, strode across the room to meet them. His matter-of-fact greeting was completely genuine, though he towered over the diminutive Frenchman. The two recognized confidence in the gaze of the other, and that, as they say, was that. There was an immediate channel of communication that opened. Gabrielle saw that the two would, with time, bond and should become friends. She excused herself after arranging dinner for the three of them, and left with a good feeling in her heart. That left only one man yet to bring into the family.

DONOVAN GOT A wagon and two men to help bring Mr. Seurat's trunks up from the ship. When they arrived at the ship and began to transfer the baggage, he could not believe his eyes, as item after item came out of the hold. He sent for two more wagons. Mr. Seurat ran the crew on the ship as if he owned it, employing every able-bodied seaman there to lift and haul the cargo. The little man had a presence, from years of power, which was undeniable. Clearly some of the crates now coming out of the ship's belly were for the hotel too. But the majority belonged to the Frenchman.

The captain came over to Donovan and said in a conspiratorial way, "Quite a character, Mr. Seurat. You get to know people who dine with you most nights for several months, you know."

Donovan didn't have anything to say, so the captain continued. "Mr. Seurat may find the West is quite different than the East. We don't have royalty out here."

That remark caused Donovan to look sharply at the man.

"I mean, Mr. Seurat is a fine gentleman. An old man like that has lifelong habits, hard to adjust." Not getting a response, the captain drifted away.

On the way back up the hill to the St. Montfort and Henri's new home, Henri ventured, "I hope that little pissant captain didn't bother you too much, Marshal Donovan."

Coming from the very refined and exceptionally small person sitting beside him, Donovan burst out laughing, but replied, "I have lots of experience not listening to pissants." The conversation picked up from there.

36

LUNCH WITH GABRIELLE HAD not gone as he had envisioned. Whereas she was pleasant and gracious, and genuinely interested in what had happened to him, there was no indication that she cared for him or had any interest in becoming involved with him again. Keeping an eye out for Corby or Donovan was also an unpleasant experience, though Zachary was curious to see, if he ran into them, if they would recognize him. In theory, he had a good cover, as a past acquaintance of Gabrielle's from New Orleans. He had spent a week riding with Donovan's posse, but not much time actually interacting with him. The same could be said of Corby, whom he had never actually had a conversation with, but had run into on several occasions in Fort Boise. The leap to identify a businessman of consequence in San Francisco from Zeke Bridges, a freight wagon hand in the Oregon Territories, might be a hard one to make. However, being high on someone's list of enemies had a way of making you stick out from a crowd. If he could avoid the meeting for a few more years, he would.

For now it was a start. Zachary had passed his story of family troubles back East, forcing him to be gone the last two years. The story allowed him the flexibility of explaining his new finances, and fabricating identities for his business associates. Supposedly he represented the western management of T.D. & Associates, Inc. His interest in the growth of California had persuaded his partners to back him in buying the Logan properties when they suddenly came up for sale. Actually his story went that the Logan gambling houses had been an item of correspondence for some time between the coasts, and really was a done deal contingent on his returning to accept ownership. As far as he could tell, Paul Logan had an interest in returning to Philadelphia; something about his family. He could be wrong, however, as he had come to find out Mr. Logan had left other commitments apparently hanging. Who could know about what was really going on? He felt the story took hold with Gabrielle, who had a poor opinion of Paul Logan to begin with.

Well, time would tell if he could win Gabrielle back. He had every confidence that he could. In the meantime, he had a selection of any of the girls that worked in his parlors and money in his pockets for any one else he might wish to meet. The extra muscle and weight had made him a little more attractive, and as always, he was a good dresser. He could well afford to bide his time and enjoy his tailor-made new life. It would be very easy to skim money off the top in the cash businesses he was running, without anyone the wiser. With the parlors doing as well as they were, it wouldn't take too long before he had a sizable stake of his own again.

Zachary was required to meet with Dan Williams and Roland Leach every week to summarize and tally the week's take in the newly acquired businesses for Günter Targon. Roland Leach would then write up a report and attach the bank receipts and presumably get them to Targon somehow. Dan Williams was the accountant of sorts, and the one Zachary targeted to befriend and work with to get richer. One hand washes the other. He sensed there was an agreeable accommodation they could reach. Leach was the one to be careful around, as his main task seemed to be to watch out for Targon's interests. Several of Leach's hires were spread out in all the businesses as muscle to police the unruly customers, and watch for cheats and thieves. Leach himself was an intimidating, nasty fellow, who had come up the hard way with Targon's smuggling and pirating ships. A confrontation with Mr. Leach was not a smart play, as Zachary schemed how he could control the businesses going forward. Targon was more likely to believe Leach than Williams and himself in a dispute. He had to figure a way to turn Targon on Leach while elevating his own standing with Targon. Getting rid of Leach would be no good if Targon just replaced him. With the possibilities of the motley crew Zachary had seen in Targon's employ, he could do even worse with Leach's successor. No, he would have to think this through very carefully, and keep his fingers light on the till for the most part, until the plan was perfected. Realizing that, Zachary poured himself a drink from Paul Logan's fine collection of liqueurs that he had discovered behind a handsome sliding wall.

He would need to go around to the parlors tonight as always. Perhaps he should invite Williams along and find Dan a girl. Zachary doubted that Dan Williams could get one without paying for one. He smiled as his first strategy started to fall into place. He would pick a pretty girl he could trust to turn poor Dan inside out.

GÜNTER TARGON HAD been keeping an eye on the U.S. naval shipyards at Mare Island. As yet there was little to no naval presence along the coast. However Commodore Perry's recent visit with his fleet to Japan, and the navy's presence in Nicaragua, meant the Pacific Ocean would soon see a police action by the U.S. government. But for now, the regular steamship mail business was shipping gold out of the California goldfields through dangerous waters, and that was just too tempting a target to let pass. With his five ships, he could trap and seize any single commercial vessel sailing or steaming in the local waters, at least for the time being. He knew his boats would be no match for a warship. His time was now.

Lying off of the Baja Peninsula in Mexican waters, near Isla Cedros, Günter removed all names and insignias he could find from his ships. He handpicked his boarding parties, to portray Hispanic nationalities, and he drilled them to say certain phrases that might lead others to suspect Central American politics. He was waiting for the regular steamship from San Francisco to Panama that would be carrying gold bullion, newly minted at the recently opened San Francisco Mint. He expected a few armed guards, but when they saw they were up against five privateers, he expected them to capitulate. The danger was in being recognized. He had thought it through, two ways: first he thought he should capture and sink the vessels, on consecutive runs, hoping the first one would not be missed or suspected of foul play before he got a second shipment. He discarded that, as he believed the disappearance of two shipments in a row would indicate an attack that the navy would have to respond to, and he did not wish to have the U.S. Navy scouring the seas to find him. He also thought it might be unlikely if he stayed in the area for close to two weeks that he would not be spotted by other passing ships. So he settled on his second plan: one attack and run, biding his time to do it again in different waters with different tactics some other time. He would only get one gold shipment, but it was safer and smarter. However, he did realize he was now taking on a government, not just individuals or companies. The risks were inherently higher, but so were the rewards. The day the first warship slid down the way into the bay from the Mare Island facility, he had decided, was the day he permanently sailed away from California. He had two or three years left on the high seas off the California coast. He would plan accordingly, for all his enterprises.

The Pacific Mail Steamship Company packet ship had gotten off to a late start, and then had run into high seas. She was a half day late on her scheduled run as she neared Targon's drifting fleet. As such, it was evening when she was spotted, throwing a wrench into Targon's well laid out plans. He had expected a daytime seizure, where the steamship would easily see its predicament and stop. As it was she kept on at full steam and nearly passed the less than vigilant pirate fleet, which fortunately had some good wind to assist in overhauling her. A couple of shots across her bow and the convergence of the five ships finally got her to heave to, but not before Günter had developed a bad temper. He allowed Ishka to accompany the boarding crews to help frighten the steamship's captain into cooperating.

While he was keeping a low profile and waiting for the gold to be sent over to his ship, a scuffle broke out on the steamship. That apparently led his men to feel justified in killing many of the passengers and crew. Targon himself then had to take charge. Once the steamship and passengers had been pillaged, he had no choice but to order it sunk with all who remained on board. At least Ishka came back happy, covered in blood. Perhaps the rough seas would be a sufficient suspect in the ship's disappearance. Targon then set sail to the West to circle the shipping lanes and return North.

However, two survived in the dark waters of the Pacific current and floated with the remnants of the sunken steamship, until a Mexican fishing boat picked them up some ten hours later the next morning. One was a young officer in the mailboat company and the other was the young son of an officer in the U.S. Army at the Presidio, San Francisco. His mother, however, who had been taking him back to New York for military school, perished in the disaster.

37

CAPTAIN FARMER'S ORDERS HAD two main directives: Survey the lands to the northeast of Fort Hall, and the headwaters of the Yellowstone River; identify a strategic position for a potential fort on the perimeter of Blackfoot, Crow, and Shoshone lands. Second, try to reach an alliance with the Shoshone tribes frequenting the Fort Hall, Fort Boise territory to safeguard the Oregon Trail and to act as guides for the U.S. Army should the other indigenous tribes cause trouble.

The captain knew they meant when the other indigenous tribes caused trouble. The recent flair ups of the Plains tribes were a precursor to every Indian Nation that would inevitably rub up against the onslaught of the Western migration. Other gold rushes would come, as would ranchers and farmers, towns, and then cities. The railroads were stretching West, and once the Indians were deemed pacified, the flood gates would open further. The magnificent wilderness that seemed to stretch on forever would permanently change. Captain Farmer was ambivalent when it came to the question of the Indians. It often depended on which Indians were being talked about and what they were doing. He was struck by the simple majesty of a scene such as he had witnessed in the Yellowstone country, where a war party of Blackfoot Indians had parlayed with Lame Elk and Waushaute. The colorful Indian ponies, and the various ornaments, feathers, and weapons on the warriors, against the larger-than-life Grand Tetons, Absaroka, and Madison ranges, and the beautiful Yellowstone Lake and River would leave an indelible picture in his mind forever. But he had also seen the wanton killing and squalid poverty that many Indians seemed to accept as a way of life. He could not fully assimilate the apparent inconsistencies, as he saw them, with the reverence for the world of nature the Indians professed and the less than Christian regard for the sanctity of human life. As an educated officer of the United States Army, he was aware of the long and less than illustrious history of man's inhumanity to man over the centuries, and he knew of the different values in each society, having studied specifically the warrior societies of past and present day. But when he saw the suffering of the women and children, and what seemed to be the callous attitude of the Indian men, his temper would rise.

His wife and daughter were somewhere back East, having eschewed the life of the military. Episodes among the Indians in particular where he witnessed unnecessary brutality toward children in his opinion, affected him the most and triggered his feelings over his own loss of his daughter. Perhaps that is why he was drawn to Lame Elk and Katy. He found that he wanted to spend more time with the unusual pair, and in time, he wrangled a fishing trip with the two of them right down in front of the fort on the Snake River.

Lame Elk sensed early on that the white captain missed his child or children, as he himself did. Katy played a therapeutic role for both men, and for a girl who had lost her father, she now had three men, including her new adopted father, Dr. Lemmins, to fog her loss and memory. The captain and Lame Elk began to slowly develop a trust between them, first based on their mutual treatment of the young girl, and then as Captain Farmer began to provide provisions to the People, per his orders to win over the local tribes.

This was a time of peace for the residents around Fort Hall. The Shoshone fallback had left a buffer zone between them and the Blackfoot. It had been a much-needed time for healing with Lame Elk's people. They turned to him for assurance and guidance, especially now that they were moving back into their old hunting grounds. Even though Lame Elk had not asked for the leadership role with his tribe, he had accepted it and, as the years started to pass, became more comfortable and assured in his role. Waushaute, while retaining authority over a larger group, the Lemhi, naturally and comfortably deferred to Lame Elk on the biggest issues for both branches of the Shoshone tribe. The Yellowstone Shoshone and Lemhi Shoshone of Round Valley were now ostensibly one tribe, with one Council, living in the Yellowstone Valley in the Fall, Winter, and Spring, and rendezvousing with the Bannock and other various Shoshones that camped by Fort Hall in the summer. The new Yellowstone Shoshone, as they preferred to call themselves, were prospering, and Lame Elk had taken another wife. Beside the trade at Fort Hall in the summer, and the small provisions Captain Farmer gave the Shoshone to retain their friendship, the Shoshone had been fortunate that the Blackfoot had kept their peace, and the Crows were busy with the Sioux and Blackfoot. The Shoshone under Lame Elk were content to live in peace and prosper, with an occasional raid into Nez Pierce and Flathead territories for the young men, and to gather fresh breeding stock for their ponies.

But Lame Elk was restless. He preferred being alone at times and exploring the mountains. He wanted to stay sharper than he had been when the Blackfoot had driven the Shoshone out of the Yellowstone. He believed the Creator had a plan for him that required he stay strong and alert. He practiced his tracking and fighting skills more now than as a young man. To do this he would go into the mountains alone, sometimes going for days without eating, or pushing his endurance climbing up the tallest peaks. He practiced with the bow and the lance, the club and the knife. He rode his pony hard and shot his rifle leaning under the pony's neck, as he had seen the Crows do. He scouted near and far, twice spying on the Blackfoot camp, where it remained to the north by the lake except in winter. Once he saw the White-man's big black horse that he had stolen and ridden briefly. It was still a very fine, strong-looking stallion, but well guarded. He watched the Blackfoot chief, Two Horns, and recognized the warrior Blue Heron from the meeting by the Yellowstone Lake. The Blackfoot were growing in numbers too. Lame Elk thought that the camp size had spread out along the lakeshore more on both sides of the camp he had seen four years earlier. They would be a for-midable enemy, but the Shoshone would be better prepared should anyone try to drive them out again. The last time he visited the Blackfoot camp, he couldn't resist, and snuck into the camp in the early hours before dawn, leav-ing his arrow sticking in the ground in front of Two Horns's teepee. He still could not get near the black horse however, as it was much better guarded. He did not want to kill to get it, so he left after leaving his reminder that Blackhand was watching and as elusive as ever.

Two Horns took the arrow to the council meeting. He passed it around.

"What does it mean?" asked Buffalo Robe, now really showing his age.

Blue Heron, a new member to the Council, suggested, "Maybe he is re-minding us that we have not returned his horse and he still wants it."

"I'm sure he still wants Messenger," Two Horns said, referring to his prize horse, "but that is not why he left the arrow. He wants us to know that he is watching us, should we wish to attack his people again, and that he is not afraid."

"The Shoshone dog should be caught and killed," said Running Bird, one of the elders.

"No, Blackhand could have killed and escaped if he had wanted. He is truly a great warrior and is to be respected," stated Two Horns.

"He spoke of Red Horses as a great warrior," added Blue Heron. "He is a man of courage and honor."

"Yes, courage and honor," said Buffalo Robe, "but a danger to the Black-foot too. We should never forget what Crooked Claws did to the Shoshone. He would kill us if he could."

"Maybe, but it shows he is a wise chief too, not to bring war on his people over his own loss," Two Horns said. "If we had not killed so many of his people, he would have made a great ally against the Crows. We should not anger the Yellowstone Shoshone, as long as the Crows continue to raid on our summer camps. And if Blackhand is friends with the Whitemen, we should be careful not to start a fight with a new enemy. Let the Lakota deal with the Whiteman."

There was a general nodding of heads around the fire. The peace had been good for the Blackfoot too, but lately the Crow had shown a storm was coming. Two Horns knew his young warriors were anxious to test their mettle.

"And I will keep the big black horse," added Two Horns.

38

E L RANCHO DE EL Viento del Norte was laid out as a fort, with a ten-foot-tall wall of wood and adobe surrounding the entire complex. A catwalk ran around the inside of the wall from which the defenders could fire down on the attackers. One side of the compound held the cabins of the vaqueros and their families and the working outbuildings such as the blacksmith and stables, and the other side housed the hacienda of Don Sebastián. The Spanish descendants had retreated within the walls many times over the centuries to fight off attacking Apaches. The hostile Indians were the main reason behind the sparse population, even more so than the surrounding desert terrain.

The hacienda was a stones throw away from the San Pedro River at a spot where there was an underground spring resupplying the river. The river came North out of Sonora, Mexico, and had a year-round flow, but it could recede down to a trickle at times. Willows and cottonwoods stood down by the river's water hole, while ash and a walnut grove were nearby. Closer to the walls of the settlement, the vegetation thinned, with mesquite trees and grass running up to about fifty yards from the wall. It was obvious that all plant life was routinely tilled over and removed for the last fifty yards up to the wall. The low hills behind the walls were lightly covered with various desert scrubs, such as acacia and creosote.

Swinging down from his horse and stepping into the courtyard of the hacienda of Don Sebastián, Corby brushed as much of the dust off of him as he could. The courtyard was an oasis in the desert, with large palm trees, probably brought from Mexico, mixed in with a riot of colors; flowers and vines covered the inner walls, bright blue and white tiles were embedded in a large water fountain and trough, and a stained-glass window dominated a small family church facing inward as did all the buildings within the inner courtyard. An overhanging trellis, also covered with vines and small yellow flowers Corby had not seen before, stood in front of the larger pillars supporting the entrance to the main house that Drego now was walking toward. Corby followed him into the shade of an open-doored foyer with its large tiled floor, and its brick covered by adobe walls. The brick could be seen as part of the decoration on the inside, along with exposed beams and many more indoor plants. Running down a stairs against one wall were large woven tapestries of green and red, on a light brown background that matched the adobe color. It was a very cheerful and light effect for so large a room.

Drego stopped and waited there, hat in hand, so Corby did the same. Then a young and very pretty Spanish girl, maybe seventeen, ran out of an adjoining room and threw herself into Drego's arms, talking a mile a minute, and calling him "Juanito." Drego turned to introduce his half sister, Maria, Elena, Alonso-Martinez de Santarosilla.

The girl shyly took his hand and curtsied, speaking in good English. "Señor Corby, welcome to the Northwind Ranch. My father will be very pleased to meet you. May I offer you some wine?"

"Be careful, my friend." Drego laughed. "We used to call her 'La Tigresa' as a child. Now that Maria ees grown up, I fear she may be more dangerous than that."

The girl flashed him a mock angry look, ignored him, and took Corby's arm, escorting him to a table and chair. She then left to get the wine. As she exited, a small, round man in an ornate beaded black shirt came into the room from an archway on the other end of the room. Drego and Corby stood up, and Drego took the man's hand and kissed it, greeting him as 'Don Sebastian.' The man embraced Drego, saying something in Spanish that Corby could not really hear. He then turned to Corby and extended his hand.

"Señor Corby, it is so good of you to come and help us. Juan has told us much about you in his infrequent letters, and I am only sorry that you have to meet us under such trying circumstances."

He then sat down heavily and began to explain to the two travelers in detail what was taking place at the current time. Maria brought in a carafe of wine and three glasses, smiled at Corby, and left.

The Don was set to ride into Tucson the next day to meet with the local authorities and several American ranchers to try and head off further conflicts, but he had little faith that the talks would be successful, as the two sides were sticking closely to intractable positions. This was the desert after all, and water was the issue. Edible grasses stayed very close to water supplies and were limited in the best years. Overgrazing could cause serious long-term shortages of the grasses, and the Don had seen it before. The Americans were desperate to grow their herds, but did not seem to understand the large acreage necessary to support a single steer on these lands. Their position was for an open range, first come first served; everyone would compete to find the available resources, which they thought were more than they truly were. The Don had tried to explain the desert to them, but they believed he was simply hoarding the best lands. In fact, he did have the best lands on the thin corridor along the river, as his ancestors had carefully surveyed the area before requesting their entitlement. But the explosion in people passing through was more than the land could sustain. There were no sweeping grasslands, as on the Plains, or snowcapped mountains with reservoirs of water. There was very little rain, which mostly ran off when it came, as the soils were too sandy to retain it. The San Pedro River did not carry the same volume as the larger Santa Cruz River did down by Tucson. Also the land had many wild cattle left by previous Spanish settlers who had chosen to return to Mexico or had been killed or driven off by the Apaches. Cattle drives had increased both from Mexico and Texas, in an attempt to capitalize on California's need for beef, and the recent mining influx to the North. Don Sebastián felt besieged. He had been reasonable but the onslaught had just continued. He had finally attempted to stop the trespassing, and the troubles escalated. Still waiting for a government or court ruling on his ownership of the land, he had not wanted to antagonize the Americans before the ruling, but he also could not stand by and watch his properties become overrun by prospectors and ranchers. Finally he had decided to fight a defensive action, turning away those who illegally were caught trespassing, but pushing it no further. What good would come from winning the court battle but losing the land to depredation or facing a criminal trial? He was on the proverbial horns of a dilemma. He was most fearful for the safety of his people, and that was why he had written Drego to come home.

After the long discussion, Don Sebastián apologized profusely for not allowing the men to wash up first, and led them to a neat cabin where they could change for dinner, and sleep during their stay.

"The Don has grown old these last few years," Drego said as he unpacked. "He does not look happy or healthy."

"This sounds like something the law should be working on. I'm going to write Marshal Donovan. Maybe he can tell us how to deal with the government," said Corby. He felt embarrassed that the Americans were not holding up their end of the law. He also wanted to hear about Gabrielle. Writing this letter would test his skill at crafting a carefully worded plea for feedback on the Countess. Describing the legal and local problems of the Don would help to disguise his other purpose.

DON SEBASTIÁN AND ten other riders, including Corby, Drego, his lawyer, and his foreman, Julio Sánchez, rode into Tucson the next morning. The town now had a few over six hundred souls, living in and around it on the banks of the Santa Cruz River. Several Mexicans were fishing in the river as they passed and took off their sombreros to nod in respect to Don Sebastián as he passed. Don Sebastián returned each of their salutes by nodding back, and saying hello by name to others. They rode into the dusty town and stopped outside of a small building that said "Gavin Dagget, Justice of the Peace, Land Office, Law Office, Post Office." A small crowd of Americans was already there, including Sam Johnson, still with a cane. No "good mornings" were exchanged, and the two parties went inside.

Gavin Dagget greeted everyone, and the main principals sat around a table for six. Everyone else was obliged to stand against the wall. Dagget began by saying, "Everyone here has come out of good will to try and resolve a conflict that has grown to threaten our peace here in Tucson. Let me start by explaining the legal bind we are all in. We all know that the United States just bought this territory as part of the Gadsden Purchase last Spring. As such, we are part of Dona Ana County, in the Territory of New Mexico for the time being, until a territorial government is set up here, in what is to be called Arizona. That's right, we are to be called Arizona. Got a letter right here from the county seat in New Mexico. Now we all know that a county seat several hundred miles away won't work for us, and the United States hasn't even taken formal military possession of the territory yet. So we are on our own for a while. We got Mark over there acting as a constable, but he can't do it alone.

"The way this is supposed to work is, the government sends in troops, and land claims and mining claims are registered with a surveyor-general appointed by the Congress of the United States. The Congress is also supposed to organize a territorial government, to handle civil disputes like these. Everyone following me so far?"

There was a general murmur of understanding and agreement.

"Now I understand that Don Sebastián, the Ortega family, and others have sent documentations of their claims to ownership in the area to Washington, right?"

Señor Francisco Morales, who had come up from Sonora, Mexico, to represent Don Sebastián and the other Spanish landowners, said, "As per the instructions of the government of the United States, we have submitted credentials and copies of documents to the government for verification. As citizens of the United States, we are awaiting their formal registration process as we speak. We fully anticipate legal compliance and assurance any month now."

"Them old maps ain't good no more. This is U.S. territory now. The Mexicans need to get over to the Mexico side," Sam Johnson burst out. He got several endorsements from the Americans standing against the wall.

"If we are to get a civil government down here, we have got to show we are law-abiding citizens. The courts will decide, not you, Sam Johnson, or any of us here today," said Gavin Dagget forcefully. "We are here today, as civilized people to find a way to cool down before someone gets hurt!"

"If that's so, then why did Don Sebastián bring in hired guns?" asked Sam Johnson, pointing to Corby and Drego. "We heard tell that one of them is a killer-for-hire."

Everyone looked at Corby. He tried to keep a neutral face, but he was squirming on the inside.

"This is my son, Juan. Many of you know that. And this is his friend, Señor Corby. I am not paying them. They have come to help me protect our home, from people like you Sam Johnson, who think you can go anywhere you like," Don Sebastián answered with some temper.

"This here is the United States. We don't believe in kings and queens, telling us where we can't go. You best learn that now. You're no longer running things around here," countered Sam Johnson.

"Don Sebastián's people settled here over a hundred years ago, fought off the Apaches, and founded this town. The Don has been a good neighbor to everyone, and that was when we were guests in his country. You've got no call to act this way, Sam. The government will decide on the land, and we should work on getting along until then," snapped Dagget.

"I can see this meeting was a waste of time," said Sam Johnson, standing up. "I ain't gonna let my cattle die while good grazing land goes unused, I can promise you that." He then headed out the door, and about half the Americans followed him out.

"The man's a hothead," said Gavin Dagget. "He couldn't stay long enough to hear what Don Sebastián is willing to concede until this land dispute is over. The rest of you should know that Don Sebastián will work with you, on a schedule, one at a time, to graze different sections of the range, so as not to overgraze and destroy any of it, much in the way the ranchos have been doing it for centuries down here."

The remaining men quickly sat down in the open chairs, eager to listen to the Don's plan.

Drego and Corby drifted off, outside to escape the hot quarters inside. They noticed the men who had left the meeting were milling about across the street. On seeing the two, the men disbanded, clearly upset.

"Looks like somebody is spoiling for a fight," noted Corby. He then remembered to go back inside to post his letter.

39

THE NEWS RACED THROUGH the city. South American pirates had apparently sunk the *Fairfield*, and mail service by steamship had been suspended indefinitely. Description of the brutal attack by the two survivors riveted the city's readers with new fears. The particularly horrific account of a knife-wielding savage, crazed and grinning as he slashed at the helpless passengers, brought revulsion and anger. A call for U.S. troops was made in the morning papers, and the naval commander at the Mare Island shipyard vowed to step up work, while requesting that more effort be put forward on Fort Point, the new project just under construction to guard the bay.

In point of fact, the United States had no forts along the West Coast, and no naval vessels. The small army presence in the Presidio (no more than an army camp) at San Francisco would not be adequate to defend against any larger-scale invasion. California was very vulnerable to attack, and the sinking of the mail packet ship drove the point home hard.

New plans for Fort Point required thirty-six-foot-thick walls and over two hundred guns. The cliff it was being built into was blasted almost down to water level to allow the lowest tier of artillery to fire across the water and ricochet off the surface into ships at the waterline. Accuracy of distance in firing would be far less important than mere directional firing, giving the batteries an enormous advantage over enemy ships. But it was estimated that it would take several more years to complete the fort, particularly since it was to be the premier fortification on the West Coast. Construction was begun on batteries on the other side of the Golden Gate Straits, across from Fort Point, and also on Alcatraz Island, with both a north and south battery. Thus any ships attempting to run away from the guns on one side of the bay would be forced to approach the guns on the other, while facing the batteries ahead on Alcatraz. The plan included that the eventual naval fleet stationed there would meet any opposing fleet under the cover of the fort guns, as the bay was wide enough to afford plenty of maneuvering. With the swift tides and strong winds in the bay, enemy ships might try to run past the guns, but the triangular placements of the fortifications, along with the water level artillery, would make for a formidable defense.

As of now, however, the citizens of San Francisco were somewhat justified in their new paranoia. Having fought local crime waves and fires and earthquakes, the city could envision an invading force from Central America, with little or no help from Uncle Sam.

There was some doubt in Zachary's mind as to who had sunk the mail ship. The question was, was there a way to take advantage of the situation. It would be unlikely that Targon would reappear in the Bay Area for some time if he were the attacker. Lifting a little more from the daily take was a forgone conclusion. Dan Williams had turned out to be putty in his hands, and together they were now skimming about 10 percent of the profits, 7 percent for Zachary and 3 percent for Williams. Zachary was also splitting the money and gifts Williams was giving to Julie, his hand-picked girlfriend for Dan. He had set up a couple of high-stakes card games that were his own, and he had begun to organize a gentleman's escort service, with the higher-end prostitutes in Targon's gambling parlors, squeezing out the assorted pimps and boyfriends as necessary, with the leverage of better money, and the muscle he now employed. But there was so much more, and he watched every week as Roland Leach left with the large sums of gambling profits to place in the coffers of Targon's front companies or wherever it went. The man wasn't spending it as far as he could tell, leaving him to wonder how much money Targon had from years of looting and other nefarious activities. And were did he take it? Was he seriously burying it, as some speculated? What a man with vision could do with money like that. He decided he should hire a detective to trail Roland Leach. It was enough distraction to send him into a melancholy mood, so he sent down stairs for Julie to come up for an hour or so.

GÜNTER WAS FIT to be tied. He had just read the newspaper brought over from the city. Already aware of the details of the *Fairfield*'s destruction, and his men's wanton killings, the story about Ishka worried him the most. Someone would make the link through the Indian to him, even while the papers were currently going with his "Spanish pirates" ploy. It was possible now the United States would be sending a squadron of warships out to take care of the pirate problem. There were enough people very familiar with his activities to point them in his direction, even if they couldn't pin the blame on him for the mail packet ship. He couldn't pretend to be a whaling fleet, or a freight line, or any other respectable occupation with the men and ships he had. His ships were fitted to raid and plunder. They could run with any sailing the Pacific, unless of course there was no wind. The navy could be sending out heavy cruisers with steam engines to supplement their sailing vessels. They would cordon off his escape once they found him, and blow him out of the water. Relocation plans might have to be stepped up, or he would have to retire to land. It was a dilemma that had been running through his mind for several years now, and just because two survivors had escaped his botched South American raid, he would possibly have to make a decision sooner rather than later. It had been simple enough: steal the gold and escape as Spanish pirates, or having made the mistake of killing some passengers, complete the job by killing them all, and scuttling the ship. His men had failed on both accounts.

Sitting at anchor in Half Moon Bay, he reviewed his options. A great deal of money was piling up from his new gambling enterprises. That son of a bitch Logan had been a damned good businessman. He already had plenty of money to live in style wherever he wished, but lying on a beach and getting fat and old had little appeal for him. Maybe he could reinvent himself and return to the Old World, but as what? Some fancy baron dressed in stockings? No, there were only two real possibilities, as he saw them. He could find new coasts, or islands to ply his trade, such as Hawaii or Argentina, and convince his crews to do the same, or he could make changes here that would allow him to escape the wrath of the navy, and continue with the lines he already had in the water. That would probably mean having to live ashore and disperse his ships, or even sell a couple of them. But he could continue to coerce the small ports along the coast through his network of agents while reaping the benefits of the Logan businesses. Maybe spending a lot of money would be something he would enjoy after a while. But to lose the sea... He closed his eyes in disgust and frustration. Someone would have to pay for the debacle of the sinking of the mail ship. It had been a long time since he had keelhauled anyone.

THE SINKING OF the *Fairfield* had a disastrous effect on Stewart Bertram's latest endeavor to raise capital for his beleaguered steamship line. Already in deeper than he ever anticipated, having purchased more ownership in order to keep the project going forward, the disappearance of Paul Logan, and the horrendous shipyard fire, had put a taint on the company. Few investors were willing to discuss the opportunity, let alone fund it. Now the pirate attack had scared the banks, investors, and creditors alike. Stewart could feel the knot in his stomach tighten as he realized, once again, the consequences of the company going under. As the majority shareholder, having had to purchase Logan's shares when Logan had not been around for the next several capital calls and had defaulted, Stewart was the target for any lawsuit that came from noncompletion of the project. He had to spread his liability, even if it meant selling some of his shares for less than he had recently paid to acquire them. The idea of being hounded by contractors and investors, and the huge financial loss were making him lose sleep nightly. Swallowing his pride, he would have to try going to the Countess again, hat in hand, and offer her a great deal. There was no other possibility left that could right this ship. The arrival of the little financier, the Frenchman, Seurat, might help to change her position. It was rumored that Seurat was well connected to financial institutions and politicians back East, and had a long history of investing well of his own. Surely he would be able to see the opportunity the young, inexperienced Countess wasn't capable of appreciating.

HENRI SEURAT WAS instructing Donovan on how to crab. They were in a small boat in the marshy tidal waters south of the city. Donovan had taken his new friend duck hunting earlier in the morning, and Henri was returning the favor with great patience as he gently pulled the crabline up toward the boat where Donovan had been instructed to scoop the net under the crabs when they got close to the surface. Donovan had been too anxious the first time and the crabs had jumped off before he could net them. Henri had reemphasized the need for more stealth, and they were trying it again. The large grayish crabs would be a good complement to the ducks. Among other things, Henri was an accomplished cook. He had promised Gabrielle and Donovan a tasty meal prepared as only he could, should they be successful in bringing home the crabs and ducks.

It was a delightful day on the water, and the waterfowl were there in enormous numbers. Had Donovan wished to keep shooting, he could have filled the boat. As it was, they would have all the catch they would need by midmorning, if he could master the net.

"So this Corby is a good match for my little Gabrielle?" Henri was asking.

"Let's just say that he has her intrigued, as he is one man she has not been able to ride over."

"Ah, yes, her papa was concerned that things came too easily for her. She has a strong will," said Henri.

"Our princess has more than a strong will, Henri," Donovan ventured. "She scares the hell out of most of the men she meets. They have never experienced a woman with her personality and power. Kind of like meeting a real czarina, and you have on your boots with holes in them."

Henri laughed. "You have a unique way of making a point, Marshal. But I see the problem too, particularly out here. Gabrielle will need a balance in her life at some point, someone to share with."

"Here we are, two old bachelors, plotting a romance for a young woman. Does this strike you as perhaps a forgone failure?" asked Donovan.

Henri, paused before answering. "We two old bachelors are all she's got. Who better to play Cupid than those who really care? I would not wish to see her make another mistake, such as Charles Loucheur."

Donovan eased the net under the two crabs feasting on the hunk of meat, and pulled them up. Henri shook them into a bucket.

"A few more, my friend, and Henri will serve you the best meal you have ever had in your life."

40

"**W**E HAVE A MISSION of mercy to perform today, my friend," said Drego when the two got up one morning a few days after the meeting in Tucson. "We are to escort La Señora Mercedes and Maria to Tucson for a meeting with the Padre and whatever else they intend to do in town. Since La Señora ees not likely to speak to me, you will carry a heavy burden today, amigo."

"From what I've seen of people moving between places out here, I gather we will have a couple more men with us," Corby said hopefully.

"Si, that is true, but you are the gringo who has captured her daughter's eye. This will be most entertaining, I think" Drego grinned.

"Who, little Maria? She's only fourteen or fifteen years old!" protested Corby.

"Seventeen, and just the age to be married. You could do a lot worse, amigo. She ees *muy mona, muy guapa,* sí?" Seeing that Corby's Spanish was overtested, he translated. "She ees a beautiful girl. A lot of spirit."

Corby just rolled his eyes. It did sound like a long day at that.

With the Apaches liable to attack anywhere, anytime, and the American ranchers stirred up, Don Sebastián wasn't taking any chances when his people left the compound. Corby had come to understand that this was the way they had always had to live. Only a couple of years ago the Apache had attacked Tucson in force in the middle of the night, sneaking right into the town before the alarm was sounded. The people had fled into the Presidio there with its twelve-foot-high walls in order to beat back the attack, but many women and children had been killed. Retaliatory raids had been going back and forth between the Spaniards and the Apache for hundreds of years around here. Drego's people were expecting something soon, having seen Apache scouts in the area, and hearing of an attack to the North on a group of miners traveling along the Gila River.

After breakfast, the group assembled in the courtyard where four more vaqueros were waiting with a wagon ready to take the women to town. Three other women were sitting in the back of the wagon, along with a small boy. There was much talking and arranging of positions before the Señora indicated she was ready to go. One of the vaqueros got up on the front bench to drive the team. A second bench was for the Señora and Señorita de Santarosillas, with their parasols. Drego and Corby rode on either side of the wagon, and the three remaining riders took positions, two in front and one in back. The other women and the boy sat down in the bed of the wagon. Out on the road, Corby and Drego moved up to just in front of the wagon in order to stay on the road. Corby could tell that the men were very vigilant.

"You are wondering why we are taking this trip if everyone ees so concerned about los Indios?" said Drego. "You must remember that it ees always this way. The women just add a little more danger."

Corby didn't answer as he surveyed the landscape. The road cut through several small canyons, ideal for ambushes. The lead vaqueros would ride farther ahead and sometimes stand sentry above if the opportunity presented itself. It was all a little bit nerve-racking to be constantly expecting an attack, so when they were about to pull out into more open countryside, there was an audible sigh of relief from everyone.

The Apaches appeared out of nowhere. As if they had sprung out of the ground, they came running, yelling, and shooting arrows from all sides at the wagon. The vaquero driving the team swept his arm backwards instructing the women on the benches to get down in the wagon. About then he took an arrow in the chest and slumped over sideways. On quick reconnaissance, Corby guessed that there were more than a dozen Indians bearing down on the wagon. Drego had grabbed the wagon team from his horse and swung to the ground to control them. The two lead riders came racing back to the wagon, and Corby found himself jumping into the wagon on top of the women, shooting as he went. The Apaches stopped about twenty yards from the wagon to pour in their fire of rifle shots and arrows. The majority of the attacking Indians were clustered on one side of the wagon, and Corby unloaded his gun into the group with a devastating effect. He was pulling the trigger on an empty gun when Drego grabbed his arm and gave him his own revolver. The second barrage from Corby sent the Apaches into retreat, and Corby realized for the first time that he had two arrows sticking in him as he fell down on top of the women. He could hear the sound of more rifle fire before he passed out.

The Apaches retreated in orderly fashion, helping those they could that were injured. As quickly as it had started, it ended. Drego paused to reload the two revolvers, sticking Corby's gun in his belt, vowing to persuade Don Sebastián to buy more revolvers for his vaqueros. The two revolvers had surprised both the Apaches and the vaqueros with their deadly repeat fire. The

Apaches had lost half their raiding party in a couple of minutes, and would not dare attack again. Drego dispatched one rider on to Tucson for the doctor, collected and distributed rifles to all the women in the wagon, and turned the wagon around with his lone remaining escort and headed back to the hacienda, as it was much closer. The women had applied a tourniquet on Corby's leg and stopped up the chest wound as well as they could. He lay in Maria's lap. The women also shared the wagon with two dead vaqueros.

HE COULD SEE the faces of the Apache Indians as they fired at him. They were so different from the Indians he had come to know in the Northwest Territories. Other than the white paint on their faces, these Indians where a perfect blend with the background colors around them. No feathers and bright beads, or prancing ponies and shining weapons like the Blackfoot and Crow. These were guerrilla fighters. Now you see them, now you don't. They wore headbands to tie back their hair, some had bandanas over their heads, but they all looked similar in dress, and color. One was about to shoot him when he woke up with a start and a grimace of pain. He was sweating and groaning. Someone put a wet rag on his head and he passed out again.

"HEY, COMPADRE, YOU gonna spend the Winter in bed?" asked Drego in sarcastic humor.

"*Vete! Que el hombre necesita dormir,*" Maria said sharply to her half brother.

"I'll come back when 'La Tigresa' is not guarding you, amigo," Drego said as Maria pushed him out of the room.

Corby found himself in a bed somewhere inside the hacienda. There were bandages loosely wrapped around his chest, and his left leg throbbed with a dull and constant pain. Maria returned to a chair alongside the bed and pressed a cup of bitter-tasting liquid to his lips.

"The doctor says you should drink this when you can. All of it," she said, tipping the cup up over his mild negative reaction. "You will need to rest here for some time, maybe two months. I will take care of you."

Corby tried to talk but his mouth was dry and his head started to spin.

"Shhh. You are to sleep as much as possible," she said, pressing her finger against his lips. She smiled at him as he faded back into a deep sleep.

He woke up again some time in the night, feeling more alert, but still very weak. He lifted his head briefly, and then let it fall back down on the pillow.

Slowly he moved his right hand over his chest, gently examining the extent of his bandages. He was surprised to find he was naked except for the bandages. There was a bandage he thought on his left leg, but he couldn't reach it as his left arm was bound up in a sling. Then he realized that there was a jar between his legs, and almost immediately he felt a need to use it. Well, this was rather embarrassing. Suddenly, Maria being seventeen didn't feel like a child. He lay awake in the soft bed listening to the night sounds outside the partially opened window. A sense of being outside his own life came to him, and the string of events that had brought him to this moment seemed unlikely in retrospect. He breathed in deeply, and immediately felt a sharp pain. Breathing shallower, he tasted the air, smelled the room, and appreciated the life flowing through his body. His previous concerns seemed small and unimportant as he enjoyed the night breeze sneaking in through the window. He fell back asleep with a contentment he had rarely felt before.

In the morning after Maria had washed his face and fed him some sort of mush, Don Sebastián, his wife, and Drego visited him.

"Good morning, Señor Corby," said Don Sebastián. "We have all been waiting to greet you for some days now."

Señora de Santarosilla bent over and squeezed his hand. "You have been sent by God, and I wish to thank you for saving my daughter and our people from a horrible death. We will be eternally grateful young man and we wish you a safe trip back to California."

"*Madre de Dios, Mercedes! Este hombre...* Never mind. What my wife means to say is you will be an honored guest at our home as long as you can stay with us. I can never repay what you have done for my family and me. Now, it is important that you rest and recover your strength. Juan, do not keep Señor Corby awake for long." Don Sebastián and his wife left the room arguing in Spanish.

"Señor Corby is not strong enough to talk yet, Juan. You must let him rest," insisted Maria.

"I will not ask him to talk, but he probably wishes to know what is going on, sí?" said Drego.

Maria looked at Corby, who indicated that he would indeed like to be filled in, so Maria sighed and said, "All right, but I will be back in five minutos, comprende?" and she left.

"To be such a hero, ooeee!" mocked Drego with a big smile. "Think of the women we will be able to impress."

Corby frowned and cocked his head at his body. "How bad?" he managed to croak.

"Well, let's see," began Drego. "You took an arrow in your chest, just missed killing you by an inch, the doctor says. Another went through your leg. It was a bleeder, big mess all over the women. The one in your chest they had to cut out. Hit a rib and broke it, or you would be coughing up blood now. You will have a big scar to show the women as the arrow skidded across your chest, until it hit the rib. Very lucky. They say you will be in pain for a while, particularly if you breathe deep. A couple of months for the rib to heal. The leg, they are most concerned for infection, but I think Maria changes your dressings more than necessary to look at your manhood. Now that you are conscious, we will get you some big diapers to wear."

It was a lot of information for Corby to take in, but the assessment left him feeling less anxious for himself.

"How did it end?" Corby asked.

"The fight? It was magnifico. You killed five Indios, and we got two more. Those revolvers made the big difference. All the vaqueros want to buy them now. I was magnifico, too. I jumped down from my horse onto the wagon team and wrestled them to a stop before they ran away killing all the women, and I gave you my gun just in time to stop the Indios from murdering the women, and I rallied the vaqueros to drive away the rest of the Indios when you went down."

Corby had to smile at Drego's self-glorification, and then asked, "Anyone die?"

"Sí, poor Diego who was driving the wagon, and Pepe who was trailing the wagon, but none of the women or the boy. They will wish to thank you when you are better. Here comes 'La Tigresa' to change your bandages again I think." Drego stood up with a broad smile with his hands up signaling to Maria that he would not fight going. "Be gentle with the poor gringo, chica. They don't have man-eating tigers where he comes from."

Maria flushed, and then looked like she was about to strangle Drego, before composing herself, and saying, "It is time to change your bandages, señor.

41

THE FIRST SNOWS WERE covering the high blue peaks, and the nights were now crisp and cold. You could hear the elk bugle in the surrounding forests as the rut began. This was Lame Elk's favorite hunting time. The Yellowstone Shoshone had fully returned to their hunting and camping grounds at the headwaters of the Yellowstone River. Soon the larger camp would break up and smaller bands would migrate out into the area for the winter, just as they had for centuries before. Down by the camp, the lake waters gave off their usual mist, as the air was colder than the water for now. Soon an edge of ice would begin to creep along the shoreline. The migratory birds had begun to leave, and others were stopping by the lake on their annual trek South.

Lame Elk stood outside his teepee, a buffalo robe wrapped around his shoulders, and looked around at the surrounding mountains. It was home. Many Flowers came out of the teepee with her extended stomach and stood beside him. They would have a baby in the Spring. The old scars were healing. He would be a better husband and father this time, he told himself, and he knew that would be true.

Waushaute walked over with their horses. Lame Elk shed the robe, and the two chiefs mounted for their morning hunt. It had been a natural pairing that both men enjoyed.

"I will kill a muledeer for you this morning, Many Flowers," said Waushaute, "while Lame Elk is pulling his arrows out of trees."

"Ho, if I do not track the deer, Waushaute will come back with a skunk for dinner," insisted Lame Elk.

Where both men were excellent marksmen with their bows, as Lame Elk had proven with the Blackfoot, Lame Elk prided himself on his tracking, and usually gave Waushaute first crack at the kill. As such, they had developed a banter that insulted each other's lesser-perceived skills, as men often do. But both men were depended upon by the camp to help provide fresh meat, and relished the hunt. Their friendship had grown to a brotherhood.

As they rode out they waved to the posted scouts, usually boys who would take turns as sentries over the encampment and the horses. Lame Elk had configured the camp differently, using a windbreak of two small hills but moving the camp further away from the forest. It might make for a little more wind at times, which was helpful in the summer, but was becoming more unpleasant as the temperature began to drop. But it would also be safer with the lake at their backs. Captain Farmer had suggested cutting away the closest edge to the forest and building a rampart facing out toward the most direct access to the camp. After Lame Elk understood the principle, the Shoshone built a five-foot-high, wide structure that they could see over, but a horse could not jump over. It had several openings that would need to be defended, but it made everyone feel safer. He had also set two guards on nearby high hills that could signal the camp, which had a greater line of vision. This would be cold duty until the snows came but practically ended any surprise threats. When the camp disbanded and the snows came, there was less fear of attacks as all the Indians were concentrating on providing for the winter months.

"Let us hunt the aspen forests today," suggested Lame Elk. "There is still plenty of ground food for the deer there."

THE FOUR MEN had been harassed constantly as they retreated South. Harrison thought there were only two Blackfoot still pursuing them, taking targets of opportunity from ambush, as the men pressed on, running from the pitched battle of three days before. Their remaining supplies were beginning to run low, having abandoned their main provisions when the Blackfoot attack overwhelmed their camp. Now his three fellow miners were losing their reason, as fear had taken control of their minds. It was all he could do to constantly give them hope that they could make it back to civilization and safety. They were lost, and he had one thought in mind. Keep going South and they would eventually find refuge.

Two Horns had led the attack on the group of miners. The Whitemen had brazenly made camp within a few miles of the Blackfoot encampment, oblivious to their proximity. The ten men all had guns and were first heard before being spotted. When the miners had discovered one of the Blackfoot scouts, they took a shot at him with a rifle. That was more than enough provocation to expel the Whitemen from Blackfoot lands. Taking a war party of fifty men, the Blackfoot had pinned down the miners in a hail of arrows, eventually killing half of them when they retreated. Blue Heron and nine others were charged with driving the remaining Whitemen out of the Blackfoot territory or killing them, whichever came first. After two days of a running battle to the South, Blue Heron's party had managed to kill one more miner, but had also lost a warrior. He elected to cut his losses, sending his warriors home, save for himself and Buffalo Lance, who would discreetly pester the miners for a couple more days until they were well out of the Blackfoot neighborhood.

RIDING ALONG WITH their guns out, expecting an attack at any moment, Harrison and his men tried to stay out in open country as much as the landscape would allow. The terrain was still mostly mountainous, but there were valleys and some open grasslands mixed in. Every now and then they would see an Indian flanking them, and that is how Harrison came to believe the attacking force was down to two, as he could identify the same two Indians each time they saw them. He concluded that they were getting an escort now, but could not calm the other men down. There was a feeling of inevitable loss growing with his men, as they continued to panic and grow more depressed. It seemed a hopeless situation to them, lost deep in the wilderness. Then one morning ahead of the retreating miners they saw two new Indians sitting on their horses, watching them as they rode forward.

Lame Elk and Waushaute saw the four Whitemen riding in their direction with their guns out. Then above the Whitemen on a hillside a Blackfoot warrior appeared, signaling them by waving his rifle. While they didn't understand exactly what he wanted, they were put on alert that something was amiss and started to move away from the advancing Whitemen. A second later a shot came whistling by them, encouraging them to move a little faster for cover. Moving up from the valley floor, the two Shoshones melted into the forest and watched as the Whitemen passed and continued on their path down the valley.

Another Blackfoot crossed over the valley behind the Whitemen, most probably to join with the warrior who had warned them. Lame Elk and Waushaute waited for the two Blackfoot.

Coming through the trees Lame Elk recognized the Blackfoot Blue Heron. The two Blackfoot warriors made a sign of friendship as they approached the waiting Shoshone.

"Have you brought my horse?" Lame Elk asked.

Blue Heron looked rather surprised, not knowing whether Lame Elk was serious or not. When Lame Elk didn't smile, Blue Heron said seriously, "These Whitemen have attacked the Blackfoot, and we have driven them out of our lands. There were ten of them."

"You are now in Shoshone lands. Are there more Blackfoot with you?" asked Waushaute.

"The others have turned back out of respect for the Shoshone," said Blue Heron.

That brought a smile to Lame Elk, who said to Waushaute, "Do not trade for horses with this one."

All four men smiled. Blue Heron then said to Buffalo Lance, "These are the Chiefs of the Yellowstone Shoshone, Waushaute and Blackhand."

Buffalo Lance sat up as straight as he could and looked at Lame Elk, saying, "I am Buffalo Lance. Red Horses was my brother in the Bull's Warrior Society. Would you tell me how he came to die?"

Lame Elk studied the man for a moment and then said, "He rode with an open wound and broken leg for four days to join his fellow warriors. He died on his horse trying." Then abruptly changing subject, he said, "The Whitemen are now our problem, you may return to your people."

With that, Lame Elk and Waushaute turned their horses and headed after the Whitemen. Blue Heron and Buffalo Lance sat there and watched them disappear into the white and yellow background of the quaking Aspen trees. Blue Heron looked over at Buffalo Lance and said with a smile, "I am a good horse trader."

"You could be on the Council with all your buffalo dung," said Buffalo Lance, as he turned his horse around.

Blue Heron, who was already on the Council, just grunted.

THE FOUR MEN came to an abrupt halt. There in front of them was a large Indian camp by a lake. Harrison calmed his men down saying it could be a blessing. If these were friendly Indians, they would be saved. The Indians did not seem to be swarming to the attack, so Harrison convinced his men to put up their guns and slowly approach the camp. He knew that further flight from a new group of savages would be futile. Might as well pretend they had come in friendship. So the men rode forward praying as they went.

As they neared the barrier wall, they received some waves and smiles, and they nearly cried in their relief. They were allowed to ride right into the camp, where they dismounted, and were surprised to see an old mountain man walking up to greet them. Fournier could see that these men had had a hard time of it. They were dirty, gaunt, and nervous, almost breaking down in their happiness at seeing him come over.

"Thank God you're a white man! We have been running for our lives for the last four days. The savages attacked us in huge numbers, and only the four of us have survived!" gasped Harrison.

"All right, slow down, catch your breath. I'm Fournier; I run the trading post down at Fort Hall. You are safe here." Fournier tried to reassure the wild-eyed men. "Where was it you were attacked?"

Harrison was regaining some composure and replied, "I led a party of ten miners out of Fort Union, up the Missouri. When we got to Three Forks, we followed the Gallatin River until we saw some promising cliffs. We hadn't been there two days before the Indians fell on us."

"That would be Two Horns's bunch," said Fournier. "Blackfoot. You almost camped in his front yard. I'm surprised you made it here."

"And these Indians?" Harrison looked around at the group that was forming in curiosity.

"Lame Elk's Yellowstone Shoshone. Blood enemies most the time to the Blackfoot. Good friends to the white man, until we mess it up. That's him coming in now with Waushaute," pointed Fournier.

Harrison turned around to look and nearly lost his balance from the weakness he felt in his legs as he recognized the two Indians one of his men had taken a shot at.

The two Indians rode casually over to the white men and Fournier. Lame Elk and Fournier began a conversation in native tongue that Harrison could not understand. At one point all three men laughed, and then Lame Elk and Waushaute turned around and rode back out.

"You forgot to tell me you took a shot at Lame Elk," said Fournier to Harrison.

Harrison looked sheepishly back and said, "We thought they were all together."

Fournier nodded and said, "That's what Lame Elk figured too. This is your lucky day. I'll guide you back to Fort Hall in a couple of days, when I'm done here. Until then, you are the guests of the Yellowstone Shoshone. I suggest you pack all them guns away securely. Don't want no accidents, or tempt anyone to steal them neither. Come on, I'll find you some food before you and your men fall over."

42

O F ALL THE STORIES circulating about the sinking of the *Fairfield*, none got as much attention as that of the wild Indian wielding two knives and screaming maniacally while doing his blood work. Ishka was well known in many quarters of the northwest coast, and it wouldn't be a stretch of anyone's imagination to picture Ishka as the bloodthirsty assassin on the *Fairfield*. There was even an artist's rendition in the newspaper from the description of the two survivors. Fortunately it erred on dramatics over detail, but no way could Targon allow Ishka to go ashore to render a comparison now. The thought had crossed his mind on more than one occasion that he might have to dispose of his assassin. But good assassins are very hard to find, and one of Ishka's special talents he may never see again, so Targon decided to roll the dice, and hope a low profile would serve his purposes.

Sitting with a shipload of possessions taken from the *Fairfield*, not to mention some newly minted gold bullion, he needed to quickly and quietly dispense with his booty. Not yet trusting Zachary and Dan Williams, he would unload the gold and personal effects from his raid and send them crated into the city with Roland Leach. Later he would arrange for the gold to be shipped South for disposal, maybe in Chile. To that end he summoned his three San Francisco managers to Half Moon Bay for a business conference.

Any meeting with Targon was dangerous, but when you were stealing from him certain fears were bound to arise. Dan Williams was a walking bundle of nerves. He presumed that Targon was on to him, and his death would be a ghastly one at the hands of the Indian. He had been practicing his report with Zachary DuPort for two hours now, and Zachary was worried about his courage. The story and the books would pass muster fine, since they had started stealing within a month of having taken over the businesses, so no anomalies of record could be compared to the past, and plenty of money was still being taken monthly by Targon's watchdog, Leach. The question was Dan Williams's backbone. Zachary could imagine someone like Targon would smell the fear and soon have Williams confessing and begging for his life. This would not do, as it of course would lead straight to himself. Zachary made his decision. He called Julie to come up and told Dan that Julie had been anxious to see him before they left for Half Moon Bay. Dan was easily coaxed to accompany Julie to one the bedrooms for a romantic interlude. He then called Shug up and explained what they had to do.

Giving the couple a few minutes to get at least partially undressed and in bed, Zachary and Shug then entered the room. Dan and Julie had gotten farther along than Zachary had calculated, but it would make no difference. Shug went over to the bed and pulled Julie off of Dan and shot Dan through the heart. As Julie stumbled backwards, Zachary ran a blade into the middle of her back while covering her mouth. For good measure, he stuck her again, holding her until he was sure she was dead. They then placed the knife in Dan's hand and tossed the gun on the floor. Going out into the still-empty hallway, they pretended to knock on the door to see what the trouble was, at last pushing the door open when a head or two popped out of other doors on the hallway set aside for similar use.

"Get the law and a doctor," Zachary commanded to one of the Targon guards that were coming up the stairs to investigate the commotion. "Just what we need around here, a double murder," he said with disgust.

His mind began to swirl. Perhaps there was a way to profit from this little setback. Could he convince Targon to let him hire the next accountant? Leach would still be Targon's man handling the muscle and the money deposits, but shouldn't Targon hire a more respectable accountant in the future; someone who wasn't sleeping with the employees and killing them? Who in Targon's group would be better suited to hire a respectable accountant than Zachary? He could get a kickback on the higher salary, and lower the new accountant's take to 2 percent on the skim. He could hire someone with a lot more sand than Dan Williams. Suddenly he was looking forward to the meeting on Targon's ship.

The two bodies were dragged onto a bedsheet where they lay side by side awaiting the police to arrive. Zachary steeped over them on his way out of the room, having almost already forgotten about them as he rehearsed his business pitch silently to himself for Targon's meeting.

STEWART BERTRAM WAS not looking forward to his meeting with Henri Seurat. He had been sitting quietly for over a half hour as the diminutive Frenchman poured over the books, prospectus, and plans. Henri had made it clear that he would be the one to meet with Stewart, not the Countess, which was actually a relief for Stewart after his last unfortunate display before the woman. Every now and then, Henri would ask a question, but mostly he just read and jotted down notes. Finally he looked up, took off his reading glasses, and folded the books shut. He slid the materials back across the immense table to Stewart.

"So, Mr. Bertram, what are you proposing as an investment at this time?" he asked.

Stewart had been running over the various answers he might give when the question came, and decided to go with, "We are flexible in that matter. As you have seen with our construction schedule, we could nurse this along, or set up a capital fund of reserves for all contingencies. The matter really rests with the upside our investors see in the future. Due to capital shortfalls at the moment and the concentration of shares in my own hands, I am willing to let you and the Countess in on more generous terms than the original subscription members were offered, should the investment amount be substantial."

Henri didn't say anything. Stewart shifted to plan B, and said, "With your background, and the Countess's reputation for honesty, perhaps you could take a couple of days to make an offer, or think of a more appropriate financing scheme. I would be in your debt, sir."

"Very well then," Henri answered. "I will run it by the Countess and let you know in three days." He reached out to shake Stewart's hand and escort him out of his office. Stewart Bertram walked down the hill to the hotel, where Henri assumed he had left his horse or buggy. Henri then went back inside and studied the letter Gabrielle had given him in the morning, addressed to Marshal Donovan from this Corby person. Only in America would someone have a single name. It was the mark he supposed of a young nation.

He reread the letter again, more interested in the account of the southwest than the problem Gabrielle had asked him to address if possible. The young man was not a literary illuminator, but he was observant and well thought out. Henri would write to his friend, the Undersecretary of War, a scolding letter asking immediate resolution for his friend Don Sebastián Drego de Santarosilla, whose family had been a pillar of the Southwest for generations. Had Gabrielle asked him, he would have done the same for the devil himself. The young man was very carefully asking about Gabrielle too. He would see how Marshal Donovan was planning to answer. Perhaps this was the beginning of his interference in Gabrielle's personal life. He would be very subtle. She need never know.

After a bit he followed Stewart Bertram down the hill to the hotel. He still marveled at the magnificent views one could have on a clear day above the city. The hotel continued to expand and become more beautiful as the gardens began to mature. Walking to Donovan's office, he spotted Gabrielle and Donovan sitting at a table in the salon, sharing a cool drink and a serious-looking conversation. He joined them.

"My relief has arrived, and not a moment to soon," joked Donovan. "Our princess would have me ride to the New Mexico Territories to see if Corby has enough pajamas to wear."

"Stop being so silly; I just was trying to understand if Corby had mentioned any plans after he single-handedly saves the southwestern United States," she said with a little sarcasm.

"Gabrielle, you are worried about this man, no?" asked Henri, as he sat down. "Marshal Donovan tells me he is a fine young man, and perhaps has some feelings for you?"

Gabrielle frowned at Donovan and said, "The Marshal has failed to tell me this."

Donovan now looked at Henri. So the game was on. He looked back at Gabrielle, and shrugged, saying, "He has often talked about a big black horse some Indian stole from him more affectionately. Besides, it is the Code of the West; you don't spill your guts about such things as women."

Gabrielle smiled a satisfied smile. "So it is true. Corby had an interest in me before he left."

"If he didn't then, your goodbye... handshake... sure got his attention, but yes, he was pretty much infected before that."

Henri looked perplexed and Gabrielle blushed. Donovan continued, "Princess, you gotta understand that your wealth and status are lures to some men, but a man like Corby would see them as major obstacles. His pride and integrity would push him away."

"That's nonsense," said Gabrielle.

"I'm afraid Marshal Donovan is right, *ma chere*. How could the man believe he could climb to your title, or even compete with your education, let alone your wealth?" Henri said gently. "And such a man would never be able to live off of your largesse."

Gabrielle had a moment to reflect on the issues. Her face remained calm and unchanged, but her eyes betrayed her, and the two men both saw the little girl with a fear and sadness inside.

"Nothing is impossible, *mon ange*, but you would ruin this man if you are not sure. That is not what you want to do, is it?" asked Henri.

"No... no it isn't," she almost whispered.

"There then," said Henri in a cheerful strong voice. "On the other hand, should you decide that Monsieur Corby is the right decision, your Oncle Henri will move heaven and earth to help you, as you already know. I think the Marshal could be persuaded to join our conspiration.

Donovan nodded his head. "But only if you are sure!"

A LETTER ARRIVED the following week, from Drego, explaining the heroic action Corby had taken in defense of his family, and the wounds to accompany it. After rereading it for the fifth time, Gabrielle was pretty sure she was sure.

43

THE AMERICAN RANCHERS SET against the idea of Spanish land grants formed an association. They called it the American Land Rights Association, and they referred to themselves as 'Soldiers of Justice.' As they saw it, this was a time to act, in the tradition of their forefathers. Let the people decide. The government would be slow in coming, and when it did, whoever was in place was likely to stay there. This window of opportunity would not be open for too long, and the more time that passed, the more scrutiny the territory would be under. Best to accomplish their goals while the dust of the new land purchase was still settling in Congress.

The first order of business was to recruit more Americans to their cause. The Soldiers were only some twenty strong, and that included a few workhands who could not be totally depended upon. It was decided that the key members would need to recruit surrounding area support, including those Mexicans that were not large landowners if possible. They would need to hire some extra guns too, to counter what the rich Mexican estate holders would probably bring in once the conflict began. Sam Johnson thought they might be able to gain financial support from the Eastern political establishments preaching a coast-to-coast manifest destiny for the American people. It was worth a try, at least traveling back to St. Louis to test the idea. Perhaps the people wanting to build the railroads would not wish to circumvent vast tracts of land, or pay high prices for right-of-way leases. Bill Tolliver, who ran the mercantile store in Tucson and a few head of cattle on a small ranch, was selected to represent the group on a trip to the city, and the association would help watch over his interests in the territory while he was gone. Until they had a few more of the pieces in place, the group decided on no overt acts to warn the Mexicans as to what was coming other than fishing for converts whenever and wherever they could.

THE SITUATION WAS an uncomfortable one. Clearly the Señora wanted Corby out of her house as soon as he was able. Combined with the obvious personal interest Maria was showing in him, Corby was willing his body to recover as fast as possible. The moment he could be moved, he requested that he be carried to the little cabin he and Drego had been sharing. But Don Sebastián and Maria would not hear of it, so another month dragged by before he could get up on a crutch and leave on his own. His ribs still hurt, and he couldn't put a lot of weight on his leg yet, but that was far better than being in the crossfire of mother and daughter, even if it was in Spanish. He was actually a little thankful that the Señora was not seeing him as a possible suitor for her daughter, as it allowed him to maintain a respectable aloofness while not offending Maria. And he did not wish to offend the girl. She had nursed him back to health with a tireless effort. He enjoyed her quick laugh and many questions. And she was truly a beauty. He could imagine her as a full-grown woman, such as Gabrielle. And that was the problem. Donovan's letter had indicated that Gabrielle was doing some serious thinking that might include him. There was no outright statement that said, "She wants you to come home," or anything like that. There was just a hint that there was a bit more than sisterly concern over his injuries and circumstance. He wondered what she would think if she saw the lovely Maria, who definitely had more than a sisterly concern, leaning over his bed fussing over him. It was more than flattering, and he could see himself getting swept up had the image of Gabrielle not been stuck in his head. But what was the use; the likelihood of either relationship working out was poor. He was a man of little means with a fast gun—hardly the candidate any girl or family would wish to team up with. The Senora was right to expect better for her daughter, and Gabrielle was never any more than a silly dream. Even if they had an affair, it would not last, and he would be left with a hole in his heart. Maybe Drego was right with all his girlfriends. Corby wished he could saddle up and go, but knew he couldn't and wouldn't.

He had shown the letter to Don Sebastián, as Donovan had indicated that some Frenchman Gabrielle knew might be able to help the Don. Donovan also indicated that through the Frenchman he might be able to convince someone from the U.S. Marshal Service to take a more active role down here. Whereas he knew these were just words, he thought the Don would be pleased to know that other Americans saw the injustice he was facing. The letter did seem to help Don Sebastián get a necessary second wind on an otherwise dreary day.

"Señor Corby, you have been an excellent friend to my family and a good influence for Juan. I see a little more responsibility and maturity in him, that is good," commented Don Sebastián.

"He is a good man, sir," said Corby.

"He is a wild mustang." Don Sebastián laughed. "Let's just hope that his bloodlines will someday lift his head. And you, it would appear that you will be back in the saddle by next month. What do you plan to do?"

"Well, it seems to me that nothing has been resolved here yet. Maybe when you have clear legal status, the ranchers will back off. Until then, I intend to honor my word, and help your family through this trouble spot," Corby said with direct candor.

"But you have almost been killed. You have already done enough for us. Providence may not be so generous next time."

"Marshal Donovan taught me that most people spend their lives wondering and worrying about what will happen to them next. It is better to decide on what is important and then try to make it happen. Even if you fail, the time you spent trying was living better than not trying. What's important now is to make sure the Rancho survives until law is established down here," Corby stated in an uncommonly long speech for him. As he said it, he reinforced his own belief in the words. It felt good to have a purpose.

"This Marshal Donovan is a wise man. Just be sure that what you are living for is also worth dying for, Señor. May God watch over you." Don Sebastián placed his hand on Corby's shoulder before walking away.

DREGO WALKED HIS horse over to where Corby was standing on his crutch.

"I must go to Tucson tonight. I have promised to dance with a pretty señorita. I do this for you, my friend. She has a sister, *una belleza*, that I save for you. But if La Tigresa finds out, even I cannot save you." Drego sadly shook his head, and then gave a big grin.

"The many things you do for me," Corby said in mock amazement. "You are planning to ride alone?"

"Do you see this horse?" asked Drego, "It is a direct descendant of the Arabians raised and bred in España for over ten centuries. They are the finest horses in the world. Borrasca here is a champion. He has more speed and stamina than any horse in northern México. No Apache pony will ever catch him, even though the wild horses here share some of his bloodline."

Corby gave the horse a good long look. It was a magnificent animal, with a barrel chest and strong legs. You could see that the horse had spirit, as the breed was reported to have in plenty. Having never seen a Spanish Arabian up close before, Corby was impressed but could see little similarities with the wild mustangs of the Plains. The thought of his lost big black, Midnight, came to mind momentarily, and the affection he had for it. This animal was smaller, but seemed to have a more muscular frame, and was bursting with energy. It had a small almost delicate looking muzzle for a horse. Its coat was a deep chocolate brown.

"Once again, I am doing you a favor," said Drego as he swung up on the horse. "I believe Don Sebastián intends to reward you with this fine horse, when you can ride again, so I must keep him in shape." And off he rode.

44

THE THIN COLUMN OF smoke twisted up in the late afternoon sky. Long Bow had been hunting waterfowl along one of the contributories of the Missouri River. Leaving his horse secured, he crept through the trees and bushes toward the fire to investigate. As he crawled closer, he could hear men talking as they do around a campfire. With considerable patience, he inched forward until he could see three Crow warriors cooking a duck over the small fire. He was instantly suspicious. What would three Crows be doing this far into Blackfoot territory, and with a daytime fire going? He sensed it was a trap. The Crow horses were set a small distance from the camp, a tempting target to steal. The Crows around the fire seemed bored; another bad sign. They should be alert in enemy territory. With all of his senses heightened, Long Bow painstakingly reversed his direction and began to sneak away from the camp at a different angle. If they had seen him come in one way, his only hope was to leave another way. Snaking along a dozen feet, he saw the first encircling Crow coming his way. Freezing where he was, he watched as the Crow looked over to his right, leading him to see another warrior also closing in. Spaced as they were, he figured there were probably a half dozen more shrinking the trap. Escape was unlikely. They would have his horse.

Long Bow was a Bull warrior of the Gray Woman Mountain Blackfoot. He sprang to his feet and raced into the camp, smashing the head of the first sitting Crow he encountered, and knocking over the second as he sprinted for the Crow ponies. Leaping on the horse, he tried to wheel it around to head for the open, when he realized the horses were hobbled and could not run. The Crows were in full pursuit now as he jumped down from the pony to run. Almost simultaneously he was hit by four arrows in the back, and went down mercifully to a quicker than normal death. He could barely feel the torture, as the Crows began to cut and burn him as he faded from life.

The mutilated body was put in a prominent place sure to be discovered, and the vengeful Crows headed back toward their territory to prepare for the retaliatory raid they knew the Blackfoot would have to make. Loud Thunder had waited and planned for this revenge. The Blackfoot chief that had killed his brother Proud Eagle would find the Crow were well prepared for the coming conflict with the Blackfoot. The young Crow Chief Loud Thunder, now a proven warrior, would help lead the Crow to victory with the knowledge he had accumulated the last few years in scouting the Blackfoot, as he never stopped in his scheming to avenge his brother's death. The Blackfoot chief must know who had brought about his destruction. Loud Thunder had rehearsed the scene many times in his mind, when he would have the Blackfoot chief powerless before him.

WHEN THE BODY of Long Bow was brought into camp, Two Horns knew that he would now have to be a war chief. So many of the Bulls had fallen in recent years. Long Bow had been a very pleasant sort, quick with humor, good with horses, never quarrelsome or whining. Stone Bear, Shining Crow, Red Horses, Howling Wolf, and now Long Bow represented half of the original band of Bulls when Two Horns had led them out to hunt Blackhand just a handful of years before. The Crows had killed the last two Bulls, Howling Wolf and Long Bow, and were pressing hard on the Blackfoot of late. The Blackfoot had been more on the receiving end the last six months or so. A superior show of force was called for. As chief, Two Horns wanted to bloody the Crows to the point where they would not wish to encounter the Blackfoot for a very long time. It would require a massive effort and help from the other Blackfoot camps.

Most of the other Blackfoot tribes lived to the North and West of the Gray Woman Mountain tribe. Two Horns knew that they had their own enemies, primarily the Cree in the Canadas. But there was a good chance to convince them to join in war against the Crows, to keep his tribe as the buffer to the South and East. He would also look to the Lakota, who were already fighting a holding action on their boundary with the Crows. If he could gather a force of five hundred warriors, he could rout the Crows and reestablish a peaceful border. He would send riders to the camps of his prospective allies, asking for a council. There would be many side deals that would have to be made ... perhaps an agreement to help fight the Crees at some later date.

Looking down at the remains of Long Bow, and hearing the cries of his mourning relatives, Two Horns knew that he must make war. Steeling himself for the days ahead, he went to console the relatives.

45

THE ATTACK ON THE miners by the Blackfoot, coupled with the trouble with the Plains Indians and now the Apache, was stirring up public sentiment that the U.S. government should more actively protect its citizens with its military. As more and more Americans ventured West and brushed up against a fading good will by the Native American population, the government felt obligated to at least respond to highly publicized incidents of violence by the Indians. Many politicians were ready for a much more aggressive approach. On the heels of its victory in the Mexican War and Commodore Perry's remarkable success in opening up Japan for trade through the threat of his armada, the United States of America was feeling rather invincible. Having pushed around great nations, it was somewhat of an embarrassment that ragtag groups of indigenous savages were slaughtering its citizens in its own country.

Lt. Col. John Barnes, attached to the War Department, was assigned the task of marshaling a response to the Indian problems along the Oregon Trail. His major obstacle in dealing any retribution was a lack of manpower in the area. An unfortunate incident had just occurred outside Fort Laramie, when an immigrant's cow had wandered off and been eaten by the local Sioux Indians. A young Lt. Grattan had led a retribution force of twenty-eight men to get the cow back. The Indians realizing their mistake offered a horse in its place, but the lieutenant rejected the offer and ordered his men to fire on the Indians instead, killing several Sioux, including a prominent chief. In the ensuing action the lieutenant and all his men were killed. The Sioux were said to be furious, and the migrating immigrants understandably were terrified.

The handful of U.S. Army forts was widely spread and severely undermanned along the Oregon Trail. Fortunately Congress had granted the funds to start building more forts to guard the trails leading West, but that would not help for some time. With its horse dragoons numbering in the hundreds and the wagon trains full of immigrants numbering in the tens of thousands, the army could not protect the settlers out West. Add the fact that posts were hundreds of miles apart, and that the Indian populations knew the land, and any attempts to redress local incidents were very dangerous undertakings. Many soldiers simply ran off after their first few months in service or on learning of potentially dangerous assignments. Few Eastern posted officers wanted posts out West. It was a sign of failure, where one was sure to be forgotten in some poorly constructed hovel called a fort in no-man's-land. And no rational officer, whether husband or father, wished to expose his family to certain and continual peril. The discipline and morale out West was spotty, and not up to the standards of the army back East. Thus, the War Department was not anticipating any strategic or impressive achievements from its men out West. It was Lieutenant Colonel Barnes's job to hold the line until circumstances (money) or politics changed significantly enough to warrant a larger presence of the army in the West, current outrage notwithstanding.

One of the few good officers he could depend on in the middle of nowhere was Captain Farmer. The stretch of trail from Fort Hall to Fort Boise was probably the safest section of the Oregon Trail at the moment, due to the current friendship of the Shoshone Indians. Colonel Barnes credited Captain Farmer with having obtained the good will of several of the major Shoshone chiefs. However either East or West of that stretch, the Trail was becoming increasingly more dangerous. Troubles with the Yakima Indians near Fort Dalles on the Columbia River, and Indians throughout the Oregon Valley between Fort Dalles and Fort Vancouver, both North and South, were stretching thin the U.S. troops patrolling that area. Fortunately for Colonel Barnes, the area was now populated enough to muster significant volunteer civilian forces under military command to assist in combating the Indians. No such population base was available to assist from Fort Dalles, in the Oregon Territory, all the way back to Fort Kearney in the newly formed Nebraska Territory. Sioux, Cheyenne, Kiowa, Arapahoe, and many others were now openly hostile. Disease among the Indians and depredation of wild life had turned the Plains Indians against the Whiteman. Meanwhile the vast emigration West continued on unabated.

The attack on the miners by the Blackfoot tribe was not forgotten, just put on a backburner. The Sioux would take center stage for a bit. It now became a strategy to pit one tribe against another through their age-old enmities, when possible, to deflect the warfare from the settlers and thin out the warring tribes. Arming one side against the other did have short-term benefits, but the guns that were beginning to fall into Indian hands would plague the settlers for decades to come.

46

HO TO TRUST? WHO not to trust was a better question. But when all was said and done, Targon ended up as always trusting no one. He could assume that in a den of thieves, there was some thieving going on. That was all right in moderation. It was by nature to be expected, and even served as a substitute bonus in their line of work, if not taken too far. Who but a fool wouldn't line his pockets as long as no one else knew? That was always the problem. They were usually too stupid to pull it off without being caught, and then Targon had to act ruthlessly to reinforce his position at the top. He worried little of the small thieves he employed, having lived by the pirate's code for so many years himself. This Zachary DuPort, much like Paul Logan before him, merited a greater risk, while offering a greater reward. Sleep with the devil, as they say.

Günter didn't believe in the coincidental demise of Dan Williams just before his accounting presentation. His instincts told him that DuPort probably was involved, but he had no proof, and DuPort was making him good money. Leach would steal from him if he could, but Leach was incapable of anything sophisticated, hence his role as custodian and guard dog. One thing was sure, he would not trust to anyone hiring a new accountant other than himself. That required him to enter San Francisco for an extended period to review candidates, albeit in the privacy of one of his parlors. To do so, meant exposing himself to some danger, which troubled him not, but he was aware that the stirred-up sentiments in the city could mean unexpected consequences. He didn't care to play poor cards when he could rig the deck. He needed another established ally in the city. Someone like Paul Logan who had credibility, but someone he could control more. It would be good to have another set of eyes on DuPort too.

Dressed in his best landlubber clothes, he knocked on the door and presented himself: "Mr. Günter Targon of T.D. & Associates, to see Mr. Stewart Bertram."

He was led into a sitting room while Mr. Bertram was informed of his arrival. Presently a gentleman came into the room with a worried face and said, "Mr. Targon, I received your note. I am Stewart Bertram. Perhaps we should discuss this in my office." He indicated a direction to walk. When the two men were seated, Stewart Bertram continued. "Your note said that you were a partner of Paul Logan's for many years, and that you had substantial cash and an interest in assuming his position in our steamship company, is that right?"

"That is correct, sir," Targon answered.

"Mr. Targon, you must be aware that I have heard many things about your other activities over the years," Stewart Bertram said.

"As have I, sir," laughed Targon. "If half of them were true, would a man such as Paul Logan have been in business with me? I must admit that in my younger days when the Russian pirates and Mexicans ran California, I was prone to take the law into my own hands on occasion. In those early days you had to, if you wished to survive. But I have been a quiet businessman for many years now. It is only when someone wishes for a colorful character to sell newspapers that I sometimes see my name in the papers again."

Targon reached inside his jacket and pulled out a handsome leather bill-fold. From this he took out several bank statements, and passed them over to Bertram.

"You will note the cash balances in each of these banks," he said. "I'm a little embarrassed to have so much capital currently not working, but then again, opportunities do keep turning up."

Stewart Bertram looked at the statements, mostly from South American banks, though reputable ones, including very recent deposits from the sinking of the *Fairfield*, and almost fell off his chair. He was looking at a fortune that he didn't believe anyone in the West, aside from the Countess, could possibly have. A partner of such substance would solve all his problems.

The investment in the steamship company would cost a pretty penny, but Günter had bigger fish to fry. Besides, there were always ways to recoup his money should he become unhappy in the venture.

"You understand, Mr. Targon, that I would need to verify these accounts, and that the other investors in the steamship company would have to approve your membership. I cannot promise you anything on our brief meeting this morning," Stewart said as he composed himself back into the businessman.

"Of course, of course, there is no rush. If you would rather keep a low profile on this because of my trangressions as a young man I would totally understand. You may keep the statements until you are satisfied. Should we proceed, I would ask you for a small favor," said Targon.

Stewart Bertram was immediately on guard.

"Traveling as much as I have been lately, your help in finding me a new personal accountant here in the city would be of great assistance," said Targon.

Letting out a slow breath, Stewart smiled and said, "I know of several top-notch accountants that would love to have an account of your size. Could I offer you some refreshment this morning, Mr. Targon?"

IT WAS SURPRISING to Donovan how much his life had changed in the last few years. He had not thought it possible that he would be enjoying his new business career (one he had really not sought out) as much as he was. He was enjoying life in a way he had not thought possible. If there was one drawback, perhaps he was getting a little soft. Perhaps he wasn't as attuned to the streets the way he used to be. But then, perhaps he didn't need to be anymore. There were others that could sweep up the dirt as he had for so many years. He had earned his second chance at life.

Therefore it was surprising to him when he thought he saw Zeke Bridges one day and the tucked-away instincts came racing back. He had wanted to rough the man up and lock him away. The blood had rushed to his face, and the anger, so reminiscent of his old life, had boiled so quickly, he could have been back in St. Louis or Fort Boise. Immediately he had shifted into the stalker, trailing Bridges through the streets of San Francisco. He had wanted to be sure, and he was not the law now. Bridges would simply deny Donovan's accusations. As the afternoon passed, he had time to reflect on the man. Surely if he was seen by Bridges, the man would feel forced into some form of action. He might just run, or he might try to have Donovan killed. Donovan had little fear of Bridges facing him as a man. So he decided he needed to gather some information in order to convince the local authorities that this was a killer from the Oregon Territories. If he could not compile a case, he wanted the element of surprise if he had to take the man down himself. He would send for the warrant from Fort Boise, and see if he couldn't get someone else to identify Bridges beside himself. Corby would have fit that bill, but another lawman like Tom Jackson would be better. In the meantime, he intended to find out where this dapper-dressed man could be found when he wanted to find him again. He also wanted to be very sure it was indeed Zeke Bridges.

It was easy detective work to pin a name and workplace on Bridges. Not surprisingly, he was associated with the gambling and whoring-out of the old Paul Logan businesses. Mr. Zachary DuPort fit into the broad timeframe of Bridges disappearance and DuPort's subsequent arrival. The more Donovan watched him, the more convinced he was this was the same man. The voice was the kicker. He might have been persuaded that the resemblance was simply that, but the voice convinced him. When the time came, he was sure he could coax out a confession.

Then he wondered if Bridges already knew he was in San Francisco. Maybe Bridges had something in the works already. Was it possible that Bridges wasn't concerned about him? Did he feel his new identity was that good? Did his new employment give him the false impression that Donovan wouldn't come for him? It gave Donovan a moment to consider, and he would be more alert and careful until he had the answers.

About that time in his surveillance, another surprise popped up. He wasn't the only one following Bridges. At first he noticed a brief shadow movement, then a person staying in the alleys, so going with the possibility that there was another tracker, he repositioned himself to find out, and confirmed to himself that an Indian was also watching Bridges. It was Targon's Indian; the one Drego had warned Corby about that was tracking him last year. The same one they had briefly met in the Oregon Territories with Targon that afternoon at Big Jake's place on the coast. Finally he was able to get an extended look at the Indian when Bridges returned to his business office on Mission Street. The Indian took up a position on one of the sand hills where he could see both the front and rear doors, but would not be seen from the building. Sitting alone on the hill, it was likely that no one would wish to bother him, particularly if they approached and got a better look at the man. He emitted an aura of death and destruction. From the pure hatred that poured out of his black eyes, to the displayed weapons and wiry muscular body, no one could misjudge his antisocial stance. If a man wanted trouble of the deadliest kind, he need look no further. Donovan watched as two policemen thought better of disturbing the waiting sentry. It was about that point when Donovan picked up on the Indian's habit of slowly and carefully examining every person he saw in a wide swing of his vision. When the Indian was about to peruse his sector, Donovan thought it prudent to duck inside the storefront he was using as cover for several minutes. On exiting, he was unhappy to find that the Indian was gone, probably taking up a different position in his surveillance. The last thing Donovan wanted was the undue attention of this Indian, so he gave up his own spying for the day and went home to think about the strange new development in his life. Donovan shuddered as he wondered if Zeke Bridges was destined to meet Targon's Indian some dark night.

47

WO TALL, RUGGED MEN stepped into Gavin Dagget's assorted businesses' office in Tucson. They were covered in dust from what looked like a long ride, but neither man appeared tired. They had a somewhat detached look about them, as if they had experienced a lot of living, and little could excite or surprise them anymore.

"You Dagget?" the first man asked.

Dagget nodded.

"U.S. Marshal Stranahan, St. Louis. This is for you," the man said as he handed Dagget an official-looking letter.

Dagget opened the letter, and was surprised to find it was from the Secretary of the War Department of the United States of America. It began, "To whom it might concern." It instructed all employees, assets, and vendors of the government to assist the two lawmen in their assigned mission in the newly acquired territory, but it did not say what that mission was. It identified U.S. Marshal Finley Stranahan, and U.S. Deputy Marshal Patrick O'Bannon, out of the St. Louis Field Office of the U.S. Marshal Service.

"Well, gentlemen, good to have some real lawmen here in town," said Dagget, handing the letter back over to Marshal Stranahan. "I guess our growing little range war has finally reached the attention of Washington."

Ignoring the statement, Stranahan asked, "Where can we find a Don Sebastián Santarosilla?"

"Don Sebastián Drego de Santarosilla lives about twenty miles Eastnortheast of here, at his hacienda on the Rancho El Viento del Norte," responded Dagget, "on the San Pedro River."

"Do you know a man named Corby, and a man named Sam Johnson?" Stranahan asked next.

"You will find Corby out at the Don's place, recuperating from a couple of Indian arrows. Sam Johnson is on a small spread a little farther North, on the East side of the river. You will see a road along that side of the river. There's a split peak to the northwest as the river bends. Head for that and you will run into his outfit. May I ask where all of this is taking us?" Dagget ventured.

Stranahan again didn't answer the question, but asked, "I understand you got them all to come in for a meeting a couple of months ago. You think you can do that again?"

"If I can say that representatives of the government are here to listen to the dispute, I could," said Dagget.

Stranahan thought that over and said, "You can say that. Now we are going to find some lodging and clean up. Talk with you later." The two men left the office and untied their horses. They began walking down the street.

O'Bannon glanced over at Stranahan. "We ain't here to negotiate."

Stranahan looked over at O'Bannon and explained. "I said he could say we were here to listen. You rather ride all over the goddamned desert?"

The two men continued their walk down the street.

DREGO HELPED CORBY swing up onto Borrasca. His ribs were still tender, and his leg had not yet healed, but he had stopped using the crutch, and was putting his full weight on his injured leg. The two were going to do some target practice away from the hacienda. Corby leaned over and stroked the horse's throat, talking calmly, to reassure the animal. He gently squeezed his knees, feeling no real pain, and began to walk the horse out of the courtyard. Maria came hurrying out of the hacienda with a basket and a look of concern.

"You must be very careful, Corby. Borrasca will wish to run. I made you some food. There is a bottle of wine in the basket too, so I will put it here in this saddlebag. Do not forget that there is food here and squish it. There is some for Juan too."

"Food for your brother, chica?" Drego said with exaggerated surprise.

Corby thanked her and nudged the horse out of the courtyard. Once past the walls of the compound, he opened him up to a trot, then a canter, and felt the power and spring in the step of the Arabian. Finally feeling a connection with the horse, he let the animal have its head and run. It was like gliding on a cloud, the smoothest gait he had ever felt, and he was really covering some ground. After a mile he eased the horse down to a walk to allow Drego to catch-up.

"Wow!" was all he could say.

"Such a horse is not for sale my friend," said Drego. "I think I should have taken two arrows for such a horse."

They rode on a distance, enjoying the crisp early morning air.

"Tomorrow will be an important day for your family, Drego. We can only hope that the government agents will bring good news."

Corby saw the tension in Drego's face as his friend thought again about what was at stake when they rode into Dagget's meeting again. There were no guarantees here. Don Sebastián could conceivably be evicted from his property. In the event that the meeting ended in chaos, the two men felt a little target practice might be valuable. Drego led Corby to a pair of small hills where the ranchhands came to practice their shooting. There were plenty of objects lying around to use as targets, and the men got busy setting them up as they wished for their revolver practice. Corby was not trying to increase his speed but rather his accuracy. Remembering the lessons Donovan had taught him, he worked on smoothing out his aiming and firing. After an hour, Drego went to sit under a tree to watch. Later on Corby noticed that Drego was sleeping. It was then that he checked out the sun and calculated he had been at it for about four hours. It hadn't seemed that long, but he quit for Drego, who had awakened and was rummaging through the saddlebag for the food Maria had packed. They took it and the bottle over under a cottonwood and sat down to eat.

"Are you planning to kill all the gringos by yourself, amigo?" asked Drego.

"Just working out some kinks in my draw. You know you can't romance the bad guys away, Don Juan Cassanova." Corby referred to the popular writings of the legendary European lover of a generation before. Drego obviously had not heard of him, but he understood Corby's sarcasm.

"It is a subject worth bringing up. What are your intentions regarding my helpless little sister, señor?" Drego demanded in mock earnestness.

"You have any advice there? " Corby asked in all sincerity.

Drego smiled and said, "It is La Condesa, is it not?"

"I have a snowball's chance in hell with her, but she is stuck in my mind. I wish she would go away," admitted Corby.

"You do not understand, compadre," Drego said. "You are afraid of women, like most men, because you must be perfecto in your opinion. Women do not want the storybook hero; they want the flesh and blood who will love them today and tomorrow. La Condesa is a woman." He raised his hands in some exasperation at Corby's obvious ignorance on this all-important subject.

"On the other hand," Corby mused, "if the Señora wasn't so against me, Maria is a wonderful girl." He raised one eyebrow and grinned at Drego.

IT SEEMED LIKE the whole town and surrounding territory came to Gavin Dagget's meeting. The possible repercussions of the government's decisions would have an impact on all of them. To accommodate as many as possible, the meeting was moved to the saloon, as it had the largest room in town. The landowners were given seats around several tables pushed together in the middle of the room, and the walls were packed with people standing. The room generally was split with Hispanic Americans on one side and Anglo Americans on the other, but because the room was so full, there was some mingling of the two groups due to available space, latecomers, and some old alliances.

Corby and Drego stood behind Don Sebastián some five feet away against the nearest wall. Corby noticed several new faces with the group around Sam Johnson, including a man dressed in a business suit, who must be a lawyer. Everyone had to adjust their eyes to the dim light inside after the bright sunshine outdoors.

Señor Morales was back to represent Don Sebastián and the other former Mexican landowners. There appeared to be some new gun hands working for the Johnson group too. One was staring at Corby with a slight smile on his face. But most interesting to Corby were the two marshals standing at the bar. These men looked like they were cut from the same piece of granite. Slightly bigger than everyone else, they had an air of confidence bordering on boredom as they waited for the meeting to get underway. Dressed in dark shirts, their badges drew his eye, and their gun holsters looked like well-worn natural appendages to their bodies. Corby couldn't help but smile, as he saw the younger images of Donovan standing in front of him. He checked his smile immediately as one of them gave him a hard look. He noticed that no one was standing in the area behind the bar. He guessed that the marshals had made sure of that.

Gavin Dagget stepped to the middle of the room and held his arms up, and everyone stopped what little talking had been going on.

"I would have guessed this was the Fourth of July," he joked, "but there won't be any beer drinking at this meeting." Recognizing the tenseness in the crowd, he got right to it. "The U.S. government has sent two U.S. marshals to speak to us today. I don't know what they are going to say, but they represent the country we live in, and the democratic style of governance that we all want, so I expect you all will listen carefully and will respect the authority they bear."

With that he walked back over to the bar, and one of the marshals stepped into the center of the room. He seemed even bigger as he moved. His voice was deep and commanding. "I'm Marshal Stranahan, and that there is Marshal O'Bannon," he said indicating the other man who did not move.

"We have been sent by the Secretary of the War Department down here to straighten out a few things.

"First off, the Comanches are playing hell with our troops over on the Llano Estacado in Texas. The Sioux are on the warpath across the northern plains, and the Apache are shootin' it up down here some. In other words, the U.S. Army has its hands full without any local war breaking out over land disputes that Congress is about to resolve." He slowly turned around and looked at the men in each corner of the room before resuming.

"Unfortunately, they haven't come to a conclusion yet." There was a general groan in the room. "But a man is on his way here from Washington with a survey team and legal experts to jump into the middle of this. Should be here by next month." A murmur of approval ran through the crowd. "Until that time, all prior boundaries are to be respected." The reaction was a mix of cheers and boos.

Gavin Dagget felt he should step in and quiet the assembly, saying, "Hold it down. This is good news for everyone. These issues are about to be addressed, and right here in Tucson, so everyone will have a chance to have their say." There was general agreement, but the men who called themselves the Soldiers of Justice saw little to help their cause, and maybe a bad foreshadowing of the final ruling with the "prior boundary" interim decision.

The man in the suit stood up from where he was sitting with the Johnson group, and said, "My name is Tobias Gresham, and I am not from this area, but I represent a large group of people in this country and in Washington who are asking the question 'What are we fighting for here and abroad?' If not for the people of the United States, why are we pushing West against Indians and weather and diseases, and yes, foreigners, like these Mexicans whose government we bought the land from. Does it seem right that we pay for the land as a country and they keep it as individuals? We aren't saying that we should own the land as individuals without paying for it, so why should they? They were given it. We say there should be a free range unless you buy the land."

Several people echoed the man's position with loud agreement. Then the man who had smiled nastily at Corby yelled, "Get the Mexicans out of the United States! This ain't their country no more!"

Marshal Stranahan walked over to the man, and before anyone knew what had happened, he hit the man along side of his head with his gun butt. The man crumbled to the floor. Marshal Stranahan calmly removed the man's gun, and stood up.

"This man is under arrest for trying to start a riot. Now the rest of you yahoos listen up ... I will not tolerate any breach of the law. Marshal O'Bannon and I will be here until this government team completes its work. Any questions?"

"Marshal Stranahan," asked Mr. Gresham, "are you denying these men the free range that everyone else in the West is entitled to?"

Stranahan took a step toward Mr. Gresham, who immediately sat down.

"This is a wild guess, but you're a lawyer, right?" he said dourly. "Let me put in plain enough terms for you, mister. This is federal territory. I am a federal officer. No other legal entity is recognized by the government of the United States down here yet. That same government has charged Marshal O'Bannon and me to keep the peace down here until they figure out what they want to do. Everything stays as is until the government says otherwise. That clear enough for you?"

Mr. Gresham did not answer. Stranahan repeated his question. "I asked is that clear enough for you?"

Mr. Gresham nodded his head yes.

"Good then, and by the way, no one is 'entitled' to free range, here or anywhere else. The government may allow free-range agreements on any land that is not privately owned. You own the land; you are entitled to keep trespassers out. Again, the government team coming down here will figure out who owns what. Is that clear to everyone?"

The room remained silent.

The man at his feet started to moan. "That's all I've got to say for now. When the surveyors get to town, we will call you in one at a time, through Mr. Dagget's office as the postmaster. You two men," he pointed at Corby and Drego, "give me a hand putting this saddle bum in jail for the night."

Gavin Dagget stepped forward again and said, "Thanks, everyone, for coming. As I get more information, you can stop by to talk."

The crowd started to move outside, still somewhat tense, but the idea of a fair process was beginning to take hold on most of them.

Drego and Corby started to lift the clubbed gunman under his arms and drag him toward the jailhouse, behind the local sheriff, Mark McGill.

Stranahan looked down at the man and said, "Just the way Donovan taught me," and smiled at the two.

"YOU AS FAST as Donovan says," asked a skeptical O'Bannon.

"If Donovan says so, believe it," answered Stranahan for Corby.

Corby guessed Stranahan to be around forty, and O'Bannon closer to thirty.

"Well, yes and no," Corby answered for himself. "Donovan says I have a reflex draw, versus an intentional fast draw. In other words, if I want to draw on someone, I'm not as fast as when someone is drawing on me."

Stranahan nodded his head. "That extra excitement you get from danger. If a bear is chasing you, you can run faster than you would in a race."

O'Bannon conceded the point. "Seen some fugitives do stuff I didn't think they could when cornered."

"You've got some powerful friends out West, young man," Stranahan said, changing the subject.

"Just Donovan," Corby said, somewhat perplexed.

"Then old Donovan's got some powerful friends," said Stranahan. "It ain't very often our branch of the service under the State Department gets a directive from the Secretary of the War Department personally. We almost never leave our own territory. The Washington bigwigs had to be together for this. Some influential Frenchman we were told, and big money, were behind it. Anyway we were instructed to hightail it down here pronto, and they asked for me by name. That would be Donovan's doing."

"Donovan is what you might call a living legend in the Service," offered O'Bannon with a smile. "All the things you are supposed to do, and a good number of those things you are not."

Stranahan had to chuckle at that. "They had to do a lot of rewriting of the training manual after Donovan left," he admitted. "They used to call the emergency ward at St. Louis Mercy Hospital the Donovan ward. The joke was he was keeping them in business single-handedly so he could see a certain nurse there."

Drego couldn't wait any longer, and he asked, "Do you know what the government is going to do about my father's property?"

"Sorry, son," said Stranahan, "but that is out of our league. I would say that they sent a pretty strong message down here that no one is to 'claimjump' the Don's spread. And if your friends had the clout to get this much done, I'd guess you would get a fair shake out of all this."

O'Bannon walked over to Corby, and said, "So if I was to draw on you, you'd be lightning fast?" He was crowding Corby a bit. Corby recognized the move from Donovan's instructions, and instead of stepping back, he stepped forward as O'Bannon drew. Halfway through his draw, O'Bannon felt the end of Corby's gun poke him in the stomach. He let his own gun drop back in his holster.

"O'Bannon never could accept it on reputation alone," said Stranahan. "Gonna get him killed someday. Damn that was fast!"

48

As Two Horns had predicted, The Gray Woman Mountain Blackfoot would have an obligation to help fight the Cree when their cousins to the North and West needed their help. But Two Horns had gotten his warriors. The idea of a crushing blow to the Crows had an inherent appeal to the other Blackfoot bands. The young men would enjoy the adventure, the spoils, and the chance at proving themselves. There would be little risk of retaliation, if they were successful, and even if there were some retaliation, it would fall on Two Horns's people. Having the pledge of Two Horns and his tribe to fight the mighty Cree was needed insurance when that danger next arose.

He didn't get the five hundred warriors he was hoping for, but he would have near four hundred. They continued to arrive each day now. If he could get a simultaneous strike out of the Lakota, or even a convincing distraction, to pull some of the Crows that direction, he should be able to deliver the kind of message he needed to. But Two Horns knew the disadvantage of such a large war party. Crow country was much more open than the mountain ranges on the edge of the plains that his people used for tactical cover. Once he was spotted, the advantage of surprise and the knowledge of the terrain shifted quickly over to the Crows. Then, a pitched battle would be better than hit-and-run warfare, where his warriors could be ambushed repeatedly. If he could strike first and by surprise, his casualties could be greatly reduced, and his enemy would be hit the hardest. Here was a lesson he had learned from his old adversary Crooked Claws.

It would be important to have a good command structure, for communications could be key. He wanted to break the larger group down into ten men units, each with their own leader, and then have a leader over three such units. He laid sticks out on the ground to see how that would work.

If he had twelve such battle groups of about thirty men each with leaders, he would still have a handful of warriors left over for scouts, and messengers to stay with him if he needed to direct a battle. Now he needed to select four war chiefs whom he could trust and get good advise from, to control three battle groups each, which amounted to approximately ninety warriors per chief. This way he could keep the tribes pretty much together under the command of their own normal chiefs and subchiefs. The less friction in command, the better.

He planned to have the warriors practice hand signals, and look to their leaders for coordinated movements. This would be an unpopular activity, but not unprecedented, and he didn't have the overwhelming numbers that he could afford any rogue activities. He would spend some time with his war chiefs devising attack and retreat tactics. If he prepared properly...

On another front, he had lost a good warrior, but hoped to gain a son, as Moon in the Daylight was pregnant. She had asked to come on the Crow war party, but he forbade it. This may be the only child he would have, and he would not risk it. He sternly told both his wives that care of the soon-to-come infant were their only priority, and he expected both to act as its mother and protect it. Two wives and one baby could be a blessing or a calamity. He intended to get out in front of this potential problem and fix it before it ever happened.

Now it was time to pick his leaders. He sent for Buffalo Lance and Blue Heron. After explaining his initial thoughts on how to organize the fighting force, he asked them for their thoughts and guidance on selecting two more war chiefs beside themselves for the upcoming foray. The two warriors swelled with pride inside but did not show it. They earnestly began discussing the politics and needs of the situation. As nearly half of the warriors would be from the northern tribes, they all agreed that one of the war chiefs had to also come from those tribes, and it was obvious whom that would be. Walking Bear of the Blood tribe of the Blackfoot Indians was a longtime recognized fighter and leader of his people, as well as a calm head and reasonable confederate. It was he who had helped sway the other tribes into the alliance to help Two Horns. The other candidates would be Rock Eagle of the Piegan Blackfoot, or Stalking Wolf of the Bulls. None of the men liked or trusted Rock Eagle, but to slight him would be an error. They decided to have five war chiefs, in order to get Stalking Wolf as the fourth battle group commander. Rock Eagle would be told Two Horns wished him to stay by his side in case he were to fall and there was no one there to coordinate the battle. They would all put up with the man for the sake of the combined force.

When the new War Council was assembled, Two Horns again went through his preliminary thinking, asking each war chief to select his three battle group commanders, and to have each of them select three unit leaders respectively. He emphasized the concern he had for communications and coordination, and got positive responses from his war chiefs including Rock

Eagle. Walking Bear suggested turning some of the training into a competition to keep the warriors attention and maximize their efforts. They all agreed that a week's worth of training was about all the war party could handle, so a rider was sent to the Lakota to inform them of the pending Blackfoot campaign and ask for a coordinated action on their part. No one was expecting much from the Lakota, but they never knew.

The rest of the day was spent in setting up the units and battle groups. The best warriors were spread out among the units in the effort to raise effectiveness within each group.

The Gray Woman Mountain Tribe was responsible for provisioning for the additional two hundred warriors. The camp was busy gathering the materials necessary for the campaign. In addition, Two Horns had instructed his people to break camp when the warriors left, and move deeper into the mountains until he returned. He would be taking as many warriors as he could, leaving the camp vulnerable to counterattack. Should someone like the Crees or the Shoshone hear about the unprotected camp, they may wish to settle old scores. Now he sent out long-range scouts with extra horses to try and locate the main camps of the Crows.

The Blackfoot had a general knowledge of where the Crows would camp, in traditional water drainage and game producing areas, but the Crows were nomadic, and intentionally shifted around. Surrounded by large and powerful enemies, the Crows had nonetheless flourished. Having only the Gros Ventres as traditional allies, the Crows had warred against the Cheyenne, Sioux, Shoshone, Blackfoot, and Arapaho, securing prime plains space to hunt the buffalo. Living as they had along some of the main water arteries across the vast northern plains, the Crows had earlier and more frequent contact with the Whiteman than did some of their enemies, in particular the Blackfoot who had tried to keep the Whiteman out altogether. An early advantage had accrued to the Crows, who had traded for guns, knives, blankets, and other supplies. However, that advantage, along with the European emigration, had put more pressure on securing territorial hunting grounds with their neighboring rivals. As the tribes expanded, and the hunting sometimes diminished, hostilities escalated. The Blackfoot as of yet saw the Crows as a bigger threat than the Whiteman, who still had not tried to settle in Blackfoot territory. The Crows had the men, guns, and will to attack the Blackfoot, and had done so repeatedly the last couple of years. It was the Crows threatening to change the boundaries as currently understood between the tribes.

The first step of the plan was to head southeast to the Musselshell River to meet the advance scouts when they returned from their mission of finding the Crow camps, training as they went. Two Horns assumed there would be reports of the Crow camps along the northeasterly flow of the Musselshell, and along the Yellowstone River as they both ran hundreds of miles to the East and North before joining the Missouri River. He hoped to find one or two major camps within a few days apart that he could inflict severe damage upon, but he also planned for a major battle where the Crows would have gathered a sizable fighting force expecting the Blackfoot to retaliate. He calculated that they would not expect quite the force he was bringing. With any luck, and luck always entered into war, he could be back home in a month's time and have the hated Crows in retreat for years to come.

49

WHEN HENRI MET STEWART Bertram to explain why he and the Countess had again decided not to invest in the steamship company, it was apparent that Bertram was not overly concerned and had found money elsewhere. It made for a much easier meeting, and in fact Bertram was so transformed that the two men quickly went on to other subjects, as if the previous crisis had not existed at all. Henri would have bet that Bertram was even relieved that another large investor such as Gabrielle had not joined in. It was possible that by the time Henri had sat down with Bertram, Stewart could not deliver the deal he had offered only days before. Bertram's demeanor told Henri many things. Henri reconfirmed his conviction that Bertram was less of a businessman than would make for a good partner. Bertram had not taken the time to review with Henri the well-thought-out reasons he had counseled the Countess against the project. His overly optimistic air was as telling as his panic had been before it. The man was blinded by his project, not realistically assessing the pros and cons. Henri had seen men fall in love with a piece of land or a business venture before. Such was the case of Stewart Bertram and his steamship company. Whoever had bailed Bertram out was not likely to be too happy a year down the road.

The times were swiftly changing, and the division between North and South back East was growing. There were even suggestions of economic separation in Washington. The slavery issue was already incorporated into new territorial lines drawn, and those territories wishing to become states were wrestling with the issue and pressure from back East as to which camp they would fall into. To Henri's thinking, the eastern United States was headed for extended conflicts, and even the agreed-upon need for railroads West languished in the political battles. As a conservative investor, it was time to consolidate one's holdings and protect against unseen dangers that were gathering. That alone was enough of a reason not to take on a new and risky venture. When looking at the particular challenges facing the steamship company based in California, one had to be pure gambler to take it on.

Before he had met with Stewart Bertram, and after he had met with Gabrielle, Henri had walked Donovan through his business analysis on the steamship company. Every few days, Henri would present Donovan with something new and educational. Donovan had understood that this education, though somewhat late in life, was a very valuable gift, coming from as accomplished a financier as Henri Seurat. Henri challenged Gabrielle as well, making her present her thinking and questioning her assumptions, rather than simply giving her the advice she wanted. He knew that this would be his best present to both of them and that his time was limited. Yet he was thankful for the opportunity to pass on the lessons he had spent a lifetime acquiring. And he was thankful that he had two such students that he really cared for. Gabrielle was his child in his mind now. All his aspirations he now wished for her. Her happiness had become paramount to his existence, and even as he knew that life would not make any promises, he would spend the last of his days working to promote happiness in her life. It gave him a reward he had not expected after all his years of bachelorhood, the love of a daughter. She had also brought him a new best friend in Donovan. The man was a true character of the West, secure in himself, and convinced in his personal principles. He had lived a life of action, yet at a point where many would be looking to ease up and relax somewhat, this man was immersed in a new world, learning a new language of business, and obviously relishing it. He was good company and enjoyed showing Henri the open West. They often had little adventures that Gabrielle would have disapproved of, but Henri trusted the man and enjoyed the small sense of danger going places and doing things he would never have done alone.

GABRIELLE WAS WONDERING where her boys were one Sunday afternoon, when they came walking back into the hotel to have a drink at the bar. They obviously had been somewhere in the countryside as they had some road dust on their boots and pants.

"Where have you two been, and why wasn't I invited?" she asked Donovan and Henri as they placed their drink orders.

"You were at church, or at least should have been this morning when I asked Marshal Donovan to take me to see the ocean," replied Henri. "I have only a few more chances to see such a marvelous thing, and I intend to take them."

"God's outdoor cathedral," Donovan offered rather sheepishly. "I can assure you, we spoke of nothing but the Scriptures all day."

"You wouldn't recognize a Bible if it hit you on the head!" Gabrielle

<m

laughed, and then wrapped an arm around the two, giving each a kiss on the cheek. "I would love to be invited the next time, then."

"It's a deal," said Henri, sipping from his glass. He had to sit as a weakness came over him. Not aware, he dropped his glass, as the room spun around on him. Regaining his senses, he was a little embarrassed, as Gabrielle and Donovan were very worried and making a fuss over him.

"This happens sometimes," he explained. "The doctors say my heart is just wearing out. I'll be fine now, if I get some rest. Perhaps you two would accompany me up the hill and I will cook a fine French dinner, oui?"

The three went arm in arm, as Gabrielle and Donovan continued to worry and fuss over their friend and teacher. Henri had to stay in bed the next day after the doctor came to visit him. Gabrielle had summoned the doctor.

"Do you remember me telling you about how I met Corby?" Donovan asked Gabrielle over breakfast.

"Of course. Who could forget a story like that?"

"Well, I've seen the man that ran away that day," Donovan stated.

"You mean the one that killed the volunteer in cold blood? The son?" she asked with some concern.

"Yes, Zeke Bridges, gunned down a man named Quaid, and may have been the one who shot old Luther in the back. Ran away not even knowing if his own father was still alive," he said with obvious distaste.

"He's here in San Francisco? Have you told the police?" Gabrielle was becoming alarmed.

"Right now it's my word against his. I wrote to Payette, Oregon Territory, to try and find the sheriff that handled the case. Hopefully they will send someone down to help identify him. He's using another name of course," Donovan explained. "Strange thing is I'm not the only one interested in him. I saw Targon's Indian tracking him."

Gabrielle was already upset with the failing health possibility of Henri.

"Promise me you aren't going to do something crazy. These are real dangerous men."

Donovan smiled at her. "Seems to me I used to be considered a real dangerous man. That is until you put a fancy shirt on me. I plan to just watch him until we have somebody from the Oregon Territories show up to help put him away." In his own mind, he said, "Unless I'm forced to take him down myself, that is."

"Lucky thing Corby isn't here. He would probably want to deal with Bridges directly."

The thought brought a dark look across Gabrielle's face as she thought once again about the man in the southwest desert. They had not heard from Corby since Henri had twisted arms back in Washington. Henri had informed her that the government would be sending help soon, but she felt that he had not told her everything he knew, which meant he was saving her from possible bad news. This was when being a woman was a disadvantage. She could not coerce with the same effectiveness as a man. Too many men, particularly if they didn't know her, just would not take her seriously on important issues. A familiar frustration welled up inside. It served to make her more determined than ever.

"Whoa! I know that look," Donovan said, breaking in on her thoughts. "Who's going to catch hell this morning?"

"When are you expecting to hear from Corby?" she asked in a matter-of-fact fashion.

"Don't know. Probably when he learns something about what is going to happen down there. But I did get a post from Stranahan. Old Henri really pulled some strings. Amazing... got a friend of mine, U.S. marshal, assigned to go down there to keep the lid on until the government can catch up on things. We told him to keep an eye on Corby for you," he smiled in some satisfaction.

"Oh," Gabrielle reacted, "this friend of yours, what will he do?"

Donovan reflected and then said, "Stranahan is as good as they come. Tough, fair, smart. If Henri had the clout to get him down there, he will understand that his government doesn't want anyone messing up. It would take a small army to stop Stranahan from doing his job."

Life was crowding in on Gabrielle this morning. A change from willing her way through the business opportunities of San Francisco, her family was under attack, but none of them seemed to notice. Corby, with the Indians and ranchers liable to shoot him any given day, didn't even write. Henri was showing his age, but not acting it. And now Donovan, who she could always depend on, was tracking a killer right here in the city, while a maniacal wild Indian was snooping around. Going to work this morning had lost its appeal.

She went looking for Barton. She wasn't about to just sit around to find out what was going to happen next.

50

THEIR MAN IN THE jail cell was named Clyde Houser, and Bill Tolliver had hired him as an extra gun during his trip to St. Louis. So it was Bill Tolliver that had bailed him out of jail the next morning and taken him to the doctor's office for the large bump on his head. However that was not before Stranahan and O'Bannon had ample opportunity to talk to him about his employers. A sketchy picture was uncovered pertaining to the Soldiers of Justice and their purpose, mostly due to the general ignorance and woozy noggin of Clyde Houser. O'Bannon was of the opinion that it was just empty talk. Stranahan tended to agree, but he didn't like the idea of the St. Louis lawyer being involved, so he sent a letter back to the service requesting information on Tobias Gresham. He also thought it would be a good idea to talk to this Bill Tolliver, and also to Sam Johnson. Maybe a talk with Tobias Gresham could shed a little light on the size of their problems in Tucson, too.

Later that morning they found Tobias Gresham having a cup of coffee at his hotel with Bill Tolliver. Approaching the table, they overheard Gresham say to Tolliver, "I'll handle this."

"Good morning, gentlemen," Stranahan said in his most pleasant voice. "Do you mind if we join you for a cup of coffee, and ask some questions?"

"Please sit down, gentlemen," the lawyer replied.

"Sorry I had to arrest your man the other day," Stranahan said to Tolliver, "but I couldn't take the chance of an escalating confrontation with so many people in the room."

Tolliver didn't answer, but didn't look convinced either.

"The marshals have their jobs to do, Bill," Gresham said in an agreeable tone. "We do not want the marshals thinking we agree with the prejudice Mr. Houser was espousing yesterday, do we?"

Picking up on his cue, Tolliver said, "No, no, this ain't about prejudices."

"We were hoping to find out a little more about what this is about," said Stranahan.

"Why, I would say that this is an honest dispute about legal rights and our country's responsibilities to its citizens," Gresham chimed in.

"How's that, Mr. Gresham?" Stranahan asked blandly.

"It is a matter of beliefs, Marshal. What did God intend when He put this country on the map? What do 'We the People' intend to do with the government we have established? Are we to become a great nation, or fall by the wayside, prey to our own weaknesses and indecision?"

"I'm afraid you're going to have to speak a little plainer for a simple man like me to understand," said Stranahan.

Gresham gave Stranahan a piercing gaze before smiling and saying, "I think you understand perfectly, Marshal. Now unless there is something you specifically require of us, I'm afraid Mr. Tolliver and I have an appointment elsewhere." He rose, put some money on the table, and ushered Tolliver away.

O'Bannon reached across the table and picked up a breakfast roll that Gresham had left. "Not much to say," he said.

Stranahan was still deciphering Gresham's reply when O'Bannon reached across the table again to borrow some butter. "Sometimes it's what they don't say," he said more to himself than to his munching companion.

SPIRITS WERE HIGH when the group from the Rancho returned after their Tucson meeting. It was at least apparent that the government intended to control a process, versus the lawless grab for land that had been threatening.

The arrival of the two marshals would cause any lawbreaker to second-guess his long-term prospects. A possible end was in sight. In a matter of months, Corby should be free to go. But where? From his perspective, nothing had really changed to guide him. He couldn't see himself returning as an employee to the Countess. He wouldn't trade off of his friendship with Donovan just to get a job. At this point, he had various experiences, but nothing that distinguished him other than his gun. Maybe a job as a lawman was appropriate, but it held no allure for him. Something out there had to be a fit. He knew that going from adventure to adventure as a saddlebum held no future. Whatever it was, he knew he wanted to be good at it.

Don Sebastián could tell that something was troubling the young Americano. The Rancho was going to hold a fiesta that evening, largely due to what the young man's friends had helped to bring about. He owed this man another debt of honor. Even the fine gift of the horse Borrasca would be paltry should he be able to retain his holdings in the United States. He was a fine young man, and despite his wife's objections, he could see Corby and Maria as a good marriage. Perhaps a marriage that could help bridge the cultural gap in the town.

"Have you ever seen it rain in the desert, Senor Corby?" Don Sebastián asked as he strolled over to where Corby was standing gazing off into the distances.

Corby shook his head no.

"It is an amazing thing. A true gift from the heavens. But the land so seldom sees the rain, that when it comes, instead of embracing it, the soils are too compact from fighting the sun, so the water runs off, down the arroyos through the seep holes, of little benefit to the thirsty ground. It is that way with people too I think. They often stick to what they know and turn away the changes that would improve their lives."

He had Corby's attention, and continued. "I am thinking that becoming Americans is a good thing for my people. This is a strong government that is going to end the Apache raids one day. It will bring a fair justice to the people, with its Constitution. Yes, I have read this document. It is a good thing." He now stood quietly, waiting while he drew the young man into the conversation.

"How do you know that the government will be fair to you?" Corby wanted to know.

"I don't know that," Don Sebastián conceded, "but I do know that the foundation for the government is a good one. You will always have good people and bad people, in any country. But few countries are willing to take the power out of the hands of the powerful and give it to the people. If the people are more good than bad, there will be constant changes made, until the desert learns how to use the water, comprende?"

"I think so, but powerful men run this country too."

"Yes, but not because they are the sons or daughters of the privileged. And they can be challenged by other powerful men at any time," added Don Sebastián.

It was a more idealistic view than Corby had of his own country, but he did not wish to dampen the old gentleman's spirits after the rare good news of yesterday. And he knew that Don Sebastián was fishing for something else.

"My daughter, has she been too much of a nuisance for you? She is young and headstrong," he casually ventured.

"No, no, Maria is a remarkable girl. She is always a pleasure to be around," protested Corby. "Your family has been most gracious and generous, Don Sebastián.

"Even my wife?" Don Sebastián said with a sideways grin.

Corby smiled back. "She is just trying to protect her daughter. Very understandable. As far as she knows, I could be gone tomorrow, never to be seen again."

The two men paused and looked at one another.

"I am trying hard to figure out what comes next, Señor. I am afraid I don't know. But you can be sure your family is the last thing I would hope to ever cause problems for," Corby said earnestly.

"I believe you. Maybe we can help you to figure out these difficult questions," Don Sebastián offered. The two men continued to look out into the desert as the sun began to set and swallows raced across the sky in search of an early evening meal.

51

T HE CROW SCOUTS WATCHED the large Blackfoot camp carefully. As the War Council took place, they sent couriers back and forth to the Crow camps. When the preparations for war started and more Blackfoot warriors began arriving, detailed accounts were regularly sent to warn the Crows. Having beaten back the mighty Sioux, and with a treaty made with the Whiteman, it was time to deal with the Blackfoot.

The Crow had been living in the Wind River Range, and North along the Missouri and Yellowstone Rivers in what would become Montana for centuries, while the Blackfoot had slowly pushed them South and East, much as they had pushed the Shoshone to the South. It was time to push back. With the signing of the treaty at Fort Laramie in 1851, which the Blackfoot did not attend, the Crow had been given 33 million acres of land stretching from the Powder River in the East to the Musselshell River in the northwest as their tribal hunting and fishing reserve. Territories had been drawn with the Plains tribes to try to stop fighting among them, but the mountain tribes had not yet entered into any such agreements, and were generally unaware of them. Even if they had known about the lines on the maps, the Blackfoot would not have recognized them as valid.

Another benefit had accrued to the Crows, with the signing of the treaty. They had been forced to come together as many bands, in order to sign the treaty, and a new tribal structure had developed, with dominant chiefs emerging over subchiefs. As such they were able to muster larger fighting forces, and coordinate a loose confederation for their mutual prosperity. With the U.S. Army now focused on many of their neighboring enemies, such as the Sioux and Cheyenne, the Crow were free, without breaking the treaty, to deal with the Blackfoot. It might even be suggested that certain interests back in Washington would approve such a campaign.

One of the chief architects of the Blackfoot strategy was a rising warrior from the bands of Crows that lived closest to the Blackfoot and had been attacked the most over the years. A tall and stately young man, Loud Thunder, had been part of the war party that had unsuccessfully pursued the Blackfoot raiding party the year before, and had led the ambush that killed Long Bow to draw the Blackfoot out. He was the younger brother of the Crow Chief Proud Eagle that had been killed by Moon in the Daylight and Two Horns three years earlier, when the two tribes had run into each other during a buffalo hunt. His hatred of the Blackfoot was well founded in blood debt. Now he had grown in esteem among the Crow leaders, and it was his initial scouting of the Blackfoot territory that had led to the advantage in spying on their enemies now. It could be argued that revenge had become an obsession for the man, and colored his everyday life. A prominent warrior, he was not particularly a likeable fellow, but in times of war, such men can become indispensable.

With the current available warriors that the Crows had at their western boundaries, the Blackfoot might have a small numerical advantage, with the combined strength of the Piegans, Blackfoot, and Blood branches, but the Crows would have a weapons advantage. Now the Crows saw that only four hundred Blackfoot would be coming. If they could pick the spot for the battle, the Crows were confident, with roughly equal numbers, superior weapons, surprise, and territorial advantage, they could crush the Blackfoot invasion. Reconnaissance would be the key to victory for both sides. As it stood, the Crows knew where the Blackfoot were. The Blackfoot were still looking for the Crows.

Buffalo Lance sat down with Two Horns. Two Horns was doing a lot of thinking and planning these days, and thus so was Buffalo Lance.

"Our scouts report that the nearest Crow camps are deserted," said Two Horns. "Blue Heron thinks that maybe the Crow have been watching us. He thinks that the death of Long Bow was meant to bring us to war. I think he is right."

"Good. Then the Crow will come out and fight," Buffalo Lance said with confidence.

"Not good. Too many will die, and we could lose."

"Since when could the Crow stand up in a fight with the Blackfoot?" Buffalo Lance wanted to know.

"You forget that the Crows have many guns now. If they have planned for our attack, they will have other advantages too," Two Horns added.

"So we don't attack?" Buffalo Lance asked, somewhat in amazement.

"We attack," Two Horns reassured him, "but we must find a way to turn their advantage into ours."

↗

"THE BLACKFOOT WILL be led by Walking Bear of the Northern Bloods," said High Feathers. "He is a strong warrior in battle, but now he is older."

"What of the warrior Two Horns? Is he not the one to call the War Council?" asked Loud Thunder.

Gray Bear interjected, "The traditional way of the Blackfoot has been to follow the greatest chief of their time. That is Walking Bear."

"Walking Bear is also their greatest warrior," added High Feathers. "Two Horns will be a subchief with Rock Eagle of the Piegans."

The Crows were in council, discussing the upcoming battle with the Blackfoot. Stands Against the Storm, the eldest chief, was there for his wisdom and experience, but he would not be fighting due to his age.

He said, "This is good if it is true. The Blackfoot of the Mountain will outnumber the Bloods and Piegans. But it is the Blood chief who will lead. It is not his fight. He will have his pride, but he will not have the anger of the Mountain Blackfoot. Still we should not underestimate the Blackfoot. It may be wise to double the scouts so no tricks can escape us."

"The Blackfoot have done as we predicted so far, and our scouts have not been spotted. We run a risk of being detected the more scouts we use. It is important that the Blackfoot do not know we are watching them," said Loud Thunder.

"If we can follow them until they are pinned next to a river or mountain, and then surprise them in ambush, perhaps drive a wedge and split their forces, that would be best," agreed High Feathers.

"But the deeper they come into Crow territory without finding our people, the more they will be alert to an ambush. You should meet them soon after they start their march," suggested Stands against the Storm.

"It might mean a less than perfect spot to battle, but the need for surprise is more important," agreed Loud Thunder. He could envision the battle and slaughter in his mind.

"We are in agreement," said High Feathers, who would lead the Crows into battle. "We should ride now to the West to be closer when the Blackfoot begin their invasion."

↗

THE BLACKFOOT WAR party was now arriving at the prearranged location just outside the Crow territory, where they would wait for the long-range scouts with news of the Crow camps. Many of the short-range scouts had come back still reporting no Crows to be found. The warriors were eager to strike out into enemy territory, but Two Horns would wait until his scouts returned.

Soaring Owl was about nineteen years old, and had been on several raids. He was an excellent rider and therefore had been selected for the longest ride to the Lakota camp. He had accompanied Blue Heron there two years before. He had delivered his message to the Sioux elders and chiefs, who were generally pleased to hear it, but had not committed to any action to aid the Blackfoot, merely saying that they would take it under advisement. As a long range scout, he had been trained to be careful and alert, but time was short, so he had turned southeast to cut across the northern stretches of the Crow lands in order to meet the war party and give his report to Two Horns at the designated meeting place by the Musselshell River. Moving along, keeping to as much cover as he could in the open rolling grasslands, he stopped to rest his mount as the sun began its morning climb into the sky. As his pinto drank by a small stream, he calculated that he was nearing the edge of no-man's-land, that thin buffer of real estate between the Crows and the Blackfoot that both tribes claimed but neither really utilized, due to their rivalry. He was now about one day's ride to the meeting place.

A pair of pheasants was flushed about a mile away, and he crept up the low hill beside the stream to see what was afoot this early morning. He expected to see a wolf on its way home from the evening's hunt, or perhaps some grazing buffalo that had stirred the birds.

Easing his head up over the hill, and peering through the grass, he saw instead the advance scouts of what must be a large war party of Crows from the size of the dust in the distance. The outriding scout who had flushed the birds would pass by without coming any closer, but Soaring Owl scurried back down the hill to stand by his horse, to make sure the animal didn't give his position away. Securing his horse where it could feed on some tender shoots of grass by the stream, he reclimbed the hill to scout some more. As the war party continued to pass perhaps two miles or more in distance from him, he judged their direction and size. There was little doubt, they were heading in the same direction as he was. They would reach the foothills by midday and achieve much sought after cover. The Crow were going to preemptively strike the Blackfoot forces. He must circle and warn Two Horns of this danger.

THE CROW WERE not the only one's who were watching the Blackfoot. Staying well above the Blackfoot war party on the mountain slopes as it moved toward the Musselshell River, Lame Elk was relieved that this large fighting force would be heading out to the East to attack the Crows. Spying on the

Blackfoot as he periodically did, he had watched the gathering of the chiefs in Council and knew that would mean something was going to happen. By the time he had gone home and gotten Waushaute and a handful of his best scouts to help him, the Blackfoot warriors were already beginning to arrive at Two Horns's camp. Keeping the scouts some distance away as a reserve, he and Waushaute had continued to observe the Blackfoot preparation for war. It was an impressive sight. Small groups were riding in unison, practicing strike and retreat tactics and flanking movements. This was all done with hand signals, and the most practice was for all the warriors to pay attention. A few were knocked off their horses by the trainers for not doing well enough. There was some sort of competition taking place between the numerous bands. Lame Elk was taking mental notes as to what he saw, as was Waushaute, and at times they would turn to each other to discuss the exercises they were watching. Should this force decide to attack the Shoshone, they would need to stand behind their barricades to thwart the horse charges and maximize their guns. The two talked incessantly about how the camp would need to be defended, and a rider was dispatched to Fort Hall for help from the Bannock and Captain Farmer.

However, once the Blackfoot left the camp, heading first southeast and then East, Lame Elk sent another rider to cancel the call for help. It was then that he and Waushaute discussed the opportunity to attack the now underdefended Blackfoot camp. It would send a message to the Blackfoot that the Shoshone had not forgotten the savage assault of a few years back, and that the Shoshone were watching their every move and were unafraid. They would not slaughter the women and children as the Blackfoot had, forcing an open war, but just the remaining men who tried to defend the camp. Of course they would steal what horses were left, and burn the camp. One hundred warriors should be more than enough to do the job. Yet another rider was sent to bring the warriors to the chiefs.

UPON REACHING THE foothills, High Feathers, Loud Thunder, and the Crow warriors staked out a hiding place nestled against a cliff in a wooded area that was out of the way for normal traffic. Two tiers of guards were posted to avoid any surprises, and fresh scouts were sent back and forth with the incoming reports on the Blackfoot war party, perhaps three hours ride away. They would wait for the Blackfoot party to emerge from the cover of the wooded foothills before selecting a moment to attack. Confidence was running high in the Crow camp. There were all the makings of a great victory in store for the warriors. They settled down to looking after their weapons and to adding touches to their warpaints. The Crow also often carried shields where the art would depict animals or acts of nature such as lightning or whirlwinds, giving their owner special powers. The shields often had feathers of eagles, or colored cloth, attached to them. Unlike their painted bodies of their own exploits, the shields were meant to intimidate their enemy or protect their owner. Many of the warriors primped their hair, which was stiff with bear grease and decorated with feathers which told of coup counted or enemies killed, depending on how the feathers were placed, notched, or stained. The Crow preferred the use of white paint on their faces, bodies and horses, giving them a ghostly appearance at times. This was sometimes highlighted with eyelids painted yellow. Brightly colored beaded warshirts, and long pants with rectangular boxes on them, gave the Crows a distinctive look when they went to war.

By comparison, the Blackfoot were rather drab. Dressed in dark brown leggings and warshirts, they tended to only paint their faces, using a variety of markings and colors. Some had black painted faces for exceptional acts of bravery or combat. They wore less beaded work and preferred owl feathers to eagle feathers. Though not as colorful as their rivals, the Blackfoot were no less intimidating in their appearance.

52

"**I** WANT YOU TO KEEP an eye on Marshal Donovan and report back to me if he is putting himself in any danger," she explained to Barton.

Barton looked rather puzzled and asked, "When you say danger, what type are you referring to, Countess?"

"He is following a killer around that he met in the Oregon Territories, and that horrible Indian everyone talks about that works for the pirate Targon is following the man too. They think that the man they found tied to the tree and mutilated that worked for Paul Logan just before he disappeared … Donovan says the police think this Indian may have done it! Marshal Donovan thinks it likely that Logan died at the hands of Targon or some other ruffian. Now that Indian might run into Marshal Donovan!" Gabrielle was working herself into an excited state.

Having watched over his charge her whole life, Barton knew how to ease her concerns. "I will follow the Marshal, carefully. He will not see me. If he is in trouble, I will assist him, and keep you informed at all times. However, you must know that the Marshal is very capable of defending himself. It is what he used to do for a living."

"Thank you, Barton. With Monsieur Seurat ailing, we could not survive Donovan meeting any foul play."

"La Comtesse de Larousseau is quite capable of surviving anything," Barton admonished her, "but we will see that no such concern is necessary."

As ZACHARY DuPORT headed out to dinner with a young girl on his arm, the three men watching him took up their positions. In reverse order, Barton mingled with a crowd of patrons standing outside a gaming parlor about two blocks south of DuPort on Mission Street with a view of Marshal Donovan. The Marshal stood at the corner of Fifth Street, alternately watching the doorway of the Blue Moon Gambling Emporium, one of San Francisco's upper-end card houses, and shifting his gaze past the building to somewhere farther up the street, where Barton assumed the Marshal had a fix on the Indian. Ishka had climbed up on a back staircase in an adjoining alley, and was not particularly concerned about being seen. To Ishka's thinking, the Du-Port man had little guile, and was very easy to keep track of. He had already discovered the late night high-risk card game that DuPort was running, and the prostitution ring. But Targon would not really care that the man was ambitious or using some company assets for additional income. Targon would want to know whom this man associated with, whether he was stealing from Targon, and if he was dangerous. So far, Ishka had found that even killing this DuPort would not be much fun. He doubted the man would put up much of a fight. In point of fact, the muscles Zachary had put on while at sea were indeed becoming soft from lack of use in his new occupation.

Donovan noted the closer surveillance by the Indian of Bridges, and figured it for one of two most probable reasons. It could be that the Indian just felt more comfortable in not being spotted by Bridges, or that the Indian was getting ready to end this exercise and kill the man. Either way, it made for an easier surveillance keeping both men in view. But he would continue to take good care not to be observed. Being spotted by the Indian would be worse than flushing Bridges.

The surprise of the evening was to be Barton's, as it became obvious that the surveillance target, Zeke Bridges, was none other than Monsieur Zachary DuPort of New Orleans. Barton had spent several months making sure Monsieur DuPort had kept his distance on the sailing vessel that had brought them all to San Francisco. The Countess would be equally surprised and dismayed that the man would again cause potential trouble and embarrassment for her. Perhaps the Indian, the Marshal, or he himself could alleviate that possibility. Another thought struck Barton then. Monsieur Corby would also know and disapprove of this scurrilous miscreant. Should Monsieur Corby ever find out about the unfortunate affair in New Orleans, La Comtesse would go from embarrassed to humiliated. Barton was sure La Comtesse was fond of the westerner, as was the Marshal. And what would the Marshal think? No, this would not do. With both the Indian and the Marshal watching the man, a quiet meeting was probably not feasible. His mind was running at an incredible pace as the worry began to take over his reasoning. Then it came to him and he relaxed as the finality of the solution worked its details through his thinking. Barton was a man of honor and a dedicated protector of the Countess's family for over thirty years. His honor and their honor were inseparable.

Zachary had selected a fine restaurant at which to dine that had a terrace out back over the water of the bay. When Zachary was seated at the table for dinner, he breathed in deeply. It was one of those rare evenings in the city when outdoor seating was preferable to being indoors. He had taken a table by the railing on the deck overlooking the bay. Seafood was something he had taken a particular liking to, and to have a beautiful woman with him for dinner was an extra bonus. She had just come into his employ, and was not yet earning her way. Zachary thought he would enjoy her for a week or two before putting her out for hire. Perhaps he could get to trust her as he had Julie, and use her for special assignments.

He was taking his first sip of wine and enjoying the men looking at his new protégé when he became aware that a man was standing next to him. Thinking it was a waiter, he did not look up until he was addressed.

"Monsieur DuPort, I presume, or is there another name?" Barton asked stiffly.

It took Zachary a second to recognize Barton. Barton had physically intimidated Zachary during their trip West, including a few convincing jabs to the solar plexus, to punctuate his point to stay away from the Countess. Well, he was not the same man anymore.

"Well, if it isn't Gabrielle's little toady man. Look, dear, this man cleans up the messes of the great Countess of San Francisco. Aren't you a little far from home, Frenchy?" Zachary snarled with heavy sarcasm. At the same time he felt for the blade he carried in his waistband, a product of his education the last few years.

Barton flushed at the insult. "Please stand up, monsieur, so I can insult you properly," he said in a loud enough voice that all the diners were now watching the drama unfold. Barton examined the man as he stood, expecting him to have some sort of weapon.

The restaurant's maitre d' hustled over to try and defuse the situation, and others became vocal in protest around them. Outside, Ishka slipped through the front door as the attention of everyone was centered on the activity out back. Donovan decided he had better close on the disturbance too.

The two men were now facing each other. Zachary pretended to turn to talk to his dinner companion while he hid his hand drawing out his knife. Whirling back on Barton, he lashed out with the blade up near eye level, sending the maitre d' sprawling backward to the floor to get away. But Barton had been ready, ducking the assault and grabbing Zachary's arm with both of his own and twisting it backwards. Losing his balance, Zachary crashed down on the dinner table, sending plates and glasses flying, and knocking over the young girl who had come with him. Barton stayed with him, repositioning himself on top of Zachary so he could use Zachary's knife against him.

People were yelling and a couple of ladies screamed, as the two suddenly rolled across the floor, banging into two more tables before struggling back to their feet. Barton maintained his two-handed grip on Zachary's arm that held the knife.

Ishka was now in the dining area, and could see that his man was in a fight with a knife. He doubted that Targon wished to kill the man, or he would have gotten the job.

Meanwhile, Barton had been able to turn the blade into Zachary's side and was about to shove it deeper, when Ishka bounded forward and ran his own large hunting knife into Barton's lower back. Almost simultaneously there was a loud report of a gun fired, and then again, as Donovan put two shots into the Indian to try and save Barton. As both the Indian and Barton sank, Zachary was about to stab Barton again with his freed hand, when Donovan strode forward and quickly whacked him over the head with the side of his gun.

Kneeling over Barton, Donovan stuffed a napkin in his wound and told the waiters to get a doctor and the police. Barton was dying, and Zeke Bridges would need hospital attention. Donovan hoped he had cracked the man's skull. Ishka surprisingly was not dead yet either.

"I was supposed to watch over you," Barton whispered to Donovan, with some irony.

"Don't talk. The doctor is on the way," Donovan said.

Barton shook his head. "La Comtesse knows this man. He would hurt her. You must protect..." Barton ran out of words, lapsing into unconsciousness.

Shortly thereafter, he died, leaving Donovan to wonder what was going on. Barton had never really warmed to Donovan, but Donovan knew Gabrielle had depended on the man, and Barton had religiously protected the girl. This would be a blow to Gabrielle.

Surveying the wreckage of tables and twisted, bleeding bodies, Donovan saw some possible closure for himself. Barton had been an unarmed man, attacked from two sides by men with knives, and killed. This should be enough to lock Bridges away until the evidence from Fort Boise closed the door on him for good.

Next he went over to the Indian he had been trailing to see how much longer he would live. Lifting his head, it was apparent that his injuries were also fatal. Ishka looked at Donovan and smiled. "Oregon Man," he said with some surprise, then gurgled and died. Donovan laid the head back down and took a close look at the man. There was a strange look of peace on his face, as if death had released him from his pain.

When the police arrived, Donovan told a convincing story about an orchestrated attack on Barton. Several of the diners saw it the same way. What else would have prompted the Indian to attack? Donovan suggested it seemed premeditated. The police took Zachary away still unconscious, to the hospital presumably, after informing Donovan that they would need to speak with him again at some later date. The coroner arrived to pick up the dead bodies, and Donovan spoke on behalf of the Countess who would wish to claim Barton's body and bury it. The coroner was thankful that someone would want it. Looking at the gruesome tattooed Indian on the floor, he seriously doubted anyone would be stepping forward for this body.

53

THE BLACKFOOT CAMP WAS completing the last chores, securing the tee-pee poles and hides to the various travois pulled by dogs and horses. The women were bickering as usual over the packing and handling of household items, and Buffalo Robe was about to shout in frustration that the camp should have been on the move hours before. Perhaps it was to be expected, as the men in large part were away, and weren't able to berate the women to work faster. Perhaps it was because there was a sullen mood in the camp, not knowing which of the warriors might come back. If they didn't finish soon, there would be no point in traveling today, and they would camp in the open with their packed possessions and start out the next day. Resigned to the delays, Buffalo Robe went to walk by the lakeshore, as he often did when he was upset or needed to think things over. Getting old had many disadvantages as he saw it. Better to have died young in glory. His teeth were bothering him the most now, and he feared he would be loosing another soon. He could live with the aches and pains, and the insolence of the youngsters, but chewing you literally couldn't live without.

JUST IN TIME, thought Lame Elk. The attack would be much easier in the open. Had the Blackfoot been climbing into the mountains, everyone would have scattered into the forest, and controlling the chaos would have been difficult.

"Listen to me, Shoshone warriors. We are going to remind the Blackfoot that the Shoshone are a great people. We do not kill women and children today. We kill the men. But bring me an old man from their Council to deliver our message after we are gone. Look for any of our people who may still be slaves. Take all the horses, and any possessions you may wish. We will burn the rest," Lame Elk told his mounted and ready warriors.

His bitter memories of the Blackfoot attack and his dead wife and son always lay just behind his consciousness and could be recalled in startling detail anytime he wished to do so. The opportunity for revenge had arisen, and seizing the moment was ingrained from his earliest education. However, Lame Elk was uncomfortable with what he was about to do. There was no glory here. No test of will or achievement. He felt a detached responsibility to settle scores and send a political message of strength on behalf of the People. But he was unconvinced that this action would right the past or secure the future, even as he felt compelled to go forward.

Breaking into two groups to surround the camp, the Shoshone rode down on the now panicked remnants of Two Horns's Blackfoot tribe. Seeing the warriors advance on the camp, Moon in the Daylight involuntarily placed her hand over her unborn baby before she ran to get her lance. A knot of Blackfoot warriors numbering about twenty, mostly old men and some boys who were yet not old enough to go on the war party, rallied behind Moon in the Daylight in the middle of the camp. Lame Elk imagined this was probably not too dissimilar to the scene his family had witnessed back in the Yellowstone Valley. Conjuring up the images of his dead wife and son again for his immediate purpose, Lame Elk led the charge into the Blackfoot resistance, swinging his warclub at any available target. The Blackfoot band made a noble but futile stand against the overwhelming strength of the attacking Shoshone warriors. Moon in the Daylight at the lead was hit almost simultaneously by two warriors, spinning her around like a top for the coup de grace by a third war club. Within minutes it was over, and his warriors were rounding up the ponies and picking through the Blackfoot belongings, as the women and children cowered or ran. Some stayed with the fallen and began loudly grieving.

Waushaute and two of his warriors brought an old man of the Blackfoot over to Lame Elk. Lame Elk dismounted, wiping some blood from his arm. He indicated the two should sit and talk. So Buffalo Robe sat looking at the great enemy of the Blackfoot, Black Hand of the Shoshone.

"I am Lame Elk of the Yellowstone Shoshone," Lame Elk stated in a business-like voice.

"I know you," said Buffalo Robe. "I am Buffalo Robe of the Gray Woman Mountain Blackfoot. I was once a great warrior like you, with many coup and many Shoshone scalps in my teepee."

Lame Elk didn't doubt that an Elder of the Blackfoot would have been a great warrior. He ignored the Shoshone remark.

"Then as a warrior you will note that my people didn't kill the women and children, and are not taking slave captives. We have punished you for your cowardly raid on our camp in the Yellowstone, but as a great people, our warriors do not kill the weak."

A bonfire started in the middle of the camp as the Shoshone warriors began to throw Blackfoot belongings onto the blaze. An even louder wail went up from the Blackfoot women.

"You have broken the peace between our two tribes," said Buffalo Robe. "Two Horns will avenge this and the death of Moon in the Daylight."

Seeing the confusion on Blackhand's face, Buffalo Robe explained. "You have killed Two Horns's warrior wife and unborn baby." He pointed over to the battle scene where the Blackfoot had put up their lone defense.

Assessing the new information, Lame Elk replied, "She chose to fight and die as a warrior. My wife and small boy were ridden down and killed in cold-blooded murder. The Blackfoot broke what you call the peace between us, as it always has been when the Blackfoot wish to take something they want. I am not here to argue. We have repaid the debt of honor for our dead families. We could kill all of you here today if it was our wish. What we have done is enough to settle the debt. It should end here. That is my message to your chief. Should Two Horns unwisely wish to continue the blood war, he will find the Shoshone are strong in our valley again, and will not be surprised or easily defeated. Tell Two Horns all I have said here today." He then rose and called for a Blackfoot pony for the old man as a token of his respect. The old Indian walked away with the lone pony toward his people as the fire raged into the late afternoon.

54

STRANAHAN AND O'BANNON SADDLED up. It was time to find Sam Johnson, and that meant riding out to his homestead. It was shortly before dawn, and it was their habit to leave with no announcement as to where they were going. They had been led to believe that it would take them several hours to get there, and they didn't relish sleeping out in Apache country, hence the early start. As usual, conversation was infrequent, particularly since O'Bannon was wolfing down some sort of breakfast food. Stranahan absently started to wonder if O'Bannon had ever missed a meal. He searched his memory, recalling the many times O'Bannon had insisted on eating at the most unlikely moments. But Stranahan trusted his colleague, and was cognizant of O'Bannon's contributions in a pinch. No one was ever going to intimidate O'Bannon. Quite the contrary, as O'Bannon had a short fuse and a thin skin. He was insulted by threats, as if his manhood had been called into question. But, as quick as he was to anger, he tended to cool off just as quickly. Stranahan had rarely seen O'Bannon end the day mulling over earlier problems. Deputy Marshal O'Bannon was large and strong, and willing to mix it up. He was determined, and honest about the important issues. He did have trouble paying his way on small items, like an apple or the last beer of the evening, which he seemed to assume people would be happy to simply give to him. But riding out to chat with an irate rancher who was threatening violence, O'Bannon was the kind of fellow you would like to have along.

About midmorning they saw the walled complex of Don Sebastián's hacienda, and O'Bannon thought they should drop in for a snack. Stranahan had been running an idea around in his head, and agreed to a short stop. The trio of Drego, Don Sebastián, and Corby greeted them. While Maria fed O'Bannon, Stranahan asked Corby if he would like to join them on their ride out to Sam Johnson's, in an unofficial capacity, sort of like a guide? Eager to do most anything, in particular to ride Borrasca, Corby quickly agreed. Drego wished to go too, but both Don Sebastián and Stranahan thought it was too provocative a measure to have the son of Don Sebastián visit the disgruntled rancher. A happy O'Bannon noticed the pretty girl who had fed him was preparing a travel basket for the threesome. She packed it into Corby's saddlebags again, hanging a while on his leg. Then they were off, with additional directions from the Rancho foreman.

Stranahan started a conversation, asking about the pretty young girl at the hacienda, but then switched to his real purpose, saying he was authorized to deputize anyone he felt he might need. The pay was poor and the job was dangerous, but Corby would have the law on his side, instead of being a target for some hothead. As Stranahan laid it out, their intentions were the same: to see that a fair deal was dealt to everyone by a legitimate authority. Corby recognized an avenue to end living off of the Drego family and still fulfill his pledge to help protect their interests. It might also allow him to find out more about who would be making the decisions, and maybe influence that process in some way. He supposed the Drego family would look upon the development positively, save for Maria. Drego would put the interest of his family above having his friend around for a bunkmate.

The wind was kicking up some as the three stopped behind a large rock, while Stranahan swore Corby in as a temporary Deputy Marshal. He then handed him a badge and walked him through the broad rules of his new employer. There would be a little paperwork to do when they got back, and Corby would be picking up his gear and moving to town. For now, the main directive was to listen to what Stranahan told him to do.

As they rode on further, purple mountains started to rise, and the land away from the river became even poorer. Rocks and sand were heavily mixed in with the low-lying plant life. Crossing the river where they had been instructed to, they saw a trail heading into a canyon that they took as their way to Johnson's camp. A mile down the trail, the canyon narrowed, and cattle tracks were obvious in the sand. Shortly thereafter the canyon opened up again, and a couple of rough-looking cabins were set against a cliff wall, with corrals and pens alongside. A thin column of smoke wafted through the late morning air, but nothing else stirred, as the canyon effectively cut off the outside wind. Dismounting they were met by a cook who told them the men were all out with the cattle, further north along the river, perhaps an hour away. Remounting they retraced their tracks back out to the river turning right to the North. The mountains were drawing ever closer, shrinking the land along this side of the river. It was true that the far side of the river appeared to be better grazing for the cattle, and it was there that they overtook the small herd and Johnson, on Don Sebastián's land again.

Following Stranahan's instructions, the three spread out a little and rode slowly toward the cattlemen who had gathered together as they approached.

Sam Johnson was cursing under his breath as the lawmen rode toward him. Even though he had seven men with him, the idea of a fight never entered his mind. His gun hand that had been hired for such an occasion had quit after being hit on the head and thrown in jail, and the cowboys he had with him were not good enough or loyal enough to stand up to the marshals. Besides which, Gresham had told him not to fight that way, and to bide his time while the lawyer stirred up sentiment for the American ranchers through his contacts in Congress.

"Marshal," was all he said in greeting when the men stopped in front of him.

"You Sam Johnson?" Stranahan asked.

Johnson nodded yes.

"You are on the wrong side of the river, Johnson," Stranahan said.

Johnson nodded again. "You see all this unused land, Marshal? This country needs beef, and these cattle need grass. I may be on the wrong side of the river for now, but not on the wrong side of the border. This will be open range soon enough."

Stranahan shifted his weight on his horse. "Maybe, maybe not. This gets decided back in Washington. I'm willing to let you off this time with a last warning, if you tell me you will stay on your side of the river until this is over," Stranahan offered reasonably.

"Seems to me that you have taken sides on this thing," Johnson said, nodding toward Corby, and evading the answer.

"Deputy Marshal Corby will act in the interest of the law. That means he will also act against any lawbreakers," Stranahan pointedly said. "Now you can start your men turning those steers to cross back over the river. Next time I hear they are over here, I come and haul you in to jail. Do you understand?"

Sam Johnson was never any good at holding his temper, but he was not a stupid man. He wanted to say a great many things, but Gresham had convinced him to hold his tongue until they could line up support. Any rash act could sour the natural sympathy they were bound to get if they handled it right. So he bit his lip, but couldn't resist saying, "Mark my words, Marshal, those Mexs will be off this land by next Fall." Angrily swinging his horse around, he yelled at his men to start herding the cattle back across the river.

The three lawmen stayed on Don Sebastián's property watching the cowboys move the herd.

"My guess is that more trouble's coming. Too much restraint by that fellow Johnson. He ain't no coward. Backed off too easily. Something else is brewing here," Stranahan muttered as he sank into thought.

55

TWO HORNS LISTENED TO Soaring Owl again, and then called in his war chiefs and had Soaring Owl repeat his story over again. After several questions, Two Horns thanked Soaring Owl and sent him to get some food and rest.

"We need to send out scouts and find the Crow war party," came the obvious comment from Rock Eagle.

"Yes, but we must assume that we are being watched right now by the Crows," said Two Horns.

"Maybe we could trap the Crow scouts, kill them and then disappear," suggested Buffalo Lance.

Two Horns frowned but did not say anything. Buffalo Lance was not in the War Council for his strategic thinking.

"We must find the Crows without them knowing we are aware of their war party," Walking Bear answered for Two Horns. "If we killed the scouts, they would know, and send out more. Four hundred warriors are not hard to track if you know where to start."

Buffalo Lance squinted in recognition of his poor proposal.

Two Horns had been quietly thinking as Blue Heron said, "We should use this knowledge to our advantage by pretending to be unaware. We can surprise them."

"What are the Crows thinking?" asked Two Horns. "They have equal numbers, better weapons, and, they believe, the advantage of surprise. What are they waiting for?"

"If I am the Crow chief, I want to use my advantage to crush my enemy," said Walking Bear. "It is easier if my enemy is in open country, and I can ambush them where my guns can be most effective."

"What about a nighttime attack?" asked Blue Heron.

"Possibly," said Walking Bear, "but there would be guards posted at the enemy's camp, and my guns wouldn't be as dangerous. I think I would attack out of hiding, from the trees, at daylight if possible, before the camp is mounted and moving, or knowing the land, squeeze in using the hills for cover and protection from behind. Someway that I can inflict the most damage and receive the least."

Two Horns smiled and asked, "When would the Crow chief least expect to be attacked?"

Buffalo Lance understood immediately and barely contained himself as he quickly answered, "When he was sure that his own attack plan was in place. Just before he was ready to attack himself!"

Walking Bear nodded and said, "It will be dangerous guessing the moment, but if I am the Crow and set my attack for a place or time, I am thinking how to attack, not defend. I might even make my warriors rest before the fight."

"We could help them decide where to attack and when," piped up Blue Heron. "We could scout ahead for a likely ambush spot, and camp there, or change our riding pace to pressure their decision. If we can know where they are."

"Dress our scouts as Crows. If we are careful and use few scouts, maybe we can trick them," said Stalking Wolf.

"They will follow us right?" asked Two Horns. "So we will have the advantage in leaving scouts hidden behind us too, as we travel. We will go forward with the normal advance scouts as if we think the Crow are somewhere in front of us, but we will leave scouts hidden along the trail to spy as they follow. We will pick the time to fight. We will have the surprise, and it will be close-in fighting to take away their advantage in guns. We do not tell the warriors until the time to attack. Pick our best scouts and bring them here for instructions."

The camp broke to head into Crow territory. Two scouts were dressed as Crows to try and infiltrate or at least approach the main band of Crows. Other scouts would drop off discreetly as they rode, and hide, hopefully following the Crow scouts back to their war party. A game of nerves began for the Blackfoot chiefs. They would soon find out if their training had been adequate and who had the better scouts.

WHEN THE BLACKFOOT started to move to the East, the Crows also broke camp to follow at a safe distance. The Blackfoot were seen to send out scouts to the South and East, and didn't appear to be setting a hard pace. They probably had not found a suitable target yet, and would begin to get suspicious in the next few days. High Feathers wanted to attack at the earliest convenient opportunity before the Blackfoot became overly concerned about a possible trap. When they continued to find evidence that the Crows had recently left the area, they would begin to suspect that the Crows had been warned and that would mean the danger of a trap. He did not want to lose the element of surprise. Instead of waiting for a good place to attack the Blackfoot, he began to look for a good place to conceal an ambush using bait. Before the Blackfoot got too far into Crow country, High Feathers planned to send a tantalizing raiding party of some forty warriors across their intended path. The Blackfoot scouts would spot the raiding party and report back, forcing the Blackfoot war party to pursue the decoy Crows who would lead them straight into his ambush. Deciding on this new strategy, he set a parallel path East, staying to the North of the Blackfoot march but angling South to narrow the gap between the two forces from a direction they would not be looking. By tomorrow he would be in position to arrange a battlefield to his liking, and spring the trap. All he would have to do then would be to dispatch the raiding party further South to wait until the advancing Blackfoot spotted them. Loud Thunder volunteered to lead the decoy raiding party.

SOON AFTER THE Blackfoot left their camp area, their left-behind hidden scouts saw three Crow scouts carefully emerge from their hiding positions and confer. One scout was sent off to the northeast, and the remaining two Crow scouts split up to trail the Blackfoot War Party to the East. Soaring Owl was one of the two Blackfoot scouts that would be relay riders working with the two scouts dressed as Crows. The four riders very cautiously followed the departing Crow scout. He made a beeline for the northeast, and after about three hours ride, they all arrived at a canyon where shortly before many men had been. The Crow rider then set out on the broad trail of the moving Crow war party, overtaking it after another couple of hours. It was apparent to the Blackfoot scouts that the Crows were now tracking and closing on the Blackfoot. Their rides back and forth would be shrinking with the hours. Soaring Owl was the first to ride with an update for Two Horns, circling South before riding hard to the southeast. He found the Blackfoot trail and followed it straight into the warriors. Two Horns had decided that in order to avoid suspicion with the ever-present Crow spies, his scouts should return to camp openly following the obvious trail. Perhaps the Crow scouts would think they were outriders, or messengers from the Blackfoot tribes back in the mountains.

56

WHEN LAME ELK AND his men arrived back at the Shoshone lake camp in the Yellowstone country, he wasn't surprised to find Captain Farmer and an army detachment waiting there for him. After all, he had sent a call for help out when it appeared that the Blackfoot might be moving to attack his people. The unexpected surprise was Katy with her father, Dr. Lemmins. Another recent outbreak of cholera with the Indians to the south had caused the men to check on the condition of the Yellowstone Shoshones. Cholera, yellow fever, smallpox, typhoid, scarlet fever, whooping cough, tuberculosis, diphtheria, and deadly influenza had been ravaging the Indian natives since the Whiteman had arrived in the New World. Diseases were so widespread and prevalent around the entire world that many cultures considered them a punishment for one's sins. As there were few real cures, the remedy when one found one's self among the sick was to leave the area, which of course carried the diseases to new uninfected areas rapidly.

The bacteria and viruses so devastated the country that the United States' mortality census of 1850 attributed 40 percent of the deaths nationwide to disease-spread epidemics. Average life expectancy was actually lowered in 1855 to 39.8 years due to the unprecedented level of deaths occurring annually. Doctors were often avoided and feared. One of the most afflicted groups at the time was the Mormons, who were settling in Utah, having carried a variety of European diseases with them across the country. The most recent cholera surge had spread to the neighboring Indian tribes around Salt Lake City, and was working its way North, including infecting some of the Shoshones and Bannocks near Fort Hall.

Dr. Lemmins and Captain Farmer needed to check on the Yellowstone Shoshone. Captain Farmer also wanted to know about the trouble between the Shoshone and Blackfoot, even though the alarm had been cancelled. Watching the Shoshone drive in a herd of new horses, Captain Farmer could tell that something was going on.

The Shoshone warriors were still in their war paint, and made a triumphant ride into the camp. As the mission was so successful, the people were happy, and members of the old Yellowstone tribe were exuberant when five captive female members were finally reunited with their families. The horses were not the best the Blackfoot had, for obvious reasons, but horses were horses. Katy noticed an Appaloosa yearling in the herd. Having never seen one before, she asked Lame Elk about it and learned that the Nez Perce, to the northwest, nurtured the breed, and occasionally a stolen pony would show up in other camps. Other than its distinctive markings, Lame Elk said the horse was usually sure footed, but not as good as the Shoshones' paints. Waushaute had a better opinion of the horse, telling Katy that the Nez Perce selectively bred the animals for speed, strength, and endurance. "If you could steal a Nez Perce 'Palouse' pony, you should."

The animal's eyes were somehow different and seemed almost human. Katy was taken with it. It had a gentle nature, and Lame Elk cut it out of the herd and presented it to Katy. The girl was ecstatic, and raced to ask her father if she could keep it.

Seeing an opening, Captain Farmer approached the two chiefs and asked about the Blackfoot. As Lame Elk had called upon the captain for possible assistance, he felt obligated to tell the man what had transpired.

Alarmed, Captain Farmer asked, "Won't the Blackfoot be coming here to get revenge?"

Waushaute smiled and explained that the Blackfoot had sent four hundred warriors against the Crows. They would be involved with the Crows for some time. When the Blackfoot wished to bother the Shoshone again, the Shoshone would be ready.

The incessant warfare didn't make sense to Captain Farmer, but it obviously was going to continue. The normal fear of retaliation that a white settlement would have after such an attack wasn't apparent with the Indians. They were content with the current swing of favor in their direction.

Lame Elk however had a lingering regret that the wife and unborn baby of the Blackfoot chief had been killed. Having lost a child, he had come to place a very high value on children in general. In resignation, he sensed that Two Horns would have to even the score. His own wife, Many Flowers, had miscarried, as new wives often do, but Lame Elk knew there would be other babies with his two young wives. He too wanted the children, which the fighting so often took away. He respected the chief of the Blackfoot, who now shared a tragedy of lost family with Lame Elk. He knew from his own experience it would be a long time before the Blackfoot chief would return to looking to the sunrise.

That night Captain Farmer sought out Dr. Lemmins.

"I consider myself a friend of the family," Captain Farmer began.

Dr. Lemmins and Captain Farmer lived together in a very small community. Dr. Lemmins was well aware that the captain was fond of his adopted daughter, and that alone put the man in good standing, but Captain Farmer was a fine officer and a friend to the doctor as well.

"Of course, Jack, what's troubling you tonight?" asked Dr. Lemmins.

"You know I have a great respect for Lame Elk and Waushaute, and appreciate their generosity in opening up their tribe to us. But eventually events will sour the Shoshone to our presence out here. Just like the Iroquois and the Huron back East, these Western tribes will be pushed aside as the country grows, and they won't like it."

"But that will be a long time from now, probably not in our lifetime. This is still a wilderness in all directions," Dr. Lemmins proclaimed, sweeping his arm in a wide arc.

"Possibly, but probably not. There will be more forts and more immigrants each year, and now the fur traders are hunting the buffalo. It has gotten pretty bad with the Sioux, between the pox and the diminished hunting. The War Department is anticipating a string of Indian revolts that could domino straight across the country at some point in time. The politicians will keep breaking the Indian treaties as they get pressure from the industrialists and the pioneers. I am thinking that a little less exposure to the Indians by your family over time might be wise."

"You mean Katy," Dr. Lemmins said with a knowing smile. "She is half Indian now, isn't she?"

Captain Farmer remained silent.

"She loves her time out here with the Shoshone. All Winter long we hear about what she will do when the snows melt and she can ride and fish."

Dr. Lemmins fell into thought. "Does Lame Elk see the problems ahead?"

Now it was Captain Farmer's turn to contemplate. "He may sense the changes will be bad, but he hasn't really seen them yet out here. I'm hoping we can insulate these people somewhat when the time comes. It would be a shame to see this magnificent area become just another farm community. But the military will be required to do as it is ordered, and if history is any guide, the Indians will become our adversaries. Those tribes farther to the North may hang on longer, but…"

The doctor was now readily concerned with the dire predictions of his friend. Captain Farmer felt a need to pull back a little on his doom-and-gloom scenario.

"I'm just reading the reports I get. They may be wrong. Sometimes our analysts overproject to drive home a point. Odds are pretty good that Katy will be of marrying age before the Shoshone turn against us."

Dr. Lemmins nodded his head, saying, "No, Jack, you are probably right in worrying about our situation out here, and the Blackfoot or the cholera will most likely strike the Shoshone first. The resulting conditions are ones I should have considered on Katy's behalf before now. She will be devastated if her adopted Indians suffer mightily. No, Jack, we need to do some thinking about Katy. She will be a young lady before we know it. Valerie has been hinting the same way. It's just that she is so happy out here, but you are right, we have to look to the future."

Captain Farmer placed a hand on his friend's shoulder, smiled, and said, "You don't have to do anything tonight, Doc. Let's go look at that pony Katy won't leave alone."

57

Zachary DuPort sat in the jail cell, gently touching the bandages covering his head. Shug O'Brien sat on the bench outside the cell, looking down at his shoes, having forgotten what they had been talking about a minute before. Shug had been filling in the gaps in Zachary's memory of the events landing him in jail. Most of what Shug had told him didn't make sense to his tender brain. In fact the whole fiasco seemed surreal to him. Barton, Ishka, Marshal Donovan, all involved in this fight. He thought there must be connections between all of these people, but his mind could not concentrate, and he felt dizzy and nauseous. His overwhelming feelings were once again of unfairness, anger, and fear. Why were these things always happening to him? His idiot brother had gotten him mixed up with the law to begin with, and he had been dodging danger ever since. There had been the vindictive Charles Loucheur that had tried to have him killed in New Orleans, and the greedy Paul Logan that had shanghaied him aboard the whaler. He had been forced to dodge meeting Marshal Donovan and that no-account drifter Corby ever since he had come to San Francisco. He had to kill Dan Williams (and Julie) to cover his tracks with that bastard Targon, and now this insanity with Barton. It was just unfair. Another ugly thought occurred to him; he could write off ever being with Gabrielle after this too.

Had Donovan come to Barton's aid, or had Donovan been watching him? Donovan obviously knew Barton, and would have tried to assist him if he saw he was in trouble. One piece of the puzzle was clear to Zachary: Targon had set his Indian to trail him. Targon probably was still fishing around after Dan Williams's death. For once having the dreadful Indian near had been a stroke of luck. Zachary knew he had been losing the fight with Barton, and Barton had seemed intent on finishing him. Targon would not like having his top assassin dead, even if it were in protecting an associate. But he hadn't asked Ishka to be there. It would be unfair to blame him for Ishka's death. No, his two biggest problems at the moment were his role in the death of Barton, and if Marshal Donovan was after Zeke Bridges, or so he thought. When his head began to clear, he started worrying more about Targon again too.

"So IT WOULD seem that your Zachary DuPort and my Zeke Bridges are one and the same," Donovan concluded his report to Gabrielle. "If Zachary Du-Port cannot provide any history prior to showing up in New Orleans, and we can get that second or third identification as Zeke Bridges, we should be able to see the man swing." Donovan referred to the still popular form of death penalty.

Gabrielle was as yet even now in shock at the death of Barton. A heavy dose of guilt surrounded her grief. Besides having been the one to send him on this terminal assignment, it was her past poor judgment and immaturity that had brought Zachary DuPort into their lives. It was not bad enough that she had sordidly consorted with a man that everyone else could see was a fraud with no honor, but then senselessly she had thrown him a lifeline, and even worse brought him along to California, where he had another chance to foul up her life. She had no doubt that Barton had also figured out that Zeke Bridges was Zachary DuPort. He had tried to save her honor. Riddled in guilt as she was, she could still not bring herself to tell Donovan how low she had sunk with Zachary DuPort. How quickly life could change its course. One day confident, ready to take on anything, and the next, wondering how could she be so stupid and whether the sun would ever shine again. The sudden shift in luck and danger had placed an awareness in Gabrielle that she hadn't felt before, on the fragility of life and those she cared about. She had lost her mother, and then her father, but in measured time, where she had been able to zero in on one grief at a time with plenty of support structure and no other large concerns. Now, her world seemed in peril, and she was at a loss as to what to do. In fact her one initiative to help had backfired disastrously; instead of safeguarding Donovan, she had gotten Barton killed. Oncle Henri was the one to confide in now.

Donovan watched as the usually alert and spontaneous Gabrielle listened to him as in a daze. Whether Gabrielle and Corby would ever get together or not, Corby could be a great assistance now. He had shared that bodyguard role with Barton, and that was probably how he came into Gabrielle's affections. He would write to Corby and explain what was going on in San Francisco, including about his old nemesis Zeke Bridges. He would push his friendship with Henri Seurat once more to apply pressure to resolve the desert politics through Washington, and he would double his vigilance where Gabrielle was concerned. He needed to speak to Henri right away.

WELL, HE COULD just rot in jail. It was not as if this DuPort was indispensable. He didn't trust the man anyway. Now what a mess he potentially had on his hands. From the frying pan into the fire. Günter Targon wasn't mourning for Ishka. No one was mourning for the Indian. But he felt a sense of loss as in a valuable asset. His anger clouded over the many headaches the sadistically gruesome Tlingit Indian had caused him over the years. He forgot that Ishka had almost single-handedly beached him from his life at sea. The Indian had been a vengeful sword for Günter. His mere presence had served notice on Targon's minions that it was a life and death game should they mess up. It was always entertaining to parade his killer out at unexpected moments to intimidate his associates.

As Günter mulled over the new problems he faced, he controlled his anger and dissected the issues. DuPort would expect his help. There was always the possibility when dealing in crime that your partners would use you to help themselves, and DuPort could shine an uncomfortable light on many of Targon's activities and contacts. True, Günter would then find a way to kill him, but critical damage might nonetheless be done. He would have to hire a lawyer and attempt to help DuPort. It would be the cheapest thing he could do. Should that prove to be unproductive, he no longer had his Indian to make a problem disappear in little pieces for the fish, but there were always killers for hire.

HENRI WASN'T IMPROVING. He had sunk to a plateau in his health that allowed him to continue his daily activities, but required intermittent rest periods throughout the day. Walking around would tire him out, and he found himself constantly scouting for the next chair he could reach. Though his mind stayed sharp, that was all the more agony of realizing that his body was failing. He could not will the flesh to do more than the most basic tasks. He took to writing as much as he could, trying to commit as many thoughts to paper as possible. The writing gave him a sense of fulfillment, as if his mind and experience would not be lost and become irrelevant. As his writings evolved, he discovered he was creating a personal and individualized guide for Gabrielle and also for Marshal Donovan, and he then crafted along that objective. Not wishing to sound pompous or unintentionally harsh, he would write out broad philosophical questions along lines his subjects would have need to explore, and then, in impersonal fashion, develop answering essays, reaching deep into his thinking to offer glimpses of truth and pragmatism that could assist his protégés when he was gone.

One thing that had snuck up on Henri was the sentimentality of his waning years. This was a new aspect of his personality. As a younger man, he had often been repelled by public displays of emotions. As a businessman, he had considered it paramount to divorce emotions from his decisions, and had done so quite successfully. His lone allowed weakness had been his love for books and paintings, translated into his recent penchant for visiting the ocean and watching the sunsets. But now as life was closing in on him, he felt the human bond as never before. Still a weakness in his mind, but it was a driving weakness that he would indulge and enjoy, almost as a reward for years of proper behavior.

He would catch himself studying Gabrielle's face as if to memorize every small detail. Then he would listen to the directions that Donovan would give to the staffers in the morning, hanging on every word, hoping the delivery was as precise and complete as could be, indicating a progression in Donovan's tutorage as a manager. He noticed the flowers, the birds, and the clouds in detail, and wondered why he had not noticed them throughout his lifetime. All of this convinced him that his time was short, and he would sit down to write again.

Gabrielle found him at his desk, pen in hand, taking a nap. Shaking him gently to wake him up for his medicine and lunch, a time they had been sharing lately, Henri did not respond. Gabrielle sat down next to him and began to cry.

58

BOTH CAMPS NOW KNEW where the other was, approximately. The advantage of surprise however had shifted to the Blackfoot, who were aware they were being spied upon, whereas the Crow as yet were confident that the Blackfoot were oblivious to their presence. It was at about this point that a very young rider caught up to Two Horns band with the news of the surprise attack on the Blackfoot home camp and the death of Moon in the Daylight. Carefully repeating the message that Buffalo Robe had taught him, the boy stood nervously in front of the War Council, answering an avalanche of new questions, as the warriors tried to determine who had been killed. Eventually there was an understanding, and some pride was taken in the elderly that had stood to fight. The few boys that died were also accepted as honored warriors, as was Moon in the Daylight. Two Horns mourned for his wife, but an anger rose as he thought of his unborn child. He understood the measured response Blackhand had taken, and respected the man for alertly seizing the opportunity. But the father-to-be had ached for a son, and this he would not let go.

News of the attack now swept through the camp, and there was actually a general relief as the small number of deaths was revealed. Blackhand's stock as a warrior rose even higher in the estimation of the Blackfoot tribe, even as they reviled the Shoshones' cowardly attack. The War Council thought it was necessary now to address the attack, and refocus the warriors on the more pressing problem of the closing Crows. Some men had openly complained that they should be riding against the Shoshone now, not the Crows. So Two Horns gathered the men in an open area where the Crow scouts could not get close enough to overhear, and told them what was currently going on.

"I have lost my wife and unborn son to Blackhand and the Shoshone, and I will make them pay for that. Our people have retreated farther into the mountains now for safety. There will be time to deal with the Shoshone later. But today we must think of the Crow, who have a fighting force and purpose far more dangerous than the Shoshone. The Shoshone wished to pay us back for our campaign under Crooked Claws. The Crow have set a trap to kill all our warriors. If they do that, is there any doubt what they would do next? The Crow see our homeland as territory they used to own. They have become strong with the Whitemen's guns. They have been fighting with the Lakota, and the Cheyenne, and the Shoshone, for more land. The Crow fight with us for our land. They have planned to draw us out of our stronghold in the mountains to use their guns on us, and might have succeeded. However, we know where they are, and we will use their plan against them. We will pretend to ride forward into Crow territory until the Crow following us are certain in their ambush, and then we will turn on them before they can attack and hit them first shortly after night falls. We must be prepared to do this tomorrow night if our scouts are right. We must crush the Crows to drive them back from thinking about Blackfoot lands, and avenge the attacks they have made on us. No warrior should die as Long Bow did. I will have Crow scalps on my belt before two suns pass. They will not have my homeland." Two Horns voice rose in strength and passion as he talked to the warriors. They responded, yelling their war chants, and brandishing their arms. The Blackfoot were emotionally charged to fight. In some way, the Shoshone attack had added to the fervor of the warriors.

"OUR SCOUTS TELL us that we are about an hour's hard ride from the Blackfoot," Loud Thunder reported to High Feathers.

"It is time then to find our battle field, and lure the dogs to us," confirmed High Feathers. Reports had the Crows a half day's ride ahead of the Blackfoot and about the same distance to the North. By tomorrow they would be lying in wait just a mile to the northeast of the projected path of the enemy. Word spread that the battle would probably be the next afternoon.

A suitable set of hills and trees were eventually found close to the assumed Blackfoot track. The hills were fairly close together with trees on the tops and sides. It would be easy to hide the Crow warriors on either side of the small valley up in the trees, where they would wait for Loud Thunder to race between with his band, followed by the unsuspecting Blackfoot in hot pursuit.

The Crows would rake the Blackfoot with gunfire from both sides, and then close the trap on the decimated and unorganized remainder. It was a good plan and would work well. To avoid any possible discovery, the Crows split their numbers and moved into the trees to make cold camps for the night, setting guards and remaining as quiet as possible. It was done so quickly that the two Blackfoot scouts disguised as Crows almost ran into the encampments before recognizing the day's march had ended. Retreating some distance to rendezvous, they agreed that this was to be the ambush spot, but they had to hide, having been caught inside the watch perimeter. It would be several hours, when night fell, before one of them could ride to warn the Blackfoot. When one finally tried, he would have to backtrack to the North and circle wide back to the West before reaching the Blackfoot relay rider, and would arrive quite late at night.

"THEY MUST BE close, but no scouts have reported in this morning, Two Horns," said Stalking Wolf. "We are blind without our scouts."

"We must go forward, and hope the scouts come before the Crows do," said Walking Bear. "We are committed to this plan and it is our best hope of surprising the Crow."

"Walking Bear is right. If the scouts do not come by midmorning, we can assume they will not come and the Crows are onto our deception. We should double our outriders. At first sign of an attack, we will assemble in the bear claw position, until we can see what the Crows are doing," instructed Two Horns to his War Council that morning. "Have the lead scouts pick a path that is clear of ambush possibilities this morning."

The Blackfoot set out on their easterly track once again. This was the day that Two Horns had expected to hear about the Crows' deployment, but he had heard nothing, and it weighed heavily on the Blackfoot chief. If the Crows met them in even battle today, the losses could be great, even crippling. Two Horns rode out ahead of the main body of warriors where the second set of advance scouts rode within sight of the lead scouts. He wanted to assess the situation as quickly as possible. Buffalo Lance rode with him.

The sun had climbed to the top of the trees in the early morning, still casting long shadows, and the grass was still wet with morning dew.

THE DECOY PARTY of forty Crow warriors under Loud Thunder had ridden out from the ambush site after having some breakfast and had taken a southwesterly track to position themselves in front of the Blackfoot. By turning a little to the West, Loud Thunder had intentionally cut down on the time it would take for the Blackfoot to discover his group. He had waited long enough to spill the blood of his hated enemy. Let it be this morning, rather than this afternoon. He wore a full war bonnet of eagle feathers, and his horse pranced such as to make a Remington painting fade in comparison. Carrying his rifle in one hand, he rode proudly in front of his warriors, at a sedate pace now so the Crows would not get too far South and possibly become cut off from a direct path back to the ambush site. Once he felt they were sufficiently in the Blackfoot's path, he sent two riders forward to give him some warning. They were instructed to race back to the main group on first spotting any Blackfoot. Loud Thunder planned to ride forward until it was obvious that there were more Blackfoot than Crows, before convincingly turning tail and running.

THE RISING SUN also told Soaring Owl that he was late. He had waited all afternoon and through the night for his message from the scouts attached to the Crow camp. He was about to give up and assume they had been caught and killed, when he had heard the signal in the early morning darkness. Returning the call, the two scouts had cautiously moved together, until they could recognize each other. Climbing Bobcat had told him about the Crows split camp and ambush, and why he could not have met Soaring Owl earlier. Soaring Owl knew that the Blackfoot plan would have been to attack last night or early this morning. He knew that the trap within the trap depended on timely information, and his was late. He rode as hard as he could now, knowing it would take him only an hour or so to reach Two Horns. But by riding hard, his pony came up lame, and now he was running on foot to catch the Blackfoot war party.

THE ADVANCE SCOUTS signaled back contact had been made. Two Horns signaled back from his position too, to the main body, telling them to come forward in the bear claw formation. He then signaled the advance scouts to stay put as everyone moved up to their position. When Two Horns caught up to the advance scout position, there was nothing to be seen. A wooded hill ran diagonally across their path opening up to a flat, grassy expanse before another wooded hill blocked further view. His scout pointed to the end of the trees on the diagonal hill and said two Crow warriors were watching from there and had turned and rode off behind the trees. The rest of the Blackfoot band was now only several hundred yards behind Two Horns and his scouts, when out from behind the spot indicated by the scouts trotted a war chief and a sizable raiding party of Crows. As of yet the Crows could not see the larger Blackfoot war party other than the six scouts sitting on their mounts with Two Horns and Buffalo Lance. The Crow party picked up a little speed coming toward the scout group. It now numbered about forty, and was clearly not the main body of the Crows that Two Horns was expecting to see. As the Crows got closer, they were able to see more behind the scout party, and at about six hundred yards out, they came to a stop, as they were now able to see the Blackfoot main body of warriors coming up to meet them. The war chief of the Crows rode out a little in front of his group showing his bravery and shouting insults.

Two Horns was thinking fast. The Crow trap must be set. Would they be coming in from two or three different directions? Should he sweep to one side when the Crows made their attack?

Stalking Wolf rode up fast with an exhausted Soaring Owl behind him, who had been running for the last half hour as fast as his feet could carry him. Now on a horse again, Soaring Owl gave his report as the two groups stared at each other.

Thinking fast, knowing he had no time, Two Horns swung around to his war chiefs who had gathered behind him and said, "They expect us to chase this bunch into an ambush to the North. We will chase for a short while and break to one side before we enter this valley, if possible, entering the trees on one side, attacking half the Crows before the others can reach them. Quickly now, chase these dogs as if you mean it, but watch for my signal when to break off."

Giving wild whoops the war chiefs flashed signs to the battle group commanders who signaled to their unit leaders to watch for hand signals and the race was on. Nervous energy flowed through all the warriors, and the horses picked up on the tension.

Loud Thunder and the Crow warriors wheeled their horses around and ran to the northeast, at a ten to one disadvantage. A horse that stumbled here would be a death sentence. But the Crows had selected their best mounts for this gambit, and the honor and excitement more than made up for the danger with the braves. Laying low on their ponies, some Crows actually tried to shoot backwards into the large group pursuing them. Within a handful of seconds, the horses had attained full gallops, extending their strides all out in a ground-eating pace. Some well-placed feathers were lost, and the two bands pounded the turf in this life-and-death game. Rounding a small hill, the Crow warriors made a direct line for some distant forested hills.

The pace was telling for Two Horns. The Crows would not be able to sustain their high gallop for much more than a mile or two, so the forested hills must be the ambush spot. He signaled the war chiefs to ease up just a little as they got within a mile of the nearest trees. The Crows continued on, whooping and screaming, at breakneck speed, making for an open valley between two wooded hills that curved away from the direct line both bands were currently on. The small hills were perhaps a quarter mile wide each as they approached. Once the Crows made their cut into the valley, they were temporarily out of sight. It was then that Two Horns signaled the Blackfoot to falloff the pursuit of the Crows and ride for the backside of the nearest hill flanking the valley.

As the Crows watched their warriors come streaking and yelling into the valley, they prepared to fire on the following Blackfoot party. They waited in delighted anticipation.

Meanwhile the Blackfoot slowed down enough to surge into the trees, and as Two Horns had hoped, found that they came up behind half of the Crows waiting to ambush them in the valley. Some of the Crows were unmounted and ready to fire their guns into the valley. The others were mounted and holding the horses for those on the ground. The surprise was complete by the Blackfoot, and hand-to-hand combat commenced. There was no opportunity to use the tactics that they had trained with. It was man to man, with little room to maneuver. The Blackfoot warriors in the rear were pressing hard to come up and help, but space was tight.

Approaching the end of the valley, Loud Thunder and the Crow decoy party had run itself somewhat out of the picture in an attempt to lure in the pursuers who never followed them down the valley. Finally stopping as they recognized that the Blackfoot had stopped chasing them, they heard the fighting coming from the one side of the ambush, but like the other side of the ambush, saw nothing. High Feathers, waiting with his men on the other hilltop, and Loud Thunder realized about the same time that they were under attack on one of the hills, and rallied their men to charge it.

As soon as Two Horns could signal his chiefs, he had asked for the Blackfoot warriors with guns, numbering about one hundred, to follow him to the front edge of the trees, as the battle raged on behind him. Knowing that the remaining Crows would come to give aid, Two Horns quickly assembled a firing line at the treeline looking down on the valley. The Crows had no choice but to attack by the shortest route, right into the Blackfoot guns. The Blackfoot had time to fire two full volleys before the decimated Crows were able to reach the treeline. High Feathers went down with the first volley, as did about thirty others. The second volley was more effective, as the combatants were closer, easier targets. By the time Loud Thunder was able to reach the battle scene, the Blackfoot victory was assured. The Crows would soon be in retreat, leaving behind fully two hundred dead and wounded. The Blackfoot hand-to-hand combat had taken its toll on Two Horns's warriors too. Close to eighty dead, and many more wounded. The men in Two Horns's own camp lost over fifty warriors, meaning a huge 25 percent loss of warriors for the Gray Woman Mountain tribe.

Beaten again by the hated Blackfoot and their chief Two Horns, Loud Thunder led an orderly retreat of the defeated remnants of the Crow's war party away, seething at his latest setback, more dedicated than ever to get his ultimate revenge.

Two Horns sat on Messenger looking over the devastation. His war party had achieved a great victory, at a great cost. Those who had survived were elated, picking up the Crow weapons, killing off the wounded, and rounding up the Crow horses. The initial one-on-one combat had been intense. With nowhere to go, and suddenly packed together, the two tribes had hacked and clubbed one another, stepping over fallen comrades to continue in a contest that had only one possible outcome: kill or be killed. Even with the two to one advantage in numbers, it was here that the Blackfoot had lost the majority of their warriors. The Crows had fought with the abandon of knowing they had to hang on until help arrived. Although they were in the forest, and surprised, the Crows' superior firepower had helped to inflict heavy Blackfoot casualties at the onset. Stalking Wolf had gone down in thick hand-to-hand combat at the front of the Blackfoot wedge, when he had been temporarily surrounded by Crows and dragged from his horse. A left arm fell uselessly beside Buffalo Lance, who had taken the full force of a blow from a Crow war club that shattered his shoulder. Though in great pain, Buffalo Lance wore his injury with pride, joking that he only used that arm to wipe his private parts. The Gray Woman Mountain Blackfoot would need their old ally Time to rebuild their strength once again, but the threat from the Crow Indians had been effectively thwarted.

Now Two Horns wished to get his warriors home to deal with the tribes' wounds and domestic woes. The Shoshone Chief Blackhand had demonstrated his uncanny ability of spying on the proud Blackfoot, and then attacking when the Blackfoot could not respond. Well if the Shoshone could do that, so could the Blackfoot. Two Horns thought it was time to not only reenergize the Bulls as an elite small fighting force, but to also concentrate on what the Shoshone had apparently mastered, the art of stealth. All these thoughts whirled through his head as he continued to tally the dead and wounded, and work with his war chiefs to organize the ride back to Blackfoot territory. Anything but think about his own loss. Two Horns wrapped his arms around Messenger's neck and buried his face in the horse's mane. This victory brought with it no joy.

59

O'BANNON STOOD IN HIS stirrups and leaned out to cut the rope. The man's hanging body fell in a heap to the ground, kicking up dust with its impact. Climbing down from his horse, he turned the body over and laid it out straight on the ground. A painted sign was pinned to the man's shirt, saying, "Mexicans go home." From the number of tracks around, it was clear to O'Bannon that at least five horsemen had been involved in the lynching of this man. He studied the hoof and boot imprints in the dusty ground looking for a distinctive mark that he could identify later, but found nothing definitive. This was the second hanging since the marshal's had been in Tucson, and they took it very personally. Stranahan and O'Bannon had already discussed the legal process for a frontier territory and decided that they had a little more leeway out here than they would have in St. Louis. In fact, without telling Corby, for his own protection, Stranahan and O'Bannon had concluded that should they catch these vigilantes outside of town in the desert, if the situation allowed, there would be a swift and sure justice dealt out in lead. This kind of killing was the work of truly despicable cowards that didn't deserve to sit in front of a jury. O'Bannon knew that Stranahan would be mad as hell when he heard about this second lynching just outside of Tucson. There would be some roughed up citizens as Stranahan went searching for answers later today. Not wanting to leave the body just lying in the dirt, O'Bannon stopped a wagon on the road and got help to carry the man's body back into town.

THE SURVEY TEAM complete with lawyers and clerks from Washington had arrived in Tucson a few days earlier and set up shop in Gavin Dagget's Post Office. The marshals now were busy escorting the surveyors around the countryside and informing residents of when they would be able to present claims to the government team. Of the several lawyers attached to the official group,

Tobias Gresham seemed to be attached to one of the government lawyers whenever they were seen in public.

As befitting the size of his claim, Don Sebastián had been one of the first asked to bring in all his original documents that he had alluded to in his letters sent to Washington. Señor Francisco Morales accompanied him, as did Drego. Corby made sure he was present also.

A Mr. Meechem was in charge of the meeting, and spread the documents out next to a larger survey map of the territory that had been scribbled on many times. A pattern of blocks lay over the hand-sketched map of the rivers and mountain ranges. Smaller blocks were drawn over towns and villages. In the broad area where Don Sebastián's holdings would have been was a stamp, reading "Disputed Spanish Grant."

Mr. Meechem pulled out a folder with Don Sebastián's full name written on it. "It is the intention of the Department of the Interior along with the Mexican Border Survey Commision and the War Department to survey all the lands of the recent Gadsden Purchase and determine what lands are privately owned, and what lands should be government property or publically owned. We intend to be as thorough and fair as possible in our recommendations to the U.S. Congress, which will have the final legal responsibility of adjudicating property lines. You are aware, sir, that the United States paid a hefty price for this strip of land along the border with Mexico?"

There was no reason to answer the rhetorical question, so no one did.

Continuing on, Mr. Meechem said, "It has been our finding in the majority of these old Spanish grant cases that there has been inadequate legal documentation to file justifiable claims. Many are based on second- or third-hand representations of original papers, and many do not have legal status with the Mexican government to start with. It appears you have an original land grant document that is also filed and accepted with the Mexican government, so legal ownership should not be an issue, but this is not an open-and-shut case. The boundaries of your claim are very vague in legal terms. The San Pedro River on your East is a clear and recognized boundary, and since the property lines between you and the townsfolk to your south have been agreed upon for some decades, we see no problem there. However the northern and western boundaries are open to interpretation. You claim land as far away as the Picacho range to the northwest, but your grant description refers to the 'mountains,' of which there are many small ranges between here and there. It is the government's wish to be fair in these matters. If you have any other legally recognized evidence as to your northern and western boundaries, now is the time to present it."

"The family of Don Sebastián has been on the land for 135 years. At times the only other people in the region were the missionaries and the Indians," said Señor Morales. "Even the Spanish soldiers abandoned the area due to constant Apache attacks. Don Sebastián's family did not. Under the principle of 'domicile by succession,' or as you say here, 'homestead,' the Don's family is protected under the law as the original and continuous users of the land, as upheld by the Mexican government."

"Again, we are not disputing Don Sebastián's legal status, Mr. Morales. The Constitution and our legislative branch are in agreement that Don Sebastián, having sworn allegiance to this government, is entitled to all the rights therein, including property rights. The question is the legal definition of the original property lines. It is the intention of our government to clarify in exact terms who owns what, and record it as a permanent and legal document. This is in your best interest too. Does Don Sebastián have any fences or buildings or boundary markers that have been registered with any official entity indicating the North and West extent of his property?"

"Do the graves of my people count?" asked Don Sebastián.

"Only if they were recorded, or surveyed in a legal filing, sir."

"And the existing home range of his cattle?" asked Señor Morales.

"That would fall under the same guidelines, I'm afraid. We have many cases of free range that have subsequently required the sectioning off of land to lay property claim to it," answered Mr. Meechem.

"Then how will you determine these boundaries, Mr. Meechem," Don Sebastián asked.

"Well, we have two fairly established boundary lines with end points to each to start with, and some language in the original grant to go by. We will take into consideration the other legal claims, if there are any, and make a recommendation to the Congress as to what seems the most logical and fairest outcome for those concerned. In the meantime, Don Sebastián can count on retaining approximately two thirds of his holdings. Look here on the map. Where the Aravaipa River joins the San Pedro will mark the northeast corner as described in all the documents. Until we resolve the question of the further extended northern boundaries, we will use a line over to Black Mountain, over here, as the guaranteed northwest corner. The San Pedro River as always will act as the eastern boundary, and this line that moves up and down along the south boundary, indicating your current neighbors' properties, is the same as before. Draw a line due south from Black Mountain until you intersect the town of Catalina for your temporary western boundary. Once we have all the information in on the lands further to the West and North of these provisional boundaries, we will inform you of our decision."

"So you mean to say that my father may lose one third of all his land that we have fought and died for when no one else would brave the Apaches?" Drego demanded to know.

"Forgive my son, Señor," said Don Sebastián. "He is excitable. We will await your justice. Thank you, Mr. Meechem."

As the four walked out the door, Don Sebastián was smiling. He slapped Corby on the back and said, "Thank you, my son, for helping my family so much. The United States is a great nation."

Both Corby and Drego were very surprised by his reaction.

"Father, don't you understand that the government may take away so much of your land? asked Drego in amazement.

"Juan, your father is neither deaf nor blind," answered Don Sebastián. "I suspect they will take all of the land in question. I am very happy that this family now has legal rights to the area we saw on the map. Let the government and Sam Johnson have the land running up to the Picacho Mountains. They can have the scorpions, and Apaches that come with it. The land is fairly useless, as you well know. Would you rather they had taken the good lands by the rivers or the forest by Black Mountain? It is of no consequence. Your heritage is soon to be legally intact, my boy. Let us go celebrate this great day at the hacienda."

Don Sebastián and Drego mounted, and rode out of town.

Señor Morales headed back into the building to get it in writing as to the current understanding, and Corby headed across the street for some lunch before he was due back at the marshal's station.

As he entered a small cantina, he noticed Tobias Gresham and Bill Tolliver having lunch. Gresham waved him over, in a jovial mood. "Marshal, may I buy you a beer?" he offered.

Corby sat down with the two to see what was going on. After his beer had arrived, the men began discussing the progress being made by the government's survey team.

"I do believe the government will do the right thing by all," said Gresham.

"How so, Mr. Gresham?" Corby asked in a noncommittal tone.

"Well, young man, no one knows for sure now, do they? But I wouldn't be surprised if some of the northern land holdings of Don Sebastián's end up as open range. It's only right that the Mexican land owner's get to keep a fair portion of their property, but it's also only right that they cede some of it to us Americans too, wouldn't you say?"

"As you say, Mr. Gresham, no one knows for sure. I'm sure you meant to say that Don Sebastián is an American now too." Corby corrected him.

"Of course, of course, a fine fellow by all indications," Gresham said continuing in his good humor.

Corby thanked the gentlemen for the beer and allowed himself a small smile as he walked out the door. Mr. Gresham's victory would look good on paper, but as Don Sebastián had said, Sam Johnson and his cattle could have the scorpions and Apaches. He began to wonder what he would do next as the situation here seemed to be diffusing. Walking back into the marshal's small area of Dagget's office complex, Stranahan gave him a letter.

"Didn't know that old coot Donovan had such an uppity upbringing," he said, examining the neat handwriting and quality envelope Donovan had sent from San Francisco to Corby.

Corby walked back outside to read the letter alone despite the obvious curiosity that Stranahan displayed. Finding a chair out on the small porch, he sat down and carefully opened the fragile document with some trepidation. What would Donovan be saying about the Countess? He realized as he thought this that the mere fact that he thought of her as "the Countess" spoke volumes of the social gap between them. But he couldn't help how he felt, and a lot of time alone this year had allowed him to come to some peace and direction, if not any good answers. Tomorrow would continue to come, and he could waffle in his indecision and emotion, or he could embrace it with its opportunities. He was learning how to live life daily, hold down his conflicting past anger, and encourage his emerging optimism. He had learned this made the day less stressful, and no one really cared about his past injustices anyway. Better to stand up and take what life dished out, and in the process, maybe dish out a little himself. So steeling himself as he did, he began to read the letter.

One thing could always be said about Donovan. He wasn't one to beat around the bush. Gabrielle's "uncle" Henri Seurat, who had in a short time become a true friend to Donovan, had passed away, leaving Gabrielle inconsolable. He had been the one to intervene for Don Sebastián's family. Barton, while fighting Zeke Bridges, had been attacked and killed by Targon's Indian. Donovan had then killed the Indian. Yes, our Zeke Bridges from Fort Boise was in jail in San Francisco, and Corby was needed to make a corroborative identification with Donovan to convict him of the murders in the Oregon Territory, and in assisting in killing Barton. Targon was involved somehow in all of this, though Donovan wasn't sure how. Donovan thought Gabrielle needed Corby there now, so if things were close to being resolved in Tucson, Donovan would consider it a personal favor if Corby would hightail it back to San Francisco immediately.

After reading the remarkable burst of news in the short letter, Corby's heart raced. Gabrielle needed him there. Did that mean as a support player or what? Donovan could have written another line and cleared up the huge question in his mind. But by not writing that line, did Donovan mean to signal Gabrielle's interest had waned? Or maybe he just didn't know. Or maybe he really had hurriedly written the letter and posted it before he thought to include such important information. Sighing a deep breath, Corby glanced at the letter again. He had no other choice than to return to San Francisco. Donovan's personal plea was enough. He owed the man more than anyone who had ever been in his life, save his mother, and if Donovan asked, he was obligated to go.

Then there was the business of Zeke Bridges. Corby had pretty much forgotten Zeke. He had always attributed the father, Ben, as the one who would have organized a manhunt for him back at Fort Boise. Zeke lay heavier on Marshal Donovan's mind, as the man who had killed two of his charges and left him to die on that mountainside six or seven years ago. He remembered that Donovan's gun had been taken too. That was the kind of thing that would bother the Marshal to his grave if he couldn't square it.

The only good bit of news in the letter had been that Targon's Indian had been killed and wouldn't be stalking anyone anymore. Just remembering the Indian sent an involuntary chill down Corby's spine. There were Indians and there were Indians, but Targon's Indian had come from hell.

So where did all of this leave Donovan and himself with Targon? Corby kills his gunman, and Donovan now kills his Indian. And how did Bridges tie in to Targon? These and other questions would have plenty of time to run through his head over and over before he got back to San Francisco.

Looking up, he saw Stranahan watching him through the open door. As a generous soul, he stood up and walked back into the room. "You won't believe what that old coot Donovan has been up to," Corby said, parroting Stranahan's earlier remark.

O'BANNON STRODE INTO the quiet office later that night. "Fin, you better get over to the big cantina, over there," he said waiving his arm in a general direction down the street. "That Drego guy is back in town, drinking and winning at cards … from Sam Johnson's boys."

Both Marshal Finley Stranahan and Corby cleared their chairs and were out the door. O'Bannon picked up a piece of chicken that Stranahan had left behind, and then turned to follow. The cantina was full of people, some eating, others drinking, and one table playing cards. All eyes were on the card table, where a very tense group of cowboys were giving an oblivious Drego hard stares as he blithely dealt the cards for another hand and talked incessantly, half in Spanish and half in English. There was nothing particularly offensive going on, other than the fact that the cowboys were losing their money to the loquacious and high-spirited Drego. There is such a thing as a bad loser, but there is also such a thing as a bad winner. The cowboys were convinced that Drego was mocking them as he took their money.

The appearance of the three marshals had the effect of letting air out of a balloon. There was now not going to be a fight. Diners and drinkers resumed their previous conversations.

"Señores," Drego exclaimed excitedly, "I am winning big tonight. Let me buy you a drink," He tossed a silver dollar from his pile to Corby.

Corby winced, knowing how unappreciated the comment would be by the cowboys. "Good idea, why don't you buy me a dinner instead if you are that lucky?" he suggested, trying to break up the game.

"No, no, amigo. I am on a streak. I can't lose. These hombres are being very kind to me." He took another shot of whiskey.

One of the cowboys spoke up, saying, "He's been winning three out of five hands all night. It ain't natural."

"You boys been passing the deal, or playing winner deals?" asked Stranahan.

The same cowboy dejectedly said, "Passing."

Stranahan gave a sympathetic smile and said, "No law against being lucky. Just not your night. Maybe you boys should hold on to some of your money and try another night."

Another cowboy said, "Marshal's right. It ain't no fun losing to a Mexican jaybird that never shuts up."

There were several grunts of agreement, and the cowboys began to collect their remaining monies and get up.

"Where are you going?" Drego asked. "Your luck will change, maybe."

His smile almost ignited a physical reaction from the first cowboy, who managed to control himself, and said, "You won't always be so lucky," indicating the marshals more than the card game, and then they left the cantina.

Corby sat down next to his friend as the other two marshals drifted away.

"Do you know how close you came to a fight, Juan?" Corby asked.

Drego shrugged his shoulders and said, "How about that dinner you were talking about? I know a special little place where the girl who serves you is magnifico."

"You will never change." Corby laughed. "What was it Donovan used to say about you, 'he's off to see the circus'?"

The two friends rose to leave the cantina. A little food would help balance out the whiskey, Corby thought as he guided Drego out of trouble this night.

60

"SO YOU WANT TO stick to a claim of mistaken identity, but you can't provide a shred of evidence or a single witness that can prove you were Zachary DuPort before 1849?" Sid Walcott asked Zachary. Sid was a lawyer of considerable skills that had been retained for Zachary by Günter Targon. Sid was now entering his seventies, and had taken on the more lucrative criminal defense clients, as his idealism had slowly and inexorably faded. A life of defending the weak and helpless had left Sid with many good memories but not enough money. Sid now worked for a different life purpose—his own, as increasing medical costs from fifty years of smoking required turning his back on principles for cold cash. In many ways, the clients were not that dissimilar: people who had run amok of the law and desperately needed his assistance. You just had to hold your nose a bit more when they tried to tell you about their innocence. There was a new coloring to his practice in defining the law, limiting the excesses of the prosecution, and advancing the cause of his clients, when you knew that your clients were probably guilty, if not of the act they were currently charged with, then definitely of others, some much worse. But the law was his mistress, and he had found new ways to please her and satisfy his changing needs.

Looking at his latest client, Zachary DuPort, accused of being Zeke Bridges, he was convinced it was Zeke Bridges, alias Zachary DuPort. There were mitigating factors in the strange tussle and death of the man Barton Villemain. It could be argued that the deranged Tinglit Indian Ishkahittaan had been the one to murder the Frenchman, without any link to his client. In fact the marshal had already stated that the Indian had been following DuPort, and though he contended that the attack was staged between them, Sam felt he could register enough doubt as to the Indian's purpose. However the purported history and warrant for Zeke Bridges was another matter. Shooting a man in cold blood, possibly another in the back, and leaving a former U.S. marshal to die alone in the wilderness left little wiggle room for Zeke Bridges. His client obviously felt that way too. However, if the prosecution could provide witnesses and the defense could not...Sid understood where his responsibility lay, first to Targon and second to DuPort/Bridges. Should the case look impossible to win, Targon wanted to know first.

DuPort had suggested that the Countess de Laurousseau, who owned the posh St. Montfort Hotel, would verify that he was Zachary DuPort, but again only after 1849. He had implied that perhaps he could get the Countess to stretch the truth, indicating a onetime clandestine relationship, but with no proof other than his say so. Such a trial and witness would electrify the community, but to no purpose if Sid could not prove Zach was not Zeke. Still, he would go interview the woman, along with Marshal Donovan, to see what might turn up.

Sid had a fair idea of what Targon might do should any of this get too close for comfort. He believed that Targon had already sent that message to DuPort, from the conversation he had just finished with the man. Zachary DuPort was sinking into a morass of fear, which grew by the day. He feared Targon foremost, and rightly so. But he feared the marshal and the prospect of dying too. Like many of the criminal ilk, there was a streak of cowardice somewhere in there that was now front and center. This was making a tougher job for Sid, as the lies were steadily increasing.

OVER BREAKFAST, GABRIELLE had come clean with Donovan over her past history with Zachary DuPort...that is, except for their romantic involvement. Realizing that it was her word against Zachary's, and that should he try to blackmail her for any reason, whatever fast-fading sympathy she might have had for him once, would not rise to cover the contempt she would have under that scenario. As a pragmatist, she realized that revealing that particular bit of information would only cause further hurt. She would internalize her guilt and shame, and take it like an adult. Having reached those conclusions, she no longer feared Zachary's shared past. If necessary, she knew how to derisively dismiss any unsavory allegation he might try to use for his defense. The fact that no one in San Francisco had ever seen anything of a relationship between him and her for the last four years should help dispel such a wild claim. She would blatantly and convincingly lie if she had to. Sometimes you had to fight fire with fire.

Only she had not yet practiced her defense when she explained her history with Zachary DuPort to Donovan, and Donovan knew she had held something back. Not that he cared what it was, but he could tell it bothered her, and with the deaths of Henri and Barton, she was in a fragile state. If Zeke Bridges did anything to harm her now, Donovan was convinced he would find a way to end the man's life personally. He had lightly fantasized on the subject anyway. Watching the poor girl fidget in front of him now over the likes of Bridges boiled his blood.

A SHORT DISTANCE down the hill near the bay, Günter Targon had just been briefed by Sidney Walcott on the DuPort mess. He too had been fantasizing about the demise of Zachary DuPort, or was it Zeke Bridges? Having used a few aliases himself, he wasn't bothered to find out the man had changed his identity. Many of the people he knew had done so for one reason or another. What worried him now was the increasing chance that the more mystery there was that surrounded the case, the deeper the prosecution would dig for answers. A simple murder/self-defense question had now blossomed into an Indian territory murder mystery, double identity, possible high society scandal, titillating mass appeal thriller. This was not good. It would only be a matter of time with such interest in an intrigue like this that Ishka could be tied to him. Any high profile of Ishka would be bad. What newspaperman could resist a sketch of the threatening looking Tlingit in its trial coverage, much as they had played it up with the *Fairfield*? When would the connection to the sinking of the *Fairfield* be made? And if he was ever tied to the *Fairfield*, he could say goodbye to this part of the world. No, this would get out of hand. Günter was not a man who waited for an ill wind to blow when he still had the ability to sail clear.

61

I T WAS WITH A heavy heart that Two Horns greeted Buffalo Robe on his return to the home camp. The tribe would be holding a feast for the victorious warriors, before the Piegans and Bloods continued on to their own homes. This would be an additional burden to the Gray Woman Mountain Blackfoot. With their heavy losses of young men, only the horses brought back from the battle were an added asset, and essential to the band's recovery, particularly since the Shoshone had stolen their reserve mounts. As was the custom, many of the best horses would be given to the Bloods and Piegans in appreciation of their supportive role. There was little upside to the victory in Two Horns's mind save the danger of the Crows being eliminated.

"It is a battle that the Blackfoot will retell over many campfires," said Buffalo Robe. "The Crows will lick their wounds and think carefully before considering stepping into our lands again."

"Yes, but in time they will again, and if not them, the Shoshone, the Lakota, or the Cree," Two Horns replied in a dejected manner.

"It is our way," Buffalo Robe answered. "It keeps us strong. It has been the way of the ancients and the natural world around us since the Creator Sun started life."

"It is a hard life," intoned Two Horns.

Buffalo Robe nodded his head, thinking he had figured out what was wrong with Two Horns. "When the Shoshone rode down on the camp, they had perhaps one hundred warriors. Moon in the Daylight led a small group of old men and boys to the center of the camp to meet the Shoshone. She showed no fear and stood firm with a lance in her hand. The Shoshone Chief Blackhand led a charge of half his warriors over the small band. All went down with the first pass. I will tell of their bravery at the fire tonight."

Two Horns looked directly at the old man. "The Mother died as she lived, with a strong spirit. It is the unborn son that I grieve for." While that was true, it was Moon in the Daylight that he had wished to see when he returned. She was his friend and adviser, and it was she whom he had planned to enjoy his family with.

Nodding his head again, Buffalo Robe acknowledged the loss. It was time to tell the chief the rest of the bad news. "There are several who show signs of the pox sickness. It showed up four days ago. I have ordered the sick into two teepees separated from the camp." He pointed at the two structures some five hundred yards from the main group.

The news jolted Two Horns. It had been about eighteen years since the last smallpox epidemic. That sickness had killed off over a third of the Blackfoot, including both of his parents. It had been worse for the Bloods and Piegans, killing more than half of their populations. Prior to the disease, the Blackfoot had been the undisputed dominant tribe in the area, numbering perhaps twenty thousand, between the many subtribes of Blackfoot, Blood, and Piegan. It was news that had to be shared immediately. Calling for his recent war chiefs, Two Horns told them what he had just learned. Having barely dismounted from their long ride back from battle, the Bloods and Piegans were quickly back on their horses and heading out within minutes of hearing about the sickness. A quick division of spoils had been made, and some heartfelt goodbyes, but distancing themselves from the sickness was uppermost in everyone's mind. There would be no feast in the vicinity of the dread disease.

The remaining Blackfoot band gathered around Two Horns for instructions. "When the great sickness came upon our people, they died as if flies, by the hundreds. No Shaman could cure them. The Creator Sun turned away afraid. We must leave here immediately and leave those sick behind. Do not touch them or take their possessions, or you may die too. Anyone that shows the bumps will be turned away into the forest. Go and break camp. We will leave before the sun reaches the treetops."

And so the Blackfoot left their families and friends that were sick with the pox and moved even further into the mountains, fearful of another devastating epidemic. The quick but brutal decision by Two Horns proved to save his people worse afflictions. Still another twenty Blackfoot succumbed to the disease before the band could outrun the infected. The recent losses by war and disease had a predictably depressing effect on the band as they split into their traditional smaller communities and prepared for a harsh winter deep in the mountains. It was anyone's guess how many would survive the disease to rendezvous by the old lake camp next Summer. Without an immediate family again save his first wife, Two Horns wished to be alone, to grieve in silence, much as Lame Elk had done in his year alone in the Yellowstone Valley. He and Messenger rode off alone into a soft but steady snowfall.

62

"YOU HAVE FORGONE TAKING a bath since I have been in jail," Zachary accused Shug O'Brien. Shug was somewhat of a lost puppy with his only friend in jail. He had taken to sleeping on the bench outside the cell when the police officers would allow it. Having slept on the open deck of a whaler on many warm nights, the hard wooden bench was not a burden to the man.

"Just forgot," answered Shug sheepishly.

"When you leave here, please go for a bath," instructed Zachary, wrinkling up his nose and stepping back from the bars of his cell. "Did you ask the nightjailer to see me?"

Shug shook his big head in the affirmative. "But he ain't here tonight."

"Well, who is out there?"

"Ain't no one out there now," said Shug.

"Go look again, and see who is on the night desk at the station next door," Zachary ordered Shug with some irritation.

The big man left to do as he was bid.

Within a handful of seconds of Shug leaving, two policemen came into the lockup area. "We're taking you to another building, DuPort. Turn around so I can tie your hands behind your back," one of them said.

"Does my lawyer know about this? You got some kind of paper on this?" Zachary asked, leaning against the cell door. He thought he saw the look of Targon's men about these two.

"Stand back from the cell door, or I'll be forced to poke you with my stick," the other officer demanded.

"I want to see the regular policemen in charge of this facility," Zachary answered as the concern began to set in. He maintained his grip on the cell door.

"We ain't got time for this, Blackjack," said the second officer. "Push the damn door in!"

The one called Blackjack agreed, and both men put their shoulders to the door and shoved on it. Bracing his foot against the bottom, Zachary was able to slow down their entry, and began yelling for help. Blackjack stopped pushing in order to pull his nightstick out of his belt to try and hit Zachary's leg or foot. Zachary tried switching feet pinned against the door, to avoid the blows.

It was at this point that Shug came ambling back into the building to tell Zachary that no one was still manning their stations. Hearing Zachary's cries and seeing the two men pushing in the door on Zachary, he charged like the bull he was, knocking both men into the cell and to the ground. With the door wide open now, Zachary jumped over the wrestling pile of legs out into the hall. Looking down on Shug and the two thugs Targon had sent to kill him, he could see that Shug was going to be overcome. Shug could see Zachary standing there, and called to him for help. Zachary's instinct for self-survival was too strong, and he turned to run out into the night.

A seething anger overcame Zachary as he ran through the streets. Somewhere deep inside was a shame for abandoning his slow-thinking friend, but closer to the surface, as always, was the rage for the unfairness of it all. He knew that Targon had turned on him, probably fearing the scrutiny of the press during his trial. Targon would have stolen whatever he could of Zachary's before dispatching the two murderers. As a fugitive he could not expect to walk into the bank tomorrow and withdraw his money. He would be forced to start over again, somewhere else. But not before he exacted some revenge for his betrayal. His fear and anger spurred him on as he ran through the vacant late-night streets, and his feelings of betrayal blocked out the fate of his one true friend, Shug O'Brien.

DONOVAN KNEW THE explanation he was receiving over the jailbreak of Zeke Bridges was full of holes. By the amount of blood still staining the floor, and the death of a citizen, a serious fight had taken place here last night. However, the police officers who maintained they were overpowered during the escape showed no signs of any damage to them, and could not explain why DuPort would have then killed a man who, by all accounts, had been his friend after, according to the police, that same man had helped him escape. The captain of police was not buying the story either, and Donovan could tell that the more the officers talked, the hotter the captain became. They would know soon what had really taken place if he was reading the captain right.

The commotion should have alerted others in the adjacent building, so Donovan surmised that a lot of money had been spent to open the cell door. Too many people to keep a secret, unless they did this all the time. But he would have heard rumors over the last few years, so he ruled that out. No, more likely there were bribes that a poor policeman just couldn't resist. Big money was easy to find. These policemen had made a very bad error in judgment, and would most likely never get to enjoy their ill-gotten gains. It was a story Donovan had witnessed several times before, and he actually felt sorry for the dumb policemen, who were digging themselves a deeper and deeper hole the more they talked.

Zeke Bridges was proving to be an elusive and lingering headache for Donovan. His years in law enforcement made him want to pick up the trail and find his quarry, but he recognized that those days were gone, and the captain would be fulfilling that role. Perhaps a well-timed suggestion to the captain at some point in the investigation would prove helpful.

Captain Thaddeus Barnes seemed to be on the same wavelength and turned to Donovan. "Marshal Donovan, with your knowledge of the fugitive, would you mind accompanying me over to his apartment for a look around?"

As the two men left the police station, Captain Barnes said, "I appreciate you not saying what a load of horse manure we just heard in front of my men."

"I figure it didn't go past the desk sergeant. You seemed to be getting at the heart of it," Donovan replied.

"Well, I appreciate it anyway. Damn embarrassing. This is going to hurt the department," Captain Barnes stared down at the ground as they walked.

"If you act on the police end quickly and decisively, you should be OK," said Donovan. "Catching Bridges could be another matter."

"I've got men checking all the livery stables, docks, stagecoaches, reported thefts... the usual stuff, but I take it Bridges is a little smarter than that. Can you tell me about him?" the captain asked.

"To tell the truth, I have underestimated the man," Donovan confessed. "He was known as a coward and a cheat as a young man back in Fort Boise. I think that had a lot to do with his older brother and father. The old man was an embittered tyrant with his family. The older boy became a bully, and Zeke suffered under both. I think he was trying to impress his father when he first killed, but you could see he liked the sense of power. When he became free of the old man, it would have been like getting out of prison. How he got the money to pull off the DuPort scam in New Orleans and here speaks to his ingenuity. Frankly I'm surprised. He has gained some muscle and confidence in the last seven years, and he is obviously intelligent. But when I talked to him in the jail cell, even though he denied knowing me and wouldn't talk, you could see he still was nervous. I suspect he is still a coward at heart, but a wily and dangerous one."

"Interesting," said Captain Barnes.

A short time later they arrived at the apartment above the gambling parlor that had served as Paul Logan's headquarters, before Zachary DuPort took it over.

"Zeke was living pretty high on the hog," Donovan remarked on entering the apartment. The wood paneling and fine furniture were apparent enough. Looking through the closet at the many fine shirts and suits, Donovan discovered the false wall. "Captain, look over here," he said as he pushed the panel open.

"Son of a gun, my old Colt Walker," exclaimed Donovan. There was some loose cash and jewelry, but not any item of other interest.

Donovan showed the black-handled gun to Captain Barnes, describing its history. If there had been any doubt that this was Zeke Bridges, it was now removed. Donovan was as happy in finding the gun as someone else might have been in the return of his or her dog. He hefted it in his hand like a piece of gold, and then switched his gun from his holster with the Walker and stuffed the extra gun in his belt with Captain Barnes's permission. Donovan saw it as a positive omen. After all the bad news, maybe things were going to change for the better.

63

"**W**ATCH. THE WIND IS shifting. Now watch the old bull," whispered Lame Elk. Crouching together just inside the treeline, the Indian chief and his little white friend stayed perfectly still. After a moment, the big bull buffalo standing some twenty yards in front of the herd shifted his feet in a short dance until, like a weathervane, he was again pointing into the wind.

"Is he smelling into the wind for wolves and such?" Katy asked.

"Yes, and listening. He can't see very well, but he can hear and smell. That is why the Creator put all the buffalo's hair on his chest and shoulders, because he usually is facing into the wind, especially in winter. It helps him in his fights with other bulls, too. That old bull has a large hump, which means he is strong, and can run fast and jump high," instructed Lame Elk.

"That big old buffalo can jump?"

"He can jump higher than a horse if he wants to. And he can run as fast for awhile, too."

Katy was now eight years old and able to ride well. She would dress as an Indian when with the Shoshone, but there was no mistaking her red hair and fair complexion. The Shoshone had accepted her as part of their chief's life. No other child had come for Lame Elk, but he had not given up, now sharing a teepee with two wives, both within childbearing years. Lame Elk had noticed the girl's interest in the natural world, and much as his own grandfather had taught and shared with him, he had a need to teach the child he still believed had come to him in his vision and helped heal his sorrow.

As he looked over at the girl now, he could see her face intense with the mystery and wonder of the buffalo in front of her. There was the intelligence in her eyes, the curiosity in her questions, and the willingness to learn, that so many children did not have. He knew that she loved him as another member of her family, and even though at times he felt awkwardness about the relationship with his people, he loved her too, in his own way. But as an adult, he felt the large distance between the world as he lived in it and what her world was and would be. He would someday have his own family again, with perhaps a daughter or a son Many Flowers would bear for him. Katy was too young to see the cultural gap. It was part of her charm.

"What would he do if I shot an arrow at him?" whispered Katy.

Lame Elk smiled and said, "I suppose he would think it was a bug flying by."

"You're saying I can't hit that buffalo with an arrow?" she challenged.

"I'm hoping you aren't going to try and get us trampled to death, Green Eyes," Lame Elk mocked great concern. "Instead of making the buffalo mad, let's see if you can circle across wind to his other side without spooking him."

Katy immediately got down on her knees and began crawling slowly off toward the blowing wind. Protected as she was from the buffalo's vision in the trees, it was a fair test of how quietly she could move in the light shifting wind. Lame Elk watched as her head popped up every so often to find her bearings. After awhile she was out of his hearing distance, but he could still see her. He began to follow so as not to be too far away should something happen. As he did so, he noticed the bull buffalo start to get agitated and interested in Katy's direction. The buffalo made a few tentative steps in her direction, at which point Lame Elk decided to end the exercise by stepping out and throwing a rock at the animal, yelling and waving his arms. The buffalo was startled, and ran off a ways before turning to reassess the situation. Seeing no further pursuit, it continued to walk away from the area.

Katy rose up and walked back to Lame Elk.

"I think he heard me," she said.

Lame Elk nodded. "When in doubt, you must not move. It takes a lot of patience to stalk like the cougar. When the prey moves, you move at the same time. If he stands still, you must too. With the buffalo, move when it eats. His grinding teeth make it harder to listen. I suggest you don't raise your head to see where you are. Find a point in the distance between the trees and grasses, to know where you are as you move, and never take your eye off of the animal's position. If you are stalking a deer and it starts to run, you have little time to stand and take a quick shot. If you don't see the deer start, you will never get that shot."

"Take me elk hunting, Lame Elk," begged Katy. "You said they are coming down out of the mountains, and their bugling is so...wild! I want to hunt the elk. You said they are the best to hunt."

"I said they are my favorite hunt. Others say the great bear or the cougar are the best to hunt, or even the antelope."

"Take me elk hunting, please, oh please," she begged.

"We shall see, Green Eyes. We must talk to your father."

Riding back toward the Shoshone lake camp, they saw some late-leaving families packed to depart to the winter campgrounds as the brisk days of autumn wound down. Snows were already falling in the mountains, and the deer and elk rut were in full swing. Waushaute and two braves rode out to meet the two as they neared the campsite. Katy and her father would be accompanying Captain Farmer back to Fort Hall soon. Flashing a sign, Waushaute told Lame Elk something in code, and Lame Elk told Katy to ride in the rest of the way by herself, as he would have to go with Waushaute.

"We will speak to your father tonight, little one. Now go and tell him how you stalked the great bull buffalo like a true Shoshone," Lame Elk said as she rode on.

"She will be a good hunter someday, Waushaute. Now what is the trouble?" Lame Elk asked.

"Come and see," Waushaute answered.

MOVING SLOWLY, TWO Horns was able to skirt the Shoshone camp higher up on the adjacent mountainside. It was a risk being this close, but he wanted to judge for himself the palisade wall he had heard about. The structure ran across the majority of the small valley floor up to a cliffside of fallen rock on one side and a narrow point of forest on the other. It was designed to force an invader into a small funnel, and thereby blunt any larger attack tactic. From behind the jagged palisade, warriors could hurl or shoot their weapons at the compacted attacking force while defending the small opening to the camp. The wall looked to be earthen with wooden stakes protruding, so a fire would not destroy it. The ground behind the wall appeared to be higher, and there were piles of spears every twenty feet or so. Behind the wall in front of the lake were the remaining Shoshone teepees of their summer camp.

Two Horns was impressed with the obvious defensive benefits. It was not that dissimilar to a Whiteman's fort, and he assumed that the Whiteman had designed it for the Shoshone. There were a handful of soldiers in the camp now with strange little folded-over teepees. He saw two scout stations in good position and surmised there would be others. The number advantage had changed in the Shoshones' favor over the last few years and the Crow war. Where once the Gray Woman Mountain Blackfoot had over two hundred fierce warriors, and the Yellowstone Shoshone about half that number, the newly banded Lemhi and the Yellowstone survivors now had the two hundred warriors. Two Horns band had been reduced to just over a hundred proud warriors, from the great battle with the Crows, and the ongoing bout with the smallpox. He could not attack and win, and he knew Blackhand knew that too. He led Messenger over to a clump of elk thistle to munch while he settled down for a longer reconnaissance of the camp below. He hoped to count the rifles and horses, knowing that many of the Shoshone had left for the Winter, but he needed to make himself useful, and spying on the Shoshone seemed the right use of his time.

NEARING THE END of the valley, where the Yellowstone River began to cut deeply through the falling landscape, Waushaute reined in his mount and jumped off to the ground. Lame Elk slid off his own horse and knelt down beside the other man to look at the track Waushaute was pointing at.

"See, it is the big black horse you speak about," said Waushaute.

Lame Elk recognized the hoof print immediately. "So the Blackfoot chief comes to visit," he said. "And he comes alone?"

Waushaute nodded. "We can find no other tracks. He crossed over here and headed up the other side. He will be above the camp on the mountainside there," he said, pointing up and back toward the Shoshone camp. "We could catch him if he returns the same way."

"Would you return the same way?" Lame Elk scoffed at the suggestion.

"No, but he may not know the area. It is worth the chance," said Waushaute.

"I think we should let him look at us and see our strength. He will go home and not bother us for many years," said Lame Elk.

"You are thinking of the woman and child he lost, but he is a Blackfoot chief, and he will kill our people if he can, Lame Elk. Do not forget he was with the war party that destroyed your summer camp before."

Lame Elk bowed his head in acknowledgement. "You are right and wise, Waushaute. We should post several warriors here for the night and following day. You and I will take a few more to track Two Horns in the morning."

THE NEXT MORNING Captain Farmer sat in thought, having read again his latest dispatches from the army. The slavery issue was heating up around the country. The army was not immune to its divisive power. As states began to declare for one side or the other, pressure on the territories soon to become states grew, and hence the army personnel within those areas were subject to the politics of Washington and the opinions of senior officers. The army had other problems pressing on it because of the times. The vast new territories, with their flood of immigrants, rising Indian problems, and thinly stretched army outposts, now had marauding bands of pro- and antislavery proponents in the plains territories/states. Increasingly bloody outcomes were becoming more common in these areas of limited law. More combatants felt it would be easier to coerce than convince their opponents, with little interference from the frontier army. As is the way with deteriorating conditions, the Indians too were acting with impunity. Captain Farmer, whose primary responsibility was for the geographic areas surrounding Fort Hall and Fort Boise, was seeing more hostile activity between the tribes and immigrants. The influx of Mormons to the South had stirred up the local Indians, and the Mormon self-government and independence had already diverted U.S. troops before and looked to again, as conflicts with that "nation" continued on a bad footing. To the West the Indians in Oregon were in an uprising with the settlers, and of course the Plains Indians to the East had become a very large and public concern.

To Captain Farmer it was only going to get worse. He had written report after report warning about the unrestricted movements of immigrants West, breaking treaties as fast as they were signed with the Indians. He could see the credibility of his government fall each year with the Indians. Perhaps there was a happy medium to the conflicts between the encroaching immigrants and the resistant Indians, but there was no authority controlling the process, much less the territory. Half the Indians in his area wouldn't even recognize the sovereignty of the U.S. government, and why should they? As yet they had not had to bear the brunt of the European explosion. He saw his government in a reactive mode concerning the Indians, patching up conflicts after the fact, and hoping that would buy time while it dealt with more political and monetary issues such as land acquisition, railroad surveys, and the establishment of local governments as the towns and territories began to require them. The more time he spent with the Shoshone, the more sympathy he began to feel for the inevitable injustice they would someday face. He sensed that a few of them were beginning to worry as the wagons kept coming by Fort Hall, year after year. Lame Elk had asked how big the California country was. The news of Indian conflicts to the East filtered into the local tribes, with mixed reactions. They were happy to hear of problems for their old enemies, but they wondered if and when they would have the Whiteman moving onto their lands too.

Of course the government representatives were told to downplay any suggestion of future conflicts, unless the Indians were unruly. Then the message would often change to one of the size and strength of the far-away government that could reach the troublemakers, with powerful impact if it had to. The changing messages helped to confuse and anger the Indians, and made Captain Farmer's job that much more difficult. Ultimately he found out that he could only speak for himself, and that was something the Indians could relate to. He found that they would disassociate the Washington talking heads from the man who spoke plainly and truthfully in Fort Hall. He figured that politics were universal, and even the Indians had their own politicians of sorts. But as a people, the needs of the immediate future almost always outweighed the out-year concerns with the tribes. And so Captain Farmer began to communicate along the same lines, even as his trepidation of pending chaos grew by the year.

Something new was happening too. The army was beginning to contract, just when one would have expected it to expand in the territories. The old trading forts in his area were losing their fur-trading profitability, and the army was simply letting them fall apart. Needing many more forts along the trails to defend its citizens, it wasn't even maintaining the old trading posts it had inherited. Resources were being pulled back East, as the acrimony between North and South grew. The more remote areas of the Oregon Trail were being abandoned to survive as best they could.

As Captain Farmer stewed about the future, Dr. Lemmins came up to him in some agitation.

"Captain, I ask that you take Katy back to Fort Hall immediately and inform the fort and surrounding area that we have a case of small pox here in the Shoshone camp. I would first like you to come with me to tell Lame Elk and Waushaute, but they don't seem to be here this morning."

64

S HE CAME UP BEHIND him as he groomed Borrasca in his stall and put her arms around him. Startled, Corby almost fell over before gently removing her arms.

"Maria, you shouldn't be out here at night alone," Corby scolded. "Your mother would be very unhappy."

"I am a grown woman, if you would take a look," she said, stepping back and twirling around in a full circle. The colorful skirt flared out around her as if she were dancing, presenting a pretty picture of youth and beauty.

There was little doubt that Corby was drawn to her. Had Gabrielle not been there first, he assuredly would have explored the moment further. But such as things were, he was now uncomfortable in their seclusion, feeling unwarranted guilt as if he had been a part of sneaking away to be alone with her. In fact, he had done a Herculean job of avoiding being alone with her after announcing his plans to head back to San Francisco.

"This Condesa, does she love you?" asked Maria.

"I don't know," confessed Corby, "but that is not why I must go back to California. My friend Marshal Donovan needs me to help put a very bad man away in prison forever." Being somewhat intimidated, he added, "Otherwise I would be more than happy to take you dancing as you have often asked."

Her face lit up a bit, and then soured again as if she detected the promise given that would not have to be kept.

"If she does not love you, then she is a fool!" Maria let a little of her pent-up emotion out.

"Hard to argue with you there," Corby responded, trying to lighten the moment as he went back to brushing the horse. "You are a remarkable girl, Maria. I pity the poor men of Tucson, who will be falling down all over with broken hearts," he added with a smile.

She smiled back but was about to take the offensive again, when Drego came sauntering into the stable. He was playing with the fancy knife that Corby had given him as a parting gift. It was the knife Corby had taken off the man Quaid, whom Zeke Bridges had killed back in the Oregon Territories. Drego had wanted it from the day he had first laid eyes on it, and Corby knew Drego could use it far better than he could.

For once Drego didn't tease his half sister, probably realizing how hard she would be taking Corby's departure.

"Well, amigo, are you ready for our ride in the morning?" he asked. Drego would be accompanying Corby in to Tucson to meet another freight wagon train bound for California. Borrasca would be tied behind a wagon for most of the trip, except for an hour or so every day when Corby would rather ride in the saddle.

"I was just suggesting to Maria that you bring her for a visit to San Francisco sometime," Corby offered.

"An excellent idea, compadre," exclaimed Drego.

Maria looked at the two of them, and without a word turned and ran back to the hacienda. Corby guessed she was crying. He looked crestfallen.

"She is a young girl, my friend. She will cry for you, but forget you by Christmas," Drego predicted.

"That soon?" countered Corby.

Drego gave him a sad look, as if to say, "I hope so."

OCTOBER 3, 1855, found Corby bouncing along the rugged trail with the wagon train, leaning up against the new Spanish saddle Señora Drego de Santarosilla had given him the previous day as a goodbye gift. She was even more relieved than Corby to see him start back for California, but over time she had come to realize it was her daughter and not the young gunfighter from California who presented a problem. She had even given him a motherly kiss and hug goodbye as they all had wished him well and a safe trip home.

As some wit had said, "Home is where the heart is." For someone who had not really had a home, the concept was especially appealing to Corby. But he had not yet found his home. Nonetheless, he experienced a pull from California, and liked the association. He would prefer to be a Californian over any place else he had traveled to date. There was the energy of the young city, being part of something new and growing. But whatever he settled on, it would have to be his own endeavor. He would not go back to being an employee, even one as well paid as he had been. Tapping his vest, he remembered that he had put the letters from Stranahan in his saddlebags. The big Irishman had written a letter of recommendation for him, and forced it into his hands along with a letter he was to deliver to Donovan. Now formally separated from his temporary status of U.S. Deputy Marshal, Corby had not earned the high praise Stranahan gave him in the letter. Another gift from Donovan. This time he was determined to use the assistance to find his place in this world as his own man. He had the bumpy road from here to California to figure out what that would mean.

65

I T WAS COLD AND wet, but safe. The chain locker on the old ship had served as Zachary's hideaway. A watchman had come on board twice but had not bothered to explore the decks. Zachary would have liked to get below decks for a more comfortable, warmer sleep, but thought the watchman might see the broken lock. He could not trust anyone. Targon's money and muscle ruled the waterfront. For ten dollars he could get his throat slit, and he knew Targon would be offering a lot more. One plan after the next was discarded as too risky. He simply could not afford to be seen. But he must strike back. Finally it came to him. An open letter to the newspapers, describing all he knew of the Targon empire, would expose the bastard to far more danger than anything he could personally conjure up. It would require stealing some writing materials and delivering the letters in the late-night hours, endangering himself to Targon's minions. It would be wise to steal some money too. Then leaving the city by horseback in broad daylight in some sort of disguise might be the safest. It would take a great deal of time, but the Eastern cities made the most sense to him now. His experiences and education should serve him well there, and as a westerner, he would have a fresh start. He knew his mother's people were in Boston, and it wouldn't be hard to invent a convincing storyline, heavy on his care for her, that would endear a little money out of them. He was after all the lone remaining bloodline of their only daughter.

There was a lot of unfinished business left in San Francisco, but Zachary was a pragmatist. Targon would eventually find him and kill him if he stayed. Marshal Donovan was currently on his trail, and Corby might be too. He had to write his letters and get out while he could. He was not one to deceive himself that things would blow over, nor was he particularly keen on facing his tormentors. Everything had been going so well. Then suddenly, after several years, Gabrielle's toadyman inexplicably confronts him. The only good thing about all of this was that the man was knifed to death. Here he was hiding in a stinking chain locker smelling the unpleasant rot of a dying ship, while

Targon, who was ten times the villain he was, could still live life to the fullest. Targon would learn well that he had tried to eliminate the wrong man. The details he planned on giving to the police would have Targon sailing the high seas to save his hide. His spirits picked up as he imagined the German on the run. If only there was a way to pick up the lucrative pieces Targon would have to leave behind. Maybe there was time to do some more thinking on all of this. Maybe a short delay in leaving was in order if he could line his pockets with some of Targon's loot first.

TWO MORE BODIES floated out to sea on the Pacific Coast current. It was so much easier than burying people. The sharks, birds, and crabs cleaned up nicely with a little time. Two more buffoons who had failed to accomplish the simple task they had been given, and now had paid the ultimate price. The fact that they had been employed by the police department too had sealed their fate as quickly as Targon could pick them up. Sailing back in to Half Moon Bay, Targon realized how much he had missed the sea. This had been his first offshore venture in many months, if only a half day to make sure nothing washed ashore. Executions weren't the same without Ishka. There was real fear, of course, but not sheer terror. Targon remembered his buccaneering days, the excitement, the women, and the treasure. Now he was actually wearing a suit from time to time, and talking to lawyers and bankers and investors. The landlubbers never understood the adventure and freedom of being at sea. They were scared of the same storms that made Günter feel most alive. Riding the crest of a big wave heeled over with full sail … They were dropping anchor now and some yahoo was waving at him from the shore.

The man on shore took a skiff out to the ship still waving his arms, in dire need of showing Targon something. It was Roland Leech. Scrambling up the ship's ladder, he nearly fell into the bay, but finally made it and handed an oversized file to Targon. Inside were two feature stories in the San Francisco paper. "Escapee Exposes Criminal Empire" read one. "Who Sunk the *Fairfield*?" read the other. Admittedly a tainted source, the papers were more than happy to print all of Zachary DuPort's accusations, including the alleged plot to kill him. A dozen names were given, and the deaths of Paul Logan and Dan Williams were attributed to Günter Targon. One editorial went on to say that "San Francisco had long known the day would come when the likes of Günter Targon and his band of pirates would have to be hunted down by the navy" and presumably blown to pieces. Half Moon Bay was mentioned as the rendezvous spot for privateering activities, such as smuggling and the shanghai trade. As expected, a small portrait of Ishka was drawn in gruesome detail, and questions of employment asked. Finally there was a plea of innocence made by Zachary DuPort, who had "erroneously fallen in with such obvious bad company." Both papers had reprinted Zachary's letters word for word to accompany their editorials. Sid Walcott attached a note: "You need to come immediately to refute these claims. It is a case of no confirming evidence, but it must be countered before it takes hold in the public's imagination."

For an instant, Günter thought he would just shuck it all and sail off, but he climbed down the ship's ladder to ride back to San Francisco. There were many opinions he could buy. Besides, this would mean he would have someone else to take on a cruise, as soon as he could find Mr. Zachary DuPort. It was a personal matter now.

66

BY AFTERNOON FEAR HAD spread through the Shoshone camp like a wild
fire. Families started leaving for their winter camps within the hour.
Dr. Lemmins pleaded with Waushaute and Lame Elk to quarantine
the tribe members, restricting them from running away, but to no avail. With
such a killer in camp, the chiefs wouldn't try to influence their people, largely
since the doctor admitted he could not cure those who would become sick.
And unlike the Whitemen who spread the disease traveling from population
base to population base, the Indians dispersed into the wilderness where they
were unlikely to meet many other people. And so, the doctor settled down
with the sick and those few who chose to stay, hoping the white doctor might
help ward off the sickness. All items brought back from the Blackfoot raid
were thrown into a fire, and camp residents were instructed to wash frequently
and limit personal contacts for the next month. So far only the one family
had shown signs of the pox, in its early stages of fever, body aches, and the
emerging rash that was beginning to define itself into bumps. The family was
isolated and monitored by the doctor. Everyone else was required each day
to visit the doctor for a quick inspection. Three more families would come
down with the disease by the end of the week. Following the progression of
the disease as the bumps filled with the opaque, thick pus that would then
scab over, fall off, and leave pitted scars on the lucky ones that lived through
it, it was easy to understand the terror and repulsion the pox brought to the
Indians. By three to four weeks, the inflicted would either die or become no
longer contagious.

THE MORNING BEFORE the sickness was reported, the Shoshone chiefs had
some other business to attend to. Just before dawn, Lame Elk and Waushaute
led four Shoshone warriors to the far side of the ridge they suspected Two
Horns had spent the night on. A party of five warriors were guarding the

trail discovered the day before, should the Blackfoot try to retrace his steps. Staying on the floor of the valley, Lame Elk's group slowly tracked across the ground looking for any sign of a descent from the ridge. Shortly after the sun had hit the top of the next mountaintop, the Shoshone had traversed the logical paths for descent to the valley floor at the rear of the ridge, and determined that no rider had come down. Knowing the mountain ridge well, the Shoshone then split into three pairs and began ascending the most likely routes to the top, spreading themselves across the base of the ridge. Lame Elk and Snow Hunter took the quickest route to get to the top. As good trackers they would find the trail on top and either work back down to meet the others or mark a trail for them to follow. The undergrowth was noisy with fir and pine needles and dead leaves from the aspens. But there were wet spots too and some open rock with light snowpatches.

UP ON THE ridge top, Two Horns had also started at dawn, as soon as it was light enough to safely travel. He continued on to the West, where the ridges grew taller as the mountains built, away from his ascent, sticking to the ridge top for easiest travel. Upon reaching the end of the ridge, he was disappointed to find an impassable cliff that would force him to retrace his path a little in order to find a way down far enough to cross over to the next ridge top. It would require descending perhaps a quarter of the way down the ridge before he could start to climb up again. A half hour of careful descent brought him to the base of the cliff he had been stuck on earlier. There was little cover on this dip between the ridges, as is often the case from snow and rockslides. About midway across the exposed area, Messenger caught the scent of the other horses climbing up with a morning updraft. Understanding immediately that his horse had sensed something below them, Two Horns quickened his pace across the divide and into the trees on the next ridge. There he reined in behind a rock outcropping, stroking Messenger to keep him quiet, and waited to catch a glimpse of what might be climbing up the other slope.

He heard the snort of a climbing horse first, and then the displacement of small rocks as the riders climbed. They would cross his old trail in perhaps ten minutes. Then he saw Lame Elk with another warrior weaving in and out of the trees. The chief would not be alone with just one other tracking him this morning. Two Horns would have several Shoshone on his trail within the hour, and he suspected that others might be setting a net below. Edging away when the Shoshone took a tangent angle in the other direction during their climb, the Blackfoot chief spurred the big black horse up the next ridge, continuing his path higher and to the West. He smiled knowing he had the advantage now with the big strong horse. The smaller Indian ponies could not climb with the sustained pace that Messenger could. While they might be able to overtake him should they spot him on flat ground, due to the nimbleness and speed of the Indian ponies, in a stamina contest the big black would leave them panting. He had barely escaped the trap Blackhand had laid for him.

Upon reaching the spot where they intersected Two Horns's trail, both Shoshones dismounted to study the tracks. They were very fresh, and both men simultaneously looked over to the next ridge, knowing the Blackfoot had successfully eluded them. It would have been a close miss. Snow Hunter thought they probably passed under the gun sight of the Blackfoot. Lame Elk felt the strange sense that sometimes comes, called déjà vu. It was on these same ridges that he had eluded the Blackfoot trap some years before. Two Horns was now above them on the next ridge, and the big black horse would carry him to safety. This time Lame Elk instigated the communication, yelling out a long and loud war cry. A moment later the call was answered somewhere above them on the next mountaintop. The warriors had once again saluted one another, and once again dodged combat.

67

S HE PACED BACK AND forth, back and forth, in her suite. Angelina rolled her eyes and finally said, "He will not get here any sooner or later because you are wearing a hole in the floor, Comtesse."

Gabrielle frowned at her former nanny turned personal servant. To Angelina almost everything was as simple as the sun rising each morning. Only this was anything but simple. What should she expect from Corby when he arrived? What should she be expected to do? The time away had not clarified anything between them. They had not corresponded. There was no indication that Corby would wish to return to the duties he had before leaving. In fact, the silence concerning his future plans was rather disconcerting, as if the St. Montfort, and her, weren't even in his thinking. The post back to Marshal Donovan had merely stated he was returning to help in the prosecution of Zeke Bridges, and indicated an approximate arrival date.

Well, she was not some little village girl who would pine away for a man who was cavorting around the country doing God knows what. Should there be no sense of interest on his part, she could continue on just "Fine, thank you." This despite the queasy stomach that would have indicated to most that she was overly upset about a man she kept telling herself really didn't matter.

So what did she expect the man to say, after riding all over the desert shooting at everyone for a year? "Can I start running errands for you tomorrow morning?" It all seemed so bizarre. He had barely had more than a handful of extended conversations with her since they had met. She had made fun of his silent, stoic personality to Donovan prior to his leaving, and then in a rush of emotions, she had thrown herself at the man. He had probably been shocked. Of course he would have been. But a year later, what would he be thinking? "That Countess is probably a good time I should have some fun with"? Or, "Once I take care of Bridges, I've got to get away from that crazy Countess quickly again"? On and on it went. The possibilities were limitless, and the clues to probable reaction nonexistent. So she paced, worrying and hoping, alternately guarded and daring in her thinking, but always unsettled.

Picking up the morning paper, she tried to turn her attention to the talk of the town, the pirate turned businessman, Günter Targon. An image remake was in full bloom, as those close to his money tried to paint a reasonable portrait of an entrepreneur with a somewhat colorful past, such as the West often took pride in, developing into a stand-up citizen who was supporting many civic and community projects. Stalwarts such as Stewart Bertram and Thomas James saw nothing past the last year that was of any importance in the man's history. Others, however, including those tied to the sinking of the *Fairfield,* wanted to examine any possibility that Targon was part of the disaster or knew about it beforehand. Still others remembered his gangs killing and looting, regardless of whether the authorities and press could conclusively tie the man to those activities. The balance of public opinion seemed to hang on the mysterious Tlingit Indian. Donovan said, should the association be made in the public's mind, then Targon's well-crafted and expensive campaign to defend himself from the damaging and graphic charges made by Zachary DuPort would crumble away. The son of one of the Presidio's officers, and the employee of the packetship company who had survived the tragedy had both identified Ishka as the wild Indian slashing and slaughtering the innocent passengers that night the *Fairfield* was sunk. Others like Donovan and Corby were aware of the relationship between the two, but no charges had been filed as yet, as there was no evidence of Targon being there at the sinking of the *Fairfield.* So two camps had formed, with Targon as the issue, and a public relations dissemination battle was underway.

Gabrielle had not taken a public side, still hoping her own name would not surface. A Sidney Walcott, attorney at law, had come to interview her about Zachary DuPort. She had traced Zachary's activities and associates for the lawyer in New Orleans, and when he had delicately asked if their relationship had been any deeper, she had brushed the suggestion away with a laugh. Walcott had seemed to expect that, not broaching the subject again. Explaining Barton's fight motive with Zachary had been a little more difficult, so she had pleaded ignorance, other than saying they had never liked each other.

The search for Zeke Bridges continued on at an unprecedented level due to the interest the case had generated. There was an official reward, and the now public reward that Targon had personally posted at Sid Walcott's advice, ostensibly to clear his tarnished name and reputation. Those on the docks, however, understood that Zachary DuPort delivered to Targon directly meant more money.

It had occurred to Gabrielle that Zachary might try to reach her for escape money. She had resigned herself to turning him over to the police should that happen, and possibly being pulled into the mess from Zachary's resentment. As she had not heard from him yet, maybe he didn't feel confident enough to test her. But in the desperate situation he must find himself, she couldn't rule that possibility out, and therefore she stayed in very public places. She hired a third watchman to the night staff at the hotel. These were draining days for Gabrielle. Up until now, even including her time with Charles, life had been an easy sea to navigate. So much seemed to be piling up on her emotionally. Her innate optimism had taken a strong hit. But it would take a great deal more to sink her.

THE NIGHTTIME THEFT of a farmer's market had netted Zachary enough food for a couple more days. He had long since stopped thinking of himself as Zeke Bridges. The recent incarceration had brought back a flood of bad memories of his previous life, but it had also reminded him about his rich relatives in Boston, a possible safety net. But now he returned to resolving his immediate problems again. Losing Shug O'Brien had been a bigger blow than at first imagined. Shug could have helped him in so many ways, or Dan Williams, or even Julie, anyone he could count on to bring him the things he needed in his time of need.

He reread the newspaper again with mixed reactions. The fire was raging over the *Fairfield* catastrophe, and had he realized when he wrote his letter that Ishka's tie to Targon would have been so important, he would have done his best to marry the two. Targon was doing a credible job of remaking his image and casting doubt about his infamous past. Zachary wracked his brain trying to think of some irrefutable evidence to present on Targon's past misdeeds. He couldn't see using the Paul Logan abduction, as he was as guilty as Targon, and revealing Logan's abduction and demise would be impossible without implicating himself. He had told everyone that Logan had gone back East. Changing his story now would cast doubt on everything else he had accused Targon of. He had no false evidence he could use in his killing of Dan Williams and Julie that he could attribute to Targon, and that too might backfire on him. There was no proof or suspects in Shug's murder either. Targon would be too smart to still have any of the contraband that would link him to any of those events. There had to be people that had witnessed some of his worst crimes. But would they risk their lives to expose the man? Unlikely, he thought, as he himself had now been in hiding for almost two weeks, in fear of Targon finding him. Suddenly he remembered he had Donovan's old gun in his apartment. They were bound to find it. Why in the world had he wanted to hold on to that obviously damning pistol? Then he realized it really didn't matter; he had already decided he had to run.

His own problem was twofold, escape Targon and escape the law, in that order. But greed had kept him in San Francisco so far. Revenge had its allure, but greed had always been Zachary's driving force. If Targon were to be picked up and held, his employees would have immediate loss of loyalty, and whatever could be stolen would be stolen while the man was behind bars. Zachary had a few hunches as to where Targon might have stashed some of his ill-gotten gains, having delivered stolen goods to various warehouses himself when he had first come into an association with Targon on the docks. He had seen a number of locked containers and compartments, as well as guards, to pique his curiosity and greed. Again, too bad he had been forced to kill Dan Williams. Dan could have helped him buy some men to raid those sites when and if Targon was put away. As things stood, he had no one he could trust or use; so much of his planning was in the dark. As such, any venture outside his hideaway was fraught with great danger. Time was running out. He would have to leave soon, and it didn't look like the law was moving as swiftly as he had hoped against Targon. Leaving with some of Targon's money in his pocket was beginning to look like a pipe dream.

HIS TEMPLES HAD turned white instead of gray, but the gray was now liberally mixed in to what had been a black head of hair only a few years ago. One no longer would see him and not know he was an older man, but he was as yet an impressive man. Donovan took pride in his strong and upright body, and felt he was still able to best anyone who he may be thrown up against. That may not have been true any more, but Donovan felt that way, and it showed in his eyes and bearing. He could tell that Gabrielle was comforted by that strength, even though he didn't feel she really leaned on him. But both had decided that staying closer to one another with Zachary on the loose made good sense. Donovan talked to the people around the hotel operation, to keep their eyes and ears open, and had by habit taken to staking out a position on a high veranda in the early evening that afforded him a good view of the back gardens where he thought Zeke Bridges might try to approach the hotel. After a short while he would leave his post, recognizing the futility of such a watch, and would then find himself drawn back again at other times. He had put an additional dead bolt on Gabrielle's suite door and checked for any way someone might possibly try to enter by the back windows or high veranda door. It would be difficult but not impossible, but very public. He made sure a night guard would check that possibility every fifteen minutes, as they rotated on their walks. He had kept up a working relationship with Captain Barnes, who had agreed to send a patrol by the hotel on a regular basis too, so there was nothing left to do but wait until Bridges showed up somewhere. Wait... the one thing he, like many, disliked the most. It sure would be nice to get Corby back soon.

68

HAVING CROSSED THE DESERT again, Corby elected to ride Borrasca North from San Diego, on the somewhat safer road to San Francisco. It was a heavily traveled road, full of wagons bound for the goldfields, or settlers on their way to the Oregon Valley. There were also freight wagons, such as the type he had teamed up with to cross the desert. They all kicked up a lot of dust, and Corby was glad he had a little more mobility being on horseback on such a road. From time to time he would ride past immigrants camped just off of the road, looking for all the world to be on their last legs. The children were dirty and ragged, and often went begging for money or food. He was sure the parents had instructed them to do so. Where it repulsed him to see children used like that, he felt a pang of sympathy, knowing that these were hard times for many of these folks, and they were desperate. He also knew that most of them would fair no better in the North.

At night he felt a need to exit the area around the road for a secure sleep, usually climbing up into the hills to disappear from sight in order to camp. He had little doubt that there were plenty of road bandits working over the already poor immigrants, and the sight of a horse like Borrasca might tempt them to try their hand with him.

The two had settled into a guarded familiarity now, not yet a team, but respecting and liking each other. The horse had enormous spirit, and seemed to prance as if on display when approaching someone on the now thinning-out road. Once when surprised by a snake, the horse literally sprang up into the air like a muledeer, a good three feet to Corby's thinking. It was high enough to almost dislodge his rider and give him a true feeling for the strength of the animal.

Corby decided he should exercise his mount a bit each morning by running him until he could feel the horse begin to tire. The first day he kept waiting, and waiting, but Borrasca didn't seem to tire before he reined him in. Over the next few days, he began to gauge the stamina, strength, and speed of Borrasca. The horse could run. It was as strong and steady as Midnight had been, eating up the miles, but it could run circles around his former horse with its speed and agility. And you could tell it loved to run. Don Sebastián had bestowed upon the young man a gift that Corby had not understood fully at the time. He was glad he had been effusive in his compliments when the Don had presented him the horse. It would have been hard to lose such an animal, even if you had a couple others. No one would have to explain the quality of a pedigree to him in the future.

In a few more days he would be back in San Francisco, and his practice lines on greeting Gabrielle were simply not working. It wasn't that he couldn't think of plenty to say; it was just that everything was inadequate and predicated on what the woman was feeling for him. This he did not know. The closer he got to the city, the more inane his greetings sounded to him.

Rising from his camp bed the last morning before riding into the city, he groomed Borrasca and then took a freezing bath in a cold stream; using a bar of soap he had seldom used on the trip, and shaved his face as smooth as he could. He then dressed in a colorful southwestern shirt he had specifically bought for the occasion, with some embroidered flowers on a black starched background. Next he brushed his teeth with the powder he had also picked up for the occasion, guaranteed to make your breath smell like a mountain stream, even though in hindsight he was aware that mountain streams by themselves didn't have a smell. It tasted like peppermint, which was all right, he guessed.

Then he polished his saddle, bags, and boots, and finally swung up on Borracsa and rode to face his fate. Borrasca wanted his morning run, and was hard to hold, but soon the horse saw they were coming toward a city and began his prance.

THE MORNING WAS like any other, except for the fact that Corby might just show up. The last week had seen an improved attention to detail in Gabrielle's morning preparations for the day. She had been seeing that she received adequate sleep, and she was selecting her own outfits to wear, and fussing over them. Angelina would silently shake her head in disapproval at the dresses Gabrielle now wished to wear, usurping her own favorite duty. But Angelina was appreciative of the upbeat mood the young Comtesse had adopted of late, and like everyone else, suspected it had to do with Mr. Corby's return. Also like everyone else, she wasn't about to suggest that conclusion to her mistress.

Today, the Comtesse had chosen what Angelina considered to be a rather fancy and bright party dress that revealed her shoulders, and a white fine-knitted shawl to protect her from the less than warm temperatures of the late Fall weather. It did compliment the young woman, but it was just a Tuesday, not a Mardi Gras social. But she wasn't going to spoil the mood, and set about helping the Comtesse complete her ensemble.

Donovan had been up for a couple of hours, as was his habit. This morning he had been cleaning his weapons, a job he took very seriously on a regular basis. Starting with the rifles, hunting knife, and new revolver, and ending with the Colt Walker, it hadn't taken very long, as they were pretty clean to begin with. But it was part of his routine, a part of who he had become, despite his last few years in tailored suits. With Henri gone, there was no one he had wished to hunt and fish with, and he missed that. The thought brought back a jolt of memory of the old man. He had known him for just over a year, but Henri had left his mark. As he thought about it, it came to him that Henri had intentionally sought him out and, without seeming to, had tutored and tested him constantly. But it had always been enjoyable learning what Henri needed to teach. An irascible little character at times, clearly Henri also had great tact when he wanted it, and Donovan smiled to himself, knowing the tact it must have taken to win over another irascible fellow, himself. He remembered one of the indelible lessons of his youth. His mother years ago had said that you should "leave your corner of the world better than you had found it." Henri had done that with him and certainly Gabrielle. Sitting there looking at the assortment of weapons on the table in front of him, he had something of an epiphany. Henri had shown how much could be accomplished in a short time if you were motivated and believed in what you were doing. Donovan had started something with the two young people, Corby and Gabrielle, but that was about it. They trusted him, maybe respected him, but like his guns, he had limited his scope of involvement, being there for the pressure moments, but staying holstered otherwise. What had it cost Henri to get deeply involved? The little man had been a very big man. Donovan would do better; he would do more.

Meeting Gabrielle for breakfast at 7 o'clock, as was their custom, Donovan suggested that they visit Henri first this morning, where they had buried him and placed a monument right in the middle of the hotel gardens alongside the one Gabrielle had placed for Barton only a short time before.

Gabrielle searched Donovan's face for something different, but it wasn't discernable. She accompanied him out the large french doors to the adjoining gardens, expecting to hear some purpose to the excursion, but Donovan only said that he missed the Frenchman. Then looking at Gabrielle, he told her if and when the time came, that this would be as good a spot to be buried as any he could think of. Then turning, he walked back into the dining room for breakfast.

Still not sure what to make of this, Gabrielle caught up to him and accompanied him back. That familiar tug at her heart told her it was not a subject she wanted to think about.

The late morning brought a hubbub of commotion out in front of the hotel. Donovan thankfully rose from his desk to go see what the problem was. There sitting on a magnificent horse, looking like a character out of a dime novel, sat Corby, chatting with the five or six Mexicans that handled the horses and buggies for the hotel guests. When he saw Donovan come out, Corby swung down from the Arabian, handed the reins to an attendant, and strode to meet him. Both wearing huge smiles, they stopped a couple of feet apart to shake hands and pat the other on opposite arms.

"You've filled out a little, sonny," observed Donovan. "Don't look the worse for wear. What did them Injuns down there use? Peashooters?"

"I brought you a letter from Stranahan, in the saddle bag, and learned enough about the 'Donovan early days' to have some fun with you for some time, so tread lightly, old man," warned Corby with a warm grin and a raised finger. "Besides, from what I've been hearing, I leave here for a short spell and all hell breaks loose. I can't keep going back and forth across the country fixing everybody's problems, you know!"

"As a matter of fact, most of us didn't notice you were gone," countered Donovan. "You steal that fine animal over there?" He walked over to inspect Borrasca.

"Given to me by Don Sebastián, in appreciation of my countless heroics and accomplishments, and on behalf of the adoring population down there. I'm thinking Borrasca here would make a fine stud for your retirement ranch."

Appraising the horse, Donovan said, "Yes, he would at that." Then remembering the imminent encounter that would take place with Gabrielle, he said, "Listen Corby, I know you must have done some thinking about Gabrielle. I ..."

"I would like to hear that too," said Gabrielle, surprising the two as she came up behind them. Looking radiant and happy, she swept forward and placed a more sedate kiss than the last time on Corby's cheek, and then backed off, saying, "Welcome home, Corby. I ... we all have missed you terribly."

Corby stood flustered, looking at Gabrielle, the scent of her perfume befuddling his mind. The moment had come and he was as unsure of what he should do as the day he left. But one thing had changed. He was determined to have a resolution, one way or the other. His downside was obvious, but at least it would then be over, and he could begin to move on with his life.

"I have done a lot of thinking since I left here. I realize that I'm just an ordinary man ..."

"Stop right there. I usually don't discuss personal matters on the street," she said sweetly, as she took his hand and led him inside the hotel and up the sweeping stairs to her apartments. Corby placidly followed, but his heart was hammering. He could feel her pulse in the hand he was holding, or was it his?

69

MAYBE THE MONEY HAD been well spent after all. The information seemed good. His informant had stuck to his story with the knowledge that his life was in the balance. So Targon had doubled his watch around the docks, feeling he was closing in on DuPort. He could have started a broader search, but didn't want to alert the police as to anything out of the usual going on. When he captured DuPort, he would take his erstwhile partner for a nice boat ride. It would be a slow death, allowing him at least a week at sea. He had not been up the North coast for some time. Why not combine a little business with pleasure? His fleet had not been very active, on his command, after the *Fairfield*, but despite the repeated threats in the papers, no navy had shown up, nor was there any expected until they built their own fleet on Mare Island. What few resources the government was spending were of a defensive nature in building up the fortifications around the bay. Perhaps he had been a bit premature in envisioning the demise of his oceangoing activities. Just a little less flamboyant might do the trick for the next few years.

But he needed new enforcers. No one had stepped up to fill the critical roles of Jimbo Fisher and Ishka. Perhaps he could test out some new talent when he sailed North with Zachary DuPort. DuPort—the man was beginning to preoccupy his thoughts. This was well past business now. DuPort had the audacity to try and take him down. The last to do so had been the Russian captain well over a decade before. Had it been that long since he and Ishka had tortured that despicable man? He walked over to a mirror on the wall. Was this the same face that had dominated the Northwest sea-lanes against all comers? Clearly he had gained some weight and lost some toughness, but the eyes never lied. He saw the confidence and command there, as always. He was uncompromising in his hold on power, and looking into that face, he knew he was unafraid of any man that would try to beat him. Time had merely lent him a different perspective. It was just as important to show his strength as ever, but the rash tendencies and techniques of his youth were being replaced by battle-tested methods that had served him well without overexposing him to unnecessary danger. The most recent example had been the *Fairfield*. It had been a bold and profitable plan, and had it been properly executed, he would not be in the tenuous predicament he now found himself. But the reckless slaughter and inexcusable escape of two witnesses were not part of the plan. He had allowed his good nature to overrule his judgment when allowing Ishka to have some fun on such a critical assignment. That excess had backfired, marring an otherwise good plan. No, there was no need for self-doubt. Just find and kill DuPort, and be more careful with his future gambles. The rat would come out of his hole before too long, and Günter would smell the invigorating ocean breezes while completing his latest victory over an enemy.

The same informant had decided to increase his earnings by going to the police after leaving Günter Targon. He would need the extra money wherever he went, because staying in San Francisco was not a smart play. So Captain Barnes also became aware of Zachary's approximate location, along with the knowledge that Targon was closing in too.

Captain Barnes had no illusions about Targon, despite the steady barrage of misinformation being circulated these days. The man was a brutal killer, who controlled the crime on the docks, and now apparently in many of the gambling halls. As to his history up and down the coastline, Captain Barnes had to accept much of it as fact. This was the most dangerous man in California to his thinking, and plucking DuPort out from under his nose would be a satisfying exercise that he would personally supervise. He would need some good men out of uniform, familiar with the docks. Considering the temptation his former officers had wilted under, he must hand pick these policemen, and do so quickly.

By nightfall the undercover police were lounging around the area identified in a variety of poses. One was even sharing a bottle with one of Targon's henchmen. Captain Barnes took up a station inside the waterfront police tower, a small two-story brick structure used by the police to temporarily hold arrestees on the docks until the wagon could come to pick them up. Should his men get lucky and pick up DuPort, they were to take him here first, for fastest security.

It was onto this scene that Günter Targon went to take a firsthand look to decide how he could close the net on his cherished prey. Upon arriving, Targon almost immediately grew suspicious. It was a little too busy on this section of the docks for this hour of the night. It could be that every cutthroat on the waterfront had heard about the reward and was out to try his luck, in which case they may send his rat deeper into hiding. A new fast gun from Kansas had recently come into his employment. Along with the usual two musclemen he had accompanying him this evening, he instructed the three to clear the area of anyone but a handful of his own paid men.

Word quickly got back to Captain Barnes that armed men were chasing everyone out of the watch area. Captain Barnes knew it had to be Targon's people, and he was stuck on the proverbial horns of a dilemma. To allow his men to be pushed out of the area would give Targon a free hand in finding DuPort first, which was unacceptable. To push back would reveal that he was also on to DuPort's relative whereabouts and tip Targon off, while creating a commotion that would probably alert DuPort. A third option was available, but wasn't the best. However, he chose to send a normal patrol of uniformed police into the area to scare off the Targon henchmen, while hopefully not showing his hand to either Targon or DuPort. Perhaps his undercover men could then resume their posts and carry out their assignments.

ON HIS WAY back from an early raid for food, dressed as a sailor, with a long pea coat with its turned-up collar, and a wool cap pulled down over his ears, Zachary approached his first observation post, routine for his return to the old ship. Slipping into the abandoned husk of a burnt building that overlooked the approaches to his hiding spot, he leaned against a wall and began to eat the bread he had stolen, from the bag of food items he was carrying. Something was going on. There was a brief scuffle and a man ran away from three others. The threesome then moved on to uncover a man sitting on the ground, who they also chased away. He watched as the men continued on in the area, finding and chasing others away. Then a squad of four policemen braced the group, and after a short discussion, the three men left the area. Continuing his watch, now fully alerted, he wasn't surprised when one of the former men that had been chased off returned to the exact spot he had frequented before. Zachary didn't need to see any more. His old hiding place was gone, and he was vulnerable on the streets again. It was time to leave that part of the city, even though it was the area he knew best. Adopting his practiced limp, he slowly and carefully hobbled up the hill away from the docks.

70

IT HAD STARTED OUT as something of a victory tour. The men had ridden out into the lands between the Tortilla Mountains and the Pichacho Range to inspect the property that Don Sebastián would soon be surrendering to the U.S. government ostensibly for open range. Sam Johnson and Bill Tolliver had convinced Tobias Gresham to join them, against his better judgment, along with a cook and two trail hands. The weather was pleasant enough, being early November, and in fact it was cloudy and rather cool at night. Mr. Gresham was very surprised by the rather dramatic temperature change when the sun went down, and was glad he had listened to the rancher who had counseled him to bring some warmer clothes.

Riding out as they had from Sam Johnson's place to the west-northwest, across Don Sebastián's property, they had quickly left the grasslands by the San Pedro River behind them, and found themselves in a vast scrubland of low-lying brush and cactus. Sam had wanted to skirt along the base of the Tortilla Mountains that ran more or less from the northwest in a line to the southeast, then cross the desert to check out the Picacho Mountains that ran perpendicular to the Tortilla Range but farther to the West. It was his thinking that these mountain ranges would have water coming down to feed unused grasslands. From his frequent intrusions onto Don Sebastián's lands by the San Pedro River he had often watched the dark clouds hovering over the Tortilla Mountains, blocking any rainfall from continuing East to his own property. You could see some fir forests high up on some of the remote peaks.

Unfortunately as they had rounded the southwestern base of the mountains there was no indication of any year-round water in the many arroyos that ran down out of the mountains. It would take a deeper investigation into the mountains to find any suitable grazing, for which they were not prepared to do on this relatively short survey outing, so they swung to the southwest to cross over to the Picacho Range to look for indications of water there.

Now three days of riding without any water to refill their canteens, they were forced to conserve and consider other options. They had sufficient extra water to get home, but no more. It would take three days to retrace their steps, or more logical to their current position, probably a day and a half to ride southwest and meet the Santa Cruz River as it flowed North into the desert. From there they could follow the river back to the town of Tucson to the southeast. They elected to reach water first by going southwest, largely due to Tobias Gresham's concerns and behavior. The man was clearly uncomfortable out in the wilderness. It would also allow the ranchers a view of the front range of the Pichacho Mountains, staying out to the West, which was after all why they had come in the first place. However, as is often the case in the desert, distances are hard to judge, and the next day the Picacho Mountains seemed no closer after a full day's ride in their direction. Sam Johnson also knew that they were deep in Apache country now, though he kept that to himself. Several rifles and pistols should be more than enough to keep the scraggly heathens at bay. No point in panicking the city lawyer anymore than he already was. On the other hand, this great land deal wasn't panning out like he thought it would. So far, there were no pastures that wouldn't require climbing up into the dangerous mountains for months at a time. The army would have to drive out the Apache before he or anyone else would be willing to try doing that.

As the fifth day dawned, the group awoke to find that three horses were missing, and appeared to have been stolen, by evidence of a cut rope. Having brought two extra, that meant they were one horse short for riding. The cook had to ride double with one of the cowhands. Now the fear of Indians was out in the open, as obviously it had been an Indian who had stolen the horses. Abandoning their idea of examining the still distant Picacho Range, they turned due South to beeline for the river. Had they continued Southwest, they would have hit the river in one and a half days, but since the Santa Cruz river flowed northwest, they actually lengthened their objective another half day by their due southerly course.

By ten o'clock in the morning, they were being shadowed by a large party of mounted Apache who kept just out of rifle range to their West, as they travelled across the wide-open desert. About noon, approximately ten riders rode out ahead of the other Indians and eventually disappeared in front of the rancher's party. It was clear to Sam Johnson that the Apaches would try to cut them off from the river to the South and, or, a clear retreat route back East to Tucson. The horses would need the remaining water if they were going to survive a race or a standoff that required them to stay in the desert all the way back to Tucson. Johnson set a slow and deliberate pace to conserve the horses, as long as the Indians were willing to keep a distance away.

Nearing a small set of bare hills, they were forced to turn to the East, when it became apparent that the Apache group that had ridden ahead had taken up positions in the hills with a few rifles. The riders were unwilling to continue to the South, as it meant running through crossfire between the hills on their left and the Indian riders on their right. Knowing that this blocked them from the river, they still had no choice but to turn back into the desert and continue riding now to the East to try and escape the Apache. It seemed that the Indians were still unwilling to come within gun range of the Whitemen, but by knowing the land, they were denying water and shelter. Tobias Gresham was now convinced he was going to die, and would not stop talking about it. Somehow he had gotten scratched up pretty badly from some cholla cactus, and not being able to drink wore on his fears. The cook had switched over to ride with the other cowboy as the day wore on.

Sam Johnson saw it first, as he had been looking for it. Off to the northeast rose Black Mountain on Don Sebastián's land. They had now loosely completed about three quarters of an oblong circle route in their travels. The mountain meant potential water and cover. Pointing it out to the others, Sam immediately set a course for the distant point. The Apache responded by pressing in and taking wild rifle shots, and the pace picked up from a walk to a steady trot and then a canter, so as not to exhaust their mounts, but to reach potential life saving cover sooner. The ranchers took turns on their right and rear flanks returning fire whenever the Apache got dangerously close. However, with many more guns, no matter how old or ineffective, it was only a matter of time before one of those wild shots hit a horse. Bill Tolliver who was trailing and covering at the time, was launched over his mount when it stumbled and fell from the unlucky shot, and before anyone could make a decision what to do in this parallel race, the Apache had closed in on him too close for a rescue attempt, and then killed him as he staggered to his feet to futilely run. The rancher's band rode on helplessly, now understanding that they could well receive the same fate before they would reach the mountain.

Within an hour, the horse with the two riders was visibly tiring, and the cowboy shouted to the group that his mount had to rest. Sam Johnson had just about had enough of the potshots too, so the group stopped upon reaching a small depression in the open desert, where they dismounted and took up rifle positions behind their mounts.

"Let's let them work up a little courage and come in a bit closer. Then when I say, we kill a few of them bastards," instructed Johnson.

The Apache sat just out of range, content to rest their ponies too, and made a display of passing around water gourds. Eventually a couple made a show of riding within rifle range, yelling and riding off.

"Hold your fire," said Sam Johnson. "They are just testing our range. When we shoot, we have to hit, understand?"

The sun was now indicating late afternoon, and the Apache just sat on their horses. The mountain was still a good distance away. After an hour of nothing happening, the Johnson party decided that they should at least continue to walk their horses toward the mountain, where they could quickly stop to fire should the Apache attack. This seemed to work, even if it was a very slow retreat to safety. But by nightfall, Gresham was exhausted from his fear and plump frame. The group was obliged to stop to rest, even though there was sufficient light to continue with a partial moon up.

Upon resumption of their walk, the Apache changed tactics, breaking into several small groups and riding out to surround the Whitemen. Suddenly one group came riding in on the Johnson party, swerving away after firing a few shots, but a second group had started from the other side, followed by another, and then another. The Johnson party had no choice again but to stop and defend themselves, turning from side to side to see where the closest Indians were. It was unnerving at the least, and allowed the Apache to get in several good shots, kicking up dust when they missed, but injuring one of the cowboys and the cook, and grazing another horse. For this they however paid a price, as four were knocked from their horses, three of which did not rise again.

An eerie silence then fell on the desert, as the Apache melted out of sight. The night sky was clouding up, and the moonlight became less of a beacon as the night grew somewhat darker. The group thought better of continuing on in the darker desert, afraid that they might walk into a trap. Watches were set for the balance of the night, save for Gresham, who Sam Johnson concluded could not be fully trusted with such an important job.

A pink sunrise colored the early morning sky, and there was no indication that the Apache were still around. What water they still had they now gave to the horses, and then mounted. From the appearance in the distance, Black Mountain looked to be only a couple of hours easy ride away, but they knew it was farther. Today was do or die. They discussed their options. They had to reach the mountain. Their own need for water, as well as the horses', combined with the probability of meeting the Apache again, meant the only feasible course was to the mountain. They all agreed that reaching the river or Tucson no longer was possible. They would try to stay together, and only as a last resort, race to the mountain. Buoyed by the new morning, they started off toward the beautiful green treed monument in front of them.

It wasn't long before they had outriders of Apache flanking them, and then they saw the main bunch, stoically waiting on a low rise directly in their path.

THE BIG CEDAR trees that the Don wanted were about halfway up the mountain on the southwestern side. The men had been cutting and loading the wagons for two days now, and as they slowly descended on the makeshift timber road cut decades before, Julio remembered to gather the piñón lower on the mountain that burned so well. It was hard work, but Julio always looked forward to these trips to the mountain, as the country was so different and green. If he were the Don, the hacienda would be at the foot of this magnificent mountain. But then the Apache also cherished these big mountains, for the hunting and the water. The men of the Rancho had learned long ago to go in strong numbers when harvesting the timber, and this time was no different. Fully a third of the Don's men, numbering fifteen good riflemen, cut the trees with their guns always within arms reach. As usual two guards were always posted when they were cutting, and now as they wound down the bumpy road in their five big wagons, armed guards preceded and followed the procession.

From their advantage point on the mountainside, they were afforded views out onto the desert from time to time, and when they heard the distant gun fire out to the southwest, they kept a lookout to see who would be out there, expecting it was Apache hunting something.

71

THE CRISIS HAD PASSED, and the Shoshone had dodged another fatal episode of death and disfigurement. Only the original warrior who had shown the first signs of the smallpox disease had died along with three elderly and a baby in the camp. Two more would carry the scars for life, but the Shoshone felt a great relief when the doctor finally said that the danger had passed. Much credit and appreciation was given to the Whiteman, though he kept telling them that they were more lucky than anything he had done. Still, he had stayed with them through their danger and fears.

Other news in the camp was that Many Flowers was pregnant again; and Dr. Lemmins spent some time instructing her on the care she should take to bring this baby to term. Lame Elk was very hopeful, but guarded. He did not wish to become too expectant should the baby miscarry again, but he had a good feeling about this pregnancy.

The few remaining family groups now broke off and left the camp for Winter. Lame Elk and Waushaute took their families a little to the South to a lower elevation, but in striking distance of the warm waters and elk and bison herds that wintered in the Yellowstone. Dr. Lemmins and Fournier headed back to Fort Hall for the long winter ahead.

TWO HORNS HAD circled back to the north through the Salmon River country, passing through the sacred mountains of the Shoshone and Nez Pierce, before finding Buffalo Lance and Blue Heron and their families. He had taken several weeks to make his circle, in no hurry to learn any more bad news about the tribe, and with little interest in returning to his first wife, who still waited for him. Messenger was all the company he required now as he sorted through his thoughts and emotions after the eventful Fall. He wasn't really angry with the Shoshone, or the Crow, and he had a more philosophical view of the Blackfoot place in the world than Buffalo Lance or some of the other prideful warriors in the tribe. Had he been Blackhand, he would have done more or less the same thing, and had the Blackfoot been in the Crows position, he recognized that he might have tried a similar baiting tactic for advantage over his enemies. He was just emotionally worn out, as chief, forever having to show strength, even when he wanted to mourn like everyone else. He was sad. He missed Moon in the Daylight and Red Horses. He remembered his mother and his father. He even missed old Buffalo Robe, who too had died of the plague. It was a good but hard life, and there were too many early deaths with his people. He wondered if it was so with the Whiteman. From time of birth to adulthood, it had seemed that someone was always dying, often unexpectedly. The boys he had run with as a child were few now, and he was far from being an old man. If it were up to him, he would not war again, but it was not. The young men would always hunger for the warpath, and the enemies of the Blackfoot would always provide ample provocation to start fights. The killing and dying would go on as it always had. Only rare respites of a year or two at a time seemed to break the monotony of war as he thought back now. And always the serious and the best were the first casualties. But what other way was there? He could not imagine a Blackfoot gathering that did not honor and praise the warrior's way. They needed their fighting culture to survive and grow as a people. The Crows and the Shoshone had just demonstrated that clearly enough for him. The weak tribes were pushed into the poor lands as they always had been, until they too were strong enough to push back or they vanished from the land.

So the lone warrior rode and thought, camped and thought, hunted and thought, until he overcame his period of mourning, and returned to his people as the leader they needed.

IT WAS A hard reality for Stands against the Storm to swallow. A lifetime of conflict with the Lakota, Cheyenne, Blackfoot, Shoshone, and others had hardened him over the years. But the last few years had shown such promise in finally getting the upper hand over these old enemies. The advent of the Whitemen's guns had created a window of opportunity for the Crow that would not have been there otherwise. He remembered the first trappers to come into Crow territory, back when he was a child. The rivers were full of beaver then, and the Whitemen had been willing to trade heavily for their pelts. Soon the Crow were wealthier than their neighbors, and that prosperity had translated to an expanding power in the area. They had beaten back the mighty Lakota and Cheyenne, and should have been able to do the same with the Blackfoot. It was a bitter turn of events. On the brink of dominating their greatest enemies, they were handed a crippling defeat. The old chief wondered if the new young leaders were savvy enough to lead as well as his generation had done. It was a squandered opportunity that would not come again soon, if ever. He could not help but show his disgust over the new circumstances the Crow now found themselves living with.

Life was even worse for the new war chief of the Crows. Loud Thunder was true to his name, as he vented his anger on everyone and anyone who displeased him, and everything right now displeased him. The Crows had figured out that the Blackfoot must have had spies to surprise them as they had. The plan would have worked, and the Blackfoot dogs would have died under the Crow guns, if not for the spies. The return to the Crow camps had been humiliating, particularly since the Crow had initiated the war. There were those who openly spoke of the poor leadership of High Feathers and the Counsel in their grief. He was not immune to the criticism either, even though he had been elevated to war chief. It was a tainted honor with so many young Crow warriors dead. The hate that burned in Loud Thunder was painful in its never-ending state. He was consumed by it. If it had been feasible, he would have taken the remaining warriors back to attack the Blackfoot again. It was his singular purpose. Eventually it led him too, to leave the Crow camp alone and head out into the blizzard blowing across the plains to the southeast and Fort Laramie to buy some whiskey. He would kill a Cheyenne he met there who had been drinking with him over a dispute he couldn't remember the next day.

72

ORBY LOOKED DOWN AT his morning coffee. He could barely take a sip without Juanita running over to refill his cup. Donovan sat stoically across the table from him, as both men struggled around the obvious subject as yet unspoken.

Eventually Donovan broke the silence, saying, "You understand that I have to pass on something to about one hundred employees eagerly awaiting this breakfast to end?" Donovan was referring to the last two days, when no one in the hotel had seen or heard from Gabrielle or Corby since they had gone upstairs to "talk" in her apartments. It was largely assumed that the two were now a couple, and they had been the major topic of conversation with the hotel crowd since Corby's arrival. However, some official confirmation was expected, and as Corby's breakfast with Donovan was the first appearance by either of the two . . .

The young man sheepishly smiled, and fidgeted. "I . . . I mean we . . . well it was . . . you know."

"A definite quote for the newspapers there," Donovan said with a straight face.

"She wants to get married," Corby blurted out in a half whisper, craning his neck forward conspiratorially.

"That's wonderful," exploded Donovan, getting several anticipatory looks from around the dining room. Lowering his voice, he repeated, "That's wonderful, Corby. The two of you will make a great team."

"Do you really think so?" Corby asked with true concern. " I mean we really got along great the last two days, but that is a lot different than marriage, and I'm still just a saddlebum, and . . ."

"Hold it there, cowboy," Donovan interjected. "The two of you obviously spent a great deal of time talking about your relationship to get to the point of talking about marriage. If Gabrielle thinks it will work, you need to look at the positive side of why it would. I think it would, but you have to believe it will work, or it can't. You understand what I'm getting at?"

"Sure, but I'm still the same guy who rode across the mountains with you, and she's still a high-society countess. You got to know that the distance between us is considerable. There may be so few things in common between us that it is impossible to forge a long-term or compatible partnership," Corby stated, having thought long and hard on the subject.

Donovan paused, realizing he wasn't going to just blow by this rather large hurdle, and recognizing the legitimate concerns his young friend had.

"All that's true enough," he said, "but let me remind you that you are not the wet-nosed kid I left Fort Boise with. That was some seven years ago, and you have come a long way. You have impressed some mighty unimpressionable people in that time, including Stranahan, me, and Gabrielle, and probably the old gentleman who gave you that grand horse, not to mention Jimbo Fisher and a few Indians." Donovan smiled. "I just believe that you can become whatever you want to become. You have that kind of ability. Gabrielle obviously thinks so too, and she's no dummy. If you start by seeing the possibilities, and let go of the reservations, you will see what we see. Kid, I can't think of a better husband for Gabrielle than you, period.

"She don't need some banker or lawyer who can talk well. She needs a man who can stand tall, and grow with her. That's you to a T."

Corby looked across at his best friend and mentor, knowing he had heard a heartfelt compliment. He would remember this moment for its own merit.

"If I do this thing... you know, marry her, you have got to stand up there too, beside me."

Donovan leaned back in his chair. "Sorry, sonny, she beat you to the punch on that one sometime ago."

It took Corby a moment to understand that Gabrielle had already asked Donovan to give her away when and if the time ever came.

73

THERE WAS NO DOUBT as to the morning's battle. The Apache were there to deny the Whitemen the refuge of Black Mountain. They intended to kill the remaining men in Sam Johnson's party. The rancher pulled up and stopped his horse, appraising the situation. The Apache had fanned out in front of him, some thirty strong, and there were three riders flanking him on each side. His group was nearing an end to its bravery and stamina. Sam Johnson was many things, one of which was a leader.

"Everyone recheck your loads," he said in an even voice. "Depending on how they come at us, we've got to make every shot count."

The four men, including Tobias Gresham, did as they were told, as all the participants to the morning's drama held their positions. With their rifles slung across their laps, the five riders started forward again at a walk. It was a beautiful, crisp morning, and would have been an ideal day to go for a ride. But as of the moment, all concentration was directed at the line of Indians still standing and waiting in front of them. Sam looked for a chief, figuring one had to be near the middle of the line, but he couldn't discern any special markings with these desert fighters. Like a light cavalry line, the Apache held their rifles upright on their thighs. They began to walk forward and then broke into a trot.

"They are coming at us head-on," said Sam. "I say we charge right through them and keep going for all we are worth." He looked at his two cowboys and the cook, and got grim nods of agreement. Tobias Gresham was now so overcome with fear that talking to the man was pointless. Sam figured they had little chance of making the mountain, but those were the cards they were given.

The Apache were now breaking into a gallop as the two sides closed in on each other. A few wild shots were now being taken, and the air was filled with the yells of the advancing Indians, along with the low thunder of the horses' hooves pounding the hard pan of the desert.

"Hold your fire until you are sure. You won't get a second rifle shot off," yelled Sam as they picked up speed forward.

Just before the two groups were to hit, two tactics changed. Most of the Apache veered away to either side, expecting to pour fire into the oncoming Whitemen, hopeful to minimize risk to themselves. And, Tobias Gresham lost his nerve on the charge and broke off to the right by himself in a panicked move to flee the conflict. By doing so he actually attracted more attention to himself, as those Apache that had split to his side of the group now had a sideways target of the fat man racing across their path. Fully half of the gunfire on that side centered on the lawyer, and with a primal scream, he fell off his horse and was dragged in one stirrup until the Apache caught up to him and captured the still alive but unconscious body, riddled with gunshot wounds.

The remaining four men on three horses fired their guns at the Apache still in their sights and spurred their mounts toward the opening hole. As the Apache swept past, both the cowboys and the cook were cut down and killed by the Apache fire, but Sam Johnson miraculously rode on untouched.

Now it was a race for his life. Even should he reach the mountain, it would be unlikely that he could find adequate cover and outlast this many Indians. However, immediate concerns outweighed thinking ahead. He had a jump on them as they had to slow down to wheel around and start their pursuit. Still at full gallop, Sam was able to cover enough distance that the Apache were quickly out of range for an accurate rifle shot from horseback. Had some thought to dismount and shoot as soon as they saw him breakthrough, they probably could have brought him down. Tucking his rifle back into its pouch, Sam hunched down on his horse and disregarded everything but the line to the mountain. In his day he had ridden enough cowponies to be a good rider, and with his life on the line, he now used everything he had learned over the years to urge his horse onward.

He heard the reports of the rifles behind him as the wind rushed past his ears, and he listened to the breathing of his horse for the first signs of laboring. The mountain was getting closer, but could his horse get there before giving in?

Two shots rang out in front of him to his left, and he saw the Mexican workers standing by an arroyo a mile distant from his line waving their rifles at him. Leaning to the left, he tacked off on the new line toward Don Sebastián's men without breaking stride, and within a handful of seconds, came under the protective fire of the Mexicans' guns.

Julio Sánchez had his men fire over the heads of the few Apache that came within range. Sam Johnson pulled in the reins enough to come to a swift halt and dismount, tripping with his momentum and rolling over a couple of times at the bottom of the arroyo the Mexicans were using for protection. Jumping right up, he pulled his rifle and ran to the wall of the arroyo in time to see the Apache nonchalantly ride away back to the desert, where they would try to revive Tobias Gresham for the afternoon's activities. Sam then slid down the slope as the energy dissipated out of his body and he began to realize he was going to live another day.

"Señor Johnson," Julio said smiling, "you are a long way from your side of the river, no?"

74

THE USS *INDEPENDENCE* HAD a long and distinguished service, dating back to 1779, when it had been commissioned as the first ship of the line in the U.S. Navy. Actually there had been two USS *Independence*s named prior. The first was bought in 1775 by the navy, a ten-gun sloop, which soon wrecked in 1778. The second was bought in 1777 as a twelve-gun brig, renamed, sold, and decommissioned two years later. This USS *Independence*, the third by the name, was built in Boston in 1814 to counter the larger ships the British were then using against the United States. She was built with seventy-four guns, had a length of 190 feet, a breadth of 54 feet, and was manned by 790 officers and men. She had served with the USS *Constitution* guarding the Port of Boston, and had sailed to the Mediterranean with Stephen Decatur. Later it was determined that she rode too low in the water for her bottom row of guns to be effective, and she was refitted to carry fifty-four guns (all 32-pounders) instead, freeing her to be one of the fastest and most powerful frigates of her time. In her prime she had delivered the U.S. Minister to Imperial Russia, and been the flagship of the Brazil Squadron, and later the Pacific Squadron during the Mexican War in 1846. She was there at Guaymas, and Mazatlan, Hawaii, and Spezia, Italy. Now she toured the triangle from Chile to Hawaii to San Francisco, as the flagship of the latest version of the Pacific Squadron. The rest of the squadron consisted of another frigate, the USS *Congress*, and three man-of-war sloops. But the future was to be steamers, and the day of the wooden fighting sailing ships was coming to a close. It would not be too much longer before she would be decommissioned for the last time.

Mare Island had yet to build a ship, but it was now capable of refitting seagoing vessels, so the Pacific Squadron rested at anchor in the bay, having sailed in from Hawaii. Also in the area was the somewhat smaller USS *Massachusetts*, a wooden steamer, carrying only four guns, but large enough for troop and armament transport. She had originally been assigned to cruise the West Coast and help with the establishment of lighthouses and buoys for navigation aids. As such, she was familiar with the traffic and ships of the area, including Targon's privateers. Lately she had been assisting the U.S. Army with its problems with the Indians around Puget Sound, Washington Territory, delivering guns and ammunition. It was in that context that she passed along information about the whereabouts of three of Targon's whalers to the U.S. Army while visiting the bay in December of 1855.

Major Conner, U.S. Army, the Presidio, had been waiting and hoping for just such a set of conditions. Personally pleading his case to the fleet's commodore, he was able to wrangle the use of one of the navy's sloops to hunt for the pirates who were within a day's sail to the South. The Major was convinced as were many in the area that Targon's ships had attacked and sunk the *Fairfield* and killed his wife. He was able to convince the navy that the ships were a continuing danger to the coast, and was supported in his beliefs by the stories the USS *Massachusetts* had heard during her service in the area. Getting assigned as a liaison officer for the sake of helping identify these vessels, the Major shipped out of the San Francisco Bay on the sloop *St. Vincent* in search of the privateers. With her sixteen 32-pounders, and six 8-inch guns, she was at least an even match for three of Targon's outfitted whalers.

HAVING THOROUGHLY ENJOYED his time back at sea disposing of the "police officers" that had failed him in their botched kidnapping attempt of Zachary DuPort, Günter had been stuck in the city for weeks fighting an image battle through his lawyer and the press. Disgusted with the whole process, he had found himself back at Half Moon Bay when his captains had reported back from their short reconnaissance sails looking for the return of any late sealing boats they might hijack as they sailed back for winter havens. Standing on the bridge of one of the three ships as he got his report, Targon saw the U.S. man-of- war sail around the northern point of land at the same time as everyone else. They could surrender or run. Neither case was appealing, but he would lose the ships if they simply surrendered.

Half Moon Bay was something of a misnomer. There really wasn't a bay as traditionally defined, but rather a break from the rugged coastline that allowed the smugglers to run in close to a beach protected by a northern spit of land and the pounding waves from the Pacific Ocean. There were large sand dunes above the beach and marshy tidal washes.

The *St. Vincent* sailed to the center of what might be called the mouth of the bay, where she proceeded to turn into the wind coming from the shore in the afternoon and sit. She had pinned the privateers against the beach before they could scramble and escape. Shortly thereafter a shell from one of her

8-inch guns whistled over the three modified whalers as they worked to hoist their sails, and exploded in the shallow water by the beach, sending a tower of sand and water into the air. The signal was clear. Stand to, or be blown out of the water.

Targon made his decision, lowering a longboat to get back to shore. He shouted to his dispersing captains that anyone who could escape would earn half shares in their ship's take next year, and $100 in gold to every man in the crew. The three ships started to separate, which brought a salvo of shells from the *St. Vincent*'s long guns again, targeting the middle ship that Targon was trying to leave with devastating effect. Knocked off his feet as he was about to climb overboard, Targon smashed his head on a metal cleat, opening up an ugly wound over his left ear. But being the brute of a man he was, he pulled himself back up and somehow muscled his way down the side to the longboat as the deck above him splintered and burned. The remaining two ships were now under full sail moving in opposite directions, trying to hug the shoreline before tacking out past the *St. Vincent* and open sea. They would try to run past the sloop simultaneously, on either side, forcing her to hold her position, or possibly lose one of the privateers. But with her 32-pounders loaded and waiting, she would be a deadly ship to pass and receive a broadside from either side. It seemed the *St. Vincent* was ready to do just that, wait and sweep the decks of both privateers as they tried to slide by as close to the opposite shores as they could. The third ship was already out of commission, back by the beach, and the crew was leaving her like rats, swimming to shore to escape capture.

The *St. Vincent* had another trick up her sleeve as she awaited the privateers in the center of the bay. Using her 8-inch guns again, she targeted the sails of the ship bearing to the North, eventually ripping through her topsails and impeding her speed. Now with only one fast sailing adversary, the *St. Vincent* swung around to cut her off. The southbound vessel made the critical mistake of firing her 6-pounders at the approaching navy sloop, in return for which the *St. Vincent* opened up with her front guns, hitting the rudder, before threatening to blow the ship apart with a now close-in broadside. The privateer lowered her flag to surrender, asking for assistance as she was now in danger of drifting onto the rocks to the South. Ignoring her plea, the *St. Vincent* jibed about, running with the offshore wind out to sea to position herself to run down the northbound ship, still under half sail, trying desperately to get up new top sails, sneaking around the northern point of the bay, and running perpendicular to the offshore breeze due North. It would take another hour before the *St. Vincent*, who had to tack out to sea, could use a swifter tack into the wind to chase down the last Targon ship. It surrendered when the outcome became obvious, and was towed back South by the *St.*

Vincent. The ship that had been left to its own devises had managed to beach on a graveled shallow, and the crew had swum ashore and were long gone. The captain of the *St. Vincent* elected to use it for target practice, as well as the first ship still burning in Half Moon Bay, thus eliminating them from ever being used again.

Riding hard back to the city, Targon organized his thoughts for the inevitable quick liquidation and escape that he now felt he must make. He surmised that the crews captured would link him to the *Fairfield*, and the hunt would be on. Unlike Zachary DuPort, he wasn't haunted by the enormous loss of money he would be forced to endure. Money had been judiciously spread around in hiding places and under other names for many years. It was the sense that he had lost the battle and would not be able to relish a victory over his enemies this time. American naval power had finally arrived and this coastline would now be too dangerous to ply his trade anymore. It was a big world, and other opportunities would present themselves as they always had if he could escape. Now he must concentrate on that escape, leaving the area silently and quickly on his remaining two ships, berthed and anchored up the American River in the San Francisco Bay for the winter. He calculated he would have two long nights to load and slip out of the bay before a possible blockade could be organized after the return of the navy vessel that had attacked him in Half Moon Bay. If the tides and winds were right, he would be long gone straight out to sea when they began to look for him. He would, however, have to sail past Mare Island to do so.

As he rode, Günter could only hope that someone might have caught the little weasel DuPort while he had been gone, thus delivering a much anticipated goodbye gift. The thought comforted him as he continued to slowly bleed from the gash on his head, and the bruising he was taking in the saddle.

75

THE COMPANY WOULD NEED another infusion of capital. Thomas James went over the numbers again. It had long ago become apparent to James that the steamship company had been a very bad investment, and he had stopped putting any more money in it some years before. However, he was the treasurer of the company, and had the very unpleasant task of reporting the health of the venture to its shareholders on a regular basis. When Targon had initially plopped down a wad of money, the company had looked like it would have a fighting chance, but Targon was overdue with the second installment promised, and with all the new bad publicity surrounding the man, the company was not immune to the occasional raised eyebrow from the upper echelon of the city. The bondholders were constantly grumbling, as were many of the original stock shareholders. Along with the tainted money, the company seemed forever plagued by bad luck, mismanagement, and a waning interest. Stewart Bertram had consistently made questionable business moves as the president, insisting on top-of-the-line materials, highly paid employees, and doomed project completion dates. The Vanderbilt executive had finally quit, saying he had seen enough handwriting on the wall. It wasn't that Bertram was incompetent—he certainly worked hard—but he was just out of his element. He had been cheated in his purchasing efforts by the handful of eastern manufacturers that built the huge boilers and fittings these new large steamers would need. Credit had increasingly tightened as the deadlines passed, due to Bertram splitting his time between his principle contractor occupation that paid the bills and the large steamship company undertaking. Friendships had suffered greatly with the large amounts of invested capital at risk. Thomas James would have loved to have taken a small loss and abandoned his role as treasurer, but it was well beyond that point now. He too had personal reputation at stake here as one of the big bankers in the city and an original touter of the project. If it was to go down, Thomas James needed to be close enough to the numbers to lay the blame away from himself.

It was with that mindset that he met with Stewart Bertram to discuss the best way to approach Mr. Targon on his overdue cash infusion. As with many of the business meetings in the city, they had arranged to have lunch at the St. Montfort Hotel. Upon arriving Thomas James could see that Stewart Bertram was highly agitated and impatient to speak with him.

"He's gone. Lock, stock, and barrel," said Stewart Bertram.

"Who are we talking about?" asked Thomas James.

"Targon, you idiot. Targon is gone," blurted out Bertram.

"Mind your tongue, Bertram," answered James. "And no he isn't. He just had to take a business trip to purchase a copper mine in Central America. I know because he had to withdraw most of his money at my bank on quick notice two days ago, to deliver the cash he would need down there. He will be back in about two weeks. I mentioned his overdue commitment to the company, and he assured me we would discuss it on his return, but that cuts things pretty short, and ..."

"He's gone, you fool! The police and the U.S. Navy are after him. The navy sank two of his pirate ships two days ago in Half Moon Bay, and towed another back. He was responsible for the *Fairfield* after all. We are ruined! There will be no more money from that ruffian, and we look like fools to have spoken up for him!" Bertram had a wild look in his eyes.

The truth sunk in on Thomas James. "It was you who sold everyone on his legitimacy!" accused James. "I will be a laughing stock in the banking community for this."

Bertram gazed over at James as if he hadn't heard him for an instant, being lost in his own thoughts, and then reacted. "What ... what did you say? We needed the money. You knew as well as everyone else that Targon was a thief and brigand."

"But he sank the *Fairfield*," whined James. "The city will turn on us. We will be ruined!"

And so the two sank down in their chairs not knowing what they would do next, but knowing, whatever it was, it would be too little.

THE NEWS REACHED Zachary the next day when he stole a newspaper. Now holed up in a livery stable on the south side of the city, he released an audible sigh. No Targon meant no reward from Targon to the denizens of the crime world. He imagined the scramble would be on for whatever assets the "Prince of Crime" may have had to leave in his abrupt departure. Zachary had been doing a lot of thinking about that himself and had chosen just one building worth the risk of exploring. There would only be a couple of other Targon associates who might know of this stash—but then again, maybe not. The night he had accompanied Targon into the city to buy opium in Chinatown, when they had kidnapped Logan, Targon had taken him to a small house he owned not far from the district but in a very upscale neighborhood, and had unlocked a simple bolt and chain. Inside had been some fine furniture, with walled up windows. Needing a lamp that had been sitting ready on a table, they had gone into a back room where Targon had unlocked a small wall safe and taken several bank notes out from a stack in the vault. Targon had been careful not to show Zachary much of what else might have been in the safe or the house, saying that he kept just enough cash here to do business on this side of town. Where that may or may not have been true, the address was nice enough that people had noticed the two enter and leave the premises, making Zachary think that this was probably a safe house and stash that Targon had established where he felt fairly comfortable about its security. If Targon had rushed to leave as the papers suggested, getting across town and being spotted in that neighborhood may have been too risky a proposition for the man that night. It would be easy enough to see if the lock was still intact, and well worth a burglary if it was. There would be no time to lose either, should someone else be thinking the same thing.

Not waiting for dark, Zachary decided he had to try this hunch now, and donning his disguise, he quickly headed back across the city to the fancier quarters overlooking the north shore of the bay. Finding a quiet park bench within sight of the house, he sat down to observe anything that might suggest trouble. It was a Sunday morning, and he quickly became aware that his dirty appearance was out of place with the church-going populace in the area. Seeing a policeman coming his way, he voluntarily waved to the officer, acknowledging that he would leave the area willingly, and ambled off, circling around to the other side of the house. Here he found a flowered alley running behind several nice homes that afforded him better cover, and he was able to attain the back door of the home, where another lock and chain stopped his progress. Looking around, he saw a second story window that he could reach by climbing up a large, leafy tree. Prying open the two- by- fours nailed over it shouldn't be too hard if he had a crowbar. The house clearly looked to be undisturbed, and Zachary began to imagine what he would find inside. He could come back late tonight and break in at his leisure. Seeing all he needed to, Zachary began to edge away from the home, back toward the alley.

"Good morning, Zachary!" someone called. Standing next to a gate that opened into the backyard of the home was Roland Leach. Several police officers now appeared and advanced quickly to cut off any escape.

A man now walked up to Zachary and said, "I'm Lieutenant Stevenson of the San Francisco Police Department, and you, Mr. DuPort, are headed back to jail."

Two policemen then bound his hands behind him, and a caged wagon was called up from somewhere. They placed Zachary inside, where Roland Leach had the opportunity to come up to quietly say to him, "You can thank Günter Targon, who also says that he will have certain friends visit you again, once you are in prison." Roland gave a triumphant smile. "You are wondering why we didn't take you ourselves? Or why I would turn you over myself?"

Still registering the obvious threat about prison, Zachary managed a nod.

"Targon couldn't wait you out, and prison will serve his purpose almost as well. As for me, money. Simply money." He then tipped his hat to the police lieutenant and walked away.

Zachary laid his head against the hard side of the police wagon, wondering why in hindsight he had risked his freedom. He could have been halfway back to Boston by ship now, had he gone to Los Angeles and taken a job as a deckhand. He knew the threat from Targon was not an idle one. So stupid! He banged his head against the side of the wagon in his anger at himself.

76

THE TOWN HAD BEGUN to accept the new boundaries and authorities. There were still many undecided disputes that would be argued in the court system yet to come, over some of the less clear land grants of Mexican owners, but the smoke was beginning to clear as to how the town and area would be governed, and a general peace seemed to be taking hold. It hadn't hurt when Don Sebastián's foreman had brought Sam Johnson into town with their tale of Indians and salvation. Old Sam was singing a different song: glad to be alive at the moment, which helped cool down some tensions. Stranahan wasn't too upset to have seen the last of the St. Louis lawyer either. It was beginning to appear that his work would be done here shortly, and Stranahan was wondering whether he should take up Donovan on his offer of work out in California. Just like Donovan, he had found out that working for the U.S. Marshal Service had less of a future than he now hoped for. California sounded appealing, as did the pay Donovan was offering for running the security for the Frenchwoman's holdings. He really had no reason to return to St. Louis, and if O'Bannon wanted to step up to his old job, he was ready to do so. Only O'Bannon had surprised him, saying he too might like to check out California. Either way, marshaling was nearing an end.

The New Mexico Territory, which included Arizona and the town of Tucson, was still a very remote part of the country. Mail service was very spotty, and the law outside of the marshal's direct view tended to be bent more often than not. The people who wished to live in peace had few options but to team together, and the old patterns of life between the Europeans and the Mexicans of intermixing in this southwest bastion in the desert began to reappear. It was nice to see, and Stranahan himself had found a Mexican woman to share some time with, and who would cook him a nice meal now and then. The lawyers and surveyors had recently left, and nothing more was to be done until after their reports had been made back in Washington. It would only be a matter of time before the two marshals would be recalled to St. Louis.

One citizen however had done anything but slow down. Whether playing cards, courting women, racing horses, or whatever else he could think up, it was as if Drego was at the center of every activity in the town, using more energy than three other men. Generally jovial, Drego simply was enjoying life to its fullest. However, as was his way, he rarely saw fences he shouldn't cross, and stepped on many toes as he passed by. Usually the offenses were of a minor nature, and were forgiven in the face of the free spirit he clearly was, but some deeper grudges were forming in particular cases. A husband had been restrained after accusing and attacking Drego in a bar, while his wife pleaded innocent to the accusation of being one of Drego's lovers. She had not fully explained how she had come by a very nice necklace. Drego had also been forced to pay a bartender some money who had complained that Drego had offered drinks to the house and then not paid up. Drego could not remember the incident and had therefore refused to pay. A fight had broken out at a cantina after an intoxicated dancer had crashed into a dinner table. Somehow Drego had been in the middle of that too.

Stranahan had seen it too many times before. It was just a matter of time before Drego would end up behind bars or worse. It was a shame, because the man really didn't mean to hurt anyone, but his lack of sense, or whatever it was that drove his "walking on a tightrope" lifestyle, was going to get someone hurt before long. The Marshal had tried reasoning with him. He had spoken to the father. He had kicked him out of town twice. Nothing would stick in the man's fun-loving head. There had to be more to it. Drego wasn't overtly stupid. You could talk to many criminals and tell that was a primary cause in their troubles. Drego didn't seem to have a 'chip on his shoulder'. It was almost like a man who had been told he only had a few weeks to live. When everyone else was ready to call it a night, Drego was just warming up.

Once back in Missouri, Stranahan had stopped a young man from trying to jump from the top of a four-story building to a three-story building top. If he would have jumped and missed, he could have crippled himself for life or even killed himself. The young man had no compelling reason to try the jump other than when asked, he had said, "because I think I can make it."

Dealing with dangerous people for as long as Stranahan had, he recognized that sometimes you would not ever figure out why they do what they do. All you can do is try to guess what they might do, and when they might do it, and hope to be there to stop it.

O'Bannon on the other hand did not concern himself with the whys of criminal behavior. It was enough for him to ascertain if what had happened was right or wrong, lawful or unlawful. And so it was that he was fairly sure the commotion coming from the saloon that was interrupting his dinner probably was unlawful. He had just sat down, and the biscuits and butter were tantalizing him, when the normal noise level in the adjacent saloon rose to what indicated a fight. He knew the sound of tables and chairs being broken and bodies slamming into walls. Reluctantly grabbing a biscuit and jamming it in his mouth, he rose to attend to the matter. As he entered the street heading for the saloon, he saw Stranahan running up from the Post Office/Sheriff's Office that they still used as their own headquarters.

Looking at each other, O'Bannon shrugged his shoulders as if to say "no idea."

Just then a gunshot went off inside, and both men burst in with revolvers drawn. Several men who had been fighting stopped for an instant to see who had shot, and if they might be aiming at them next. In the confusion it would have been hard to tell, and Stranahan took the opportunity to fire two shots off through the roof of the one story building, causing everyone to look his way.

With the freeze in the action, the marshals saw two bodies not moving on the floor. Both were Mexicans. One had been shot, and one had a knife protruding through his chest. As the combatants began to get up off the floor, Drego went over to the man with the knife in his chest and pulled it out, wiping it on the man's shirt before sheathing it in his belt. Then rather nonchalantly he said to Strananhan, "My knife," as if the question of ownership might be disputed and he wouldn't get it back. They all knew the knife. It was the one Corby had given Drego when he left, and Drego proudly displayed it whenever he could.

Stranahan's eyes flared open a bit at the incongruous comment.

"O'Bannon," barked Stranahan, "please take Señor Santarosilla over to the jail, and then come back and help me figure out what happened here. The rest of you will place your two hands on the bar, and you," he indicated the bartender, "will put all their weapons on that table over there."

When O'Bannon got back, he found six men sitting on the floor leaning against a wall with their hands on top of their heads. Stranahan was sitting at a table interviewing the bartender.

"Pick one and get his story. Go over there," Stranahan said to O'Bannon, indicating the far side of the room. O'Bannon pointed to one of the men on the floor, and then jerked his finger directing the man to follow him.

"Then it looked like Estaban cursed and stood up. Drego cursed back and they lunged for each other," the bartender said. "I don't know who killed Paco, but that was Drego's knife in Estaban. He throws it you know. Real well."

It took about two hours to interview and unravel the course of events at the saloon, and there were still some questions about timing and motivation that were unclear. What was clear was that Drego had killed Estaban, and a fellow named Raúl had killed the other man Paco. All had been drinking together and discussing women. According to most accounts, the evening had started like many others, but had escalated with the alcohol into a mean-spirited confrontation between Drego and Estaban. The men had been childhood rivals, coming to blows on many occasions. From what he could discover, Stranahan pieced together a conversation line that had started with young men boasting about their prowess with women, and had abruptly ended with accusations about Don Sebastián's life as a young man and Drego's mother. The actual fighting tended to get blurred, with no one really sure who had drawn weapons when. The evidence suggested that Paco and Raúl had squared off in some fashion, as the gun of the dead man was found on the floor. Drego claimed that Estaban had reached for his gun, but there was nothing to corroborate that suggestion. Raúl, who was Estaban's friend, claimed that Drego had pulled and thrown his knife when Estaban had insulted Drego's mother. Everyone was well aware of how sensitive Drego was about his unwed mother, and being the bastard son of Don Sebastián, even though Don Sebastián had treated his mother well, and considered Drego as his son.

Other than sticking to his claim that Estaban had gone for his gun, Drego refused to talk about the reasons for the fight. Stranahan charged him with murder and sent O'Bannon out to tell the Don.

Book 3

1856

77

I T HAD BEEN A hard, cold Winter in the Oregon Territories. Heavy snows had cut deeply into the elk and deer populations. As Spring approached, frozen carcasses were revealed and thawed by the sun, and the carnivores had a feast. The great bear had many months to catch up on, and was ravenous. The Winter's kill would quickly help the bear begin its annual campaign of devouring everything it could find and catch. Beneficiaries of the Spring's harvest included cougars, wolves, coyotes, foxes, badgers, wolverines, martins, birds of prey, and the ever-present magpies and crows. But when the great bear spotted the dinner party, everyone else gave way to his size and strength. Needing to regain much of the fat it had lost during the Winter's sleep, feeding was its only thought in the first Spring months. It was still a little early for the traditional grasses and roots that were a staple of the bear's diet, as intermittent patches of snow covered the shaded hillsides. Stealing nuts from the squirrels' caches wasn't as satisfying as the big carcasses being uncovered everyday by the sun. Killing an occasional elk calf was also more work than necessary with the larder lying about. But soon this easy bounty would be gone, picked to the bone by the forest denizens. The bear would then hunt in earnest as the Spring months gave way to the next feasting occasion, the summer fishing and berries harvest. For now life was good, as the sun rose higher each day in the mountains. The big bear stood on its hind legs sniffing the breeze for another easy opportunity, but smelled the Indians instead, and ambled away up the hillside into the forest.

It had been almost a year and a half since the smallpox had struck the Blackfoot. When they had met at the lake for their summer camp, families had eagerly, yet carefully checked to see who had returned and who had not. Fortunately not more than forty more had died that Winter, and with no warring for another year, and no more diseases, the Blackfoot were just now beginning to think hopefully again. There had been a high number of births lately, in the relative calm.

Buffalo Lance could still not use his left arm, and it had begun to atrophy. However, he had a new son and as much energy as ever. He had worked to learn a new balance with the one arm as he swung a war club or threw his lance. He had taken to using a buffalo shield similar to the Crows that he fastened to his left side. Two Horns had been pushing the Bulls to redevelop and enhance their fighting skills, and Buffalo Lance was not going to be left behind. He practiced long and hard with his disability, working to turn it into a new fighting style and advantage. His right arm grew stronger. His kill stroke grew deadlier. His spirit was strong.

Blue Heron had also taken up the challenge. It felt good to train with his brothers again and gain vital skills. He had finally spent the time he had wanted as a rider, working his pony over the toughest terrain, racing with the buffalo, honing his riding skills to match his fighting skills. He had always felt uncomfortable on his horse compared to the great riders in the tribe, but no more.

The Bulls were a smaller group now with Running Wolf Leaps and The Badger rounding out the old group of five surviving members. Their sixth and newest member, whom they all teased as the boy was the now twenty-two-year-old Soaring Owl, who had won his membership during the Crow war. Suffering the good-natured insults of his betters, Soaring Owl was learning from the best and very proud to be there.

Two Horns had the Bulls on a training mission. He wanted to make them more than the best fighters. He had been impressed with the tracking and stalking skills of the Shoshone Blackhand for years, and knew if they too practiced, they could become a more silent and invisible force, and therefore more deadly to their enemies. He had made them play hide and seek games throughout the summer and winter, setting traps and sneaking up on everyone in the Blackfoot camps. They had hunted together, camped together, thought up new training techniques together, and finally were thinking together. It was time to test their new abilities as a single unit. There was no better test than the Shoshone who had crept right up to the Blackfoot camps before. Two Horns wanted to let the Shoshone know that the Blackfoot could appear and disappear too.

As it was just springtime, the Shoshone would be scattered, but slowly beginning to move back to the barricaded camp by the big lake that fed the Yellowstone River. They would scout out an opportunity to demonstrate their elusive skills.

Dressed in wolf skins, Two Horns led the small horseband southwest through the area he had scouted some eighteen months before. They would approach from the West and higher elevation to help avoid detection, even though it would require more time and colder temperatures. But the Bulls were eager to see what they could do, and what kind of a story they could come back home to tell.

Messenger smelled the bear, and snorted. It was a fading scent, and in the company of the others, did not alarm the big horse. There was a bounce to his step, as if realizing the group was up to something different.

Above on the mountain slope, the bear now angled across a meadow re-testing the wind, hoping again to smell that decaying odor of meat uncovered by the sun.

78

I T HAD BEEN A small wedding by most high society standards, but Corby wasn't sure he would survive the day. Gabrielle had spent such large sums of money for a one-day ceremony, and to entertain the handful of guests she had chosen to invite. Far from it being a happy moment in his life, this was extremely uncomfortable, and he could hardly wait for the wedding to be over and the people to leave. Gabrielle had coached him on the small talk he would be encountering during the festivities, and they had agreed to certain statements explaining what he would be doing in the future. That did little to mask the awkward feelings he had every time someone asked him a question about his life going forward. To be totally truthful, Gabrielle had been beautiful, and he had been very proud to stand up as her husband, but they could have done that at the small chapel on the ranch. The wedding just proved to him again that he lacked in the social graces and business acumen of Gabrielle's circle of friends and associates. But it was done now, and he could apply his hand to running the big ranch and seeing where it would go from there. He had some plans for the place, including building more reservoirs, starting a timber company, and commercially raising a larger herd. The Montara Ranch would have been heaven to any cowboy who loved the outdoors. The projects would be endless and the potential vast. Corby could envision the day when the ranch provided everything he would ever want or need. He doubted that would be true for Gabrielle. As out of his element as he had been during the wedding impressed upon him that he would have to make some changes if this union were to last, and he was convinced that he would do his part. If it took learning how to be a businessman, then so be it; he would learn. He knew he had a huge opportunity to learn whatever he was capable of learning, and he knew that was a rare circumstance in his world. Most of all he didn't want to let either Gabrielle or Donovan down, and he knew they wanted him to succeed. Logically it would take time, but he had time. He could do this.

After the wedding Gabrielle had gone back to running her businesses, and as he was deeply involved with the ranch, they would sometimes not see each other for a week at a time.

He made a point of always being at the hotel on Sundays, and she would try to visit the ranch for two days at a time when she could, for him. But it worried him that she needed to continue building her empire, and that he was just a part of her life. He rationalized, and he reasoned, but he worried. Somehow, with all the changes in his own life, a woman he loved, a fantastic ranch to run, and the ability to be anything he could possibly want, he felt he had lost something. The pressure to change was always there, even if no one was telling him to. But he would see if these feelings were simply adapting to all the new pieces in his life. If he changed, maybe how he felt about the changes would change too.

FOR GABRIELLE, LIFE was wonderful. Corby was the remarkably sensitive man she had thought he was, and went to great lengths to show his love. He was strong and quick of mind, and determined. She had her partner for life. She was aware of his apprehension of fitting in, but felt confident that in time that would fade.

The hotel was almost completed now, and Gabrielle had a sense of fulfillment about her life. The wedding had been exquisite. Donovan had been so handsome in his tails, showing as much concern as any father would have. Her dress had been made to her specifications in New Orleans and had fit to perfection. The hotel staff had provided everything else with such attention and care that she was sure San Francisco had never seen a finer wedding. And she had kept it small and simple to please Corby. She found herself humming at her work, something she had not done since being a child. Corby had thrown himself into pulling the ranch together and had some interesting plans for its future. He certainly did love the place. Perhaps it would take awhile before she could pry him away for a honeymoon, possibly back East, or to New Orleans.

Another venture had been running around in her mind for Corby. Bertram's steamship company was now bankrupt and could be picked up for pennies on the dollar. She didn't believe in a luxury steamship line out West, but the shipyard was there to build anything else anyone might want. Trade continued to grow at an incredible rate in the city. Eventually there would be overseas trade from Japan and China. Right now there was a need for an independent West Coast mail service from Alaska all the way to Chile, and more ships for whale and seal hunting, not to mention the transports for local goods and services. Corby would know how to deal with the rough and tumble customers out here, and together they could build a company attuned to the changing needs of the West. With a bargain price start, it would be hard to fail. She thought she should talk to Donovan to help explain the idea and convince Corby to take the plunge. She knew he could do it, but she sensed he wasn't as sure yet.

THE HOUSE THAT Gabrielle had built for Henri Seurat was filled with the books he had collected over his lifetime. These he had left to Donovan. With nowhere to put all the books, Donovan had bought the house to live in. He really had stolen the house, as Gabrielle had given him a ridiculous price and would not take any more. He had never imagined living in such a fine structure, and the views of the bay were incredible. Henri had left something of a guide to follow, instructing Donovan how he had grouped the books on subject matter, and where his favorite passages were. Looking for a shortcut, Donovan had gone to some of the listings, where it became instantly clear that Henri Seurat had been a very complicated and studied man. This was not a surprise to Donovan, but the more he read, the greater his appreciation became for the little man's vast education. Donovan had learned from trial and error, and while he recognized how important book learning could be, he had never seen it as a form of entertainment or a quick reference service before. You could probably find an answer or at least an opinion on just about any question that might come to mind in Henri's library. There were even books about plants and animals, weather effects, and growing conditions necessary to maintaining a healthy garden. Some of this was applicable to the common man, and the more he read, the more seemed to apply. So this was what Henri had intended, he surmised. His last gift, a never-ending companion in books. What a shame he had known the man for such a short period.

Donovan had also been thinking about his horse ranch again. He had more money now than he had ever dreamed of making. It was over eight years that he had been with Gabrielle, and he didn't regret any of them, but he was beginning to feel his age for the first time. He had mastered the businessman fundamentals and was proud of what he had done, but he missed the hunting and fishing, working with animals, and meeting the morning sun outdoors. With Corby now out at the Montara Ranch, Donovan found himself paying a few more visits to the place, and remembering his former surroundings.

When he had left St. Louis back in '46, and ventured out to the wilderness of the Oregon Territories, he recalled the massive buffalo herds he had passed and the beautiful rivers he had crossed. He remembered the trip over the Cascade Mountains with Corby and the nights they had camped out by the sparkling lakes on the range top. A good campfire seemed a lifetime ago. But he didn't want to disappear into the wilderness alone. He still enjoyed the people he worked with, his newfound talents, and the challenges the businesses brought each day. But something would need to change soon. Henri had harped on the need to constantly adapt and change.

Something had already changed, particularly the rewriting of the history he had already lived. Over breakfast one morning Gabrielle had shown Donovan another Eastern newspaper that had been shipped out West, lauding the pioneer's bravery and love for country. It went on to say how these modern day Pilgrims were bringing much needed civilization and religion with them to the indigenous peoples of the plains and forests. Once again Donovan had grunted, but this time he decided to enlighten Gabrielle a little about the heroes of the West.

"More like the dregs of society, they ought to have said," he explained. Many of the people that had gone West were looking for something for nothing. Quick riches in the goldfields, free land, escape from criminal prosecution. Rather than the intelligent entrepreneurs and good Samaritans they were painted as, Donovan knew a large portion to be cowardly, lazy, and not smart at all. Of course there were many exceptions, but the West had primarily called out to the failures from the East and the oppressed from overseas—hardly the ideal stock for forging a great nation. They came with their small-mindedness into Indian Country, where they saw what they considered their inferiors who they treated openly as such. They died by the thousands having not properly prepared for the trip, and they brought the diseases of the unclean and unwitting. They killed each other as quickly as they killed the Indians, and they failed to learn from their experiences. But the West was being romanticized for many economic and political reasons, along with the idealistic and uninformed writers who liked to think it was so, and who profited by telling it as such.

A classic example had been Zeke Bridges. Never wanting to actually work for his money, he had constantly been drawn to the lure of fast riches. Devoid of a moral compass, the man had squandered above-normal intelligence with less-than-normal common sense. He was serving a ten-year sentence in the new San Quentin State Prison across the bay, rather than risking the trial in the Oregon Territories where he might be hung.

And Targon. There was another jewel of the West. Hopefully he was long gone not to return. Donovan could have listed his examples by the dozens, but to no point. Let the newspapers say what they wanted. You were a fool to believe them if you wished. Having expounded like a grumpy old man,

Donovan said he was going down to the livery stable to see if they had any new stock.

Gabrielle watched him go, and made a mental note to have a longer conversation with him soon, just to make sure everything was all right.

79

THE WINDS BLEW HOT and dry as always. Big Jim sat with the rifle across his lap, leaning back against a rock in the shade, seemingly staring out into space. Drego wondered if the man had learned how to sleep with his eyes open. Working with the other inmates on the road-building crew, he had taken to watching the guards' behavior, hoping to find a flaw to the security. He had tried to escape once before, getting into the surrounding mountains before the dogs found him and he was dragged back. He had learned that he would need some help from the outside, or some better luck to have a real chance of escaping. Thereafter he had been a model prisoner the last six months, even refusing to join a break by some other prisoners, whom he considered to have little chance of escaping. He had been right. Two came back dead and the other two looked almost dead. The prison was somewhere near old Santa Fe, and Drego knew that meant it was far from anywhere. The best escape route would be straight north for water and woods in the San Juan Mountains, but to get there you would need a horse and water. The hard, sunbaked local mountains were too sparse of cover to hide in, and the round-up system, which likely had been used many times, was effective in returning escapees. Drego was of the opinion that he would die in this camp long before he served his sentence, therefore he must escape.

The prisoners were a mix of Anglo, Mexican, and some Indian, but the guards were all Anglo, and the Indians and Mexicans fared the worst. There were some very bad men in the camp, and he had been forced to make alliances with the Mexicans for his personal safety. He told no one his real name, and the guards seemed unaware that he was from a good family. He had written to his father, Don Sebastián, once, carefully crafting the suggestion that a visit from anyone would be to his detriment. The guard who had read his letter had not picked up on the subtlety.

The meanest Mexican in the prison was called El Cacharro, loosely translated to mean "boneshaker." He was very large, standing a full head above most of the other inmates, including Drego. He had a sullen manner to him and a quick temper. He too had no intention of staying a prisoner, and had been sorting through the population for potentially intelligent accomplices to help him in his escape. He had decided that Drego was the right caliber to assist him, and had basically threatened Drego to be an accomplice in his escape. Drego's life in prison became markedly better, once his loose association with El Cacharro was known. Where the man was definitely a danger with his brute strength, Drego did not fear him, as he came to know him. El Cacharro was an illiterate but intelligent man. There were few really intelligent prisoners in the Santa Fe facility. A respect and something of a bond was formed between them, in an otherwise bleak and mind-numbing daily routine of supervised work in the hot temperatures. In a short time, the two men were in position to gather what little information was available around the prison camp, and recruit whatever help they would wish from the limited offerings available.

The lockdown each night took them through a series of fences and gates into a complex of small brick and adobe sleeping quarters. There were no individual locks on the buildings, which backed up to a rock cliff. Drego thought the compound might have been a rock quarry before becoming a prison. The inmates' quarters were separated into sets of three buildings each, housing only twelve prisoners per building. A high wall, except where the cliff served as an enclosure, surrounded each set of buildings. Guard towers were placed on two of the four corners, enabling the guards to look down on at least two yards each. There was also a guard structure halfway up the cliff that wooden stairs had been built to reach, allowing the guards there to view the entire facility. Inmates were never sure what housing complex they would be placed in, as the policy was to keep them from getting too familiar within one yard. Like most such policies, there were ways, should someone really wish to find them, to communicate between yards. Work groups were also kept relatively small most of the time, but on occasion, a large project required a large group of workers and extra guards.

Many of the prisoners had assumed that they were here until they died, and that was often true. Once an inmate was too weak or sick to work, they were transferred to the prison hospital, from where they seldom returned. A few would serve out shorter sentences, and a few of them would return again, never to leave again.

So it was that Drego, El Cacharro, and anyone else that spent any time there quickly concluded that escape was an option that had to be evaluated. Most evaluated and gave up. Some tried escaping, and were brought back or killed in the process. If anyone had escaped in recent years, it was unknown in the prisoner population. But with the prospect of a slow death in prison staring them in the face, the two men agreed that they would find a way.

Breaking out of the camp was discarded as an idea versus the potential for breaking away from a work group. The obvious advantages of escaping during time outside the prison focused the two on planning accordingly. Smuggling and hiding scant available supplies on the outside became their first objective. Buying outside help would be more problematic, but very helpful if possible. Having an escape route and horses would of course be essential, and obtaining weapons would be a major plus. Drego understood that should he actually be able to escape, he would have to leave the Southwest forever. There would be no chance of ever seeing his father and half sister again. He would return to being a drifter, probably out West or in Mexico, and he would have to get away from El Cacharro and his friends in the process. But for now the big Mexican was a needed ally, albeit a deadly one.

80

HE VIEW WAS MAGNIFICENT—THE bay, the hills, and the city. But life in San Quentin Prison had been a daily torture for Zachary. When could he expect a visit from one of the German's henchmen, if ever? Was Targon simply playing with him, and long gone, lying on some island beach enjoying his riches? He would have preferred knowing who might be the assassin behind the bars with him. He found himself searching faces, looking for an expression that might give away a potential attack. This was a dangerous thing to do, as most prisoners had learned that it was best not to call attention to themselves, or inadvertently anger strangers, who might not like being stared at. But soon the word was out, as to why this inmate was so nervous, and it became a source of amusement to some, who would laugh and pretend to scare him.

After several months had dragged on to over a year, and no attack had materialized other than local disputes and turf struggles, Zachary began to become more angry than scared. He had physically regained his edge, and with little else to do, had added more muscle and more confidence while incarcerated. His above average intelligence had made him the necessary contacts and alliances to become 'secure' in his new world to the extent that anyone was. He had in fact found his niche, and was growing as a criminal in stature and ability. The time in prison would serve as a sheepskin of sorts, elevating him as a bona fide and seasoned leader.

Sidney Walcott had continued to be his lawyer, first out of a sense of fulfilling his obligation for being paid by Targon, and later by having some success in the high profile case, keeping jurisdiction in California through a plea bargain, that had sent Zachary to prison, but kept him away from being charged on the crimes pending from Fort Boise. The State of California it seemed took precedent over crimes in unincorporated territorial jurisdiction. And since the state actually had the man, the case for the conspiracy to murder had gone forward, along with the plea bargain for extended prison time of five years to nominally cover the allegations from the Oregon Territory.

Considering the possibility that there might not be a trial or extradition to Fort Boise, Marshal Donovan had reluctantly acquiesced to the plea bargain on the state prosecutor's recommendation. On Sidney Walcott's side of the ledger, the risk of a trial that included testimony about possibly two murders attributed to his client was a must to avoid. He convinced Zachary DuPort that a seven- to ten-year sentence beat a possible hanging in Fort Boise.

After the San Francisco case was settled, and Zachary had been sent to San Quentin, Sidney Walcott had been able to get time reduced, as more evidence against Ishka subsequently established the tie between the Indian and Targon as long-time associates. Zachary's efforts to discredit the German were seen as further proof that the Tlingit Indian was Targon's agent, not Zachary's. And so it was now possible that Zachary would be out of prison with further negotiating by his lawyer within another year, having by then served only a little over two years, and he would be a free man, with no charges against him.

Sidney was very pleased with the final outcome. Zachary, who had hoped to escape with a lesser sentence, was about to get one, while Donovan and Corby, who already saw a travesty of justice in the deal made, had not yet heard of the reduced sentence.

But Zachary was not out of prison yet. There was the ever-present reminder in the back of his head that the closer he got to freedom, the more likely he would come under attack from Targon. Targon was not a man to make idle threats; that was if Targon were still alive or even in this part of the world.

GÜNTER TARGON WAS still alive, very much so. A rebirth of sorts had brought Targon back into American waters after a successful season of pirating the whaling and sealing routes off of Alaska. Now, too far away from his new home base in the Hawaiian Islands, he would try to sell off his stolen furs and oil barrels to his old trading partners in the Puget Sound to the South of his current sailing position, where the possibility of running into any angry Russians would be less. Targon had purposely singled out Russian seal hunters and whalers in this part of the world, as the relationship between Russian Alaska and Imperial Russia was poor, and protection of the Russian boats out of Alaska was near nonexistent.

Targon had not forgotten about Zachary DuPort. He received a written update every so often from either Roland Leach or Sidney Walcott. Both were still on his payroll as were dozens of others in the Bay Area of San Francisco. He had been able to continue running the gambling houses after some legal obfuscation by Sidney Walcott. The operations weren't as tightly run as before, as even Roland Leach had found ways to steal in Targon's absence, but huge sums of money continued to flow into his many accounts, and were systematically transferred to other banks in Chile. More importantly, Targon was back at sea, where he vowed he would never consider leaving again. The money was more or less just a way to keep score. He had no real interest in the vast fortune he had tucked away. Life back at sea had trimmed some thirty pounds off of his large frame, and returned to him his zest for life and adventure. He had bought some better ships; though still sailing vessels, they were sleek and fast, and better armed. Staying away from the equatorial doldrums as much as possible when plying his trade, his new fleet would be harder to locate and farther away from the military powers of the world. The ambush at Half Moon Bay had taught him some lessons on securing his most frequented harbors, and liberally spreading some money around to act as eyes and ears for trouble. Running for his life from the U.S. Navy had reminded him that he too could lose everything, and could not control all he wished to control. It was a lesson in sanity he would remember. It had been a setback, but only a temporary one, and he liked to think that he was wiser and stronger for it.

Life was good, and as part of his return-to-basics renaissance, he intended to keep his promise in killing Zachary DuPort and anyone else that tried to cross him, but he would be more deliberate in his planning. He did not wish to ever be so close to losing again. He had even found a partial replacement for Ishka, a brutish little Nipponese man who could do remarkable things with a sword. One could imagine Bhutto slicing and dicing, piece-by-piece, his former employee, Zachary DuPort.

After making his profits on a sale of his season's loot in Seattle, he decided that he would continue South staying well out to sea with two of his ships. A quick slip in and out of the Bay Area to do some clandestine business should be simple enough considering no one had seen him for some time and the new ships were unknown in those waters. It was time to deal with the rodent DuPort, as only Günter was capable of doing.

81

THE CALF HAD BEEN half eaten when the vaqueros found it from the circling buzzards. This part of the ranch was rarely visited, due to its rugged nature. Only a big grizzly could have killed like that, breaking the back of the large calf. They would have to hunt the bear, which would now have learned how easy it was to kill the young livestock. Reporting back to Corby, Paco had recommended a hunting party of five men, pulling two men off of the much-needed water reservoir and a hand off of the fencing crew. Donovan, who had happened to be there at that point, had suggested that the three of them, along with one more good hunter, could try to do the job first. It would be a nice break from the city for him. Corby also thought it would be good for Donovan to breathe the mountain air, and so along with Paco and Roberto, the four headed for the kill site, to stake out the calf for the bear's return.

They elected to ride the road above the ocean beach for as long as it went, until they got closer to the far south end of the ranch where the bear had struck. Cattle had been wild down there for many years, living in the lower valleys out to the shore, but they also would climb into the mountains seeking better pastures when conditions below weren't to their liking. It was a great day for a ride along the beach, with the salty smell of the ocean blowing onshore. There were many flowers of brilliant orange and purple colors above the dunes where the rough road ran. Almost overgrown with grass, the two wagon wheel ruts that served as the road began to climb as the coastline became more rugged with cliffsides meeting the ocean waters. The road ended at an impassible point of land that jutted out into the sea, looking over large rocks in a turbulent stretch of waves pounding against mountainside that had long ago crumbled into the waters below. Now the men turned inland to complete their travels to the remote kill site. They had to lead their mounts over some of the rougher terrain, where it was too steep or too tangled with underbrush to ride. As always the big trees dominated the forest here, rising to unbelievable heights. As with all old growth forests, they had to make many short detours around the huge tree trunks that had fallen over the years, now moss-covered monoliths, too large to climb over. Once past the first rise of the coastal range, they were able to find many game trails that ran along the streams between the ravines in the forest. And there they followed Roberto back down to the small valleys nestled within the Montara Mountain Range where the calf had been discovered.

It was late afternoon when they arrived at the kill site. Borrasca and the other horses were very nervous, smelling the bear in the area. The grizzly had been back fairly recently, by the indications left on the carcass, having consumed a large amount of the calf's hindquarters since Roberto had last seen the animal. The men all pulled their rifles and led their horses across a small open meadow to the edge of the surrounding redwood and Douglas fir forest. These coastal inland valleys tended to be wet from the winter rainy season and the summer's persistent fog banks, and dominated by the big trees, but some open areas with a wider variety of trees and grasses cropped up now and then. This was such a pocket in the forest, and from the abundance of tracks in the moist soil, they could see that cattle had been here recently. The bear tracks were there too, indicating a well-fed, large animal. There was little doubt in anyone's mind that the bear would return to feed again, with little or no fear of the men. It was very possible that the animal had never seen a man before or heard a gunshot. The danger was in the bear surprising the men or the horses, but Paco felt that a well-fed bear was less likely to be aggressive.

They decided to build a small, simple corral to contain the horses, halfway up the gently sloping hillside, on the far side of this small opening in the forest, away from the kill. They could see the remains of the calf from their camp but would have to move in closer for a better shot when the bear came back. Right now a little safety margin of ground between made good sense. They then elected to set a camp next to the corral and settle in for some dinner and their wait. A fire would be necessary for their welfare should the bear return to feed in the dark. Paco suggested that they could approach the large stream in the center of the valley to fish without disturbing their stakeout. It was his opinion that the bear had eaten his fill and would be sleeping somewhere, probably for several more hours. Roberto was charged to stay with the horses, and the other three men went to catch their supper.

Sitting around the campfire, eating the trout the men had caught, Donovan felt at ease in his old clothes and gear. Throwing another branch on the fire, he looked around at the setting as if he were recording it in his mind. In fact, he felt differently, as if he were a watcher from outside, observing the scene, rather than just living it. He and Paco were seasoned and hardened veterans of living in a hard land, but for the first time he acknowledged, looking at Roberto and Corby, that the two young men had a bounce and vigor that the two older men would never have again. He felt a pride as he watched Corby move about the camp with his good nature and able body. The kid had become a real man, quick and attentive, aware and alert. Yet Corby showed a caring side that had eluded Donovan most of his own life. Donovan thought Corby was better for having it. You could see the respect the two vaqueros had for their jefe. It was a loyalty Corby had built up with them by listening and learning, yet leading with authority. Corby had taken the lessons Donovan had given him to heart, but he had gone further as his own man, and become a better man, thought Donovan. He would show Corby Henri's library when they were back in San Francisco. If Henri could impact Donovan at his age, there was no reason Donovan couldn't continue to share with Corby the new ideas he had stumbled over. Maybe he and Corby could make a little more sense out of some of it together.

A GENTLE SHOVE on his shoulder woke Donovan up. Corby, Paco, and Roberto were crouched down beside the slow-burning fire, looking across the meadow. The bear had returned and was not happy. Donovan heard the low bawls the bear made as it pulled the carcass around. The presence of the men and horses within sight of the calf had put the bear on edge. It was too dark to really see the bear well, other than a large shape moving against the background of the trees. Paco was lighting the torches he had made, and passed one to Donovan. Corby and Roberto would be the shooters, while Paco and Donovan would provide the much needed light. Holding the torch in one hand and his pistol in the other, Donovan moved forward with the others across the dew-covered grass toward the snarling bear. They could see the bear's eyes, red from the torch's reflection as it stared at the approaching men. With such a large and dangerous animal, it was imperative that they get close enough for good kill shots. A wounded but unimpaired bear was the last thing any of them wanted to see.

As the men narrowed the distance with the bear, the bear became more agitated, swinging back and forth, and then taking some quick steps in opposite directions. Suddenly it disappeared into the trees behind it. The men froze where they were, waiting for the bear to reappear. They could hear it crashing about just out of vision up the hillside. The bear did not come back but continued to protest a short distance past the treeline. The men decided to move slowly forward, hoping to get a good line on the bear. Within twenty yards of the treeline, they still could not see the bear, and it was no longer making any noise. The hunters moved a little closer to each other, in the uncertainty of the moment. It was possible that they had driven the bear away, or the bear might re-emerge from the darkness at any second.

"Maybe we should back off a distance and allow him to come back, but not so far that we can't get a good shot," ventured Donovan. The others nodded and began backing away.

It was then that the bear rushed out of the underbrush without a sound, heading like a freight train for the group to their immediate left. Donovan, on the party's left, was blocking a good shot from either Corby or Roberto as the hunters swung around to face the new angle of the bear's attack. With unreal swiftness the bear slammed into Corby, and swiped a huge paw at Roberto, knocking the man over as if he were a small child. At the same time, as soon as he had a clear shot, Donovan snapped off a couple of rounds with his revolver at the blur that was the bear going past him. Changing direction in an instant, the big grizzly bore down on Donovan with its full weight, its jaws stretching for Donovan's head. Paco, who was the only man left standing, had a clear shot and fired his pistol, aiming behind the shoulder. Corby, who had been dazed but essentially unharmed, rolled up on one knee and emptied his revolver into the bear too. The big bear then collapsed on Donovan, covering him completely. Paco and Corby ran over and pushed the bear off of a still-lying Donovan. Blood flowed freely from the side of his head, and a great rip of clothing and blood ran down Donovan's shoulder and chest where one of the massive claws had raked across his torso. Corby began applying pressure to stop the blood flow on Donovan's head, and sent Paco to check on Roberto.

On first examination, it appeared that the bear had been able to sink its lower teeth into the left side of Donovan's face and eye socket. The back of Donovan's head showed the marks of the top teeth and fangs. The chest wound, though ugly, didn't appear to be dangerous. The eye, however, in Corby's opinion, would be lost. There was a bloody gouge where Donovan's left eye had been only seconds before.

Paco returned, reporting that Roberto was dead from a broken neck. He had brought up some water from the stream, and they began the process of cleaning and bandaging the wounds as well as they could. Donovan had not regained consciousness yet, and they took the opportunity to clean out his wounds with the camp whiskey, pouring essentially the full bottle over the damages. Bear wounds were known to be some of the most prone to infection one could receive. With tight bandages stemming the flow of further blood loss, they quickly built a travois for Donovan, tied Roberto to a very skittish horse, and headed back as fast as they could for civilization.

82

THE DISCUSSION CAME UP every so often. What should you do with a ten-year-old little girl in Indian country? Dr. Lemmins was not a rich man by any means, but he could afford to send Katy to school somewhere back East, like St. Louis. They wanted to give their girl the opportunity to experience something other than the rugged Fort Hall life, even if she didn't seem to have any aversion to it at this point. What kind of a marriage could she expect if she were to grow up half Indian? But sending her away seemed an extreme measure. The thought of the whole family moving on to California had been discussed many times, and one day soon might prove to be necessary, should they hope for a good life for Katy. There was still time, but the clock was ticking. By fifteen, Katy might be too far behind her contemporaries to ever adjust well enough. They could foresee an embarrassing transition for a girl from the wilderness trying to fit in with young ladies of the cities. As mother's do, Valerie worried the most, while Dr. Lemmins and Katy were more optimistic about the future.

At ten, Katy was more than a tomboy. She could ride and shoot well, and had gotten into more than one scuffle with kids passing through Fort Hall, primarily over her defense of the Indians. Valerie had to apologize along with Katy when it was revealed that Katy had told a boy that she wouldn't be surprised if her friends, the Shoshone, were to scalp him some dark night. It had sent a shiver down Valerie's spine, picturing her girl showing proper young ladies in San Francisco how to throw a knife.

Fortunately for the Lemminses, the local Indian situation continued to be nonconfrontational, and Captain Farmer's grim predictions had not materialized so far around Fort Hall. Across the country, however, one treaty after the next was being broken, and the fallout was escalating. The old Hudson Bay Trading Company was actively pushing government policy in both the United States and Canada for removal of Indians from those lands that they could sell to settlers. A growing number of citizens saw the Indians as a hurdle to progress that should be swept aside in the greater interests of the country.

With the coming of Spring, Katy was looking forward to the return of the Yellowstone Shoshone to rendezvous both at Fort Hall and at what was now called Shoshone Lake in the Yellowstone River country. Her father would make a spring trip to check on the tribe, and she would be able to join him and Captain Farmer, riding her Appaloosa, Snowflake. The red-haired girl and the white-spotted horse were unmistakable together, particularly when she would race across the Fort Hall camp grounds to greet the new wagon trains with her long hair flying behind her. It was a ten year old showing off, but it was a heart-warming sight to see such a happy, healthy child enjoying herself so much. What was it about girls and their horses? Dr. Lemmins wondered. Something akin to the instincts of motherhood? Whatever it was, the girl was bonded to the horse, and treated it as a family member, and sometimes better—something else Dr. Lemmins could thank the Shoshone chief for. The idea of removing this child of nature from the great loves of her early life after the tragedy she had suffered as a toddler was hard to imagine at this juncture. Hopefully, as she became twelve or thirteen, the priorities in her life would naturally start to change, and a break from the Indians and the wilderness would be more amenable to her. The doctor could only hope. Until then, unlike his wife, he would try to enjoy the happiness she now exuded.

FOURNIER HAD FINALLY sold out to a new American company. Now well into his seventies, and freed from his trading post business, he found that his services were still in demand when it came to the surrounding Indians. Few could speak the various dialects, and fewer still had much of a relationship with the tribes. Every time some government team would show up looking to appraise this or survey that, Fournier was almost commanded to accompany them to communicate with the Indians. He didn't mind, as he would set his own rules, and overcharge for his services. He always accompanied Dr. Lemmins on his forays out to the tribes, as did Captain Farmer. It was unthinkable to lose the doctor out here. Fournier was set for free medical attention for the rest of his life, and he enjoyed the doctor's company anyway, along with the missus and of course Katy. It was Fournier who often kept Katy company through the long Winter months with his stories and teachings about the mountains. She was such a pretty and happy child. They had adopted a teasing relationship some time ago, him calling her "that little stinkerpot," and her warmly referring to him as Mr. Grumpety. Most of her Indian questions, and there were hundreds, were directed to him. It was a rare week during the winter that Fournier didn't wrangle a dinner invitation from Mrs. Lemmins from Katy's persistent harping, often on the same night that Captain Farmer would come to dinner. As no one was really any good with an instrument, after dinner they would tell stories, tailoring some of the worst violence out for the sake of Katy's young ears. On other occasions the men would get to speaking seriously about the events of the day back East and out West, and Valerie would have to take Katy into her little bedroom and read to her from one of the earmarked books that they had read many times before, or work with her writing and reading skills until it was bedtime, when she would then chase the men from the small house over to the tavern if they wished to continue their conversation.

Now Fournier lay on the mountainside listening for the approach of the sheep. He had helped deliver the military's spring goods to the Shoshone with three of Captain Farmer's soldiers. He would stay with the Shoshone for a week or two and do some hunting before heading back, probably accompanied by a few of the braves who would trade some Winter furs back at Fort Hall now that the mountain passes were open. With the high country game still within reach, he had convinced a couple of Waushaute's braves to accompany him on a bighorn sheep hunt. The Shoshone had always hunted the sheep as a staple of their winter diet. They used the sheep as a favorite source for making their bows. The snows higher up were keeping the sheep at lower elevations even as mid springtime neared. While the sheep sought safety on the high and jagged rock walls, they preferred to graze on open grass patches, and could be hunted there if one knew where to look.

The two Shoshone and Fournier had spotted a nice pair of sheep moving across an open ridge toward a sprinkling of aspen trees a couple of miles to the northwest of the camp. Moving around in front of the sheep required a slow and careful stalk, which took them out of view of the animals until they settled on a spot where the sheep looked to eventually graze into their range. The three hunters settled down to wait, lying on their stomachs and peering forward in anticipation of the slow-grazing sheep approaching their hiding places. Being in the mountains again filled Fournier with a thankful joy. This was as close as he came to worship, but he figured it was closer to God than listening to some lowland preacher. It always reminded him of his youth as a trapper and mountain man.

Something was not right. He sensed it but could not identify what it was. As a seasoned veteran of the mountains, he became instantly alert. All was quiet, maybe too quiet. He rolled over onto his back, and then he smelled them. Blackfoot!

IT HAD BEEN easy to watch the Shoshone camp from up on the jagged ridge

Two Horns had brought them to. There was snow lying under the trees, but the open areas had melted and sprouted new growth. The brighter green of the Springtime growth was everywhere, on the branch ends of the tall firs and the new tassels, the budding bushes and emerging grasses. The six warriors had infiltrated the area as they had hoped, without being seen. They had cautiously scouted the watching post area for the best escape routes, and had found an excellent perimeter point out on a rocky ledge that could survey almost every approach to the watch post. Soaring Owl of course pulled that duty most of the time. Then it became an exercise in choosing their objective. They had not yet picked one when the three sheep hunters came almost straight toward them.

Blue Heron had seen the old Whiteman before in the Shoshone camp, and they knew of his life in these parts. Killing an old Whiteman and two Shoshone braves was not much to be proud of, but it was Two Horns's plan on what to do with them next that would tax the Blackfoot warriors' skills. But first things first. The Whiteman had a fine looking rifle, and Blue Heron had no doubt he knew how to use it. As the old mountain man rolled over on his back, Blue Heron knew that his stalk was discovered, and let fly his arrow. The planned silent kill was gone. As the arrow sunk into the man, he fired his gun in the direction of one of the charging two Blackfoot. Fighting and yelling broke out with the other two Shoshone warriors and the remaining Blackfoot. Blue Heron's arrow had been true, and Fournier was unable to really rise to defend himself when The Badger cracked his head open with a powerful swing of his tomahawk. He had picked the weapon up off of a dead Crow after their battle two years before and had kept it as his new favorite weapon. It was Whiteman-made, with a heavy iron blade on a sturdy oak handle. He had not yet mastered throwing it, and was reluctant to do so anyway, but as far as smashing power, it was more effective and easier to use than the larger warclub he had carried before.

When the gun spoke, the two Shoshone warriors had been surprised and rose from their positions to look Fournier's way, wondering if he had seen something they had missed or the gun had gone off by accident. In doing so, they became better targets for the Blackfoot, who had all tried to use their bows and arrows to see if they could surprise the Shoshone. Two Horns had been very close to his victim, and along with Soaring Owl, he had quickly dispatched his target. The final Shoshone had been momentarily luckier, as both arrow shots missed their target when he continued to roll upon seeing the Blackfoot ready to shoot. Jumping to his feet, he had charged the closest Blackfoot, landing a glancing blow on Running Wolf Leaps, before Buffalo Lance ran his lance through the Shoshone warrior so hard it nicked Running Wolf Leaps on his hip. Within seconds the three hunters were dead. Over seventy years of experience and two Shoshone warriors had not been enough to warn Fournier in time, but true to his storytelling, death had struck with suddenness once again in the mountains he had so loved.

The two small injuries to Running Wolf Leaps were the material for many jokes later as the Blackfoot gathered their spoils and planned their next move. Confidence increased, and bragging about their stealth did too.

The sound of Fournier's gun was heard faintly in the Shoshone camp, and soon forgotten, as it was known the mountain man had gone sheep hunting.

83

"NONSENSE! YOU ARE MY lawyer. You take the money and do as I instruct," thundered Targon.

"I have become many things of late," Sidney Walcott calmly replied, "but a merchant of death I will not be. Please take your money and leave, Mr. Targon. I can no longer represent you. If we meet again, I will be obligated under the law to turn you in." Sidney lifted the short stack of bank notes and handed them back to Targon.

The big German towered over the frail old man, but Sidney Walcott stood his ground. His office was in a very public area with a glass window to the busy street. Targon shook his huge head, smiled, and said, "You want more money. It is a risk to your profession. This I understand. I will pay you double on the completion of your assignment."

"I'm sorry, Mr. Targon, it is something I cannot do for any price. I am seventy-five and failing of health. I have sailed close to the edge of ethics in my profession, but I have never committed a criminal act, nor will I. Delivering a bribe for you that would result in the death of another human being is something even my weakened moral code cannot abide. I will truly miss your money, but I must decline. I suggest you use the back door, as the street has gotten rather busy, and your face still graces the newspapers around here from time to time."

Targon admired courage in all its forms and allowed himself a small laugh. "You would have made a fine pirate, Sidney. I will find another way to skin the rat."

He took Sidney's suggestion and left by way of the back door. Sidney then allowed himself to collapse back into his office chair and exhale deeply. So, his soul was not for sale after all. He had been brave and he had drawn the line. No one should be above the law in this new country of such moral promise. All was not lost yet, and the day took on a brighter light. Later he took a walk around the town, feeling better than he had in years.

IT WAS ROLAND Leach who had originally found the right person to bribe at San Quentin State Prison, and he could probably deliver this bribe as well. It was just that Roland was never one Targon could really trust in executing anything requiring any finesse. But Roland was the next best option after the lawyer. It would require some organization. Guards would have to be pulled, and Zachary would have to be isolated. But it certainly wasn't a job that couldn't be handled if enough promise of monies was spread around. It would be good to have his name whispered around again, too. Maybe profits would magically pick up in his gambling parlors.

Sitting across the table now with Leach, Targon couldn't help but enjoy the uneasy glances Leach would give Bhutto every so often. Leach had to assume that Bhutto was Ishka's replacement, and the fact that Bhutto spoke even less English than Ishka had gave him an immediate sense of mystery and danger. As things were, Bhutto apparently saw himself more in the role of Targon's bodyguard than Ishka had ... something to do with his culture and training. He would probably never find a similar assassin to Ishka, but Ishka had his own drawbacks too. The silent and ominous Bhutto would do for now, since the role's reputation had been so well defined by Ishka.

"And I want it to be a slow death, unmistakably a murder," Targon concluded. "Oh, and make sure afterward that it gets around in the prison that I had this done because he crossed me."

Roland Leach kept nodding his head, hoping that his informant at the new San Quentin Prison was reliable. He had witnessed Ishka's work twice before, and far more than the money he would get from completing this job, he wanted to avoid the fate of failing. He had already concluded that he would disappear should this assignment go wrong, leaving the best income stream he had ever known from the gambling parlors. What good would being rich do, if he were spread all over the ocean's floor?

THE EXTENT OF Zachary's newfound power had reached the guards and ward supervisors. Like others of influence, he could now buy commodities by trading influence with the other prisoners through the middle management of the prison staff. Soon he found he could barter special rewards for his supporters, securing better jobs, more outside contacts, and some freedoms inside. These in turn fostered some loyalty and control, along with inside information, helpful to the guards. It wasn't that much different than the city government...just played on a different field with different incentives and punishments. In another life, Zachary could have been a fair alderman, or even mayor. However, this was not where Zachary wished to be, and the news of a shorter term was very encouraging. Sidney Walcott felt he could get Zachary released within a year. He also felt obligated to inform Zachary of his visit from Targon. Targon was clearly planning something and Zachary had better be on his toes. The old lump of fear returned to Zachary's stomach. But now he could begin to prepare for the assumed attack. He began spreading his growing capital to gain firsthand knowledge of any whispered threat that would be coming his way. He overcommitted his resources with barely believable promises of payoffs for the right information, and began a listening network throughout the prison. He now went nowhere without two bodyguards that were very expensive to keep.

A week went by after Walcott's visit without a sliver of news about Targon. Then the grapevine picked up the news that a high-ranking prison official had intermediaries snooping around for a few guards that could assist in an isolation of a prisoner. A day later it was learned that Zachary was the target, and the game was on.

84

THE CREW HAD BEEN removing large rocks from the fields along the Sante Fe River, and building a levee with them along the riverbank. The area was soon to be irrigated for either pasture or crops. It was backbreaking work, and required the prisoners' cheap labor. They had been supplied with a few tools to dig out the small boulders, and a couple of horse-drawn wagons were necessary to carry the rocks down to the riverside. Actually, Drego was taking some pride in the levee he was building. As a crew leader, he was instructing the haulers where to put the largest boulders before they scattered the remainder on the ground for Drego's crew to plant into a base wall to be covered with gravel and dirt. Even the minimal use of his brain was welcomed, but he also kept aware of the comings and goings of the guards and prisoners as he worked. Today was the day he and El Cacharro had picked for their escape attempt. Four others thought they would be going too. The plan had been set as well as possible, and Drego had to be at the right place when the events unfolded. He knew that there was a possible clock ticking on the last minutes of his life as he lifted and dropped the rocks onto the levee. Half of his instinct's told him to walk away when the time came. It would be better to continue living versus dying. As long as he was alive, there would be hope. But he knew that was a false path. There would be no miracle to save him, save himself. He would only be gaining many more years of misery, and a slow, debilitating demise. So he worked and watched, ready to assume his position when the time came.

A farmhouse stood a half mile away down the river, surrounded by a barn and pens. There was a bunkhouse of sorts, along with a small irrigation aqueduct from the river providing water for a pond next to the barn. The prison officials had spent a good deal of time with some men who had appeared to own the property, and Drego assumed the land and levee were being cleared and built for the same men. It really didn't matter, other than providing the possible opportunity the prisoners had been searching for, for several months now.

It started with the cry of "Fire!" down by the barn, and Drego quickly moved over to the wagon team next to the horses, as did El Cacharro over in the field with the other team of horses. As expected, the guards called for the wagons to assist with the fire, and the close-by prisoners were told to quickly run to the barn to form a water bucket brigade from the pond if possible. The horses were unhitched from the wagons to be used to drag whatever they could out of the barn to safety.

The fire had been set well, and it roared up one side of the barn as animals and people ran in different directions to escape and fight the fire. A group of prisoners were wheeling a wagon out of the barn when they uncovered a handful of machetes lying in the back of the wagon. Encouraged by the prisoners in on the escape, the others grabbed the machetes and whatever other makeshift weapons they could find, and suddenly charged the guards who had temporarily been distracted in their attempts to combat the fire.

In the confusion, El Cacharro and Drego were able to lead the horses they had around the backside of the barn and quickly mount. Shots rang out as the guards and machete-armed prisoners mixed it up back around the front where the fire raged. The guards were retreating in face of the surprise attack, but the prisoners were paying a high price. Two other prisoners ran after El Cacharro, who led an extra horse, but were not quick enough. He and Drego urged their horses away under cover of the barn toward the beckoning line of trees by the river and then across the shallow river into the surrounding barren foothills. Not a single shot had been fired in their direction during the escape. They could hear the gunshots and yells steadily fade as they pushed their horses away from the farm.

Circling quickly to ride behind the cover of the foothills on the other side of the river, the two men headed upriver to the small cache of food they had buried weeks before on another job down by the river, and then heeled their horses away to the North in a effort to confuse those that would follow later. It had always been assumed that should they escape, particularly with horses, that North was the best direction to run, to the San Juan Mountains, where the wilderness could hide and shelter them. They would then work their way deeper into the Rocky Mountains, where they could eventually exit in any direction. It wasn't a bad plan, if they had horses and food, which they did. Therefore it would be a very risky strategy to reverse direction and head out into open country, going South to the Rio Grande and El Paso. This had convinced them to do just that. A run for Mexico meant a daring doubleback along the Sante Fe River and slow travel just when they would most likely be expected to take advantage of their head start. It would mean, having nerves of steel, great patience, and some luck, but if they could get South of Albuquerque undetected, they could follow the rivers straight into Mexico. They had placed a heavy bet that the men coming after them would discount the difficult route for the better possibilities to the North.

As it turned out, they were aided in the success of many other prisoners escaping the farm fire and scattering across the area, stealing what they could in hopes of also finding freedom. Local lawmen were called out in full force, hunting down the many leads they were receiving in the expanding prison break. The Sante Fe prison guards raced to their preset tracking locations to close the net that had effectively worked for them before, but by then, the two southbound escapees were outside the net's circumference, and wouldn't have a dedicated tracking team assigned to them until the night's chaos started to come to a close.

Morning found the duo circling South well to the East of Albuquerque, in open, desert-like terrain. The new clothes, taken from a farm fence, were too big for Drego and too small for El Cacharro. They decided they would sell the extra horse for more food money, better clothes, and weapons when they were able to rejoin what was now the Rio Grande River, flowing South to Mexico.

85

THE HORSES HAD BEEN restless as the dawn broke over the Shoshone Lake. Herded as they always were to the edge of the lake just inside the barricade wall for the night, they had milled around and snorted as the light began to fill the morning sky. The two boys who had been charged with watching over the small herd had been playing stick games and telling stories to ward off sleep. Now they walked into the herd to see what the problem was. Maybe an animal was down and the owner would wish to know immediately. In fact, that might be the problem, as the horses were definitely upset about something on the ground that they had encircled. Breaking through to see what was the matter, the two boys almost stumbled over the carefully laid out bodies before turning to run back to the camp and sound the alarm.

Ten minutes later the majority of the half-filled Shoshone camp was standing looking down at the bodies of the two Shoshone warriors and Fournier, lying side by side, each with an arrow stuck in their necks. One of the three arrows was Lame Elk's, and a Blackfoot lance stood planted in the grass at their feet.

Waushaute was building up an anger. "Only a Blackfoot son of a motherless dog would sneak up on us to kill in the night!" he blurted out. His reaction to the deaths of two of his braves was expected. The message was a clear one to Lame Elk. Two Horns was returning his arrow and telling Lame Elk that the Blackfoot considered the Shoshone their enemies, and had the ability to strike right into the heart of the Shoshone camp without being detected. This was inevitable to Lame Elk's way of thinking. The cycle of violence and pride was simply returning as the Blackfoot healed from the losses caused by the Crow war. He was not overly concerned for the safety of his people, as he knew Two Horns's band could not face him in open battle yet, and the other allied Blackfoot tribes would be unlikely to rally to Two Horns in another war against his enemies so soon. The Piegans and Bloods were owed a debt that would require the Gray Woman Mountain Blackfoot to fight their enemies next. No, this was a personal vendetta, aimed at Lame Elk for killing Two

Horns's wife and unborn son. It was a personal challenge being made from one warrior to the other. How it would play out from here was unclear, but Lame Elk understood that it would probably end only with the death of one or the other.

THE DIFFICULT TASK of delivering the three bodies right into the thick of the Shoshone campsite had lifted the spirits of the Bulls. They had been skeptical that it could be done. To sneak up to the edge of the camp past the watch positions and drag along three bodies had taken great patience and no small amount of muscle. But they had carefully followed their leader and they had succeeded. The aura of Blackhand was somewhat diminished. They too could move with the shadows and pass over the land as the wind, leaving no trace. They too could shake the confidence and security of the enemies' stronghold.

As always it was Buffalo Lance that led in the banter on the way home. His boasts and exaggerations about the raid raised everyone into high good humor. It reminded Two Horns of Red Horses's personality of some years ago, but instead of bringing him sorrow in remembering, this time he felt good about being reminded of his lost friend. He even told a funny story about Red Horses that had the men laughing so hard, Blue Heron started to cough. This was the Bulls he remembered from the past, the brotherhood that had felt invincible. Here was the foundation for the future, the much needed boost to tribal morale. The only drawback was that it required more confrontation. But it was worth it, if only for the pride and spirit the Bulls enjoyed this fine day as they headed back to their new summer camp, farther to the North, and better protected from their enemies. Even the horses seemed to pick up on the mood, and Messenger practically pranced as he set the steady pace home for the group.

86

I T WAS HARD SEEING Donovan this way. The doctors had kept him sedated with the new but widely used drug chloroform. The hospital smelled of chlorine, as the works of Florence Nightingale and her crusade for hygienic practices had forced hospitals and doctors throughout the civilized world to wash with chlorinated water regularly. You really needed to step outside to get a fresh breath of air or you would taste the effect of the smells on the roof of your mouth after a while.

Eventually they had stopped operating on Donovan and placed him in a room with a partially opened window, but he was still unconscious with a morphine drip. Lying as he was with his head bandaged, unmoving save for his breathing, Corby could barely recognize his friend. All his hair had been shaved off, even where he had not been hurt. He seemed to have lost a shade of color in his skin, and it also looked somewhat waxy in appearance. There were some kind of stains on his face and scalp that the nurses told him were antiseptic in nature and would eventually disappear. It just didn't seem possible that this was Marshal Donovan, the indestructible tower of strength and will that Corby had gotten so used to.

Stranahan and O'Bannon had been regular visitors as had Gabrielle, but it was Corby who insisted on staying at the hospital through the long nights. Gabrielle understood, and supported her husband in his vigil. She had wanted to stay too, but Corby had insisted that she get her sleep, as she would have to hold the company together by herself for a while and would need all her strength. While this was perfectly logical, somehow she felt that once again the rules for women were at work against her here too. But now was not the time to enter into such thorny debate. She found she was keeping her own vigil alone at the hotel, worrying about Donovan.

The doctors, and there were many that Gabrielle had employed, had declined to say much other than "time would tell" and that the Marshal was a strong man. However he had lost a lot of blood during the long journey back to the city, and an infection had started, according to the doctors.

That was their main concern, as an infection could spread through the eye socket into the brain and kill Donovan. They were always removing the bandages, and trying to keep the eye socket wet and clean, as well as allowing it to drain regularly. The area around the gashed-out eye had turned a deeper red, and then a purple. Corby had learned that the line marks on Donovan's face were the doctors' measurements of how far the infection had expanded then contracted. He had been told that the injury would be extremely painful, even with the narcotics they had given him. That was why he had been strapped down on the bed. A pain that would not quit and would throb from the infection would from time to time wrack Donovan in agony.

Corby thought he smelled sulfur's rotten egg smell when he was close to the injury. Some doctor had put Donovan on his stomach, having read in an Italian medical journal that this would help with the critical drainage from the eye's socket. Later he found out that they had continually removed any scabbing during the infection period to prevent stopping the drainage. Finally, about ten days later, the skin around the eye began to look less angry, and as his pastiness improved, they allowed the scar tissue to now grow in and cover the socket. There was the stubble of hair returning on his head, and the doctors gradually reduced the amounts of narcotics, as they gauged the lessening of pain. The patient would live.

Several days later Donovan came out of his morphine-induced daze, unsure of what was happening around him. An ability to concentrate eluded him, but he was aware of a very heavy feeling, as if someone had covered him with stacks of horse blankets. He had no energy, and breathing alone was a chore. Then he felt the throbbing pain, but he couldn't place its location until a sharp, localized dart of pain jolted him in his left eye. He tried to open his eyes, but failed, not being quite in control of his motor functions yet. He moved his lips and felt his tongue, which tasted awful. Maybe he was dreaming. But the pain felt so real. He began to distinguish a little light, and worked on opening his eyes again. Light flooded into his right eye, forcing him to shut it momentarily before blinking open again. His vision was fuzzy but clearing. He moved his head, rocking it in a small arc.

He was lying on his back in a room. He could hear some birds from what appeared to be an open window. It was daytime. The throb of pain continued, but he ignored it. He now began to recognize that his head was bandaged. He tried lifting his hand and could.

There was a scraping sound and Corby was in his vision, looking down at him and smiling.

"You gave us a real scare, partner," Corby said, as he gave Donovan a small sip of water from a glass. The taste in his mouth was really lousy, as if he had been sucking on a tin cup, but the water was cool and refreshing despite it. He tried to talk, but it came out as a weak rasp.

"The doctors say that you will be able to talk real soon, but you need to drink and wake up some more. You've been doped up for a couple of weeks now. Had an infection from where the bear got you, which almost killed you."

Corby paused and sighed as he looked down at Donovan. "I'm afraid you lost your left eye."

Donovan closed his right eye on hearing the bad news, but opened it again, indicating to Corby to tell him the rest.

"The bear took off a pretty good piece of scalp, but the doctors say that they were able to stitch it back, and other than a scar on the back of your neck, you will have a full head of hair again, but I figure it will be a little grayer. Only fair for the gray you probably put in mine.

"You will have an attractive scar on your chest, kind of like the Indians do to themselves, where the bear clawed you. Hell, I figure you could get a dime novel written about you. 'Crusty old lawman defies death in battle with a grizzly bear,' told in his own words."

Donovan found he could barely smile, and then a wave of pain hit him again.

Seeing the two reactions on Donovan's face, Corby said, "The docs say that you will experience pain for awhile. Two kinds. A sharp one from deep in your eye socket, where your eye was connected to . . . where it was connected in your head, and a steady pain as the general area heals. They say that the infection could have made it all the way to your brain and killed you, but it didn't. We were lucky that a couple of doctors seemed to have learned some new things about germs and infections and such."

Donovan managed a "when?"

"When were you brought here?" Corby guessed.

Donovan shook his head no.

"When will you be up and about?" Corby tried. Getting an affirmative blink, Corby said, "The doctors are playing that real close to the vest, depending on all kinds of things, but as best as I can figure, you are out of the woods now, and will be on your feet in a couple of weeks. That doesn't mean they will let you go though. I think they are real proud of their work and plan on selling tickets for a while.

"Gabrielle has been coming to see you every day about dinnertime, and is having a rough time keeping all your friends at the hotel working, rather than visiting. I think she plans on mothering you for a few months. Milk it, I say." He stopped, feeling like he was rambling on, when he felt Donovan's hand cover his that had been pressed down on the bed so he could lean over. He looked down into Donovan's one eye, and was overcome for a second, tearing up, before he could regain control. He had told himself that Donovan would not like the intense emotions that he was going to get from Gabrielle regard-less. He needed to cheer his friend up. He gave Donovan another sip of water. Donovan indicated he wanted a little more, which Corby gave him.

Donovan whispered, "Did you get the bear?"

Corby nodded.

"Make me an eye patch out of the bastard's balls, for my dime novel," Donovan instructed in a hoarse rasp.

The weight of the world seemed to slip off of Corby's shoulders with that comment.

87

I T WASN'T HARD TO follow the six Blackfoot once their trail was finally detected. Lame Elk and Waushaute, along with Snow Hunter and ten other warriors, had struck it about midday as they worked back and forth covering the ground where the Blackfoot would have had to cross in order to deliver Fournier and Waushaute's two Lemhi Shoshones. The trail through the grass where they had dragged the bodies was very apparent, but the trail under the trees and up through the rocks had been brushed well. It wasn't until they had deduced the logical possible paths and ridden out some distance to scout them that they had picked up a still well-concealed partial track, and it wasn't until they had climbed all the way up to the snow that the Blackfoot had ended their attempts to erase their movements. Here it was determined that there were six mounted ponies and three unmounted ones, assumed to be the ponies of the three murdered men.

Considering that the Blackfoot had done much of their elusive work in the dark impressed Lame Elk. However, he or Snow Hunter would have discovered their trail even had they had a day to hide it. Now they could see that the pace home had picked up and there was little they could do to close ground. The Blackfoot knew where they were going and the Shoshone had to pay attention to the trail, slowing them down. For now it would be enough to follow the Blackfoot.

The more Lame Elk rode on, the more time he had to try and think of a solution to the escalation of hostilities. This could become a very costly problem. While the Blackfeet of Two Horns's camp were no longer the imminent threat that Crooked Claws had been in his day, the confederation of Piegans, Blackfoot, and Bloods certainly was too dangerous to ignore. He could easily imagine a series of counterstrikes bleeding the two camps until a larger battle became unavoidable. The Shoshone would need the help of the Bannock or the Whiteman to have a chance against the combined strength of the Blackfoot alliances should it come to that level. And who could be called a winner then? Hadn't the Blackfoot had enough death with their war with the Crows? But then he understood that they could not simply let the razing of the camp by the Shoshone stand unanswered. It had been a measured response, just as his own attack on the Blackfoot camp had been. In this he had to admire his adversary again. Crooked Claws or the Crow would not have reasoned in their response, as had Two Horns. Were it up to him alone, he would have let it end there. But there were no guarantees that it would end there. Warfare among the tribes had taught them all over the long span of many lifetimes that each incident must be addressed lest the sign of weakness bring even further destruction down on the tribe. There was the remote possibility of a brokered peace, but the people would probably not wish to hear it, due to the many deaths at the hands of Crooked Claws and the Blackfoot almost a decade before, still within the active memories of too many. And now the Lemhi Shoshone had suffered their first unprovoked attack, as if that was ever a possibility. But to Waushaute right now, the Blackfoot were devils that needed to be exterminated. Only time to cool down would help his friend regain his normal, collected reasoning. All these and many other thoughts ran through the Shoshone chief's mind as he tracked the retreating Blackfoot deeper into the Absaroka Mountain Range, before they began to swing more westerly in their run back to the Missouri River headwaters and traditional Blackfoot hunting grounds. There had to be another way to stop all the fighting yet to come.

Once it was agreed that they would not overtake the Blackfoot, they took a slower and more careful pace. There was the possibility that the Blackfoot would lay in ambush, but neither Waushaute nor Lame Elk thought that likely under the circumstances. It was more important now to discover where the Blackfoot were going so they could re-establish reconnaissance of them for when they would decide what was to be done next. It was now incumbent on the stalkers to become stealthy. By slowing down they helped to avoid detection. Retreating parties often dropped off a scout to determine if they were being followed, to protect themselves, but if there was no pursuit within a couple of hours, the scout would need to report back to the party, or risk being left too far behind to effectively communicate or even regroup. Lame Elk slowed the Shoshone down, as the trail was now one he could follow for several days given good weather. The farther they went into Blackfoot country, the more they needed to take a defensive posture. Roles had been reversed. The pursuers were now the smaller fighting force in unfamiliar territory.

The game went on, as it had for centuries. The major difference now was the speed that the horses brought to close on the warring tribes. Before the horses, there had been less constant fighting. Hit-and-run, and the popular art of horse thieving, were not motivating factors then. The tribe really had to want to go to war to march on an enemy, because escape was much more difficult without the ponies. Lame Elk was recalling the stories his grandfather Swiftsnake had told him about the old ones. They had been great hunters, and fighters by necessity. The children had been taught how to hide and provide for themselves at the earliest of ages, in order to maximize their survival. But the enemies of the people had been fewer, while the dangers had been just as great: weather, the wilderness, and starvation.

The horse had brought a wealth through hunting, thus lessening the constant need for food gathering and shelter seeking. The hunters could cover large areas if the game had moved away. They learned how to hunt the buffalo by horse very effectively, which provided the tribes a wide range of resources besides food and clothing, items like needles and thread, glue, ropes, robes, spoons, toys, even buckets and drums, fashioned from the stomach and untanned hide. But with this great improvement came the dramatic increase in warfare. Those tribes that mastered the horse first had a huge advantage over their neighbors, and took full advantage, pushing them out of the better hunting grounds. The Plains tribes had swept to the West to the foot of the mountains, pushing the Shoshone back. The People had retreated into the Yellowstone where they had found a haven of sorts, surrounded by mountains but fed by a fire under the ground that kept the animals in the region during the winter. They too began to master the horse and to fight back. But the larger tribes had expanded and grown, becoming increasingly more aggressive. The Shoshone were forced to adopt many of the ways of their tormentors in order to survive. This was the hard part for Lame Elk. He had been taught that the Creator wanted the Shoshone to cherish the land He had made for them, to respect the creatures He had provide for their sustenance. The Creator visited the People in their dreams to remind them of the bounty He had given them and to make them proud and resourceful. Lame Elk did not see the hand of the Creator in the tribal greed, and he knew that the cries of the women and children who lost their husbands and fathers would not be something the Creator would have wanted. But, there seemed no way to stop the violence, and the young men clamored for more, as they would for a good piece of warm buffalo liver.

A fleeting image of his lost son, Beaver on the Rock, passed through his mind and disappeared. He tried to recall the image, but time cruelly had erased his ability to do so. Fortunately he could still conjure up pictures of his first wife, Dancing Clouds, and their years together, which he did now.

88

THE IDEA HAD BEEN spinning around in Zachary's head ever since he had come into the prison. Despite his disclosure about the ownership of T.D. & Associates, Inc., the city government had not closed down the gambling houses that he and Targon had run. Sidney Walcott was pretty sure Targon was still running the businesses by proxy. Zachary had signed the papers along with Targon as the principles that ran T.D. & Associates, Inc. Ownership was Targon's, but legally, unless there had been changes made, he was still the titular director of the entity. With Targon chased out of the country, why couldn't he reassume the role of director and steal the company? Even if he couldn't legally steal it, why couldn't he simply confiscate it with muscle, much as he and Targon had done before with Paul Logan? His time in prison had given him all the muscle he would ever need when he got out. He could enlist twenty Shug O'Briens to take down the remnants of Targon's thugs, and what could Targon do about it? Sure, Targon would counterattack, but he would be ready. It wasn't as if Targon wasn't already trying to kill him.

Word had come through the yard trustees that the blood money had been paid, and Zachary quickly had been able to identify whom Targon had picked to do the job. His name was Moog to those inside, and he was a lifer. Targon would be taking care of someone on the outside for him, or settling an account, or any other of a variety of services unavailable to a man in San Quentin. It didn't matter; the man had accepted the assignment to kill Zachary DuPort, and was now probably working out the details of how he would do it. Moog was a mountain of a man, who had killed before (and since) coming into the prison. He had spent considerable time in solitary confinement, but also mixed with the general population before, and now was back in the main yard. He was a logical nominee for such a task. Moog could overpower just about anyone, and would enjoy doing it. People like Moog had no illusions of ever getting out of prison, and had become warped into a brand of sadistic killers that were sprinkled throughout the prison system. They hated everyone with a vengeance, and took their pleasures in poking the system in its eye whenever they could. For someone like Moog, killing Zachary would be a treat, a challenge to do it and escape getting caught, an opportunity to further his reputation and ability to strike fear in the house.

Zachary had witnessed several attacks and reprisals in his time here. He had hardened and survived, and now he was ready. Before learning who had accepted Targon's assignment, Zachary had already narrowed it down to a handful. It would have to be someone that was a loner, since Zachary's connections throughout the prison were excellent. It would have to be someone who wasn't expecting much of life anymore, so losing his own life wasn't too distasteful, and it would have to be someone capable of either surprising him or overwhelming him. Moog had been near the top of the list. It was the sneaky little murderers that had concerned Zachary the most, perhaps someone that he had overlooked or trusted. When word came that it was Moog, he had been rather relieved. Not that Moog would be easy to kill, he wouldn't, but then he had been able to zero in on his assassin's moves and relax a bit rounding every corner. He had people watching and warning him when Moog came anywhere near him, and he had planned his counterstrike.

Targon had made a mistake in trying to kill Zachary DuPort. Zachary felt he now had a destiny in replacing Targon as the crime lord of San Francisco, provided no one else was out there beating him to it. If there were, they too would have to be swept away.

Now he crouched up on the ledge six feet above the ground on the small passage that ran between the library and the wood shop. He had picked this spot as it gave him the ability to drop down unseen as Moog turned the corner into the passageway. He could have hired two or three other big men to kill Moog for him, but he instinctively knew that if he could do this himself, his prestige in the prison would reach a new height, and he could use that when he left the place. All he would require was the sharpened thin iron bar in his right hand and the courage to jump on the man's back.

When the time came, it had been unbelievably easy. Using the bar as an ice pick, he had sunk it into the man's huge neck at the same time that he had landed unexpectedly on him, buckling Moog's legs and forcing the big man to catch his fall with his hands. By the time they had hit the ground together, Zachary had already pulled the weapon out and stuck it back into another side of Moog's neck, were he left it as Moog twisted around and threw him off. Zachary crashed into the wall in the narrow passage, but quickly leapt to his feet to defend himself with a smaller knife he drew from his left shoe. But the fight was over. Moog's eyes were bulging as he tried in vain to pull the iron bar from his spurting neck. His blood was everywhere, and he was stumbling around indecisively. Zachary backed away to watch. Finally giving up on saving his own life, he turned on Zachary but now no longer had the strength to cross the small divide and use his massive hands and arms to harm his killer. Zachary watched him drop, gurgling and grunting, unable to speak, until the man lay still. Then with a sense of great accomplishment and relief, he literally skipped down the hall and out of the area. In about ten minutes as previously arranged, a guard would discover the body with no clues as to who had perpetrated the murder. That night several inmates started calling Zachary "Mr. D."

Two days later when Roland Leach found out about his foiled murder attempt, he failed to deliver that day's receipts from the gambling halls, filled several trunks with as much contraband as he could personally make off with, and bought a ticket for the southbound stage to Los Angeles, where he planned to catch the first eastbound ship he could take. It didn't matter where, as long as he could get away before Targon came looking. When the stage reached the outskirts of San Francisco, Roland Leach was still looking all around him, sure that someone would be coming after him with death on his mind. Too many years with Targon made him a mass of nerves as the coach kicked up dust clouds on its way South.

Up on the hill, O'Bannon sat in the hotel kitchen devouring a second helping of some new creation Philippe had cooked. One of the best benefits of his new employment had been the one free meal that came from the hotel kitchen every day. O'Bannon had also teamed with head chef Philippe as a guinea pig for Philippe's testing of new entrees for the hotel menu. Philippe could count on O'Bannon to heartily endorse anything set in front of him.

Lately, O'Bannon's visits to the kitchen had been more erratic, appearing for breakfast one day, lunch another, and dinner yet another. This was because O'Bannon had been placed in charge of the security team for the shipyards the Countess had just purchased. Corby, who O'Bannon still called Corby, unlike everyone else, who now called him Mr. Corby, was setting up an office out at the yard, getting a handle on all the employees and, as Corby put it, the flow of the business. O'Bannon and his team were to make sure that no one but authorized personnel was on the property. It was O'Bannon's first crack at leading a team, and he took it seriously. Stranahan had told him if he messed it up, he would personally mess O'Bannon up. Stranahan was the chief of security for all of the Countess's businesses. To listen to Stranahan tell it, the two of them had arrived in heaven. In fact, pay was excellent, far more than either had anticipated. The work kept them busy, but it was pretty easy, and not nearly as dangerous as being marshals. And San Francisco was a great place to be. O'Bannon still felt like he was on a vacation, with the variety of strange sights and people to see every day. Marshal Donovan had insisted that he hold onto 15 percent of the men's pay in some kind of forced savings plan, and since Stranahan thought it was a good idea, O'Bannon went along with it. There were times when he could have used that extra pay, like when he had to leave a marker after losing his week's pay in the gambling halls, but usually he had plenty of living money. He had more clothes than he had ever owned before, and they were new clothes. He had a nice little apartment not far from the hotel, and he found that his steady employment was really admired by the girls in the halls. In summary, life was good, and he was not that far removed from his previous life that he didn't appreciate it. Besides, Strananhan was constantly reminding him of how good he had it, every day when he showed up for work.

When Marshal Donovan was in the hospital, O'Bannon and Stranahan had visited every day after work. Stranahan had seemed really shaken, and O'Bannon had never seen that in his colleague before. He had come to like Donovan before the hunting accident, but he had not known him as Stranahan had before as a marshal. Stranahan had tried to explain that Donovan had been his teacher, like Stranahan had been for O'Bannon, and it made some sense in that context. O'Bannon would feel a little lost if Stranahan were to disappear he guessed.

Fortunately, the old man had pulled through and was now back at work, with a black eye patch. Donovan still had a bandage wrapped around his head. Stranahan thought Donovan was waiting until his hair grew back in before he would take it off. Donovan was a little jumpy if you approached him from his left side, probably from years of instinctive reaction to danger. But everything seemed to be settling down again, as Donovan reinserted himself back into the heart of the Countess's businesses.

THE MOST MARKED change these days seemed to be in Corby. He was no longer just trying hard to do what he should do. He had taken ownership in his tasks. Almost losing Donovan had an enormous impact on him. Donovan had saved Corby's life when the bear had run over him, drawing the beast instead to himself, where it almost killed him. Had Donovan died, Corby would have been wracked with guilt at surviving. The realities of the sudden and huge changes that could slam into one's life had taken root in Corby's mind. He woke up to the wonderful wife he had, the incredible opportunities lying right out his front door, and the binding glue that held him to those whose lives intertwined with his. His prior fears and concerns seemed petty in nature now. He was determined to live up to the good opinions his family had of him. He could and would bring a measure of security to them and a return of the love they had shown him.

Gabrielle noticed it immediately. There was a new air of confidence and determination about Corby. He became the initiator, surprising her with his interest levels in all her businesses and willingness to tackle any task that came forward. Before he had been attentive and loving to her, but now there was almost an immediacy to his affection, as if it might be the last time for everything. Day by day and week by week, Corby was taking over more and more of the work of running the company, first filling in Marshal Donovan's role, plus running the ranch, and then sitting with her in her meetings and working incredible hours. When Donovan came back to work, he simply was freed up to insert himself more into other areas, and now he had taken control of the shipyard with the same passion. Her only concern now was that he was working too hard.

There was one other issue on the table. Corby wanted children. Gabrielle was both pleased and concerned. She could think of no greater pleasure than children, along with the running of her business. Corby had understood that, and promised that she would not lose that part of her life.

"Are you kidding?" he had laughed. "We will be running papers to you up until the moment you give birth, asking you what to do! This hotel and all these businesses are yours, forever. If all this is what makes you happy, we will grow it and then some. Or if the day comes that you ever wish to sell it all and move into the wilderness, the kids and I will be there with you, with Donovan, Stranahan, and O'Bannon riding shotgun."

The hotel was just about complete, but the joy of running it was still a big part of her life, and would be hopefully for years to come. She wondered how Corby would feel about naming the boys Pierre and Henri.

SOME SAGE HAD suggested that a close encounter with death would enhance a man's appreciation for living. As many times as Donovan had cheated death, he had come to a somewhat different conclusion. Life could be a daily battle, and to continue to live in a highly risky world, he had to have a little anger in him, a "fight back" mentality that said he can take whatever was dished out and then some. That assumption of toughness had been a second skin for the lawman through countless scrapes and more than his fair share of bumps. The spirit was still there, but he felt tired. That damned Frenchman had put too many questions in his head, questions that he had never cared about in his previous years of black and white reasoning. He remembered the night Henri had talked about the stars. Donovan had taken the old man out to the Montara ranch to witness the calving season, and that night they had walked under the stars while Henri pointed out the constellations. The stars had always been a great comfort for Donovan, a constant that was never disappointing in their splendor and magnitude. But as Henri had rambled on about the Greeks and Romans, the early sailors, longitudes and latitudes, and the possible makeup of the stars themselves, Donovan saw for the first time the difference between himself and a true thinking man such as Henri, with his insatiable appetite to learn and question. Now when he looked up into the night sky, he still appreciated the beauty of the heavens, but those incredible questions plagued him and entertained him.

"How far do you think the universe goes, Marshal Donovan?" Henri had asked. In hindsight, Donovan now grasped that it had been a rhetorical question, one that no one had the answer to, designed to trigger more questions and stimulate his mind. And it had. Henri had effectively knocked him off of the simple rail he had been traveling on all his life, and thrown him out into a sea of uncertainties, but a sea that more realistically represented the true world he lived in.

So his latest brush with death at the jaws of the great bear of California had begged new questions that he could not answer, while taking away a bit more of the great strength and certitude he had so long relied upon. But this was his life, the cards he had been dealt, and Henri could watch from wherever he was, because Donovan intended to play out the game harder and smarter than he had up to this point. Somehow he would find the capacity to read and understand the books sitting in his home overlooking the bay, and he would pass the "curse" on to Corby, as Henri had done to him. That thought brought a smile to his rugged face, and he took off the cosmetic bandage he still had wrapped around his scalp and looked in the mirror. Not that bad. In fact he needed a haircut. Putting on a new black hat to compliment his black eye patch, he stared down the mirror with his remaining eye, while shaping the wide brim of the hat to his preferred angle. Not bad at all. Time to join his two adopted charges for dinner, and badger them about raising a family again.

89

THINGS WERE CHANGING AT Fort Hall that Dr. Lemmins had been noting for some time. Now with the surprise death of his old friend Fournier came the just-as-unsettling news that Captain Farmer had been called East, and would be leaving within two weeks for good. Combined with the general deterioration of the Oregon Trail military posts, and more Indian uprisings being reported all the time, the doctor knew his family should be moving on.

East or West? His ongoing dialogue with Captain Farmer had convinced Dr. Lemmins that despite the sometimes lawless nature of the West, should they reach San Francisco, the opportunities for both himself and his adopted daughter would be better than the upheavals that appeared to be taking place back East. Word had reached Fort Hall, as it had most of the country, that the divide between North and South over slavery was being fought more and more out West in the developing states of the Great Plains. The question of whether to restrict the new territories from allowing slavery, or whether to allow them to decide by region for themselves, was becoming a moral debate all over the country. Captain Farmer had gone so far as to reveal that the army believed that violence was imminent, and troops would become embroiled in trying to keep the peace, while the leadership back in Washington wrestled with the complex and troubling issues.

Dr. Lemmins did not want to be a part of it, and after years of watching mindless violence among the immigrants and also the Indians, he chose California. With the arrival of Spring, it would be easy to attach themselves to the best-looking wagon train to come along in the next two months and cross the mountains in the middle of summer, reaching California safely before any weather problems.

The soon-to-be-realized departure of Captain Farmer had sealed the deal with Valerie. Now it had to be conveyed to Katy in such a fashion that the young girl would see the need to leave and the opportunities ahead. The three adults talked the matter over and decided an open discussion with all of them present might help to soothe the pain of leaving "her Indians."

To their absolute surprise, Katy had seen it coming from overhearing snippets of conversations and had prepared herself for the inevitable. Her only open regret was whether they would be leaving before the Yellowstone Shoshone came to Fort Hall or she had an opportunity to visit them one last time. No one had an answer to that. The girl quietly left the small house and walked to the stable, where she began grooming her Appaloosa.

Talking to Snowflake, Katy found herself expressing the fears she had kept to herself while listening to her parents and Captain Farmer. Maybe she was just a "wild Indian" and the children in California would laugh at her. What if there was no place for Snowflake living in a city? If she left without talking to Lame Elk, would he ever forgive her? What would happen to her Yellowstone Shoshone? Was she to read someday of their ruin, as Captain Farmer had prophesized to her father was the fate of most of the Indians? There would be no wilderness to ride through in San Francisco. She sank to the corner of the horse stall, her head in her hands, as the tears began to fall.

90

THE NIGHTS WERE FINALLY cooling off. As Drego lay in bed next to the lightly snoring young woman he had accompanied home earlier that night, his thoughts returned, as they always did, to his father and to Tucson, his home. He rationalized, once again, that perhaps in a year or so he could secretly visit and not cause trouble for his family. One Mexican could look a lot like another to the Americanos if he were careful. But then he worried for the thousandth time that he would bring hurt and humiliation back on his aged father, and discarded the idea again. What he could do, he had, and that was to write a letter to his father telling him he was fine, having escaped prison and fled to Old Mexico, where he was working on a rancho near Chihuahua. This was partly true. He had found light work at several ranchos, but had sustained himself primarily as a bandito, still in the company of El Cacharro.

El Cacharro had formed a full-time band of desperados that ranged from Ciudad Juarez as far West as Nogales, and South to Chihuahua, hiding in the Sierra Madre Mountains anytime the Federales made their weak attempts to bring some law and order to the vast northern provinces. El Cacharro, whom Drego had come to learn was named Pedro Mendoza, had turned out to be a fairly reasonable person once out of prison, and they had actually become something approaching friends during their travel down into Mexico. When Drego was in need of money or became frustrated with the low-paying jobs he was offered, he would find El Cacharro and ride with the bandits for a couple of months, before guilt would consume him and force him to try an honest lifestyle once again that would make his father less ashamed of him.

Currently he was with the outlaws who had just ridden into the outlaw-friendly town of Baceras in Old Mexico for a little rest and relaxation. Since the outlaws spent more money in the town than anyone else and the government had never been of any assistance, the wise residents of Baceras had formed a benevolent relationship with the bands that moved through the territory, and it was understood that no robbing or killing would be done in town in exchange for safe haven, women, and food.

Increasingly, the rather slim pickings and the ever-present risk of Indios in the mountains of northern Mexico had driven El Cacharro and his men into a pattern of raiding across the border, primarily around El Paso, where they could quickly slip back across the Rio Grande river and disappear into the Mexican countryside. It was a more risky proposition because the Texas Rangers who had been fighting various Indian campaigns for years were not to be taken lightly. If caught by the Rangers, it was unlikely that the bandits would make it back to prison alive. But it was an occupation built on risk taking, and they had to go were the opportunities presented themselves, and that meant the border.

Having just raided a nice little settlement on the outskirts of El Paso, and gotten lucky with a stagecoach coming in from somewhere to the east, the band had headed straight back to Baceras from there. After a hard week of riding, they had descended on the small town intending to stay until their money and credit ran out. Other than El Cacharro, Drego had little use for anyone else in the band. They were of low moral character, illiterate, and highly offensive of odor. Besides that, they were thieves who had to be watched all the time, and were capable of doing some very stupid spur-of-the-moment things, which tended to get them killed on a fairly regular basis. But finding replacements was always easy in a country as poor as Mexico. There were no outside qualifications for joining the band other than having a gun and doing what El Cacharro said.

Such as thing were, Drego and El Cacharro tended to spend more downtime together, in order to have any kind of a conversation with another person. They learned a great deal about each other, except Drego would not talk about his family for fear of further possible harm he might bring their way. However, El Cacharro was able to discern that Drego had a better education, similar to the wealthy families that had dominated throughout Mexico since the coming of the Spaniards centuries before. He had figured out that Drego had lived his life North of the border, and probably would have been living a better life had he not run afoul of the law. He could also tell his friend was not happy. Neither women nor gambling could cheer him up for long, and it was only a matter of time before Drego would risk going back to live with the gringos. This was too bad for El Cacharro, as Drego had not only been his friend, but when they rode together, his most dependable colleague. And El Cacharro had seen what Drego could do with a knife. This bandit life had little future to it even in El Cacharro's eyes, and he had begun to ask more questions about Drego's time in California.

When dawn began to break, Drego slipped out of his night's accommodations and headed for the stable to check on his horse, a good one he had stolen in El Paso. He was still grooming it when El Cacharro found him there and offered to buy him a cup of coffee and a burrito for breakfast. Sitting alone at the sleepy cantina, El Cacharro brought up California once again.

"Do you think I could become an honest hombre, compadre?" he asked with a smile.

Drego glanced up from where he was sipping his coffee. He knew that El Cacharro was asking about a clean start in California again.

"Do you think you can be an honest man is the question," he said without a smile. "My friends in California are honest men, who would feel obligated to turn us in if we robbed or killed anyone."

"These men are your friends? They would turn you in for a simple robbery?" Pedro asked with incredulousness.

Drego sighed and said, "It is different with the gringos." He did not mention that it was different with his own family. "Maybe that is why they prosper. No one is always taking their money away from them."

El Cacharro tilted his head in consideration of that idea. "But they must have banditos. The prison was full of them."

"Oh yes, they have banditos. But the lawmen are mostly honest too, and do a better job of putting them in jail. You have seen the Texas Rangers, no?"

"The Rangers are killers with badges," spat Pedro.

"But who is it they are killing?" countered Drego.

El Cacharro conceded the point with a facial contortion, and took a different tack. "How cold is it in California in the winter, hombre?"

"No colder than the worst nights in the desert, unless you are in the mountains there, and you can buy a good coat. What is in your head, Pedro?" Drego asked as he wrapped his hands around the warmth of his coffee cup and leaned back in his chair.

"I think we will die poor here in Mexico, or the Rangers will get lucky someday. I think we should go to California. You speak the language."

"And what will we do there, my friend?" Drego asked. He did not want to be an outlaw in California.

El Cacharro sat up like a schoolboy and solemnly said, "My father was a blacksmith. In a rich country it would be a good life."

That totally surprised Drego, who took a double take on his partner in crime. El Cacharro was serious.

"I have not given the men all their money yet," Pedro added. "We could leave tonight with enough to get to California and start an honest business."

The incongruous comment made Drego choke on the coffee he was sipping. Shaking his head, he asked, "So you would be an honest businessman from the money you stole from your men, who stole it first from the gringos? Pedro, I am afraid you do not understand the concept of honest." He grinned at El Cacharro and shook his head again.

"I understand the concept of dead!" El Cacharro snapped back, somewhat insulted by the remark Drego had made. "Do you intend to stay here for the rest of your life?" He swept his arm out in a broad arc over the poor Mexican town. "Is this what your father would hope for you?"

Not knowing the how close he was hitting to Drego's own thoughts, he continued. "If I had friends in California, and a chance for a better life, I would not be sitting in this hellhole trying to argue with a burro!"

There was a short silence as the two looked at each other. Then Drego slowly said, "If we ride to California, and my friends help us to start new lives, and you decide to steal or kill, I will not stand beside you. Do you understand this, Pedro? I will not participate in anything that would hurt my friends, and I want to try being an honest hombre."

El Cacharro chose his words carefully too. "This I understand. I do not know if I can be this 'honest hombre' or not. If I fail, it will be my failure, and I will go my own way. But to die here or fail there are very poor choices, no? I think we can succeed there, or at least try." Then smiling, he said, "And if you do not wish to share my stolen money, I will have to learn to live with that."

91

I T WAS EARLY MORNING on a bright sunny day. Sidney Walcott stood outside the big iron gate with a horse and buggy waiting for the gate to open. Twenty-two months had passed since Zachary DuPort had been incarcerated. It was a long time to be in any prison, but a short time considering his sentence. Sidney reflected on his work. His job was to serve his client, and he had ably done that yet again with the case of Zachary DuPort. But the older he got, the more he questioned the sense of it all. The law had many flaws, and the system was abused. He had abused it. As a younger man he had rationalized that away rather easily, as a balance to an imperfect system. His clients had been the weak and poor, who needed a good lawyer lest they be trampled under by an uncaring behemoth, the odds stacked against them. He had learned his craft well. He had served his clients well, but it seemed that little had changed in the world for all his efforts. His opinions of the human race had deteriorated over time. People didn't seem to be evolving. Science marched on. Maybe even the standard of living was improving, but Sidney saw no improvement in his fellow man. If fact, mankind was depressing him more each year with its pettiness, stupidity, greed, and inhumanity. He was appalled by the brutality many people were capable of.

As a reader of the classics, the intellectual tone of the ancient philosophers was more uplifting than anything he had read that was written in the last one hundred years. Of course they had been at the top of their societies and the suffering was below them, but at least they saw it and wished for better. Sidney wasn't sure the top of his society had anything on their minds but getting richer, as fast as they could.

And here he was, waiting outside the San Quentin Prison walls to greet a thief and murderer he had helped to commute a long sentence to a short one. He was disgusted with it all.

THE GATES SWUNG open, and out came Zachary DuPort all by himself, beaming from ear to ear. The man sauntered over to Sidney and smacked him on the back, saying, "Let's get to the city and start making up for lost time."

Zachary DuPort promptly climbed into the passenger side of the buggy indicating that he expected Sidney to get moving and drive him down to the ferry service that would deliver him back onto the streets of San Francisco.

The old man reluctantly climbed into the buggy, still tired from his early morning start to cross the bay, with the knowledge that Zachary DuPort would resume his nefarious activities with a new vigor and a better criminal education for having served his time in "criminal college." Sidney decided then and there that he was done. He would collect what was due and retire to quietly read until his emphysema consumed him.

For Zeke Bridges, now forever more Zachary DuPort, it was a new dawn. He had the knowledge necessary to run the gambling halls. He had the ambition and the will to take on Targon, and he now had the reputation and contacts to enlist the muscle he would need. In hindsight, his circuitous route to this point had prepared him well for the next steps in a rise up the criminal ranks. He had come a long way from the bullied younger son of an embittered and distant father. His imagination had taken flight as a conman in New Orleans where he had figured out that he was smart enough to take easy money without working. But his time at sea and in jail had been necessary to toughen him up in order to deal with the element of people his chosen profession threw at him. He even owed Targon a debt of gratitude in allowing him to learn the gambling business. Now he was ready. He would not shirk the task before him, as he knew what the prize was worth. A fortune was waiting for him, and he was just the man to step in and build a new empire, first by wrestling away the old Logan/Targon properties, and any others now under different management since Targon had been forced off premises, and then by using his God-given talents to pool the other lucrative underworld trades that a big and growing city like San Francisco had to offer. All he would need was a decent stake to start the ball rolling, but he would worry about that tomorrow. Today, he was a free man, with a clean slate, and today he would enjoy all the city had to offer.

One man rode down to the ferry full of optimism and energy. The other, who had spent a lifetime primarily helping his fellow man, was resigned and deflated.

92

I T WAS JUST BEFORE sunset. The bay sparkled like a jewel, and a V of pelicans were winging their way toward their roosting area for the night. The garden was a quiet haven for Gabrielle at this time of the day. Soon she would go upstairs and change for the evening, as befitting, to greet her guests arriving for dinner. There was time yet to relax a moment, and she chose to sit on the little bench next to Henri's marker. She was having one made for her father to place beside Henri's and Barton's, even though his remains would stay in New Orleans. It was simply a comforting gesture she could afford to have.

Now approaching thirty, she reflected on her life and what was ahead. Her emersion in the world of business had taken her farther than she had imagined, even though it was what she had wanted. The arrival in a fast growing city with significant working capital had touched off a series of start-up businesses that seemed to pull in more and more opportunities. She had made numerous mistakes, primarily in the people she had chosen to do business with, but she had picked many more winners than losers, and had learned from each endeavor.

Under Henri's direction she had been buying up large tracts of timberland along the coastline, both to the North and the South. The huge redwood trees in particular were becoming increasingly valuable. Along with the land came other natural resources, such as a lime producing plant she now owned down near Santa Cruz. The open land was converted to pasture, and again with Henri's help, she had a couple of small government contracts for beef that could only grow with time. Her original investment in the brick factory had continued unabated, boosted by the never-ending cycle of fires that seemed to plague the area. With the expertise of three ex-marshals, it had been only natural to develop a security service in a town that bordered on lawlessness from time to time.

With all of these investments, along with the St. Montford Hotel, the Montara Ranch, and now the shipbuilding yard, and no national or state run bank yet in the State of California, her assets alone were more than enough to open the Montara Trust Bank. It quickly doubled in size, as many of her business associates felt obligated or compelled to move their resources there. The Mexican American community made it their bank too, as did other foreign-born immigrants arriving daily to the area.

Following a complicated scheme Henri had put together for her, profits were divided between reinvestment needs, more venture capitalism, and stockpiling of cash vehicles, such as gold, reputable notes, and other liquid safeguards. The empire she now sat on was seemingly invulnerable, but Henri had drummed it into her head that there was no such thing, hence the large cash positions she was forced to take.

Marshal Donovan was now a complete businessman, albeit one who looked more like a riverboat gambler with his eye patch, western hat, and solid frame. Any thought of retiring to a little Oregon ranch had passed by the wayside, and she knew she could depend on him as her right arm for many more years. The family of employees she had built within the businesses over the last eight years had proven to be loyal and fairly trustworthy, with the Marshal looking over everyone's shoulder.

And what to think of Corby? He was transforming in front of her very eyes. The bug had finally bitten him too. He could see the potential of the city. He could envision their role in building it. But there was also the mark of the Westerner that would always be on him. The need to look around the next bend of the river, over the following hill. To brace the worst weather, testing his mettle. The unique love for his horse Borrasca, and the great outdoors. Those parts of Corby would always compete for his soul with the new world she had brought him into, and she wouldn't have it any other way. It was the hard tempered edge of the Westerner that had first drawn her interest, and now that she knew the complete package, she couldn't imagine her life without her cowboy.

BORRASCA WAS PAWING at the ground. It was time to go home, and that meant Corby would run him. Corby knew the horse looked forward to his morning and evening runs . Otherwise most days were spent in a stable or pasture, and a horse like Borrasca needed more.

Corby looked up at the same squadron of pelicans flying by that Gabrielle had watched. The tinted sky suggested he had perhaps an hour before dark, and he was already overdue to leave the shipyard and get back to the hotel for dinner with Gabrielle and a group of businessmen who were interested in building some tanneries using the oak groves prevalent in the east bay area.

He needed to take the direct route home, if he were to have adequate time to clean up and be on time for the dinner.

Swinging up on Borrasca, he felt the energy and impatience of the horse as he started out of the shipyard. There was another way home that ran along the beach before a steep climb up through the scrub brush hillside to the hotel, but that took nearly twice as long, and usually covered him with dust. But it was a good run for Borrasca, and he certainly enjoyed it too. With a small smile he turned toward the beach and let the Arabian run.

93

THE BLACKFOOT CAMP WAS nestled in a mountain valley some thirty miles to the northwest of their previous home base, at the foot of the mountain they had called the Gray Woman. Two mountain streams came plummeting out of the surrounding hills and met on the valley floor to form a swift but not overly deep current that raced to the southeast through a series of smaller valleys and ravines below the campsite. This was a higher elevation, but not too far from a plateau that opened up and dropped down to grasslands to the northeast, allowing access to buffalo hunting.

To Lame Elk's thinking, it had probably been a Blackfoot village a long time before, and probably served as a retreat when hard times or enemies pressed on the Blackfoot. A few well-placed guards high up on the adjacent mountainsides could see a long way and warn of any impending threat. The mountainsides would be too steep to attack down, so a defensive stand at the valley ends could hold off a larger force, and it appeared that some large rocks and trees had been placed for just such an occurrence. He had managed to elude the guards in working his way down through the timber to the closest point above the camp, still some six hundred yards above and away from the camp.

Here he selected an arrow, inspecting it very carefully. It had a very close-cropped fletching, and was the longest arrow he carried, one that he had kept for a long shot. He restrung his elk horn bow, wrapped in buffalo sinew for extra strength.

DOWN BELOW THE Blackfoot women were beginning to stoke their fires to cook the evening meals. The Bulls had informally gathered and were once again telling the details of their successful raid on the Shoshone camp. The Badger was wearing Fournier's beaver hat and laughing as he described the Whiteman's look when he cracked his head open with his new tomahawk.

Sitting a little to the side in a more dignified manner as bespoke the chief of the Blackfoot, Two Horns recalled the moment as The Badger embellished it a bit. It had not given him the satisfaction he had hoped it would, but there was a satisfaction in seeing his warriors revel in their exploits. The tribe was regaining some of its swagger, and the sound of the babies laughing and crying was good to hear too. His people thought well of him, and the hurt of losing Moon in the Daylight and his unborn son, though still with him, was lessening. On the ride back he had been wondering what the Shoshone Chief Blackhand might do in response to his raid. It had been a Whiteman and two Lemhi Shoshone warriors, but Two Horns knew that would probably not make a difference to the Shoshone chief. They seemed destined to match wits and arms, ever since the ill-advised raid by Crooked Claws years before. One's own stature and prowess are marked only with the aid of an esteemed adversary. Blackhand was the most notable enemy of the Blackfoot in many decades. Two Horns and the Bulls spoke of him often and with admiration. To kill him would be a great achievement, but Two Horns did not ache to do so, as he had the Crows when Long Bow's mutilated body had been discovered.

The arrow whispered on its long, arcing flight through the air. Shot as it was from up on the mountainside, it carried a remarkable distance and stuck with a thud and a quiver into the ground two feet from where Buffalo Lance was sitting gnawing on an old bone in anticipation of his upcoming dinner. With a shout, Buffalo Lance jumped up onto his feet and pointed at the missile, now a stationary marker for all to see. The markings of Blackhand on the arrow were familiar to all the Blackfoot. Yells erupted from the northwest end of the camp, and Blackfoot men, women, and children came running and pointing up the slope on the northern mountainside. Riding slowly out of the woods was a lone Shoshone warrior dressed in war paints that everyone knew was Blackhand.

Two Horns held up his hands for silence. The Blackfoot people sensed the drama of the moment and became very still. Up on the mountainside, Lame Elk gave his battle cry and sat upright on his pony. The lone war cry reverberated throughout the valley. The challenge had been given. Two Horns had been called out for personal combat. Higher up the mountainside, a dozen more Shoshone warriors appeared to witness in silence as their chief met in combat with the Blackfoot chief.

Blue Heron said, "He comes for me, Two Horns. He twice warned me."

Two Horns smiled at the weak attempt to shield him. "The Shoshone and I have known this day would come. He does the honorable thing to avoid further bloodshed for his people. Would you have me do less?"

"Take my lance," said Buffalo Lance. "It is the best in the camp."

"And the heaviest," said Two Horns, walking over to pick up his own weapons. "Bring Messenger to me that I may show Blackhand what the Blackfoot warrior can do."

When the big horse was brought over, Two Horns swung up on him and rubbed his ears. "I'll bet Blackhand would rather be seated on you my friend."

The two warrior chiefs began to move toward the valley floor to the North of the camp where there was some room to ride and fight. Two Horns rode at a sedate pace to allow the Shoshone chief time to descend down to the flat ground. At last he would meet this great enemy in battle. He felt pride in the oncoming struggle. However it turned out, his tribe would watch their chief fight his best, and there would be great honor in battling the Shoshone. Red Horses would be smiling down on him now, as would Stone Bear, Long Bow, Stalking Wolf, and the other warriors now gone to the next life. He heard Moon in the Daylight whisper to him, "Be strong, my husband," as she had done whenever he had ridden out to danger. His chest swelled, and his eyes misted momentarily.

When Lame Elk reached the valley floor, he stopped where he was, war-club across his lap and lance in his right hand. He saw the Blackfoot chief was thick through his arms and chest, and the big black horse Lame Elk had stolen from the Whiteman years before set the big Blackfoot well above him. The Whiteman's horse jogged his memory. The horse had been in his vision, leading him to a happier future. That stormy night in the mountains and the little red-headed girl he had rescued had set his life in a different and more meaningful direction. The Creator had known, and now he too knew. Life had taught him many lessons, given him much joy and sadness. What he did now he did for the People. He smiled, satisfied in his decision, and then he refocused on the warrior before him. Lame Elk started his pony forward at a trot.